MR CAMPION'S WINGS

MR CAMPION'S WINGS

Mike Ripley

SEVERN
HOUSE

First world edition published in Great Britain in 2021 and the USA in 2022
by Severn House, an imprint of Canongate Books Ltd,
14 High Street, Edinburgh EH1 1TE.

Trade paperback edition first published in Great Britain and the USA in 2022
by Severn House, an imprint of Canongate Books Ltd.

severnhouse.com

British Library Cataloguing-in-Publication Data
A CIP catalogue record for this title is available from the British Library.

ISBN-13: 978-0-7278-5040-9 (cased)
ISBN-13: 978-1-4483-0639-8 (trade paper)
ISBN-13: 978-1-4483-0638-1 (e-book)

All Severn House titles are printed on acid-free paper.

Typeset by Palimpsest Book Production Ltd.,
Falkirk, Stirlingshire, Scotland.
Printed and bound in Great Britain by
TJ Books, Padstow, Cornwall.

For

Tim Coles,
loyal scientific advisor and totally innocent
resident of 112 Barton Road in 1965

CONTENTS

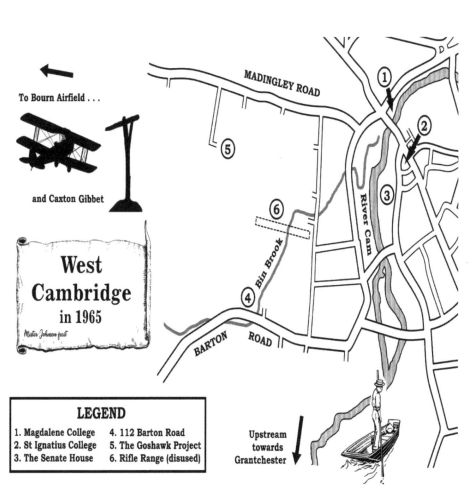

To Bourn Airfield . . .

and Caxton Gibbet

MADINGLEY ROAD

River Cam

Bin Brook

BARTON ROAD

① ② ③ ④ ⑤ ⑥

West
Cambridge
in 1965

Mister Johnson fecit

LEGEND

1. Magdalene College   4. 112 Barton Road
2. St Ignatius College   5. The Goshawk Project
3. The Senate House   6. Rifle Range (disused)

Upstream
towards
Grantchester

ONE

Scarlet Robes, Soft Bonnets

The procession processed, as all processions should, with a fair amount of pomp and not a little circumstance. The bells of the university churches chimed through the warm morning air across the rooftops and trumpets, mostly unseen in hidden courtyards, sounded the lower notes at street level.

The procession itself moved in near silence, apart from the swish of silk-lined robes and the click of heels on cobbles, its progress regal and dignified as befitted the occasion, the way ahead of it paved by two formidably robed figures, each wielding a distinctly unwieldly ceremonial mace.

'They're the Bedells,' said Mr Albert Campion. 'Their weapons are purely for show, but I would still advise not making eye contact with them.'

'So what's a Bedell, then?' asked his companion, a large gentleman of a similar age, whose vulgarity was masked for the occasion by his formal dress, which included frock coat, striped trousers and bowler hat. In the snug of The Platelayers' Arms, where he would naturally feel at home, the fat man would have been ridiculously overdressed and the object of a campaign of scorn and derision from fellow patrons. In Cambridge, on the occasion of a university congregation to award honorary doctorates, he blended in perfectly.

'A Bedell is an official of the university; in your world they might be regarded as the strong-arm boys or "the muscle" but their purpose is mostly ceremonial, organizing and officiating at events such as this. The spelling is peculiarly Cambridge; most other institutions call them Beadles and you find them, famously, in Dickens, running workhouses and refusing that second helping of gruel, and in the Worshipful Companies of London. Most of the livery companies have a Beadle to organize their dinners and their cellars.'

Campion was convinced that the rim of his colleague's bowler elevated a quarter-inch as his ears pricked up.

'You mean like the Distillers or the Vintners or the Brewers?'

Campion eyed him thoughtfully. 'I was thinking more on the lines of the Goldsmiths or the Scriveners and, my favourite, the Worshipful Company of Lightmongers, but I see the way your mind is working. You know, my dear Lugg, you should consider trying your hand at Beadle-ing. You are now of pensionable age and really ought to be thinking of a comfortable sinecure to ease you into retirement. You brush up quite nicely, and with your stentorian voice and tracer-bullet eyes, you could impose order on any unruly gathering.'

'And what about yerself? You qualified for the pension last month. Sixty-five on yer birthday, though everyone's agreed you could pass for eighty in a bad light.'

'I will ignore both the fact and opinion expressed in that statement and demand that you button your scurrilous lip and concentrate on the reason why we are here lining this historic street with this adoring crowd, for the object of our adoration approaches. Not, I hasten to add, that I have done anything *but* adore her for more than a quarter of a century.'

'I knows 'ow to behave.' His companion sighed. 'Stommick in, chest out, eyes front. 'Ere comes the wife.'

The object of their attention was dressed in scarlet robes and a soft black felt bonnet, a form of headgear which did its best to contain unruly strands of hair which now, with age, glowed rather than blazed red, but failed entirely to shadow its wearer's perfect heart-shaped face. In spite of impractical, though impressive, black high heels, she was dwarfed, almost hidden, by the clutch of taller, black-robed, ermine-trimmed academics shielding her as the procession moved across the Great Bridge from the Magdalene side. It was almost as if a garden robin was being escorted out of town by a court of crows, but the crows, being intelligent birds, knew better than to get too close to the fearless and often aggressive robin.

It was not a large procession on the scale of, say, a state funeral or an arriving circus, but a few strategically placed uniformed policemen made sure that it took precedence over motorized vehicles and the cyclists which outnumbered them, as well as pedestrian residents blasé about such disruptions to their daily shopping, and a small throng of tourists for whose benefit the whole spectacle had been carefully staged.

Campion, standing at the old (Anglo-Saxon) Quayside end of the bridge, swelled with pride and affection as the procession swished by imperiously and he caught the sideways glance and brief pursing of ruby-red lips in what was surely a surreptitious blown kiss, aimed in his direction by his wife.

'Talk about a guard of honour . . .' muttered his companion. 'They don't mean to let her get away, do they? Got her well and truly surrounded. Mind you, if she broke cover and ran for it, none of them old crows would catch her, even in them heels.'

'Why on earth would she run away?' asked Campion. 'It is, as you say, a guard of honour, not a police escort. Those distinguished dons and officials of the university are taking Amanda to receive an honorary doctorate, not pursuing a suspected shoplifter. It's a very moving ceremony, conducted in Latin, but no doubt you will be in the nearest pub by then.'

'Do we 'ave to call her Doctor Amanda after she picks up her Pee-Haitch-Dee?'

'For you, she'll probably insist on it, though here at Cambridge it's not a PhD, it's an ScD, a doctorate of science.'

'So why does the poor little thing 'ave to give a speech in Latin? Seems a bit steep to me.'

'The recipient does not have to speak at all, let alone in Latin, but a little thing like that would not have daunted Amanda. Keeping quiet during the ceremony might be a trial for her, but once the formalities are over, the National Anthem sung and there is one last blast of the trumpets, the chancellor invites all those assembled to a jolly spiffing garden party. Not you, of course – they don't want to have to count the spoons afterwards.'

'Cheek!' bristled the fat man, his face contorted into his favourite expression, that of a bulldog sadly betrayed by life's unfairness, but if he was summoning a cutting rebuttal, he was not allowed to deliver it, as Mr Campion was hailed by a figure hurrying across the bridge from the Magdalene (Norman) side in the wake of the elegant convoy of academics.

'Albert! Albert Campion, it is you. Older, greyer and much wiser, I suspect.'

'Marcus Featherstone,' Campion said quietly once he had focused on the balding man in a dark three-piece suit making a beeline for them. Then to his companion, out of the corner of his mouth: 'You might want to make yourself scarce, old fruit. Marcus is not the sort of chap you'd prop up a bar with.'

'Copper's nark, is he?'

'Worse; he's a solicitor. Now go and explore the town whilst I support my wife in the gown. Rendezvous back at Gnats about teatime.'

By the time Marcus Featherstone was close enough to offer a handshake, the big man had silently disappeared into the pedestrians along Bridge Street, his formal dress providing perfect camouflage on a day when sartorial excess was the norm.

'My dear Campion, you haven't changed a bit. Knew it was you the minute I spotted you, even though it must be twenty years since that business in Socrates Close and those Faradays. What a family!'

Mr Campion, with his instinctively impeccable manners and an inherited steely resolve, did not point out that it was much more than twenty years since he and Marcus had had dealings, nor acknowledge the compliment that he still retained the poise and energy of a thirty-year-old, or point out that Marcus, with his thinning hair and thickening waist, did not. They were, in fact, of the same generation, although Marcus was four years the younger, and both were *alumni* of St Ignatius College Cambridge, known high and low, though mostly low, as 'Gnats', where, according to a scurrilous rumour started by Campion, Marcus had achieved a Blue in deportment. The thing was Marcus had aimed at acting sixty ever since their undergraduate days; a race Campion had been more than happy to let him win for, if nothing else, such an attitude to life made him the perfect solicitor.

'Yes, the Faraday household was something of a menagerie,' Campion admitted, though he had no particular wish to dwell on the unsavoury incidents surrounding the Faraday family, clients of Marcus's solicitor father before the war, 'and we all thought the police would be needed at the funeral. But you appear to have done well for yourself, expanding the family firm, I hear' – he did not add *and waistline* – 'to show that crime really does pay.'

Marcus chuckled and feigned modesty.

'We are now Featherstone and Devine, and one of the largest firms in the city. We still do a lot of work for St Ignatius, of course, to keep up the Faraday connection.'

Campion nodded approval as etiquette, if not interest, dictated whenever the name of Dr John Faraday, revered Master of Gnats in the 1880s, was mentioned in polite society.

'I'm sure the college continues to provide a steady flow of cases for you,' said Campion, 'unless the very nature of students has changed since our day. Getting young gentlemen out of scrapes was bread-and-butter work for solicitors trying to explain youthful urges to put policemen's helmets on lamp-posts or Austin Sevens on the roof of Senate House.'

'Yes, they do get overenthusiastic when it comes to the Rag, but it's usually all in a good cause,' said Marcus seriously, and then a lighter thought struck him. 'There was a famous stunt, years ago, when an undergraduate, fully dressed, complete with cap and gown, jumped off the Great Bridge here using an umbrella as a parachute. The whole thing was caught on film by Lord Burghley; you know, the Olympics chap who ran the hurdles. There was a rumour going the rounds for years that you were that parachutist.'

'On my oath, it was not I who took the plunge,' said Campion, glancing towards the river as a punt slid silently under the bridge, 'though I know of what you speak. It happened a few years after our heyday, Marcus, after David Burghley had missed out at the Paris Olympics in '24 and before he got his gold in '28. He had acquired a cine camera, or whatever they were called in those days, and he showed me the film he took of that undergraduate's energetic self-baptism, though I don't think the chap was doing it for a Rag; I think he was just hard up.'

Marcus Featherstone sighed loudly. 'Those were the days, eh, Albert? We had some fun, some larks, didn't we?'

Mr Campion smiled in polite agreement, though in his

'Varsity days', as his maiden aunts might refer to them with
more than a hint of disparagement, he had never associated
Marcus Featherstone with the concept of 'fun', nor could he
remember a single lark in which either of them had conspired.

'Shall we process in the footsteps of the scholarly elite?'
Marcus asked, his reverie over. 'I assume you are heading for
Senate House.'

'Naturally. My wife is the guest of honour, though she did
look like a prisoner being taken to the block as she passed. I
expected her to wave frantically or at least tip her bonnet.'

'Come, come, Albert, this is an occasion of great dignity,
though Lady Amanda did look a little like the proverbial rose
among the thorns. You must be very proud; not many women
are so honoured. In fact, I cannot think of another.'

'Queen Elizabeth the Queen Mother was the first,' said
Campion slyly, 'in 1948. You might have heard of her.'

'Well, of course, but I meant in Amanda's particular field
of expertise, which you must admit is rather a masculine one.
Come, I'll walk with you as far as Gnats, where I have a
meeting, and you can tell me all about it, and who that large,
rather fearsome character was you were talking to. He looked
like an overweight undertaker and undertakers should not be
fat and jolly. No one expects them to be jolly.'

'Rather like solicitors. What was it Caesar said about preferring men who were chubby rather than the lean and hungry
ones? Mind you, it didn't go well for old Julius in the long
run. The stout fellow you caught me exchanging racing tips
with was Magersfontein Lugg, who is not so much a family
retainer as a family heirloom. If I'd thought of it, I would have
bought him an umbrella and told him it was a university tradition to parachute off Great Bridge – though I must remember
to call it Magdalene Bridge or I will be in trouble with my
son.'

'How so?' Featherstone seemed genuinely curious, as if a
new point of law had just sneaked up on him. 'Both names
are in common Cambridge parlance.'

'In *this* Cambridge, perhaps, but son-and-heir-to-not-very-
much Rupert is a bit of a traitor to the cause. You see, he
chose to go to Harvard, which is in another Cambridge in

North America and they have a Great Bridge there across the Charles River.'

'You couldn't persuade your son to go to St Ignatius? I'm sure Gnats would have welcomed him with open arms.'

'I'm sure they would have,' said Campion as they eased their way through the crowds on the pavement, 'but Rupert, probably wisely, chose not to follow in father's footsteps and, to be fair, Harvard does have something of a reputation for academic excellence which has never exactly been a strong point of St Ignatius.'

'Now who's being the traitor?'

'Steady on, Marcus. Gnats was great fun and I don't regret a minute of my time there, but you remember our graduation, when the graduands were called up in the order of precedence of their colleges?'

'A proud moment.'

'Until you realized how far down the list St Ignatius came.'

'At least we were ahead of Girton.'

Campion smothered a smile. 'Yes, but everyone was back then. It's 1965, not 1922, and women are allowed to collect their degrees like men, even in Cambridge.'

'And receive honorary doctorates,' said Marcus, almost whispering into Campion's left ear, as if passing on a piece of scandal, 'in the most manly disciplines such as . . . engineering.'

'Not exactly,' said Campion.

They crossed the road by the Round Church and for a moment were separated whilst navigating a brace of women wielding pushchairs outside the tailor's shop on St John Street. The procession they were following was momentarily out of sight until they allowed the stream of pedestrians to sweep them round the narrow curve which led into Trinity Street and their *alma mater*, Gnats.

Outside the gates of St Ignatius, Campion paused for Marcus to catch up. 'Amanda's honour is for services to aeronautical engineering and she was sponsored by John Branscombe, the Emeritus Professor of same. He's a Magdalene man, which is why the procession started there.'

Marcus looked surprised. 'So Gnats didn't offer to put her up?'

'Our dear old college is still rather queasy about female visitors,' said Campion wearily, 'and Magdalene offered a decent bed and breakfast and a chance to snoop around the Pepys Library, though I'm not sure she managed that. When we spoke on the phone last night she was furious at one of the dons, who'd apologized to her for not having the latest copy of *Woman's Own* for her to read.'

'You would have thought the university might have taken out a subscription to *Aviation Weekly*, if there is such a thing, or . . .' Marcus's face bloomed with surprised delight, which Campion took as advance warning sign that a witticism, or what passed for one among solicitors, was on its way, '. . . arranged a showing of that new film, you know, *Those Magnificent Men in their Flying Machines*. It's supposed to be jolly funny, though I suppose Lady Amanda would prefer it to be *Those Magnificent Women*.'

'I am very proud of the fact that my wife has reached the top of a male-dominated profession and has done so whilst keeping her temper and not leaving a trail of bodies a mile long in her wake. I am especially proud that the university is honouring her achievement.'

'I would think her bringing the Alandel Aeroplanes research team to Cambridge weighed in her favour,' said Featherstone waspishly.

Campion did not rise to the bait. 'Alandel is part of a big national concern now, and Amanda's Goshawk Project is merely a small cog in a bigger, well-oiled machine, but the university seemed keen to have it based here.'

'I suppose it's all hush-hush, most secret, this Goshawk Project. If you explained it to me then I suppose you'd have to kill me.' Marcus gave a patently fake laugh.

'I'm not sure I could explain it to you, Marcus. Most of it is way above my head, but I could try and then, yes, I would have to kill you, so could you recommend a good solicitor before we start?'

'Naturally, I wouldn't want you to break any confidences,' said Marcus, clearly unnerved by Campion's deadpan expression, 'and I was not suggesting that your wife's honorary degree was in any way recompense for bringing Alandel to Cambridge.

After all, we all have to embrace the white heat of modern technology these days, don't we? Even in Cambridge.'

Mr Campion's expression softened and his eyes twinkled behind the lenses of his large round spectacles. 'I would never suspect a solicitor of such venal thoughts, old boy, especially not one who cites speeches by Harold Wilson, a prime minister I suspect he did not vote for, but it is all about modern technology and science, and it's all too modern for me. The Goshawk Project is researching the possibility of producing an advance agile fighter plane and looking at structure and stress on metals. And that is the sum total of my knowledge, but fortunately Amanda and Professor Branscombe both know what they are talking about so I don't have to.'

'It's based out on Madingley Road, isn't it?'

'So I believe. Somebody found them an old aircraft hangar now surplus to requirements, but I have not yet had the grand tour. I suppose that will follow when she shows off her honorary doctorate from an open-top bus to the adulation of the staff there. I got the idea from the Cup Final where the winning team parades the trophy around their hometown streets.'

Campion extended a forefinger and gently poked the solicitor above the second button of his waistcoat.

'Don't look so worried, Marcus. It was yet another of my brilliant ideas to be instantly rejected by my sensible wife, but I think some sort of party is planned for the boffins out at Goshawk this evening, after the jollities in Senate House.'

'An odd career for a woman, aircraft design,' said Marcus, as if the thought had been bothering him since birth.

'I don't see why. There have been numerous famous aviatrixes – or should that be *aviatrices*? I'm never sure. Lots of women flew during the war, ferrying Spitfires and Lancaster bombers all over the place, and the Russians had female fighter pilots. Why shouldn't they have a say in how the planes are built?'

'Perhaps Amanda could plead her case with the chancellor when she meets him.'

'Lord Tedder? It's a nice touch that she's getting her doctorate from his hand, him being Eisenhower's deputy during the war and a former chief of air staff. A very famous hand, come to think of it, a hand which signed the instrument of unconditional surrender in 1945 – for the Allies, of course.'

Marcus Featherstone pulled back his neck and gave Campion a steady, studied and no doubt legal appraisal.

'You know, Albert, one is never sure when you are being serious or ridiculously frivolous; that's your problem.'

'Oh no, Marcus, that's not *my* problem at all.'

A hush seemed to fall over the whole city as the procession reached Senate House Yard. All traffic noise seemed to disappear on cue and only a lone bell rang out somewhere from a rogue college chapel. Campion was sure that black-gowned officials were already hurrying to seek out and silence the rebellious ringer.

He watched the last ritual turns of the academic quadrille which took place before the formal entrance, nodding to the few faces he recognized and the even more who seemed to recognize him, then he took his place for the ceremony at which his wife was confidently taking centre stage, even if in a non-speaking part.

She entered to a final fanfare of trumpets and took her place between her mentor, Professor Branscombe, and Jolyon Livingstone, the master of St Ignatius, who had clearly decided to claim credit by association for any Campion so honoured, even if it had to be a female one and in such an unusual field of expertise.

The proceedings, as he had warned Lugg, were in Latin, and the recitator, reading from a delicate scroll, declaimed an account of Amanda's achievements which must have taxed the most fluent scholar who composed it, not only for the use of so many feminine pronouns but for the approximation of Latin terms for aeroplane, aerodynamics and jet propulsion. Mr Campion was confident that the text would pass muster, as this was a university where notices warning students not to chain their bicycles to college railings were in Latin – *duae rotae* or 'two-wheel' being, apparently, what an Ancient Roman would have called his bicycle had he had one. (After all, Campion mused idly, they did have the roads for them.)

Through it all, Amanda sat gracefully and delicately

impassive, yet in no way aloof from the regal theatricals going on around – and because of – her. In Campion's eyes, Amanda appeared ethereal and luminous and, at that moment, in those surroundings, only a Botticelli could have done her justice.

A choir Campion had hardly noticed began to sing something he did not recognize and then the National Anthem, to which he reacted automatically, struck up to signal the completion of formal procedures and the senior university dignitaries led the charge to the waiting garden part outside.

Campion remained on the rim of the circle of black gowns and mortar boards which surrounded Amanda as she clutched her scroll in one hand and had a glass of champagne thrust into the other. The soft black bonnet she wore had slipped slightly to the back of her head, releasing a shock of auburn hair, but the female French-beret-style suited her perfectly and was being much admired by her all-male audience as she raised a glass in a polite toast to the university.

'You'll not get your wife back for hours,' said Jolyon Livingstone, appearing at his elbow. 'The dons seem entranced by her. An attractive and intelligent woman who has succeeded in that most masculine of professions has a certain . . .'

'Novelty value?' Campion suggested.

'That's rather harsh, Albert, although I admit that one or two of them may be thinking of the story of the dog who was supposed to have been tutored in arithmetic but, when asked what two plus two was, answered five.'

'The point being that the dog could speak at all, though the mathematicians hardly noticed that.'

'I'm a mathematician, Albert.'

'Of course you are, master, and a distinguished one, but you must admit that is a very masculine discipline as well.'

'Not necessarily.'

'Name a female mathematician in a senior position at Cambridge.'

'Mary Cartwright, at Girton. First-class mind.'

'I'll give you that,' said Campion. 'She did valuable work on radar during the war.'

'You knew about that? Oh, of course, I was forgetting you had an interesting war yourself.'

'Can you name another?' asked Campion, but the Master of St Ignatius had decided that the topic had reached its natural conclusion.

'Come on, Albert, let us grab a glass and make inroads into the smoked salmon before it's all gobbled up. You can introduce me to Lady Amanda.'

They eased their way through the press of bodies and the rumble of conversation, with Amanda's beaming face as their target, totally oblivious to the fact that two other men were on the same trajectory.

The two intruders reached her first. They were not dressed in academic garb, but were hatless and wearing raincoats, despite the fine weather, and as they reached Amanda, they took up position on either side of her and both placed a hand on her arms.

That gesture alone was enough to disturb the background hum of a dozen conversations, and an ominous silence descended on the gathering.

'Amanda Campion?'

'Yes.'

'Come with us, please.'

'Who are you?' Campion, still out of reach, heard his wife speak clearly in the sudden quiet.

'We're from Special Branch, ma'am,' said one of the men politely. 'Please come with us without making a fuss.'

'Am I under arrest?' said Amanda loudly for the benefit of the curious crowd.

'Just come with us quietly, please.'

'Surely I'm allowed to know why I'm being detained,' Amanda demanded, her voice rising in anger.

Her outrage did not intimidate her two oppressors, who tightened their grip on her arms, and one of them seemed to take an inordinate pleasure in saying loudly: 'For breaking the Official Secrets Act.'

TWO
Meet and Greet

'I am so sorry, Campion. These are the most abominable of circumstances in which to give you the guided tour.'

'They are, but you are certainly not to blame for them, Professor.'

The casual observer might have thought that, of the two men walking across the floor of what had clearly been an aircraft hangar, it was Professor Branscombe rather than Albert Campion who was suffering the most from the aftershock of the events a few hours before. Without doubt he seemed the more anxious of the pair; his physical movements were best described as edgy and his demeanour tense. There was even a definite tick in his right eyebrow when he spoke, and changing out of formal academic dress into a comfortable Tweed jacket with leather elbow patches had done little to relax him.

'That was a truly awful scene at Senate House,' said Branscombe. 'Are you sure you want to do this? You must still be shaken to the core.'

Mr Campion considered that as it had been his wife who had been very publicly accused of high treason and dragged away screaming in chains (for surely that would be Lugg's version of events as he recounted them in The Platelayer's Arms), his core had every right to be agitated. He did, however, have a sneaking suspicion that John Branscombe's sensibilities had been troubled by the fact there had been a *scene*, rather than any alleged breach of national security. If Amanda – whom he clearly saw as his appointee for the honorary doctorate – had tripped and broken one of those spectacular high heels in full view of the academically great if not good, he felt sure the professor would have been equally devastated.

'I have often said that my wife is a constant surprise to me, but for once I understate the case.'

'There must have been some dreadful misunderstanding.'

'Of that I am certain, just as I am that Amanda will easily clear things up, but given the nature of the alleged offence, I'm unlikely to get to see her while enquiries are being made. That's the most frustrating thing.'

'Do you know where they have taken her?'

'In the first instance it will be to the new Mid-Anglia police headquarters in Brampton, over at Huntingdon. A solicitor chum I ran into this morning, Marcus Featherstone, offered to go out there and find out what he could. If it's serious, then I would think they'd cart her off to London.'

'Not the Tower of London?' The professor was genuinely aghast.

'Oh, Amanda would insist upon it! But until we find out exactly what secrets have been divulged and to whom, there's very little I can do, for you see I have no idea what secrets she was privy to. Well, obviously, otherwise they wouldn't be secrets. The fact is I am disgracefully ignorant about the Goshawk Project, but as we are standing in what seems to have been an aircraft hangar and the fact that my wife has just received an honorary doctorate for her contribution to aeronautical engineering, would it be a fair guess that the Goshawk is an aeroplane?' Campion presented his blandest, most vacuous facial expression to the professor in an appeal for understanding and sympathy.

'Not yet it isn't,' said Branscombe, and immediately suspected that Campion was no wiser for the information. 'By which I mean there will be a Goshawk one day if the research being done here gets the right results. Or might be – one can never be sure when it comes to aircraft production these days, unless there's a war on.'

'Wars are good for the aeroplane business?'

'Of course they are – look at the last one. We started with biplanes held together with string, fought off an invasion with Hurricanes and Spitfires and ended up with jet fighters.'

'So the Goshawk is a jet fighter – or might be. Do I take

it that my wife is merely waiting for a convenient war to break out to boost her research?'

'No, not at all,' said Branscombe, retreating. 'The work here is mostly theoretical.'

'Good. I would hate to think of my darling wife as a latter-day James Puckle.'

'I'm sorry, Campion, you've lost me. Was he a Cambridge man?'

'That I do not know and, forgive me, I'm rambling. James Puckle invented the machine gun, a flintlock machine gun, back in 1718, which was supposed to have round bullets to fire at Christians and square ones to shoot at Ottomans. It was the first nasty thing which popped into my head when I considered the overlap between Amanda's work and the more belligerent aspects of aviation.'

'The connection is inevitable,' said Branscombe, 'and always had been. When Blériot flew across the Channel, the powers-that-be didn't think here was a new way to attract tourists, they instinctively thought how many bombs could he have brought with him? Developments in aircraft design and engines are interchangeable between the civil and military sectors. After all, the Spitfire was a racing seaplane until somebody thought to put guns on it.'

'But the work here is civilian, not military?'

'It's *theoretical*,' Branscombe said carefully, weighing his words like a lawyer, 'but it would be naïve to think it did not have military implications. This is, though, a civilian establishment with only a minimal input from the military.'

'How minimal?'

'We have been allocated an air officer as a sort of consultant. He's only a part-time visitor and he's American, from one of the USAF bases; he's a token gesture to keep our major ally happy.'

'And the rest of the personnel? Can you give me a brief run-down, without breaking any confidences?'

'Certainly, you would have met them this afternoon anyway, under . . . normal circumstances. As it is, all the workshop technicians will have gone home by now, but I asked the senior engineers to stay behind. They had their lunch hour disrupted while we were at Senate House. Two Special Branch chaps turned up to take statements from them and they are dying to know what's going on.'

'So am I,' said Mr Campion.

Transcript of STATEMENT (Voluntary): My name is Kevin John Loder, I am 46, married with two boys and I am a senior engineer on the AAF-003 project in the airframe section. I attended Birmingham University where I got a first-class degree in engineering and my first job was local, at 'The Austin', which is what we called the British Motor Corporation. In 1940 I was drafted to Vickers in Weybridge to work on the Wellington bomber. Inspired by Barnes Wallis – you must have heard of him – the Wellington had a geodetic structure which was light but strong. Lady Amanda said my subsequent expertise in wing structures and stiff, twist-resistant structures made me crucial to the Goshawk Project, which is flattering coming from someone like her who knows what she's on about when it comes to aircraft.

'The command structure here is somewhat fluid,' said Branscombe, as he led Campion across the concrete floor of the hangar, the taps of their heels echoing off the corrugated metal walls. 'I am the overall director and the official link with the university. Amanda is, officially, our technical director, and of course our main liaison with Alandel, as was, though it's now part of Hawker Siddeley, and any government department which wants to stick its nose into our business.'

'And that happens often?' Campion carefully sidestepped a puddle of glutinous oil which someone had begun to soak up with shredded cotton waste, but then abandoned.

'More and more these days. There's a saying in this business: all modern aircraft have four dimensions – span, length, height and politics. You know who said that?'

'No, but it sounds rather clever. Do tell.'

'Sir Sydney Camm, the chap who designed the Hurricane and went on to work with jets. Brilliant man.'

'So I believe. Amanda's mentioned him; one of her heroes.'

'I think he's a hero of all the senior engineers here. They're the chaps who direct operations at the coal face, as you might say.'

Campion made a show of turning his head to take in the array of welding, cutting and grinding machinery, now silent and at rest, as quiet as a petrified forest of tree stumps.

'Shouldn't that be metal face, rather than coal face?'

'There are times when this place resembles a foundry and, you know engineers, they do like to get their hands dirty. Which is why we have these.'

Branscombe pointed his right shoe and gently kicked an open drum at the end of a workbench. The contents, green and gelatinous, quivered under the strip lighting.

'I assume that's not lime-flavoured jelly,' said Campion, 'though it does remind me of the school dinners I still have nightmares about.'

'Swarfega,' said Branscombe, 'the mechanic's friend. Best known substance for cleaning greasy hands, once you get over the counter-intuitiveness of dipping your hands in green slime in order to get them clean. It's also remarkably good for the skin, leaves your hands nice and soft.'

'I'm sure Amanda swears by it and carries a small jar of it in her handbag.'

'Wouldn't surprise me,' said Branscombe, considering the matter seriously. 'She's not frightened to get her hands dirty, that's why the staff here all love her.'

Transcript of STATEMENT (Voluntary): I'm Melvin Barnes and I'm the grumpy old sod the young 'uns are supposed to look up to, though they never do. [indistinguishable] Me? I'm 52, so there's life in me still. Got my HND in mechanical engineering at Aston Technical College, specializing in aircraft engines, and went straight to work at the Bristol Aero Engine Company in Filton, which made me a reserved occupation when the war came and I worked mostly on the Centaurus engine. After the war I moved on to work on jet engines with Bristol Siddeley Olympus. After the wife died a few years back, I took up with Alandel for a quieter life. When Goshawk came up, I volunteered, thinking it would be an even quieter life. Didn't realize there would be all these students needing mollycoddling.

'I promised the senior engineers I would brief them on . . . events,' said Branscombe, 'though I really don't know what to say.'

They were halfway across the hangar, having passed a large, vicious-looking lathe, and walked under a motorized travelling crane spanning the entire width of the space, rolling along steel girders high up the hangar's side walls. The far end had a wood and glass partition protecting what was clearly an office space, though Campion doubted it was soundproof and, when all the machines in the hangar were going at full speed, would hardly be a place for quiet, considered meetings. Leaning casually against the partition were four men, standing apart, not talking, three of them smoking pipes. They might have been commuters waiting for the 7.32 to London Bridge and, though they had caught the same train together for ten years, being English they had never introduced themselves.

'I wondered if you might like to say a word . . .?'

'I'm not sure I could tell them anything,' said Mr Campion, 'though I would like to meet all the staff at some point. But as of now, what could I say? *My wife is innocent of all charges, whatever those charges might be?* To misquote a famous legal maxim: I would say that, wouldn't I?'

'Perhaps we'll know more tomorrow,' Branscombe spoke as if to convince himself, 'when the junior staff are here. They're a mixture of Alandel technicians and postgraduate students from my department. They are all quite in thrall to Lady Amanda.'

'Isn't everyone?' asked Campion.

Transcript of STATEMENT (Voluntary): My full name is Nugent Cyril Monck and I am 38 years old. I did my National Service in the RAF and decided to stay in the service. I got my qualifications in engines and airframes at Cranwell and held the rank of squadron leader on leaving the service to join Rolls-Royce Aero Engine. My speciality is the link between engine design and airframe application, which is, obviously, critical to a successful outcome for Goshawk. [indistinguishable] No, I am certainly not married and I have never worked for a woman before, but I fail to see what that has to do with anything.

'Left to right,' said Branscombe quietly, his chin on his chest, so that only Campion could hear, 'we have Melvyn Barnes, who regards himself as something of a father-of-the house figure, then Kevin Loder, who is our main airframe chap, and Nugent Monck, who is ex-RAF and therefore knows everything worth knowing about aircraft, or assumes he does.'

Campion scanned the line of men, who had now, in his imagination, undergone a radical transformation from expectant commuters to a line of apprehensive stage-door johnnies, as his mother might have called them.

'And the fourth?' said Campion. 'Is he the American air-force liaison man you mentioned?'

'No, he's one of our engineers, but he is American. How did you know?'

'He's a foot taller than anyone else, he's wearing jeans and a short-sleeved shirt with a bow tie, and there's a packet of cigarettes in the breast pocket. Elementary, my dear Branscombe.'

Transcript of STATEMENT (Voluntary): Do I need a lawyer here? Or somebody from my embassy? It's a big building in Grosvenor Square, I'm sure even you guys couldn't miss it. [indistinguishable] OK, OK. My name's Gary Cupples and I am, as you might have guessed from my accent, not from around these parts. [indistinguishable] Originally? I'm from Fresno, California, but went east to graduate from Harvard, then back out to the left coast for life in the skunk works at Lockheed Martin in Burbank. I'm what you'd call a design engineer and I came over here to see if I could help you Brits with your TSR-2 and we all know how that turned out. Then I got the royal summons to join Goshawk here in Cambridge. [indistinguishable] OK, so she's not actually royal, but me and some of the guys do call her Your Majesty when she's not around. We colonials tend not to be very respectful of your lords and ladies.

'Actually,' said Branscombe, 'all the senior staff wear bowties when the machines are running. You don't want a normal tie dangling into your work when you're leaning over a lathe or a spinning saw.'

Campion nodded agreement. 'Same principle as surgeons and snooker players, and they should be compulsory for waiters serving soup. Now, will you do the honours?'

'Of course.' Branscombe steered Campion towards the man on the far left of the line. 'Gentlemen, thank you for staying behind on what has been a most unusual and upsetting day for us all, but especially for Albert Campion, who has asked to meet you all. Albert, this is Kevin Loder, our key man on airframe structure.'

The first man in the line-up – for Campion thought of it almost as a police identity parade rather than a receiving line – stepped forward and offered a handshake.

Kevin Loder was a small, solid man with a firm grip, and when he spoke it was still with traces of a Birmingham accent in spite of conscious attempts to control or eradicate it.

'Is there any news of Lady Amanda's . . . do we call it predicament?'

'I think that's a very good word for it,' said Mr Campion, 'but I'm afraid there isn't. The little I know points to it being connected to the Goshawk Project and, as I know little, if anything, about that, Professor Branscombe offered to give me the guided tour, so I can get an idea of who you are and what you do here – see you in action, as it were.'

'Not much action today,' said Loder, 'not with the kerfuffle at lunchtime. Thought it best to give the workers the afternoon off, but if you can pop by tomorrow, I'll get Alf to show you the ropes.'

'Alf?'

'Alf Bagley, the workshop manager. Rules the shop floor with a rod of steel. Salt of the earth, came with Lady Amanda from Alandel.'

'Most of us here did,' said the second man in the line, who

stepped, or rather limped forward, offering his hand. 'I'm Melvyn Barnes, the old man of the hills as they call me round here.' His voice also betrayed traces, deliberately supressed, of Black Country origins.

'Melvyn takes great pleasure in his great age,' said Loder, 'though in fact he's only six years older than I am.'

'But a mere chicken compared to a fossilized pensioner like me,' said Campion with a grin.

'No offence meant, I'm sure, my lord. I wasn't implying anything specific.'

'None taken, but we'll both be in hot water if you call me a lord. Lady Amanda certainly is a lady, as the daughter of an earl, albeit one nobody remembers much. I have never accepted or admitted to a title, although I have been given several; usually when I am out of earshot. I'm happy to stick with Mr Campion, or Albert, if you're happy for me to call you Melvyn.'

'Happy to make your acquaintance I'm sure, Albert,' said Barnes, and with a twinkle in his eyes he nodded to the next in line. 'We don't go much on titles here, do we, Squadron Leader?'

The third man did not step forward but drew himself up parade-ground straight before thrusting out a hand. He was a good six inches shorter than Campion; a thin, sallow-faced individual with a pencil moustache, which had probably taken three or four years to grow and had not been worth the wait.

'Nugent Monck,' he said in a voice which betrayed a slight lisp, 'and I was a squadron leader in the RAF in a previous life. If some people insist on continuing to use my rank, I do not take umbrage, for I am rather proud of my service career. It makes me appreciate leadership, hard work and a loyal workforce, especially when the work is sensitive and involves military assets.'

Campion was not sure how to take this strange little speech from a rather strange little man, who seemed almost perfectly named, as there was an ascetic, almost monkish quality about him.

'I am sure you're right,' said Campion, not quite sure what he was agreeing to, 'and I hope my wife keeps you all on a tight leash with noses pressed to the grindstone, assuming that one of the fearsome machines in here is a grindstone.'

'Lady Amanda is truly an inspiration to us all,' said Monck, 'and I for one am happy to serve under her, even if we have disagreed on certain lapses of discipline.'

'Discipline? I would have thought Amanda ruled with a rod of iron.'

Melvyn Barnes jabbed the air with his pipe, now fortunately dormant. 'Don't pay Nugent too much mind, Mr Campion. He has a bee in his bonnet about things going missing or mislaid.'

'Going missing? Not secrets going missing? And can you mislay a secret in a moment of forgetfulness?'

'No, no, nothing like that. Nugent's convinced somebody's stealing offcuts of tubing.'

'Tubing? Now I'm really confused.' Campion turned to Professor Branscombe for both elucidation and rescue.

'It's an internal matter,' said the professor. 'Nugent discovered certain *discrepancies* in our stocks of raw materials. Amanda did not think it very serious, but Alf Bagley, whom you'll meet tomorrow, is dealing with it. It's a minor matter of no great consequence.'

'But much of the work we do here is of consequence,' fumed Nugent Monck. 'Possibly great consequence to the nation's defence through the capability of our air force.'

'It must, therefore,' said Campion carefully, 'be reassuring for Amanda to have a flier who has seen active service advising her.'

Monck's cheeks began to glow pink. 'To my eternal disappointment, the war was done and dusted before I joined up,' he said, his teeth clamped tight.

'Of course,' said Campion. 'I forget how young people can be these days. And here's another one who makes me feel like a dinosaur.'

He had passed smoothly by Nugent Monck, and now stood in front of clearly the youngest of the four engineers on show, the tall, strapping American, his crew-cut blond hair and sun-tanned arms declaring his nationality better than his passport.

'Gary Cupples, Your Honour,' said the fresh-faced young man with an impressive display of perfect, and perfectly white, teeth.

'This is becoming something of a record,' Campion laughed, 'having to deny both a peerage and a judgeship in the space of two minutes! I am not a member of the judiciary and these days rarely get asked to judge the local flower and produce show. If I had ever held court anywhere, it would have been in the 4-Ale Bar of The Panton Arms.'

'Hey, I know that pub! We drink there with some of the students.' The American's smile widened.

'Students always have, but I'm so ancient I remember the old brewery, Bailey & Tebbutt as it was in my day. Does it still serve a decent pint?'

'I'll say. Hey, sorry about the "Your Honour" gaff, I just assumed that any Brit married to a lady must have some sort of title, even if your government is full of socialists.'

Campion peered over the top of his spectacles, giving Gary Cupples what he liked to think of as his 'disapproving Latin master' stare.

'Unlike you Americans, we tend not to see a Red under every bed—'

'Perhaps we should,' interrupted Nugent Monck.

'And why should we do that?' Campion asked him.

'In view of the events surrounding your wife, Campion.' Monck blustered. 'If Lady Amanda has been arrested . . .'

'Detained,' said Campion firmly.

'Detained, then, under the Official Secrets Act, it must suggest that there has been some sort of leak of confidential information or sensitive research. I'm not saying for one moment that your wife is guilty of anything herself, but security round here is notoriously lax. I have raised the topic with her on several occasions.'

Monck fell silent, as though he had run out of steam. An embarrassingly loud squeak of expelled air as Melvyn Barnes blew through the stem of his pipe seemed to provide a full stop and introduce an uncomfortable silence.

'Don't mind Nugent, Mr Campion,' Gary Cupples smirked, 'he sees more Commies under more beds than J. Edgar Hoover, and if your FBI guys are looking for spies when it comes to aircraft, then they'll start with me.'

'Now why on earth would they do that?'

'Because we Americans have form, as you might say. We have a track record in stealing British designs and there's plenty who think that the cancellation of TSR-2 was all part of a plot to make Britain buy the F-111 from Uncle Sam.'

Nugent Monck glared, Kevin Loder stared at the concrete floor and Melvyn Barnes noisily cleared his pipe again as Gary Cupples held out both wrists towards Mr Campion.

'Go on, snap on the cuffs, clap me in irons, do what you have to. If it gets Amanda out from under the bus where she's been thrown, then lock me up and throw away the key.'

THREE
The Goshawk Project

It was a very nice house, there was no denying it; a family house with a long verdant garden, complete with summer house, ideal for children and other pets, convenient for the town centre and, directly across the fields beyond the garden, the Goshawk Project itself. It came with a telephone and a housekeeper who could also cook meals, and Mr Campion could have the run of it.

'For the . . . duration . . . or until things become clearer,' said Professor Branscombe.

'That's really most kind of you,' said Campion, surveying the well-appointed kitchen in which they stood clutching mugs of tea, 'but I could not deprive your family of such a lovely home.'

'Nonsense. I will be perfectly happy in my rooms in Magdalene – I spend most of my time there anyway. Of course, you may prefer to stay in St Ignatius. I'm sure they could find room for you.'

'Jolyon Livingstone did offer, but I could tell he wasn't keen and I cannot blame him. When the press get hold of the story, I am bound to draw some unwanted attention to the college in the general hue and cry. Still, I feel I need to remain in Cambridge until I have a better idea of what Amanda is supposed to have done, so your offer is tempting, but no, I really could not impose on your family.' Campion paused as a tiger-striped short-haired tabby cat appeared as if by magic from behind his legs and strolled casually across the kitchen to examine, with disdain, an empty dish on the floor by the sink unit.

'But you wouldn't be imposing on anyone, my dear fellow. I live here quite alone and I actually prefer to be in college rather than rattling around in this place.'

Mr Campion pondered the professor's sudden, enthusiastic outburst, and also noted the withering look given by the cat as he said the words 'quite alone'. At least Branscombe had not suggested he became a lodger or that they moved in together as roommates.

'Quite alone, Professor?' he asked, frantically trying to remember what, if anything, Amanda had told him about her fellow Goshawk Project director.

'I'm afraid so.' Branscombe bowed his head for a moment as if in confession, then looked Campion full in the face. 'You may as well hear it from me: my wife has left me. She ran off a month ago with an *astrophysicist*!' He almost spat the word out, as though denying Satan and most, if not all, of his works. 'She took the children and the dog and moved into a big house on Hills Road with him. I'm supposed to sell this place before the end of the long vacation in order to help keep her in the style she has become used to.'

'I am sorry to hear that.'

'Don't be, I'm beyond sympathy. Look, Campion, you'd be doing me a favour in a way. You need a base while you're in Cambridge, and here's a ready-made one, if you'll just keep an eye on the place so I don't have to. Astra will do the house-work, feed the cats and cook for you if you ask her nicely.'

'Astra is the housekeeper, I presume.' He pointed at the cat now sitting upright and looking bored. 'You said cats, plural.'

'We have two, or rather I should say I have two: Pratt and Whitney. They keep the mice down. That's Pratt, Whitney must be out killing something. There's a stream at the bottom of the garden, part of a thing called the Bin Brook. It's posi-tively heaving with water voles and rats.'

'Unusual names,' murmured Campion.

'I did some work for Pratt and Whitney in their Canadian plant some years back. They always made dependable engines, that was their slogan, though it's probably not a description applicable to cats. My wife never liked them, she's a dog person – and she hated Canada.'

Campion bowed graciously. 'I'd be delighted to keep company with Pratt and Whitney, Professor, and keep an eye on them, though hopefully only for a few days until things get sorted out. Let me telephone St Ignatius and get a message to my colleague, who will be lurking at their gates if they haven't had him arrested or carted away by now.'

'Is there anything I can get you?'

'My chap can take the car back to London, pick me up some stuff from my flat and be back here before the pubs shut. I'd better tell him the address, though.'

'112 Barton Road.'

'Thank you, now show me the telephone and then tell me all I need to know, or am allowed to know, about the Goshawk Project.'

'Certainly. Where should I start?'

'With whatever came immediately after the Wright Brothers,' said Mr Campion.

'I won't go quite that far back,' said Branscombe, and then shocked Campion into total silence. 'Let's start with the Nazis.'

It had been the Germans, during the war (Professor Branscombe explained), who had been the first to experiment with the concept of 'swept-forward wings' in aircraft design. Well, perhaps not strictly true, as the Americans, Russians, Poles and Japanese had all done some work before the war, but the Germans brought the idea into the jet age.

Swept forward? Well, most jets have wings which are swept back. Think of the English Electric Lightning, now available as a Dinky Toy. Swept-back wings are vital in reducing drag when the aircraft is flying close to the speed of sound. Should he go into Bernoulli's law, Mach numbers and spanwise flow? Perhaps not. (Mr Campion was relieved and still thinking about Dinky Toys.)

But the idea of sweeping the wings *forward* was to imitate the action of birds, who can sweep their wings forward to increase manoeuvrability by reversing the normal spanwise airflow, the logic being that it would improve performance in terms of lift and drag, which could offer high manoeuvrability and agility, both desirable qualities in a military aircraft.

The Germans, as we all know, developed an effective jet fighter during the war and it was perhaps lucky for the Allies that they tried to put swept-forward wings on a bomber, the

Junkers Ju 287, which had four jet engines. That was in 1944, but by 1945 the Junkers factory had been captured by the advancing Russians and, in very short order, the factory and all its personnel were uprooted and moved to just outside Moscow in order to develop a Russian version, the EF 131. That made its debut in 1946 but was not a success despite having an impressive *six* jet engines. The professor even had grainy black-and-white photographs of the Junkers, complete with Lutfwaffe markings and a swastika on the tailfin, and its Russian copy. The two bombers looked remarkably similar, but therein lay the problem; they were designed as bombers and, for a bomber, the key thing is carrying bombs.

The reason the designers used swept-forward wings on the Ju 287 was that they put the centre of lift forward, allowing the main spar to be placed behind areas of load in the fuselage, such as the bomb bay, instead of right through it. That, *at least theoretically*, made the structure of the fuselage lighter while maintaining its strength. Wings could be smaller and perform-ance improved, offering better manoeuvrability and agility. But – and it was big 'but' – with the materials and technology available back in the 1940s, this meant such a design was fundamentally unsound for a bomber carrying a full payload and, with jet engines, travelling at higher and higher speeds, putting enormous stresses on fuselages which simply could not take the strain.

(The professor offered to go into more detail on the topic of 'spanwise flow' and the dangers of a 'Dutch roll' thankfully at a later date.)

Despite multiple jet engines, those bombers were relatively slow, but the theoretical advantages of a swept-forward wing design could apply to fast modern jets which fly near and beyond the speed of sound. The extra agility and increased manoeuvrability could give a fighter jet a real advantage in aerial combat.

Of course, the professor assured a slightly glazed Campion, it was not that simple (at which Mr Campion nodded wisely), as much research had to be done on the strength and stiffness of the wings and how they might twist under aerodynamic strain, and that research was a key component of the work of the Goshawk Project, the long-term goal being to overcome all the hurdles and design such a fighter, hence the official classification as AAF-3, or Advanced Agile Fighter, the 'three' being the third attempt by the government to get such research off the ground. The name Goshawk coming from the northern goshawk, which is supposed to be the most agile of birds at high speed.

There was, of course, a very long way to go before this particular goshawk flew at all, or even got built. The joint Alandel/university project was a theoretical exercise to see if the problems inherent in swept-forward wing design could be solved by an assemblage of first-class engineering brains (the professor had the good grace not to identify himself in this category, leaving the obvious unsaid) outside the whole sphere of government defence spending and thus free of political interference.

Mr Campion finally found himself on more familiar ground and seized the opportunity to ask a question. 'You mean political interference as with the cancellation of the TSR-2?'

'Exactly. That was a world-class aircraft but it has been axed by this Labour government for political, not aviation or defence reasons. It's a great shame and we'll come to regret it.'

Campion suspected he had discovered the professor's hobby-horse.

'You mark my words. In ten or even twenty years' time, the TSR-2 will still be ahead of its rivals.'

'Unless the Goshawk replaces it.'

'No, don't mix apples and oranges. The TSR-2 was designed as a Tactical Strike and Reconnaissance aircraft, hence TSR, which could deliver a nuclear weapon and bombs; hence it was a bomber. The Goshawk, if it ever exists, will be a fighter.'

'But subject to the same political pressures.'

'I'm afraid so.'

'Your young American engineer – Cupples – referred to them this afternoon and, if I understood him correctly, he was implying that the cancellation of TSR-2 was all part of a plot to get us to buy American aircraft, and that it wasn't the first time it had happened.'

'Well, that depends on how cynical is your view of aviation history.'

'I am disgracefully ignorant of that speciality, given my wife's profession. In general terms I followed the maxim that to be ignorant of history is to have the mind of a child, until I discovered that was coined by Cicero, who was a lawyer and therefore probably not to be trusted. Anyway, having the mind of a child has kept me blissfully happy for most of my sixty-five years.'

Campion noticed the frown forming on Branscombe's forehead, and the way the professor was looking at him with increasing concern. 'I'm sorry, I must sound as if I'm rambling. I do if I tend to have more than one thing on my mind and today has been a bit busy for the old brainbox. Please continue to pile on the pressure. I'm sure I can take it.'

'Then let me give you the cynical version, which I have to admit is the popular one with most of our engineers over at Goshawk. During the war, the British company Miles was given a contract by the government to develop a supersonic plane and the result was the Miles M.52, which I worked on myself in a minor capacity at their place in Berkshire. Naturally, we were all sworn to the utmost secrecy because we were aiming for a jet aircraft which could reach 1,000 miles per hour. In 1944, our American allies were informed of the project and they suggested a joint venture with their plane makers at Bell. You will recall that joint ventures and cooperation on scientific research were rather vital back then.

'In due course, a delegation of American designers and engineers came over to examine the plans for and calculations behind the Miles M.52, even taking the initial designs back to America with them to "run the numbers" as they put it. For whatever reason, the joint venture never materialized and the silence from across the Atlantic was deafening. As soon as the war in Europe ended, the team at Miles contacted Bell and politely asked for their plans back, along with the results of any work the Americans might have contributed. They were told, in no uncertain terms, that the research was classified top secret and further enquiries were unwelcome. Towards the end of 1945, the Miles company was told, on the quiet, to forget about the M.52, and in early 1946 Atlee's Labour government formally announced that the project had been axed.'

'Hence the similarity with Wilson's Labour government axing the TSR-2,' said Campion. 'Yes, I can see why people might think there's some bizarre conspiracy being perpetuated.'

'Conspiracies tend to be in the eye of the beholder, of course. There may have been legitimate reasons – political or economic – for both decisions. It's common knowledge that the TSR-2 went way over budget and the Atlee government had to face huge domestic problems after the war, rebuilding and feeding the country as well as introducing the National Health Service. A jet plane attempting to break the sound barrier perhaps wasn't seen as essential, however brilliant the design. The thing that niggled those of us involved in aviation, though, was that shortly after the Miles M.52 was consigned to the dustbin, the Americans produced the Bell X-1, which looked suspiciously like the M.52; *very* similar, in fact. The Bell plane went on to famously fly at supersonic speed, piloted by a chap with the unlikely name of Chuck Yeager.'

'Do you think history has repeated itself? Our TSR-2 has been consigned to the flames, but an all-American version will pop up out of the ashes to replace it?'

'I doubt that as the Americans have an aircraft, the F-111, which they are more than willing to sell us and which the RAF will be told to buy. You find this amusing?'

Campion realized he had allowed himself what Amanda had christened his 'most inane grin'.

'Not really, it's just ironic that in the middle of a Cold War, where the Russians are supposed to be our deadly enemies, we don't seem to trust our American allies very much, at least when it comes to aircraft. Perhaps Gary Cupples was right – we should have him arrested on principle.'

'That would be on the assumption that someone is leaking the Goshawk research, which we do not know for sure is the case.'

'No, we do not,' said Campion, all smiles, smirks and grins erased. 'But if the Official Secrets Act and Special Branch are both involved, that would seem a good guess. I take it the Goshawk Project does have secrets worth stealing, just as the Miles project had during the war?'

'Naturally it does on the technical level, but in all fairness I must point out that the designs of the Miles M.52 were not stolen by spies, they were given to the Americans in a spirit of wartime comradeship and cooperation.'

'And why would the Americans spy on Goshawk when one of their own is involved in the research?'

'You can't seriously suspect Gary Cupples of any misbehaviour,' said Branscombe with feeling. 'He's a Harvard man.'

'So is my son Rupert, whom I love dearly, but I'm not sure I would trust him with the keys to the wine cellar, let alone official secrets. I did, however, get the impression that Gary Cupples expects to be suspected. Would he know about the Miles affair? He would have still been in short trousers at the end of the war.'

'He's an aeronautical engineer who has worked for some big American companies; of course, he will be familiar with the case.'

'I'm afraid I wasn't.'

'Well, you should have been.' The professor scolded his guest with the voice he had used on a thousand slow-witted students. 'There was quite a furore in the papers back in the thirties when Maxine, Viscountess Ratendone, got divorced after an affair with her flying instructor. She would have been a great inspiration for your Amanda.'

'I certainly hope there were other reasons . . .' Campion let his voice trail off.

'Of course, I wasn't implying . . .' Branscombe cleared his throat. 'What I meant was that Maxine, once divorced, married her flying instructor who was Frederick *Miles* and she, Fred and his brother George went on to form Miles Aircraft, with many of their designs being adopted by the RAF during the war. The thing is Maxine, who was always known as Blossom for some reason, was a damn fine aviatrix who had her own plane which she called *Jemimah*.'

Campion smiled.

'Yes, Amanda would like that.'

'Not only could she fly, but Blossom also turned out to be

an excellent designer and draughtsman, previously thought an unsuitable job for a woman. She became a member of the Women's Engineering Society.'

'As was Amy Johnson,' said Campion, 'and as is Amanda. You see, I do pay attention sometimes.'

'And now you know some of the background to our Goshawk Project.'

'Oh, I haven't been paying *that* much attention,' said Campion lightly, 'but I do get the feeling that mistrust is rife in the world of aeronautical engineering.' He prodded the photographs that Branscombe had left on the kitchen table. 'The Nazis come up with a plane with forward-swept wings which the Russians steal; the British develop a supersonic jet plane, which the Americans then appropriate. Today, politicians cancel advanced airplanes seemingly on a whim in the middle of a Cold War, bringing comfort to our enemies and spreading doubt and misgivings among our own troops and supposed friends.'

'I told you not to worry about Gary Cupples. He's one of us, an engineer and a good one who has worked on front-line aircraft.'

'But he's not – I think you said – your official liaison with the American air force.'

'No, that's a chap called Luther Romo, whom you have yet to meet. He's a serving officer and a different kettle of fish entirely; doesn't trust us an inch.'

Mr Campion spread his palms in supplication. 'Can you blame him, or the Americans in general? By the way, he's not actually a general, is he? They can be awfully difficult. But my point is they have every right to be suspicious and mistrustful of us, given the constant stream of spy stories and revelations our newspapers have revelled in over the last few years. There was Philby finally nailing his colours to the mast and hitch-hiking to Moscow, the Portland spy ring, George Blake, Gordon Lonsdale, Vassall, Profumo . . . No wonder the Americans think we can't keep a secret.'

Having shown Campion the house, Professor Branscombe then showed him the garden as dusk started to fall. It was a long rectangle of a garden dominated by rambling rose bushes and apple trees desperate to be thinned out, along with a raised vegetable patch which still housed last year's crop of carrots and potatoes. Mr Campion did not think himself much of a detective to deduce that it had been the former Mrs Branscombe who had been the gardener at 112 Barton Road.

At the bottom of the garden was an octagonal summer house, made up of panels which opened like hatches to allow a flow of fresh air, or removed entirely so the structure could be used, should the unlikely need ever arise, as a bandstand, assuming the band contained no more than four musicians, none of whom played anything larger than a French horn. From the age and state of its wooden frame, Campion was sure it would sway and creak in a strong wind, perhaps even collapse, were it not propped up by a large wooden sherry barrel adapted as a water butt with a lid made of roughly cut planking. It may formerly have been a Butt or perhaps a Puncheon, Campion was not sure, but made a mental note to raise the matter the next time he dined at high table in St Ignatius. Someone there was bound to be an expert on the sizes of sherry casks.

Behind the summer house, marking the boundary of the garden, was a narrow stream, no more than two feet wide and overhung with long grasses and guarded by an impressively lush growth of nettles. This was, Branscombe repeated, part of the Bin Brook – the happy hunting ground for his cats Pratt and Whitney – which ran alongside the sports fields and tennis courts of several colleges parallel to – it was thought – the line of an old Roman road. To the left of the Bin Brook, untended fields concealed a disused rifle range used by the wartime Home Guard and, beyond that, further over to his left, Campion could make out the stark outline of the aircraft hangar which housed the Goshawk Project.

'Good place for a dog,' observed Campion. 'You could walk it to work across these fields.'

'Yes, well, I did have a dog, but my wife claimed him when she deserted me. You asked about a dog earlier . . . have you got an aversion to them?'

'Not at all, but I'm more of a cat person. Dogs can be loud

and enthusiastic and overfriendly. Cats, I feel, can always keep a secret.'

At Branscombe's insistence, they walked into town and found a Chinese restaurant where neither were likely to be recognized, something Campion thought highly unlikely, but the professor was clearly wary of running into any of his colleagues who may have witnessed *the scene* at Senate House.

As they finished their meal, Branscombe handed over the keys to 112 Barton Road and asked, for the sixth or seventh time, whether Campion would mind if he retired to his rooms in Magdalene and left Campion to his own devices.

Having repeatedly assured the professor that he was a big boy now and that he knew Cambridge of old, Mr Campion again thanked him for the loan of his house and set off alone to thread his way through the dimly lit Petty Cury and the lanes surrounding the Corn Exchange. By the time he emerged at the bottom of King's Parade, he knew he was being followed.

He crossed the river by the Silver Street bridge and stopped to gaze down at the dark, still water of the Cam and across Laundress Green to the armada of punts tied up for the night outside The Anchor. Glancing casually over his left shoulder as he leaned on the parapet of the bridge, he saw an all-too-familiar silhouette emerge from the shadow of Queen's College.

'It's all right for some,' grunted Lugg.

'Was that you pressing your nose against the window of the restaurant, salivating at the thought of a crispy Pekin duck?'

'Nah, Chinese nosh is not for me; too fiddly. I was round the corner 'aving a medicinal lemonade and a meat pie in the window seat of the snug of a very friendly boozer.'

'That was very abstemious of you, old fruit.'

'Well, you said I had to keep a clear head and watch your back. There was nobody after you, leastwise so far there ain't.'

'Give them time,' said Campion. 'I haven't made my presence felt yet. Where's the car, by the way?'

'Parked up down Barton Road, beyond the 'ouse, which looks a nice piece of property.'

'Amanda said it was and it's a perfect base for me.'

'Have much trouble getting your feet under the table?'

'None at all. Amanda was dead right about that too. I think the professor secretly likes the return to his bachelor days in college, with me looking after the family home and feeding his cats.'

'Cats? But no dogs?

'No dogs,' said Campion. 'I checked.'

From the back of Campion's Jensen, Lugg removed a smart new brown leather suitcase and an old army kitbag so tightly stuffed it could have doubled as a punchbag. He deposited both at the foot of the stairs in the Branscombe house and followed Campion into the kitchen.

'Do you need a bed making up?'

'There's a guest bedroom primed and ready,' said Campion. 'Branscombe has a housekeeper who comes in and does for him.'

'Probably some sour-faced Scottish hag who'll stick her nose in everywhere and give you cheek in an accent only Highland cattle can follow.'

'I have no idea whether she is a Scot,' said Campion serenely, 'or what dialect she might speak. Her name is Astra, which is rather appropriate to our current situation – *Per ardua ad astra*, if you remember your schoolboy Latin.'

The big man snorted in contempt. 'Leave my schooling out of it, but don't think I don't know the motto of the RAF when I hears it.' Lugg's eyes fell on the photographs on the kitchen table. 'An' I know enough about the RAF to know that *them* two aeroplanes 'ave got their wings on backwards! Do they only fly in reverse? No wonder the country's in a state.'

Campion shuffled the photographs away. 'Pretend you didn't see those, old fruit, and don't you worry about Astra McTavish or whatever her name is. The plan is to keep well out of her way. Now you'd better get off back to London – *again*. I take it nobody saw you this afternoon?'

Lugg's face crumpled in disappointment that such a question needed to be asked, then he drew himself up to attention. 'I followed yer orders blindly. Waited at St Ignatius like you said, then this flunky comes beetling out and says you're on the phone and could I step into them there 'allowed 'alls and take the call. I listens to your blather about going and fetching your washcloth and your unmentionables from Bottle Street and makes sure all those in earshot knew what I was up to, even that po-faced head porter, Gilbert.'

'Actually it's Gildart, but never mind. Then what?'

'Then I picks up the car, drives out into the countryside, finds a shady lane, changed out of my funeral gear into my civvies and caught up on a bit of shut eye. At the appointed hour I drive to the appointed map reference, which turns out to be an Iron Age hill fort, so the Ordnance Survey tells me, though I couldn't make it out. Anyway, your man turns up as promised and gives me these to give to you.'

Lugg's left paw reached into the inside pocket of his black blazer, the breast pocket of which displayed the crest of a minor public school, which Lugg had certainly not attended, but may well, in a past life, have burgled. He produced a few sheets of thin, carefully folded paper.

'They're carbon copies – "flimsies" he called them – and he said they were the introductory interviews, all conducted very gently and friendly like. No thumb screws involved. I suppose they come later.'

Campion took the sheaf of papers. 'Thank you for that. As far as anyone is concerned, you've just made it here from Bottle Street with my shaving gear and spare pyjamas and now you're going straight back there to stay by the telephone.'

'You sure I can't be more use here?'

'Positive. Even in a town full of eccentrics, you'd stand out like a sore thumb and the Bulldogs would be on to you like a shot.'

'Bulldogs? You said there was no dog.'

'Bulldogs with a capital "B",' Campion explained. 'They're the university police. A small, dedicated force, appointed by the vice chancellor to patrol the precincts. The porters are scary enough but the Bulldogs have powers of arrest.'

'Fair enough,' said Lugg with a shrug of his massive shoulders. 'If I put my foot down, I might just make last orders.'

'You be careful with that car. Undue wear and tear will come out of your wages.'

'There are wages for this job? Blimey! It must be serious.'

Campion slept well and in the morning was inordinately pleased that he had, first, mastered the plumbing of the house and drawn himself a hot bath and then, secondly, located a teapot, tea and a kettle in the kitchen. The morning then started to go downhill when he failed to find any milk either in the fridge or on the doorstep. He did find a supply of cat food, though, which at least reduced the howling of Pratt and Whitney who were circling his ankles.

Dressing quickly, he ventured out and found a corner shop, which sold him a pint of milk and two newspapers, the local *Cambridge News* and *The Times*.

As he strolled jauntily back down Barton Road, he saw that a shiny new black Ford Zephyr had parked outside number 112. It was hardly the vehicle in which an ancient Scottish crone (according to Lugg) transported her mops and buckets, so it seemed unlikely to be the transport of Branscombe's housekeeper – or if it was, the professor was paying her too much.

It was, on the other hand, exactly the sort of vehicle in which the forces of law and order tended to travel, and Campion was still fifty yards away when he identified the two men on the doorstep as plainclothes policemen.

'Good morning, officers. Can I be of assistance?' he called out cheerfully.

The rain-coated, trilby-wearing one who had been pressing the doorbell with some venom, turned on his heels. 'Are you Albert Campion?'

'Does he owe you money? I'm sorry, that's my flippant response to questions at this time in the morning. Yes, I am he.'

'Then you'd better come with us.'

'Where to?'

'Round to the Madingley Road, to a research facility.'

'The Goshawk Project?'

The second, younger policeman tried a less aggressive approach. 'If you wouldn't mind, sir.'

'I was just about to brew some tea,' said Campion, waving the milk bottle. 'May I offer you a cup?'

'No time, sir. Professor Branscombe said you ought to come straight away.'

'Well, he is the boss there. Is anything wrong?'

'There's been an accident, sir.'

'A pretty bloody one,' said his companion, who did appear a little pale and queasy, 'and a death.'

FOUR

A Deadly Span

It was near impossible to identify the deceased as there simply wasn't enough of him left undamaged for anyone to make an accurate facial recognition, but everyone knew it was Alan Wormold, a twenty-one-year-old postgraduate student whom Professor Branscombe had regarded as one of his best and brightest. Though not, unfortunately, any longer.

What there was of Alan Wormold was carefully hidden by a woollen blanket, fortunately a red one, provided by the two ambulancemen in attendance who were part of a small crowd of men gathered in a circle in the middle of the hangar floor.

The two plainclothes policemen who had denied Campion a leisurely breakfast cuppa steered him to the right-hand edge of the crowd, where Professor Branscombe was speaking rapidly to a man writing very slowly in a black policeman's notebook. Beyond them, through the large glass windows of the office at the far end of the hangar, he could see another ambulanceman leaning over and administering to a man sitting in a chair, whose mouth was opening and closing as if silently shouting.

'Ah, Campion, I'm glad you're with us. I didn't want you to have to hear about this second-hand.' Branscombe shook his head. 'It's shocking, quite shocking.'

'What exactly has happened here?'

'Alan Wormold, a former student of mine and one of our production engineers on the shop floor, as you might say. He was working at the big lathe here when the accident happened and he fell into the gap between the lathe bed and the spinning chuck.'

Campion was conscious that the word 'spinning' produced sharp intakes of breath from several of the assembled congregation.

'Fell?' said Campion, who was immediately confronted by the man who had been taking notes.

'You don't think so, sir?'

Branscombe interposed himself between the two. 'This is Detective Inspector Mawson. He's a policeman.'

'Obviously,' said Campion.

'He's from Cambridge CID.'

'We're now Mid-Anglia,' corrected Mawson, 'and I know who you are, Mr Campion.'

'I'm flattered.'

'You shouldn't be. Now what makes you think this wasn't just a tragic accident?'

'I never said it wasn't, but must we do this with an audience?'

'Good point,' said the policeman, closing his notebook and slapping it against his thigh as if calling for order, which he was. 'Sergeant! Get the gawkers outside, line 'em up and take all names and addresses. Only these two gents' – he waved his notebook at Campion and Branscombe – 'and the ambulance boys stay inside; and find out where our photographer is! Soon as he gets here, put him to work. Then we can remove the deceased, or what's left of him.'

'Has a doctor seen him?' asked Campion, and the policeman misjudged curiosity for criticism.

'The doc's been and gone. Took him about two seconds to declare the poor sod dead. Massive blood loss due to contact with violently spinning metal.' Mawson looked around the hangar floor. 'There's some pretty lethal machinery in here if you don't know what you're doing.'

'Our safety record is second to none,' Branscombe protested.

'Not any more,' said Campion, 'but if it was an industrial accident, it would hardly be a matter for the CID would it?'

The inspector skewered Campion with the unblinking stare he probably used in court when being cross-examined by an aggressive barrister.

'After yesterday's little incident with your wife, anything untoward to do with this place is a matter for the CID until proved otherwise.'

'So you are treating this as a crime rather than an accident?'

The detective raised a forefinger and pointed upwards. Beyond the lathe, which measured ten feet by four, and the shrouded body of its last victim, a heavy block and tackle arrangement hung down from the travelling crane at what would have been head height. Its pendant control unit, which reminded Campion of an old-fashioned wooden pencil box, dangled even lower on a thick black cable. It took only a glance back down the workshop to the hangar doors where the crane span normally rested to realize that the travelling crane had travelled three-quarters of the length of the building. The block and tackle it carried had traced a route neatly bisecting the hangar, directly in line with the large lathe.

The crane, being able to move forwards and backwards and presumably crabwise to the left or right along its span, had only limited ability to take evasive action if an unexpected item such as a human being got in the way of the block and tackle dangling from it. A human being, seeing or hearing its approach, would surely have got out of its way, or shouted an angry warning to the crane's operator.

'We think Wormold was working at the lathe with his back to the main doors,' said Mawson, looking to the professor for confirmation. 'He had a reputation for getting in early to work before anyone else showed up.'

'He was very keen,' said Branscombe sadly, 'and a very good worker.'

Campion surveyed the metal detritus scattered on and around the lathe, consciously averting his eyes from the blood splatters and the red blanket, from the bottom of which protruded a pair of feet in badly scuffed brown suede shoes.

'So he was alone in here, using the lathe and the crane . . .'

'He wasn't using the crane,' said Mawson. 'It came up behind him and if the block and tackle hadn't been hanging, would have passed over his head. As it was, it clobbered him and sent him into the gap between the lathe bed and the revolving chuck, which is what did the damage. The fatal damage.'

'But that block and tackle arrangement, it doesn't usually hang down like that, does it?'

'Of course not,' answered Branscombe. 'It's usually stowed away along with the control box at the far end of the workshop, by the doors. Normally whoever needs it uses the pendant control box and walks along with it as it moves until they get to where it is required. The winch on it can lift up to five tons and move things around the hangar. As we're modelling and researching light materials, we don't actually use it that much on a day-to-day basis.'

'Who would know how to use it?' Campion asked, noticing a wry smile creasing the detective inspector's lips.

'Everyone who works here, including Lady Amanda.'

'Fortunately, she has a cast-iron alibi thanks to Her Majesty's Secret Service,' Campion said with a trace of bitterness. 'But unless Alan Wormold operated the crane in one of the most bizarre suicides ever, somebody else must have.'

'I never said Alan Wormold was alone in here,' said Mawson. 'I said he was usually the first in before anyone else.'

'So there was someone else here who set the crane moving.' Campion paused. 'Which could make it manslaughter rather than an accident.'

'Or murder,' said the policeman. 'Shall we go and ask him?'

On entering the office area, Detective Inspector Mawson asked the uniformed ambulanceman to wait outside. As he sidled out of the door, Campion noticed the shiny metal hip flask he was attempting to hide under the skirt of his uniform jacket.

'That's not exactly doctor's orders, is it?' said Campion under his breath.

'He needed it, poor sod,' came the whispered reply, 'and so did I after what I saw first thing after breakfast . . .'

The poor sod in question was sitting in a high-backed chair as rigid as if he had been welded to it. His hands gripped his knees and his cheeks inflated and deflated like a frog's, but a pallid frog from which all the colour had been washed. He wore a blue boiler suit pocked with small burns and pinholes caused, Campion presumed, by shards of hot metal; it was open at the neck to reveal a grubby white shirt collar and a tie pulled askew. His complexion was that of a ghost, but at least it was a ghost with the power of speech.

'Mr Campion.'

'Alf Bagley . . .' Campion stopped himself before adding either 'fancy seeing you here' or 'as I live and breathe', neither of which was appropriate, and he settled for, '. . . you've had a shock.'

'You two know each other?'

'Alf is a faithful, long-standing employee of Alandel Aircraft,' Campion told the inspector. 'He's worked for my wife for several years.'

'Came to Goshawk at Lady Amanda's personal request,' said Bagley, every word an effort. 'She thought I could keep the young 'uns on the workshop floor in order, mebbe teach 'em a few things. Now look what's happened.'

'What exactly did happen, Mr Bagley?' Mawson flipped open his notebook with a flourish. 'Please go through it one more time, for Mr Campion's sake.'

Campion admired the shrewdness of the policeman. He had clearly heard one version of events and was now seeking confirmation, and if questioning Bagley, who was plainly in shock, was ethically dubious, then it was Campion who would be to blame. Yet Alf Bagley, perhaps out of loyalty to the Campion name, steeled himself and gave a lucid, almost emotionless, account of the ghastly events of that morning.

As workshop foreman, Alf prided himself on being the first into work each morning and, usually, the last to leave in the afternoon, but here at Goshawk things were different. Aircraft designers and draughtsmen always were a law unto themselves, but here, mixed with bright, young university types who thought they knew it all, systems and working practices were elastic, to say the least. For a start, because some of the production engineers preferred to work late into the evening, not having wives, children, choir practice or a darts match to go to, just about everyone had been issued with a key to the large padlock which secured the main sliding doors. As foreman, though, Alf held keys to the office section and the safe there, and opening up the office was the first of his daily tasks.

Not that he was the first in to work. When he arrived, Alan Wormold was already busy, bent over the large flatbed lathe, the screech of metal being worked and the buzz of the lathe's engine making any early morning greeting – other than a brief nod and a wave of a hand holding that morning's *Daily Express* – impossible, as Alf walked by him to the office. It was not unusual to find Wormold already at work, and Alf suspected he was involved in some private project or hobby at these times, but once the senior engineers arrived and began allocating the day's tasks, Wormold followed orders to the letter and was a good worker. Alf had never pressed Alan Wormold on what he was doing in those early hours as he was one of Professor Branscombe's postgraduate students and had letters after his name, which Alf did not.

Wormold had his own key to get into the hangar and would have closed the circuit breaker for the central lathe as it was the only machine he needed to work. It was Alf Bagley's first task to throw the other circuit breakers to power the other workshop machinery, his second to open up the office, where he would check the worksheets for the coming day and put the kettle on.

Once he flipped those circuit switches, the travelling crane must have started to move inexorably across the workshop, and under normal circumstances would have passed way above Alan Wormold's head, but the block and tackle winch dangling from it made it a deadly, head-height weapon.

Alf had not checked that the block and tackle were not stowed out of harm's way because he was not expecting the crane to be used that morning and, in any case, forward travel of the crane was controlled by the pendant control box attached to it. But that morning the crane moved without anyone operating it and – with the flatbed lathe going full pelt – neither Alf Bagley nor Alan Wormold would have heard it as it traversed the workshop in a straight line to its victim.

Bagley did not so much pause in his recitation as deflate, as if he had run out of steam.

When Inspector Mawson, poised over his notebook, made no comment but flashed Campion a glance, it was clearly a prompt to ask the all-too-obvious question. It seemed the policeman was hoping that some imagined old-family-retainer relationship would produce a result.

Mr Campion, not relishing his role as interrogator, took on the task with reluctance. 'So who set the crane moving, Alf?'

Bagley looked up into Campion's gentle face, seeking sympathy if not redemption. 'I did, Mr Campion, when I turned the power on. It must have been me . . . there was nobody else here except Alan.'

'And he couldn't have done it himself, accidentally?'

'Don't see how. Like I said, he'd closed the circuit breaker on his lathe, but he needed power for just that machine and he must have been here working for twenty minutes by the time I clocked in. It definitely wasn't travelling when I came through the door – I would have noticed. There was no reason for Alan to use the crane anyway; he was working light tubular metal, nothing that needed heavy lifting.'

'Could he have done it deliberately?' Mawson asked, which produced a loud gasp from Professor Branscombe.

'Inspector! Are you suggesting suicide?'

'And an extreme and utterly bizarre method at that,' said Campion.

'Just ruling things out,' said the policeman, writing a note in his book.

Their attention returned to the seated Alf Bagley, who was slowly shaking his head. The fingers of his hands, resting on his knees, began to flex nervously and individually, like the legs of a spider which had just woken up.

'However you look at it, Mr Campion, it was me that killed him. I didn't mean to and I didn't know I had, but I did it. As soon as I turned the power on, like I do every morning, I set that crane moving, and it didn't stop until it knocked poor Alan into the spinning chuck.'

'How did it stop, Alf?'

'What?'

'How did the crane stop after it had hit Alan?'

'I turned the power off. I'd just opened up the safe and was going to ask him if he fancied a cuppa as I was planning a brew, but then I saw the blood . . .'

'You didn't stop it with that pendant control box?'

'No, I never touched that, I just cut the power.'

'But I thought the idea was that the crane only travelled with somebody holding that control box, pressing the button. If no one pressed the button, the thing didn't move.'

Mawson scribbled furiously.

'That's certainly how they work normally,' said Branscombe. 'Whoever is using it guides it to where they want it positioned in the workshop using that control box. It's a fail-safe, the crane can't move unless the "Go" button is pressed. Unless something has short-circuited somewhere.'

'Can you check for that?' asked Mawson.

'Of course. It's the only logical explanation.'

Mr Campion reached out a hand and gently squeezed Bagley's shoulder. 'There you have it, Alf, a quirk of electricity. It was an accident which no one could have foreseen or prevented,' said Mr Campion, not believing a word he said. 'There was no one else here when it happened?'

Bagley shook his head. 'Young Alan was already a goner by the time the others got to him.'

'Others?'

'The others who had just turned up for work to find the place looking like a slaughterhouse. There was Mr Barnes – it was him who rang for the ambulance and then rang the professor.'

Branscombe nodded his agreement.

'Cuthbert was with him. Cuthbert Snow, another one of the professor's students and a big pal of Alan's, and then all the staff seemed to be here, gawking. The wing commander took one look and went outside to get some air. Looked as if he was about to lose his breakfast.'

'That would be Nugent Monck?' asked Campion, and Inspector Mawson scribbled furiously as Bagley said it was.

'Did any of them try to help Wormold?'

'No point – he was beyond help. Somebody – his mate Cuthbert mebbe – threw a tarpaulin over 'im until the ambulance arrived, and then the professor turned up and took charge.'

'I telephoned the police as soon as I got here,' said Branscombe.

'And asked for Mr Campion to be rounded up and brought

here,' Mawson observed pointedly, then made a show of flipping back several pages of his notebook. 'Is there anything you would like to add about the deceased, Campion?'

Surprised, Campion said, 'Alan Wormold? I'm afraid I never met the chap and had never heard his name before today.'

'You were not aware,' Mawson read from his notes as he spoke, 'that Mr Wormold had been reprimanded at least twice by your wife, Lady Amanda, for misuse of machinery and possible theft?'

'Goodness me, no! Is it relevant to anything?'

'Just pursuing a line of enquiry, sir.'

'Really, Inspector, I think that is entirely uncalled for,' blustered Branscombe, and his forcefulness seemed to inject new energy into the despondent Bagley.

'Don't you go blaming Lady Amanda for this. If there's fault, then the fault was mine when I turned the power on.'

'That will be a matter for the coroner,' said Mawson dryly, then turned on Campion again. 'Is there anything you would like to contribute that might be useful?'

'I assume you will be dusting that control box for fingerprints.'

'Of course,' answered Mawson, resisting the urge to make a note as if the idea had only just occurred to him, as it had.

'You'll find mine on there,' said Branscombe, 'along with those of everyone who works here. We've all used the crane at some time.'

'Then I have nothing useful to contribute, but I would like to talk to some of the staff gathered outside . . . if the professor will introduce me, and if the detective inspector has no objections.'

'In an unofficial capacity only,' warned the policeman.

'Of course.'

Campion's attention was drawn to the far end of the workshop, where the main door had slid open and two uniformed policemen had entered accompanying a harassed civilian bedecked with cameras and carrying a folded wooden tripod.

'Your photographer has arrived,' said Campion, 'so we'll leave you to it. Will you be all right, Alf?'

Bagley looked up, his face hangdog and drawn, his voice weak and uncertain. 'Am I under arrest?'

'I don't think so,' said Campion looking at Mawson.

The policeman shrugged his shoulders. 'Nobody's under arrest – yet.'

Branscombe and Campion took a circuitous route across the workshop, giving the central lathe and its gruesome adornments a wide berth as the police began to photograph the scene. Their footsteps echoed on the concrete floor and the flash and click of the photographer's camera added to the unreal atmosphere and a setting which Campion could only describe as that of a nightmare cathedral.

When they neared the dangling rectangular box which controlled the travelling crane, Campion peered at it closely from a distance of two or three inches but made no attempt to add his fingerprints to it.

As they moved on, skirting other machines, most still covered with tarpaulins but now all looking as potentially dangerous as the central lathe, Mr Campion seemed to be dragging his feet, or rather scuffing them as a child might carefully test the depth of a puddle (and his mother's patience) with a new pair of shoes. 'Does anyone sweep the floor here?' he asked suddenly.

'Every night at close of play. Alf will have a rota. It's not a popular job, especially if you're one of the young ones dying to get round the pub or go on a hot date, as I believe they call it nowadays. It's a mucky job with all the sawdust we use to soak up the . . .' Branscombe hesitated, his gaze fixed on a small pool of red, '. . . oil we spill, plus dust and metal shavings.'

'Can you get one of your chaps, someone you trust to keep quiet, to do a thorough sweep up as soon as the police and the body have gone? Before anyone starts work again, and to keep the sweepings separate from any other rubbish; bag them up so I can see them.'

'What an odd request, Campion, but of course I can. I'll get Crocodile Snow to volunteer.'

'Who?'

'Oh, sorry, that's his nickname. I mean Cuthbert Snow, one of my postgrads. Good chap.'

'Would this Cuthbert Snow by any chance be the son of Marmaduke Snow, who was something of a legend in my days as a student?'

'Not son, *grandson*.'

'My goodness, more of a legend than I thought. His nickname was "Crocodile" as well.'

'Another fine Cambridge tradition. I'll introduce you, though the lad will be upset, I fear. He and Alan Wormold were close friends.'

'Another good reason for meeting him,' said Campion so quietly that Branscombe hardly heard. 'But before we go outside to meet the workforce, we should clarify two things.'

'Which are?'

'Firstly, they will have a hundred questions to ask us and we must be careful how we answer. I think the best policy is to say there has been a tragic accident which has led to the death of Alan Wormold and that Alf Bagley is explaining the machinery and electrics to the police. I think it best to avoid the phrase "helping the police with their enquiries", as that has certain connotations. It might be best if you tell everyone to go home and come back after lunch, as long as the police do not require a statement from them, as there won't be much work done here until things have been cleaned up. Though don't forget to put Crocodile Snow on sweep-up duty, but do it quietly.'

'I understand and agree completely. What was the second thing?'

'Alf said one of his regular early morning jobs was to open the safe in the office. What do you keep in the safe?'

Professor Branscombe's head jerked back in surprise. 'Why, the blueprints of our Goshawk research. We can't just leave them lying around; they're top secret, don't you know?'

The staff of the Goshawk Project were lined up against the long side wall of the hangar, as if facing a firing squad or awaiting a summons to the headmaster's study. A lone policeman patrolled to keep order, though the line-up was silent and passive, offering an array of white, shocked faces. One figure had turned to the wall, his forehead pressed against it. From his height and haircut, Campion recognized him as the American, Gary Cupples who, given the way his body jerked as he dry-retched spasmodically, had probably witnessed the scene inside. His colleagues, being English, preserved his dignity by totally ignoring him.

Down the line, Campion acknowledged nods from the other senior engineers he had already met, Loder and Barnes, and gave a half-hearted wave to Nugent Monck, who stepped one pace forward and solemnly offered an air-force salute in his direction. He had no time to dwell on the rather bizarre behaviour of the 'squadron leader', as Professor Branscombe was – mercifully – introducing him to two of the younger staff, their faces pale and straining to hold back tears.

'Campion, meet some of the chaps I was telling you about. This is Cuthbert Snow, who might look and behave like a prop forward with a hangover, but is actually quite a reasonable design engineer, and this other chap, who looks exactly like an engineer should – neat, polite and with a mind like a Swiss watch – is Edward Toomey, Ted to his colleagues. Both of them were chums of Alan Wormold.'

'We all share the same digs, round on Pound Hill,' said the taller, more muscular of the two, 'but we can't go back there until the police have been to look through Alan's things. God knows what they're looking for.'

Campion studied the young man; he could imagine that unruly blond hair and moon of a face with its crooked nose coming hurtling towards him to dispute the possession of a rugby ball.

'If it is any comfort religiously,' said Campion, 'I don't think the police know what they're looking for either. I understand you were one of the first on the scene . . . the scene of the accident.'

Cuthbert Snow swallowed hard and caught his breath. 'I went in with Mr Barnes, as we'd arrived at the same time. Ted here was a minute or so behind me because he's as slow as a snail on that old boneshaker of his.'

'You are both cyclists?'

'Isn't everyone in Cambridge?' Cuthbert turned on his friend. 'Some of us, however, have dispensed with training wheels.'

Ted Toomey, clearly having suffered the jibe before, merely raised his eyebrows in exasperation.

'Actually, most of us turned up around the same time for an eight o'clock start, but Mr Barnes and I were the first inside. Alan was lying across the big lathe and there was blood everywhere. Alf, Alf Bagley, was in the office, tearing about like a blue-arsed fly, pardon my French, and the whole place was deathly quiet. Sorry, bad choice of words again.'

'Don't worry about that,' soothed Campion. 'I'd like to speak to you later, after the police have finished here. I doubt there will be much work done today, so how about a drink this evening? But only if you feel up to it.'

Snow nodded like an excited puppy. 'I could be in The Pickerel about eight thirty, if that's any good. Do you know it? It's near Magdalene Bridge.'

Campion, making sure Professor Branscombe could hear, agreed. 'Of course I know it. Eight thirty in The Pickerel it is. I'll see you there.'

Branscombe took his cue. 'Cuthbert, walk with me, would you? I'd like a word.'

Although he was sure he could make out what must be the back garden of 112 Barton Road in the distance across the fields and open ground, Mr Campion chose to walk back to the house by the longer, more conventional route, via Madingley Road and then Queens Road and along 'The Backs', which offered, across the river, the most reproduced picture-postcard view of some of Cambridge's finest colleges. It was a perfectly splendid place for a morning stroll and the view was picturesquely enhanced by the first punts of the day scudding up and down the Cam, their tourist passengers busily clicking away with their cameras. In his student days it had been a source of beer-fuelled rivalry that, from this aspect, Trinity College completely masked any view of the smaller, less boastful St Ignatius.

As he turned into Barton Road, he half noticed a large black motorbike which pulled away from the kerb near where he guessed number 112 to be. The bike accelerated and passed him at speed, heading into the town, its rider an anonymous, helmeted figure in black leathers.

He opened the front door to Branscombe's house with the key he had been given and made immediately for the telephone he had spotted the night before. It was located on a small card table, which he suspected was a temporary replacement for a decent hall stand lost when Mrs Branscombe evacuated the premises. Picking up the receiver, he dialled a number he had memorized which was answered on the third ring.

'Jackdaw to Hummingbird, are you receiving me?' he said, and then froze as a figure emerged from the kitchen and stood less than two yards away from him.

It was not that the apparition was a Gorgon with the power to turn men to stone with a single glance, but it was female.

Instead of a blue-rinse perm of writhing snakes, it was the long and clearly sharp carving knife she held in her right hand that had transfixed Mr Campion.

'I'll call you back,' he said into the receiver, before dropping it back on to its cradle as though it had stung him.

FIVE

The Hired Help

'You like shepherds?'

Given the size of the blade the woman was waving, Campion considered his reply very carefully. 'I think they are a fine body of men, and probably women, who do a marvellous job in all weather conditions, valiantly resisting the urge to fall asleep every time they count their flocks . . .'

'I mean the pie of shepherds – no, *shepherd's pie* – with lamb and onions and carrots.' The woman waved the knife as if to indicate that it was only a threat to mutton and vegetables.

'Oh, I see,' said Campion with exaggerated relief. 'Forgive my idiocy. You must be Astra. I wasn't sure when to expect you.'

'Yes, I am Astra, Astra Jarvela, and you must be Mr Albert. The professor told me about you on the telephone last night. I am to look after you.'

'You'll find I need very little maintenance, and though Professor Branscombe has generously allowed me the run of his house, I doubt I will be here much. I will, however, need to know when you will be here.'

'This time, every morning. Make beds, clean, do laundry, make supper if required and leave in oven, feed cats.'

She spoke rapidly from a well-memorized list, her accent – which Mr Campion could not quite place – thickening as she did.

'That sounds comprehensive, and I trust neither of us will get under the other's feet, though please do not go out of your way on my account. I am a man of simple needs and I have no real idea how long I will be here, but for tonight, as you've gone to the trouble, shepherd's pie sounds admirable, as long

as all I have to do is turn the oven on. But do tell, your accent
. . . where is it from?'

'Finland, but not Helsinki, which is what all people say
when I say Finland.'

'Forgive my compatriots for their limited grasp of geog-
raphy. I'm surprised they don't say Lapland and that you must
know Father Christmas.'

'Lapland is actually correct,' she said without a smile, but
at least the knife had been lowered, 'and a place called Salla,
but instead of your Father Christmas, we have Joulupukki,
which I am told translates as a "Christmas goat", because men
dress in animal skins for the winter festivals.'

'Fascinating,' said Campion, 'but please don't let me keep
you from your culinary skills. I need a wash and a shave and
then I have work to do, but first I could murder a nice cup of
tea.'

'The kettle is on!' The woman spoke as though announcing
that a church fete was now officially open. 'That was the first
thing I learned to say in England.'

'And it is the most important, possibly only, phrase you'll
ever really need.'

He followed her into the kitchen, noting that the knife was
held by her thigh, pointy end downwards, and took stock of
his temporary housekeeper. Or should that be caretaker? Or
perhaps au pair? She was certainly young enough – early
twenties perhaps? He had heard Nordic au pairs were all the
rage in Cambridge that year, just as 'having an Italian girl'
had been a domestic stipulation for any middle-class wife with
four children and a Labrador to manage a decade earlier.

Astra Jarvela was only a wisp of blonde hair more than five
feet tall, but most of that long, thick mane was captured in a
single, tightly braided plait tied off with a small red bow,
which contoured her spine when still and swung like a metro-
nome as she walked. Her figure was what Amanda would have
described as 'sturdy'; not stocky and certainly not plump,
unless compared to some of the increasingly brittle models
being used to promote the new season of miniskirts. And
judging by the muscular efficiency with which she chopped
onions and carved the meat from a pair of chump chops,

Campion decided he had been right to be wary of the arm which had wielded the kitchen knife.

On the surface she seemed ideally suited to her tasks, at least as Campion imagined them. She obviously had the strength and stamina to handle all household chores, certainly if the house had a log cabin sauna in the garden; she could rustle up a shepherd's pie with ease and make a half-decent cup of tea, and clearly got on well with the professor's two cats who affectionately circled her ankles, though that might have been something to do with the scent of fresh meat.

'Have you worked for the professor for long?' Campion asked, still not sure what her actual job title might be.

'Half a year. First for Mrs Branscombe, but then she upped stumps and left with her boyfriend. That is how you say it, is it not, when couples get divorced?'

Campion hid a smile behind his teacup. 'I've not heard the expression in that context before, but it probably describes the situation accurately. I take it you volunteered to stay on and look after the professor.'

She moved to the sink and ran the knife blade under the cold tap before chopping a large onion. Clearly, the Finns did not approve of crying over vegetables.

'Professor John is much easier to look after than his wife. She was . . . difficult. Is it polite to say such a thing?'

'If she's not present,' admitted Campion, 'and I assure you I will not be a trouble to you. In fact, you might take a short holiday while I'm here.'

'No!' said Astra with some force as the knife blurred the onion into thin slices with frightening speed. 'I am paid to come here every morning and that is what I must do. You will not know I am here.'

Campion doubted that but conceded the point. 'Very well. I admire your work ethic, but I must insist that you limit your hours to between nine and eleven each morning. I have some confidential work to do over the next few days and really must not be disturbed.'

Or surprised by a knife-wielding woman whist trying to make a telephone call.

'That is agreeable,' said the woman, nodding sagely. Then

she turned and looked at Campion as if she had noticed him for the first time. 'You are working with the professor in his big shed?'

'In a way,' said Campion cautiously.

'You have much trouble there this morning.' Astra was making a statement, not asking a question.

'Yes, we have. How did you know?'

'When I let the cats out into the garden. I had to because nobody else had.'

Campion blanched, realizing he had forgotten to perform the one domestic duty his host had entrusted him with.

'From there I saw the police cars and the ambulance.'

'There was an accident, a tragic accident, involving one of the professor's postgraduate students.'

'Not Teddy?'

'Teddy who?' Campion was disconcerted by the emotion in Astra's voice, but the lack of expression on her face.

'Toomey, Teddy Toomey, he is a nice boy.'

'Ah yes, young Mr Toomey. I met him earlier, he's fine, although very upset, naturally. I'm not sure I should say any more at this stage, though. Friend of yours, is he?'

For the first time since he had encountered her, Astra's lips curled delicately into a lascivious smile. 'All the young men in Cambridge want to be my friend.'

When Astra had gone, having left strict instructions about turning on the oven a good forty-five minutes before he planned to eat that evening, Mr Campion made two telephone calls and then took a stroll in the garden, shadowed by the felines Pratt and Whitney and with the pair of binoculars he had made sure to pack in his luggage hanging around his neck.

He examined the octagonal summer house and found its interior dry and generally weatherproof. It was not connected to the electricity supply and, with its shutters closed, the only light came through splinters and knotholes in the planks of the eight wooden walls. There was a lock on the flimsy door, with the oval bow handle of a metal key protruding from it. Campion tried the key and found it did work, but only after a struggle, and made a mental note.

Branscombe's cats found little of interest in the musty interior and were easily shooed out when Campion closed the door, both of them leaping majestically over the small stream marking the garden boundary and disappearing into the open field beyond.

From there, across what appeared to be rough pasture, but with occasionally more manicured areas, which might have been sports fields, and several random sections of barbed-wire fencing, he could clearly see the Goshawk Project building. Deferring to Astra's superior eyesight, though, he needed the binoculars to get a detailed view, not that there was much activity to see.

The ambulance and police cars had long departed, and the only vehicles parked outside were two cars and a Land Rover, but it was impossible to tell whether there were lights on in there as the hangar was a sealed metal shell, ideal for keeping any activity inside away from prying eyes.

Campion judged the distance and memorized the line, where he could see it, of the Bin Brook, as the professor had called the stream. He was sure that if he kept the brook on his right and then cut diagonally across the flattest piece of open ground by the second wire fence, he could reach the Goshawk Project unseen without getting his feet wet or suffering physical damage; unless, that is, he wandered into an unexpected minefield.

Yes, it was certainly possible, even for a man of his advancing years. No more than a strenuous walk in the country, really. Of course at night and in the pitch-dark it would be more difficult, but still possible.

The Pickerel Inn on Magdalene Street was said to be owned by Magdalene College just across the road. Whether this was true or not, Magdalene men, back in Campion's day, were always expected to buy the first round of drinks.

Mr Campion thought it only polite to ignore that tradition, given the gulf in difference between his circumstances and those of Cuthbert Snow, who might soon have a doctorate attached to his name, but was still some way off a decent regular income. Unless, of course, Cuthbert Snow as a

Magdalene man insisted on treating an alumnus of the far less prestigious St Ignatius. He did not, and was genuinely grateful for the pint of bitter Mr Campion placed in front of him on one of the rickety wooden tables in the dark, smoke-stained bar, from which the Cam could just be glimpsed through the one clean diamond segment of a particularly filthy window.

'We call this place the Little Pike,' Cuthbert enthused.

'That's what a pickerel is,' said Mr Campion.

'Exactly, and there's not another pub in the country called that.'

Campion did not challenge the young man, although he personally knew of three other 'Pickerels', all in East Anglia.

'We came here quite a lot, Alan and me, and Ted of course.' Cuthbert's voice changed down a gear from jovial to sombre.

'The Three Musketeers, were you?'

'Not really. We were friends and colleagues, but we didn't live in each other's pockets.'

'But you roomed together?'

'Well, we shared a rented house once we started our post-graduate work, and then the placement at Goshawk came up . . . but we all had different interests. I'm quite sporty, Ted is a bit of a weed and a wimp on that score – decent enough chap, though.'

'And Alan Wormold?'

Cuthbert sighed and sipped his beer before answering. 'Alan was his own man and kept himself to himself most of the time. He only had one interest beyond engineering and that was aeroplanes.'

'Then working at the Goshawk Project must have suited him down to the ground, engineering aeroplanes.'

'Well, yes, it did, but Alan was into flying real planes, not just drawing blueprints. He was a member of a flying club out at Bourn and he spent all his spare time and cash there, zooming around like the Red Baron in an open-cockpit biplane.' He looked up from his beer. 'And yes, I know, the Red Baron flew a triplane, but you get the idea.'

'First rule of an aeronautical engineer,' Campion laughed, 'should be to count the number of wings accurately, even if they're pointing the wrong way.'

'I see your wife has briefed you on her hopes for swept-forward wings. She's quite inspirational on the subject.'

'I'm sure she is, but she knows I am too dull-witted to follow half of what she says when she talks shop, so she rarely bothers to baffle me with science. Professor Branscombe did try to explain the principle to me yesterday, but most of it went over my head at the speed of light.'

'Sound,' said Cuthbert, 'speed of sound. We haven't got to light speed yet.'

'There, you see, it would be useless to entrust me with anything technical, that's why I would make a pretty poor spy.'

'Is that what Lady Amanda is charged with, being a spy? It's the current rumour.'

Campion raised his eyebrows in what he called his 'outraged aunty' expression. 'I do not think my wife has been charged with anything as yet, and there has been no sound of a headsman sharpening his axe – or do they use swords these days? I am rather out of touch on such matters. Do you think she has a case to answer?'

Cuthbert Snow did not miss a beat, even with a mouthful of ale. 'Good heavens, no! Why would she spy on herself? If she wanted to give her Goshawk research, or any of the work she was doing on high-bypass jet engines for Alandel, to the Americans, she could sell it to them and they'd pay handsomely. Not that I'm suggesting she needs the money . . .'

'My dear boy, I have recently achieved pensionable age and so an additional source of income to put bread on the family table might be a temptation, but only to lesser mortals, not my Amanda. Still, I am intrigued that you said Americans rather than Russians. I thought one was our ally, one our Cold War enemy. Have I got them confused? Politics, like aeronautical engineering, is not one of my strong suits.' He rolled his eyes upwards to the nicotine-stained plaster ceiling as if in contemplation. 'Perhaps I don't have a strong suit.'

'That I do not believe,' said Cuthbert, collecting their empty glasses and pointing himself towards the bar, his head bowed to avoid collision with the low beams, his upper body swerving impressively to avoid collision with other customers.

He returned to place two glass tankards of beer with not a drop missing on the table and sat down with a self-satisfied smile.

'You see, I'd heard of you, Mr Campion, long before I got the chance to work for Lady Amanda. My grandfather told me all about you.'

'Nothing good, I hope.'

'Well, nothing bad. He was not an exact contemporary of yours, but he became aware of your – shall we say – reputation?'

'As I was of his, but we must not wallow in nostalgia, we should be concerned with today's sad events.'

Cuthbert frowned. 'A sad, and bad, business. We all know the machinery we use can be dangerous, that's why we keep our hair cut short and we count our fingers at the end of every shift. Alan was always very careful when he was cutting metal and had never had an accident until today. It was an accident, wasn't it?'

Campion avoided the young man's puppy-dog eyes. 'I'm sure it was – a bizarre one, but an accident nonetheless. Who would wish such a thing on him on purpose?'

'I can't think of a single person,' said Cuthbert. 'The professor thought very highly of his work – he got a First, you know, and his PhD thesis was right up Branscombe's street. You might say he was the prof's favourite – academically, that is – but Alan also got on with the professional engineers from Alandel. He soon got very chummy with Melvyn Barnes, who used to give him a lift out to Bourn.'

'Bourn? Oh yes, his flying club.'

'That's right. We all thought it a bit crazy that Alan had got himself a private pilot's licence when he was seventeen but had never learned to drive a car.'

'Clearly a bright chap,' said Campion. 'We were not allowed cars in my day, though I understand students can have them now.'

'More trouble than they're worth in Cambridge. We go everywhere by bike.'

'So I gathered this morning. Now what about the other staff at Goshawk?'

'Like I said, Alan got on with them all, even the wing commander.'

'Nugent Monck? You call him that too?'

'Not to his face, but yes. He's a bit of stickler, the sort who would be a bully if he could, but he left Alan alone because Alan was a flier and he never was, despite his time in the RAF. In a way, I think the wing commander actually envied Alan.'

'I think that could be a shrewd judgement on your part. I'm finding your insights very useful.'

Cuthbert tried to conceal his surprise. 'Nobody's accused me of being insightful before. They usually say, "Here comes the big beefy rugby player who only has small talk about engines and beer," and they always put the fine china out of sight if they invite me for tea.'

'Well, I certainly recognize your inner depths,' Campion grinned, warming to his companion, 'and I want to hear more of your insights about Goshawk staff. They will go no further, unless, that is, they are particularly scandalous.'

'I can't think of any juicy gossip,' Cuthbert admitted, 'but then juicy gossip doesn't come my way much, and certainly nothing about Alan. He got on with Mr Loder well enough and didn't even take the mickey out of his Brummie accent, though the rest of us did. Mr Loder doesn't mix much with the university crowd, though. I think he's got a wife and kids somewhere, so he doesn't socialize much outside of work. And Alan went out of his way to be friendly to our resident Yank, Gary Cupples, though there's no love lost with the Americans professionally because they steal all our best ideas and then sell them back to our government.'

'I think that may be an over-simplification,' said Mr Campion, 'but I am aware of the background to your suspicions. Isn't there another American attached to the Project?'

Cuthbert nodded and pulled a face as if his beer had soured in the glass.

'You mean our liaison officer, Luther Romo. He's something called a senior master sergeant in the air force – their air force, that is. He turns up when he feels like it and snoops around. If you're looking for a spy, he'd be a good bet.'

'I'm not particularly looking for a spy, but if I need one, I'll keep Mr Romo in mind. What about Alf Bagley?'

'And Alan?' Cuthbert shrugged his shoulders. 'They got on fine; everyone gets on with Alf, he's old-school engineering. If something doesn't work, hit it with a spanner until it does. He was always willing to help us students as well.'

'He had no quarrel with Alan Wormold?'

'I don't think Alf quarrelled with anybody, and nobody had a beef against Alan except . . .' He covered his mouth with his glass.

'Let me guess,' said Campion, reaching out to give Cuthbert's arm a reassuring pat. 'You were about to say "except Amanda".'

Cuthbert slowly lowered his glass until it was firmly back on the table, as if it could no longer betray his emotions.

'I'm sure you've already heard about it, but it was not really anything serious.'

'Assume I know nothing, my boy – most people do.'

'Alan did get a bit of a dressing-down from Lady A, but it was hardly a firing offence. There were some discrepancies over the amount of Reynolds 531 Alan had been working with.'

'You'll have to explain what that is.'

'Reynolds 531 is steel tubing. It's light and it's strong and we use it for making models, for stress-testing among other things. Alan was always finding new uses for it and was probably sneaking out a few offcuts for his own experiments, but he'd never do anything really dishonest.'

'Did Amanda accuse him of stealing?'

'I don't think it went that far, but she put a scare into him and told him to keep better note of the materials he was using.'

'And I am sure he did; my wife can be very forceful at times.'

Cuthbert picked up his glass and toasted Mr Campion. 'I'm just glad I never got on the wrong side of her.'

'I wish I could say the same.'

The hand holding Cuthbert's pint glass began to shake slightly. 'I didn't mean anything by that, it's just that we engineers aren't terribly familiar with girls . . . women.'

Campion repressed a smile. 'I am given to understand one of you has some familiarity with the ladies – your chum Edward Toomey, or Teddy as I suspect he's known affectionately in some quarters.'

Cuthbert's eyes widened. 'You must have met Astra, the professor's housekeeper? Ted certainly has the hots for her and would pop round to Barton Road on any excuse if he knew she was there. He's been smitten since he first met her at his Russian class.'

'Russian?'

'Yes, he's been learning Russian in his spare time for the last six months. You wouldn't think it to look at him, the little swot, but he has hidden depths.'

'As, I am sure, do you, Cuthbert.'

'Hardly! I'm just your average hail-fellow-well-met sort of chap. What you see is what you get.'

Mr Campion peered over the top of his large round spectacles. 'Oh, I don't know about that. I hear you've inherited your grandfather's nickname, Crocodile. Do you know how he got it?'

'Of course,' said Cuthbert with a proud turn of his head. 'It's a family legend.'

'Good,' said Mr Campion, 'then we must go punting on the river together.'

SIX

Two Pounds of Swarf

I f there could be such a thing as a normal working day at the Goshawk Project after the alarums and violent excursions of the previous forty-eight hours, then John Branscombe was determined there should be.

From the garden of the Barton Road house earlier that morning, Mr Campion had – through his binoculars – observed the staff arriving, identifying Professor Branscombe's car, two other small saloons and a Land Rover amidst a flurry of bicycles. It seemed that no police vehicles or other emergency services were required today.

He left a note for Astra, thanking her for the shepherd's pie and telling her not to cook anything for that evening as he would be out, and then he left the house by the back door to the garden. Crossing the Bin Brook with one lengthy stride and keeping the stream on his right side, he followed the line of it until bearing diagonally left at the first section of barbed wire. The side wall of the Goshawk Project hangar became fully visible across one and a half fallow fields and two more random sections of waist-high, three-strand barbed-wire fence, which seemed capable neither of keeping livestock in nor trespassers out.

The disparate sections of fencing did not appear to be protecting anything, certainly not the Goshawk hangar, for that was still at least two hundred yards away, but then Campion stumbled as the ground level changed and he understood.

Before him was a deep dip in the earth, a long, rectangular, clearly man-made depression, almost as if someone had landscaped three sunken tennis courts, which only allowed the occasional high lob or return serve rather than the actual players to be seen by any passing fan of the game.

Mr Campion quickly dismissed such a surreal idea and

realized that this must be the overgrown remains of the rifle
range Branscombe had told him about on his orientation tour.
Campion could imagine a Boys' Brigade or OTC, or even a
Home Guard rifle section lying prone at one end of the depression, shooting at targets at the other, probably with small-bore
weapons. At this end, where he presumed the targets had stood,
the sunken range was a good eight feet below ground level,
and the earthen side banks provided a soft and safe home for
any wayward bullets, though he guessed that not a shot had
been fired in anger here for many a year. The only relic of
human occupation was, at the far end, a rusty oil drum lying
forlornly on its side.

Mr Campion was still spry enough to clamber down the
bank, which was rough and steep but far from vertical, without
the need for crampons or guide ropes, but he did not linger
crossing the 'killing floor' of the range. In fact, he walked
with such energy, it was almost as if he were weaving his way
between flying ghost bullets, and he released a long sigh of
relief when he reached the opposite bank.

The sunken feature reminded him of the excavated swimming pool he had once seen in the gardens of a Roman villa,
destroyed – yet also preserved – by a furious outburst from
Vesuvius. That too had been colonized by grass and weeds,
and now the vegetation assisted him in his attempts to climb
out of the rectangular depression, as he used tussocks of
greenery as handholds to pull himself up the bank, all the time
bemoaning the fact that such cross-country rambles were best
left to younger men. Reaching ground level again, he brushed
dirt from his trousers and plucked grass seeds and half a dozen
'sticky buds' of burdock from the sleeves of his jacket.

As he straightened up he felt dangerously exposed, as if he
was the first man out of the trench and over the top, facing the
daunting walk into no man's land. He shook his head to dispel
such fancies. He had just walked across a rifle range and no
one had shot at him. Why should they now? True, he was
walking across what some may call 'dead ground', but as a
setting it was no more threatening than the sites of a hundred
other industrial estates across the country, albeit few of them
were located so close to the echoes of church bells, chapel

organs and the underlying hum of disputing Dons which for Campion always provided, along with the lapping of the Cam, the background music he expected to accompany Cambridge.

To him, the clatter and whine of the machinery inside the Goshawk hangar were alien sounds, discordant and, as had been shown, potentially violent. It was, he knew, all in the service of supersonic flight involving slipstreams, air flows, airframe stresses, twist-resistant structures and turbojets. Yet the workshop seemed less an example of the white heat of modern technology than it was almost a throwback to a Satanic Victorian factory. All that was missing was a large brick chimney belching smoke, and a furnace blazing away somewhere to drive steam engines for power. The rest of the set dressing was in place: sparks flew from grinders, metal screeched against cutting blades, drills whined, and the air reeked of scorched metal and oil.

Which reminded him.

Professor Branscombe was enclosed alone in the office section of the hangar, seated at the desk and doing a fair imitation of a swimmer breast-stroking his way through waves of paper. There were typed sheets and forms, work dockets and invoices, pencilled drawings on flimsy tracing paper and large ammonia blueprints, and the professor seemed to be failing in an attempt to control the swell, let alone turn the tide.

'Good morning, Campion,' said Branscombe, a pencil clenched horizontally between his teeth. 'Just trying to bring a little order to the chaos.'

'I can see you are busy,' said Campion, noting that the door of the office safe was open. 'I don't suppose there's anything I can do to help?'

'I doubt it. I'm putting off the nightmare of telephoning Wormold's parents, but first I have to go through all this lot to see where we are with various things and work out who is supposed to be doing what for the next week. Normally Alf does the legwork on the rotas, work schedules and so on.'

'He's not here?'

'I told him to take the day off to recover from the shock of the accident.'

'The police have decided it was an accident?'

'What else could it be? Alf will blame himself though, he's that sort.'

'How are the rest of the staff taking it?'

'Not well. The overwhelming atmosphere is glum. Alan Wormold was well liked.'

'He was a flyer, so I understand.'

'Cuthbert filled you in, did he? Yes, Alan used to go off to Bourn and take up the club's Tiger Moth every chance he got. You wouldn't catch me in one of those things, far too flimsy, but then I'm not keen on flying at all.'

'Really?' Campion's expression of surprise made Branscombe look up from the pool of papers.

'Truth is, Campion, I get terribly airsick.'

'That's quite an admission for an aeronautical engineer, isn't it?'

'No more unusual than a nautical engineer who can't swim. I'm sure some of the chaps who designed the *Titanic* couldn't swim. No, wait, that's a bad example and probably in very poor taste. Forgive me, I have a lot on my mind. I have a load of work to complete at my college before the summer vacation and now I'm tied down with this place doing Amanda's job, and Alf Bagley's as well. I don't suppose you've heard any news of Lady Amanda?'

'None at all,' said Campion blithely.

'How's your grasp of the theory of spanwise airflow and the problem of out-of-phase yaw?'

'I'm afraid I only understood *some* of those words, Professor.'

Branscombe sighed and examined a page of mathematical calculations scribbled in pencil at an angle.

'Is that my wife's penmanship?' Campion asked. 'She normally has such immaculate handwriting.'

'We don't go in much for calligraphy in our line. Things get written down, or drawn, as they occur, and all the notes are gone through at a meeting of the senior staff once a week.'

'But until then, they're just stuffed in the safe?'

'We don't run to secretaries and filing cabinets. Everyone working here can file the results of their work and then the design engineers put the pieces together – like a jigsaw.'

'Don't any of the pieces get lost, or taken out and not put back?'

Branscombe looked up with suspicion. 'What are you suggesting?'

'My wife,' Campion said softly, 'has been arrested under the Official Secrets Act. Now I am not aware that she has any – shall we say domestic – secrets worth passing on to a third party, so I conclude that any valuable secret must have something to do with her professional life. You told me yourself yesterday that the safe here is the repository of all Goshawk's secrets, yet it seems access to it is rather free and easy.'

'All papers, blueprints and calculations are locked away at the end of every day's work. Only Alf Bagley, Lady Amanda and I have keys.'

'And all the pieces of your Goshawk jigsaw are present and correct?'

'Of course they are. The contents of the safe are checked by Alf and he keeps a log of every scrap in there.'

'How often?'

'I beg your pardon?'

'How often does Alf Bagley take stock of the documents in there, which I presume are being added to all the time as research progresses?'

'Every week, on Friday evenings, then the safe is locked, as is the hangar. Neither is opened again until Monday morning.'

Campion slowly turned his head so he was looking through the glass windows out over the workshop where the staff were bent over machinery or seated at drawing boards.

'I am no engineer, Professor, but thanks to a misspent youth and over-familiarity with some of a recidivist tendency, I suspect that in this hangar you have the machinery and the raw materials to make keys to fit most locks, should the fancy take you.'

'Preposterous! Are you snooping, Campion?'

'Well, yes, I suppose I am. It's what I do, and I will continue to do so if it clears my wife's name.'

Branscombe cleared his throat with a bark of a cough and flapped the edge of a sheet of blueprints as if folding a bedsheet. 'Of course you must, old boy. How do you want to play this?'

'For the moment, I'd just like your permission to wander around and chat up the staff here; see if I can learn anything to Amanda's disadvantage, as it were.'

'With the amount of work I have on, I'm happy to leave you to your own devices. Have you settled into the house?'

'Very comfortably, thank you. Hopefully, I will not impose on your hospitality for too long.'

'Is Astra looking after you?'

'Very well – far too well really. She seems an interesting young woman. How long has she worked for you?'

The professor, who no doubt could do calculus whilst drawing circles on his stomach with one hand and patting his head with the other, had to think long and hard about such complex domestic conundrums.

'Getting on for a year, I think; yes, it was about the time we were drawing up the plans to move Goshawk here. You're not connecting her to what happened to poor Alan Wormold, are you?'

'Not especially, but I hear one of your students was rather keen on her.'

'A lot of young men are attracted to the Nordic type. I suppose Cuthbert told you young Toomey was a bit moonstruck.'

Campion nodded.

'I don't think there was much going on between those two. Astra's very capable of fending off unwanted suitors. By the way, Cuthbert did the sweeping up last night as you suggested, and the results are in that fire bucket over there. What do you want to do with it?'

'What time is tea break?'

'Ten thirty. Since it's a nice day, everyone will go and sit outside.'

'Excellent. I will sneak in here and have a rummage then.'

'What the dickens do you expect to find in a couple of pounds of swarf?'

'Swarf?'

'It's what we engineers call the muck, the dust, the detritus we sweep up from a workshop floor.'

'No idea, really,' said Campion, 'but I'd appreciate it if you would stop anyone putting out a cigarette in there between now and then.'

In the workshop, Campion found that the four senior engineers worked at tables or drawing boards ranged against the north wall of the hangar, leaving three-quarters of the floor space for the various bits of machinery operated or tended by the technicians. There seemed to be no set hierarchy or structure and the labour force was distinctly fluid, no one sitting or standing still for long as they moved between machines or desks, chatting and comparing notes. As far as Mr Campion was concerned, they might have been discussing their forecasts for the football pools or gossiping in Swahili, such was the technical jargon they had adopted as a second language.

One thing he did understand, however, and that was the way all the junior technicians glanced nervously upwards as they crossed the hangar floor to make sure that the travelling crane and its block-and-tackle were secured and not moving.

He was not surprised that it was Nugent Monck who reacted first to his presence, working on the ancient military principle that the junior officer should always appear alert and on point when the general makes a surprise visit. Not that Campion thought of himself as Monck's superior officer, but he clearly regarded Amanda as such and Campion as the next best thing, as he was not a natural fit with ivory-tower academics like Branscombe and his bright, and frightfully young, postgraduate students. He was that shallow sort of man who would tell his former messmates that it was better to take orders from a strong woman than a long-haired student 'who had never had a proper job'.

'Campion! Good morning to you.'

Monck stood up from his drawing board so abruptly that Mr Campion was sure he heard a *snap*, and for one terrible moment he thought the man was going to salute him.

'And to you, Mr Monck. Don't let me interrupt anything. I'm here to get a feel for the work of the Goshawk Project and the last thing I want to do is disrupt it by getting under the feet of you boffins.'

Monck shivered at the word 'boffin', but Campion could not tell whether it was with pleasure or distaste.

'Mere engineers, proud to be doing our bit. Good of you to come and inspect the troops.'

'I'm not here to inspect anything, merely to check on morale. I doubt I would find anything here I could understand, let alone inspect intelligently.'

Monck brushed the front of his jacket with the palm of his right hand, as if removing cat hair, then leaned forward at the hip until Campion had to steel himself from recoiling at his breath.

'Between me and you,' he said quietly, though there was little chance of being overheard, 'half the stuff being worked on goes over the heads of some of the people here.'

'That sounds rather sweeping.'

'But it's true. Branscombe's students have never worked in industry or been in the services, and those of us brought in from Alandel are either engine specialists or airframe men, like me.'

'And the two don't mix?'

'Well, of course we mix, but it's a question of priorities. Designing an aircraft with swept-forward wings is essentially a question of getting the wing structure and the airframe right and that's where Loder and I come in as that's our speciality. Barnes, the Yank, and most of Branscombe's boy scouts are engine men, only interested in producing more thrust, not whether the Goshawk can actually fly.'

'You have considered this carefully,' said Campion, keeping his voice, and his opinion of Monck, as neutral as possible.

'I say what I see,' said Monck, thankfully straightening up and standing at attention, 'and, when asked, I give my thoughts to Lady Amanda.'

'Didn't somebody say that you had *seen* some discrepancies in your stocks of raw materials?'

Monck cleared his throat nervously, disconcerted by Campion's change of tack. 'Yes, I had picked up on the fact that some of our steel was going missing. Somebody has to keep an eye on such things.'

'And you reported this to Amanda?'

'What else was I supposed to do?' he blustered. 'I was following the chain of command.'

'Of course you were, but I am curious to know if you named Alan Wormold as a suspect.'

'Not as such, but one of Branscombe's students must have been responsible. What would one of the senior engineers do with Reynolds steel tubing?'

'What indeed?'

With all the workshop's background noise and Nugent Monck's secretive theatricals, Melvyn Barnes, seated at his draughtsman's board at the next table along, could not possibly have overheard their conversation but, as he leaned back in his chair and puffed on an evil-smelling pipe, he gave the smug impression that he had taken in every word.

'Nugent whining again?' he said. 'He always is, and whatever it was about you can be sure it wasn't his fault.'

Campion smiled thinly. He had no desire to add fuel to the flames of workplace rivalries and disputes, though in the present circumstances he was naturally interested in them. 'I think he's a man who is not completely happy with his lot,' said Campion, conscious that now he was acting as if frightened of being overheard.

'Who is?' said Barnes between puffs of acrid smoke.

'Oh, I think I am, generally speaking.'

'Even when your wife has been hauled up before the Star Chamber, accused of treason?'

'I don't think the Star Chamber has tried any cases for three hundred years,' said Campion, 'and Amanda hasn't actually been accused of anything specific yet.'

'Well, that's good to hear. I had assumed you were here drumming up the case for the defence.'

'Unofficially, that's exactly what I am doing, but the events of yesterday have rather thrown things up in the air.'

'You mean poor Alan's accident? Yes, terrible, quite terrible.'

Campion wondered whether to question the word 'accident' but decided on another approach. 'You got on with him quite well, I hear.'

'I certainly did. I used to give him a lift out to Bourn Airfield.

He was a really keen flyer, just about the only one here who could actually fly an aeroplane, unlike certain people who boast about their time in the RAF.'

'I think' – now Campion deliberately lowered his voice – 'the wing commander suspected him of appropriating materials from the Project.'

Barnes took his pipe from his mouth by the bowl and used the stem to describe small circles in the air, just as a stage magician would wave a wand. 'Nugent suspects the students of everything, from fiddling the petty cash to plotting the international Bolshevik revolution. The man has a sixpenny-worth bag of chips on his shoulder – chips that have been soused in vinegar at that. He can't stand the fact that none of us was in the services and he didn't go to university.'

Campion said nothing but his expression prompted an answer from Barnes.

'During the war, Kevin Loder and I were in reserved occupations. Nugent was just too young to see active service, which he sees as a missed opportunity, the fool.'

'Forgive me,' Campion said, 'but when I saw you limping I assumed . . .'

'No, that happened before the war. Mind you, if I had a real war wound, it would irritate the wing commander no end.'

'And the American, Cupples? He doesn't seem to like him much.'

'Thinks he's a draft dodger, only over here to avoid being sent to Vietnam.'

'Really? How old is he?'

'Twenty-five or twenty-six, I reckon.'

Campion did some mental arithmetic. 'Then he's actually too old for their peacetime draft. I think the favoured age is nineteen, which is terribly young to be sent to fight Communism half a world away. Our son, who is a bit younger than Cupples, studied in America; he had a lot of friends who were worried about the war.'

'They're right to be worried,' said Barnes, 'and they call it a police action, not a war, but it's a war all right.'

'And wars, hot or cold, are good for business – your business – aren't they?'

'Sadly, they usually are, but it's not just my business, it's your wife's as well.'

Campion moved down the workshop and realized he must look like a casual visitor to the National Gallery, gawping at one exhibit then having his eye caught by a more interesting one across the way.

On his mental checklist, the next senior engineer on his list was Kevin Loder but, before he could make contact, Loder sprang up from his workbench clutching a sheaf of papers and headed for the office.

'Morning, Campion,' he said as he scurried past. 'Were you looking for me?'

'Just getting myself orientated,' said Mr Campion. 'Don't let me disrupt anything, though.'

Loder waved the papers, which Campion recognized as official government requisition forms.

'Got to ring some damn civil servant about these,' he said cheerfully, 'and it's always best to catch them before their tea break. I won't be long, but our resident cowboy, young Cupples, will show you around and fill you in on what's on my plate. Sometimes I think he knows what I'm doing before I do it!'

Loder scurried away before Campion could say anything, but he saw that his arrival had been anticipated. Buttocks perched on the edge of the last table and drawing board before the east end of the hangar were Gary Cupples', his long legs stretched out and crossed at the ankles, giving him a casual salute.

'Mr Campion.'

'Mr Cupples.'

'Actually it's Doctor Cupples, but I don't play that card around here, so it's Gary, or The Cowboy, or That Damned Yank, if you don't mind.'

'Then Gary it is. Tell me, how are you chaps holding up since the accident?'

'Apart from me, everyone here is British, and so naturally it's stiff upper lips all round and polite enquiries about when the funeral might be. There's more nervousness about the fate of Lady Amanda and what that might mean for the Goshawk Project in the long run.'

'A nervousness I share,' said Campion, 'and I have no news on that score.'

'Pity; she's a great loss to us.'

'And to me.'

'Sure, of course. What I meant was she's a natural leader and can inspire a real team effort, which ain't easy given the circumstances.'

'Which particular circumstances did you have in mind?'

The American seemed to stretch his legs out even longer, leaned back and put his hands in his trouser pockets. The thought occurred to Campion that if he became any more relaxed, he would slide off the desk.

'We may look like one unified team,' said Cupples, 'but in fact there are three interests working here. Among the senior engineers there are the pure engine men like Melvyn and the squadron leader, who were working on high-bypass jet engines, whereas the more artistic among us, such as Kevin and little old me, are airframers, more concerned with a beautiful design to give a plane agility rather than just thrust.'

Campion furrowed his brow and peered over the rims of his spectacles. 'Are you saying that you "airframers" don't get on with the turbo-jet boys?'

'I wouldn't go that far, but there's a lot of drama between us at times over how a by-pass engine can be tied into an airframe.'

'I will pretend I understood the gist of that,' Campion grinned, 'and guess that the third interest you mentioned is having to working with the university crew.'

'Oh, they're a good bunch of guys in the main, but they're green and haven't seen much life outside the classroom.'

'Yesterday would have been a big shock to them, don't you think?'

'It would, but the disadvantage of being young is that some-thing even more horrible will soon be coming down the pike at them – except for Cuthbert Snow, that is. Life just seems to bounce off him. He doesn't let anything worry him.'

'You've just reminded me, I need a word with Cuthbert,'

said Campion, 'but whilst I've got you, can you spare me a drop of oil by any chance?'

'Oil?'

'It's for the hinges on an old suitcase. I am afraid – like me – they are rusting up with age.'

'Got just the thing,' said Cupples, opening one of his desk drawers and handing Campion a small aerosol can bearing the legend WD-40, as manufactured by the Rocket Chemical Company of San Diego. 'That'll unstick anything. They're sending cans to our boys in Vietnam to help keep their weapons operating smoothly in the jungle.'

'Thank you,' said Campion, pocketing the can.

'Let me guess,' added the American, misjudging Campion's expression, 'the wing commander told you I was a Vietnam draft dodger.'

'I long ago learned to listen politely to almost anyone speaking on any topic, though with some exceptions, such as National Socialist foreign policy from 1933 to 1945, and whether the cream or the jam goes first in a Devon cream tea, but I quickly realized there was a scientific law I could invoke.'

'Which is?'

'Light travels faster than sound, which is why some people appear bright, until they speak.'

Campion wandered across the workshop floor between the islands of machinery until he reached the bench where Cuthbert Snow was hunched over a large pad of tracing paper, sucking on the end of a pencil like an addict. He had a slide rule in one hand and a spare pencil behind each ear, as if he was rehearsing the role, perhaps forty years hence, of the absent-minded professor.

'I hear you were on sweep-up duties yesterday.'

'Was it you who volunteered me?' Cuthbert said with a cheeky grin, pointing a pencil as if it was a rapier at Campion's chest.

'I'm afraid so.'

'Why me?'

'I knew I could trust someone called Crocodile Snow to do a good job.'

Cuthbert pursed his lips and blew a raspberry of disbelief. 'Well, there's a bucket full of muck in the office for you. How do you want it wrapped?'

'What usually happens to the sweepings?'

'Alf Bagley usually goes over them with a magnet to pick out shards of metal, then it gets dumped round the side of the building in a big wooden box next to the dustbins. About once a month the council comes and empties it.'

'Could you smuggle the bucket out without looking suspicious?'

'I suppose so; when it's tea break. It'd certainly be less suspicious than you doing it.'

'Good lad. Then can you give the contents a going-over with Alf's magnet before you dispose of them?'

'What am I looking for?'

'I'm not sure, but perhaps something round and metal, which may have some black insulating tape attached to it.'

'I take it this is a secret mission?' asked Cuthbert, with an enthusiasm that betrayed his age.

'Most secret and highly confidential and, if anyone catches you at it, say you're mining for loose change which, by the way, you may keep if you find any.'

Cuthbert went into conspiratorial mode. 'Are you acting on a tip-off?'

'In a way.'

'From an engineer?'

'No,' said Campion confidently, 'from a recidivist.'

SEVEN
Wild Blue Yonder

At tea break the Goshawk workforce followed the industrial tradition of segregation which prevailed in most British factories. 'Management', the senior engineers, gathered in the office and stood stiffly in a circle, whilst the 'shop-floor workers', the postgraduate students, preferred the warm sunshine outside to the gloom and dust of the hangar. In the fresh air they leaned against the hangar wall or sat against the wheels of the parked cars or simple stretched out on the patchy grass. Like most energetic young people, they could relax anywhere in the most uncomfortable of positions, and indeed one or two seemed to have nodded off completely, though the majority were drinking tea from enamel mugs with their names scratched on them and munching on Marathon or Mars bars.

It was Ted Toomey who offered to act as a waiter when Mr Campion opted to mingle with the lower ranks outside, proudly presenting him with 'one tea, dirty brown, no sugar, as ordered', but immediately looked crestfallen as Campion tried it.

'It's just how I like it, it really is,' said Campion. 'I know it may be odd but I am sure there are other people who do not take sugar; it's just one doesn't meet many of them. Couldn't get any during the war, so oldies of my generation either accepted their lot like me, or are now greedy for it by the tablespoonful.'

Teddy shook his head.

'It's not that, sir, it's the mug. I didn't realize . . .'

Campion held the enamel mug at arm's length and saw that the word 'Alan' had been neatly embossed in silver solder on the side.

'Ah,' said Campion, 'but never no mind. I will treat it with reverence and drink to Alan's memory. You were good friends with him, I understand.'

'We share – shared – digs, with Cuthbert.'

'Did you share his hobby?'

'Oh yes, we trained together on our bicycles whenever we could.'

'I meant his flying hobby.'

'Not likely! You wouldn't get me up in one of those string-bags! I know enough about airframes and stress patterns to know they can be death traps, especially with an inexperienced pilot.'

'Dear me, the devil-may-care attitude students here were once famous for seems to have slipped a generation. A bit of looping-the-loop or naughty sky-writing would have been a hoot in Rag Week in my day.'

'Perhaps it's all the sugar we consume,' said Toomey, a cheeky grin twitching his lips.

'And chocolate,' said Campion, pointedly looking at one overweight student sitting cross-legged on the grass whilst 'dunking' a two-fingered KitKat into his tea and then trying to work out the quickest path into his open mouth.

'Your hobby is learning languages, I hear,' said Campion casually, turning back to Toomey. 'Why Russian, though?'

If Ted Toomey was surprised at Campion knowing that, he did not show it. 'I thought it would help reading some of their technical papers. The Russians are very interested in the thermo-dynamic issues of high-bypass jet engines, and occasionally some of their scientific journals appear in the West. Plus, you can study anything in Cambridge if you can find someone to teach you.'

'And you found a tutor willing to take you on?'

'Easily. Some of the new young lecturers are grateful for a bit of extra tutoring money a couple of evenings a week, especially the foreign ones.'

'Your tutor is a Russian?'

'No, he's a Finn, but Russian is his second language, and it's quite an honour to be taught by an Olympic athlete.'

'Really? I know the Finns are awfully good at throwing the javelin. Can't think why; must be something to do with hunting reindeer. Personally, I could never hurl a pointed stick at a Rudolph . . .'

'He's not a javelin-thrower; he did the biathlon, which involves at lot of skiing. He was with the Finnish team at the Winter Olympics in Squaw Valley in California in 1960. I think the Finns took a silver medal.'

'Interesting,' said Campion. 'What's the name of this Olympian?'

'Jaris Jarvela.'

'And does he have a sister?'

'Oh, you've heard,' said a deflated Toomey. 'I suppose Cuthbert's been sniggering behind my back. She's called Astra and I think she's rather fine.'

Campion thought 'fine' an unusual way of describing the object of a young man's first love, but he had no wish to deepen the blushes reddening Teddy's cheeks.

'Young Mr Snow is probably jealous,' he said, 'and so he should be. Astra is an impressive young lady. I've met her.'

'You have?'

'Professor Branscombe has kindly given me the loan of both his house and his housekeeper whilst I'm here.'

'She's only doing that while her brother settles in and her English improves and she finds something better,' said the young man defending his young love.

'Her English seems more than adequate to me, and I am sure she will succeed at whatever she puts her mind to. I get the impression she knows her own mind.'

'She certainly does.' Toomey grinned.

But you don't, thought Campion, *and in this case, ignorance may be well be bliss*, but he was immediately distracted by the deep growl of an approaching engine from somewhere behind him. As he turned slowly, he became aware of another sound – whistling – coming from the students, which became more off-key as more of them contributed to the tune.

It was, however, still recognizable as 'Here We Go into the Wild Blue Yonder' and although he made no attempt to join in the rendition, Ted Toomey clearly thought he should explain to the Project's distinguished visitor.

'Oh, hell! The Yanks are coming!'

'But aren't they here already?' asked Campion. 'I've just been talking to one inside, Gary Cupples.'

Toomey shook his head. 'We don't count Gary, he's one of us. This is a *serious* Yank.'

It was certainly a serious car, thought Campion, if you liked a lot of metal for your money, that is. He recognized the model, on the principle of once-seen-never-forgotten, as a red, two-door Chevrolet Bel Air, which approached with the grace of a destroyer coming into harbour, its twin headlights staring back at anyone who dared to gaze at it. Stretching in the distance behind the driver would be a boot, or 'trunk' as Americans insisted, big enough to take the contents of a small cottage. It sighed to a rest parallel to the hangar; of all the other, British, cars parked against the hangar, including the Land Rover, it was the only one which seemed to be in scale.

As the driver switched off the engine, the sarcastic whistling died away, though the Chevrolet, as a thing of engineering wonder, still drew the odd low wolf-whistle of admiration, until the driver's side door opened – the left one, naturally – and a tall, rangy figure seemed to peel itself away from the brightly coloured metalwork.

His blond hair was cut short in the military style which Campion could never decide was either a crew-cut or *en brosse*, and he wore a blue military-style short-sleeved shirt with epaulettes and a buttoned-down collar, the ensemble completed with sharply pressed, powder blue trousers and topped off with wire-framed aviator mirrored sunglasses.

'This must be Luther Romo,' said Campion.

'It is,' said Ted Toomey, 'and he's come to look down his nose at us.'

'Now, now,' scolded Campion, 'let us not be boorish. I understand that he acts as the liaison officer between the US air force and Goshawk, so we must be diplomatic and liaise, and as with all diplomacy we must do it with a thin veneer of politeness.'

Campion handed his mug to Toomey and briefly enjoyed the confused look on the young man's face, then strode casually towards the Chevrolet where the driver was taking a slim brown leather document folder from the passenger seat.

'Good morning, Senior Master Sergeant,' Campion hailed him. 'Have I got that right? It's not a rank I'm familiar with. My name's Albert Campion and I am unencumbered by rank.'

'Now that I just don't believe,' said the American from behind his mirrored glasses which, disconcertingly, reflected two small images of the approaching Campion. 'If Amanda is a lady then you must be a lord.'

'A common enough misconception. My wife is a lady in every sense of the word, but her title comes by virtue of her being the sister of an earl, albeit of a rather obscure earldom. I remain simply Albert. I take it that the two of you work together.'

'If you're Al, then I'm Luther,' said the American with a broad display of perfect white teeth as they shook hands, 'and she does all the work. I just peek over her shoulder occasionally to see how things are going.'

Campion glanced at his reflection in Romo's sunglasses, wondering if he had visibly flinched at being called 'Al'. Perhaps it had been a test.

'I'm sure you do more than that. Amanda has always valued the opinion of the American air force, who, after all, may well be one of her main customers if her research is successful.'

'That remains to be seen,' said Romo, slowly peeling off his aviator glasses the way a movie star expecting a close-up would, 'but if the Goshawk ever flies, I'd like to be the guy at the controls.'

'So you are an active pilot?'

'Yessir, I earned my wings flying F-100 Super Sabres at England.'

'England?'

'I like telling people here that just to see their reaction.' Romo illuminated his smile again. 'Actually, I trained at England Air Force Base, Louisiana, before going operational.'

'And was that in Vietnam, may I ask?'

'Uh-huh.' He shook his head in the negative. 'I was sent to the front line of the Cold War, a place called Ramstein in Germany, to eyeball the Russians.'

'And now?' asked Campion.

'Based at Alconbury, just down the road and taking things a little bit slower, learning to drive on the wrong side of the road, trying to figure out cricket and getting a taste for warm, flat beer.'

'That sounds like my ideal retirement.'

'But you're far from retired, are you, Al?'

'What makes you say that, Sergeant?'

'A man of your reputation, his wife detained by the authorities, would spring to her defence and investigate the trumped-up charges thrown at her. No, you're not retired, Mr Campion – far from it, I would guess.'

'And just how do you know what reputation I may or may not have? Not that I'm not flattered that my fame has spread through the American air force from Louisiana to – where was it? – Ramstein and even, most impressively of all, to Alconbury.'

'The workings of the Goshawk Project require a considerable level of security clearance, not just for those doing the grunt work, but sometimes those nearest and dearest to them. Part of my job, to protect American interests, is to check those security clearances. Your name cropped up several times.'

'Delighted to be a person of interest,' said Campion, giving a short bow of mock deference, 'and you are quite right in that I am anxious to clear my wife of the suspicions of an insensitive *gendarmerie*, but I am here in a purely unofficial capacity trying to get a feel for things without getting in the way.'

'I got the impression, from my contacts in your British police, that you were pretty good at getting in the way.'

'I will take that as a compliment, though it was probably not intended as one.'

'Have you got anywhere?'

'Hardly. Things were rather disrupted by yesterday's accident.'

'Accident?'

Campion realized immediately that this was news to the American. 'With the crane that travels across the ceiling in there.'

'Who got hurt?'

'One of the workshop technicians, a postgraduate student called Alan Wormold; and he didn't get hurt, he was killed.'

'*Goddammit!*' Romo's hands clenched into boxer's fists in a sudden spasm. 'He was a good kid. What happened?'

'First thing in the morning, Wormold was working at the central lathe when the crane must have malfunctioned, possibly due to a power surge, and started across the workshop. He was in the way and got knocked into a spinning blade. The only mercy was that it must have been quick.'

Luther Romo clenched and unclenched his fists several times before asking: 'Are we sure it was an accident?'

What an unexpected question, thought Campion, even though it was exactly the question that had worried him for more than twenty-four hours.

'You're upset,' he said. 'Did you know him?'

'Sure did, we were fly-boys together.'

'Wormold was flying jets out at Alconbury?'

'Jeez, no. We both used the flying club's Tiger Moth out at the Bourn Airfield. I like to take it slow and easy some days.'

'When you get to my age,' said Campion, 'you don't get the option.'

Romo smiled politely at that but – significantly, thought Campion – did not refute the suggestion.

'How's the prof taking it?'

'Not well, but not as badly as Alf Bagley, who thinks he is somehow personally responsible.'

The American narrowed his eyes as if regretting he had removed his sunglasses.

'Was it an accident? You didn't answer my question.'

'No,' said Mr Campion, 'I did not.'

Detective Inspector Mawson was 'resting his undercarriage' (as Lugg would have said) on the bonnet of a police-liveried Morris Minor and smoking a cigarette when Mr Campion rounded the corner of Pound Hill.

'I'm not sure I should be doing this,' said the policeman in greeting, 'and I'm certain you shouldn't be.'

'Come now, Inspector, what harm can it do? Think of it as pastoral care. These are impressionable young men and, on behalf of the Goshawk Project, I have taken it upon myself to ensure that they are holding up psychologically after the experience of such an horrific accident.'

'And you're doing that by searching their digs whilst they're at work?'

'I have to get a feel for the young minds I'm caring for,' said Campion, 'but if you believe that, you'll believe anything. Have you spoken with Charlie Luke?'

'I have, otherwise I wouldn't be here, but when Scotland Yard tells a regional CID inspector to jump, he jumps.'

'I'm sure Superintendent Luke didn't order gymnastics.'

'Maybe not, but he told me that I should assist you with your enquiries, which is the other way round to how we normally deal with the public.'

'Well, I am immensely grateful for your forbearance. Before we proceed, can I just check one thing. We are still dealing with an industrial accident – officially, that is?'

'Unless you're telling me something I don't know but ought to.'

Campion smiled his patented high-beam smile, which Amanda always referred to as his 'immaculate idiot' face.

'Shall we proceed?'

The students' house was a small, terraced cottage, possibly built a century ago to accommodate a family of lace-workers or weavers given the generous size of the windows. It had been modernized by the introduction of electricity, and by capturing the outdoor wash-house and lavatory in the small backyard and dragging them into a ground-floor bathroom. There was a tiny front room, full of mismatched and distinctly uncomfortable furniture, which could have been mistaken from the street for an antique shop, were it not for the permanently drawn thick brown curtains, and there was a kitchen which showed all the signs of student habitation in terms of dirty dishes, spilt milk, open packets of breakfast cereal and a frying pan with what appeared to be the bottom half of a fried egg welded to it, though only a pathologist could confirm that.

Mr Campion followed Inspector Mawson up the uncarpeted stairs to the three bedrooms, the first they encountered having a picture of a crocodile cut from a comic glued above the door handle.

'I take it that is Cuthbert's room,' said Campion.

'Who?' said Mawson, fumbling at the door opposite with a bunch of keys.

'Cuthbert "Crocodile" Snow, one of the workshop technicians like Wormold. He inherited the nickname from his grandfather, another Magdalene man.'

'You Cambridge men all stick together. Thick as thieves, you lot.'

'And policemen do not? Stick together, I mean, not act like thieves.'

'Out of loyalty and tradition and the need to keep the Queen's peace.'

'One can say exactly the same about the students at this distinguished university if one glosses over the part about keeping the peace, of course. I do hope you won't be too shocked if we find a couple of traffic cones or a policeman's helmet in there.'

'We'd better not,' muttered Mawson, holding the door open. 'Well, go on, have a snoop around. See if you can find anything we missed.'

'I'm sure your chaps didn't miss anything important, Inspector,' soothed Campion. 'I'm just trying to get a feel for the poor chap. I take it you have removed any personal documents?'

'A diary with not much in it and some bank statements, but there was nothing like a suicide note if that's what you were hinting at.'

'I wasn't, but the bank statements might be interesting.'

'His academic papers and drawings we've left until Professor Branscombe sees them,' said Mawson. 'He might know what he's looking at. That stuff's beyond me.'

Campion nodded sympathetically, realizing that he did not actually know what he was looking for, let alone at. He wandered aimlessly around the bedroom, noting that the only personal additions to the decor were schematic diagrams of famous aircraft, pull-outs from comics – most likely the *Eagle* – which had been stuck to wallpaper above the bed with yellowing strips of Sellotape. The wardrobe revealed nothing other than that the late Alan Wormold had a limited and conservative range of clothing, although it did include a rather shiny dinner suit which Campion suspected was a family heirloom. There was a desk by the window, which groaned with technical papers and magazines, drawing paper, slide rules and set-squares, and a small shelf of books. Close examination of their spines revealed they were all technical manuals about aircraft or bicycles, apart from *Biggles Learns to Fly* and *Biggles Flies East*, plus a Hodder paperback of Gavin Lyall's *The Wrong Side of the Sky*, with a picture of the author in full flying gear on the back cover. Wormold's choice of fiction, though limited, displayed a theme which did not surprise Campion.

What his wandering foot made contact with under the bed did.

It was a wooden crate which had once contained beer bottles and still retained the name of Lacons Brewery stencilled along the side, but instead of bottles of pale ale it now contained coils of greased bicycle chain, pedals, rubber handlebar grips, two padded bicycle seats, brake blocks and a selection of spanners of sizes to fit any recalcitrant nut or bolt.

'Well, that explains it,' he said aloud.

'Explains what?' asked Mawson, hands in pockets, staring down at the crate of metal flotsam.

'What Nugent Monck, and indeed my wife, suspected. Wormold was filching lengths of steel tubing from the Goshawk Project. Reynolds something-or-other, they call it, and they use it to make models of airframes to test stresses and strains.'

'So what?'

'Given this box of bits and pieces, I would say Mr Wormold was building himself a bicycle.'

'Seems a bit of a redundant thing to do in Cambridge,' said Mawson. 'There's a fair trade in second-hand ones and, if he had his wits about him, he'd go to the police pound on Mill Road. We have a couple of hundred lost or stolen bikes there on any given day. If he turned up with a convincing story of it being pinched, he could take his pick. Some students go through nine or ten bikes in their three years without ever actually owning one. Frankly, we're glad to get rid of them.'

'You're forgetting that Wormold was an engineer as well as a keen cyclist, like his friends. He'd want to build – to engineer – his own.'

'I thought his hobby was flying.'

'A young man can have two hobbies,' said Campion, 'though perhaps rarely do they both involve means of transport. You are quite right, though. Everything I have heard about Alan indicates that he dedicated every penny and spare moment he had to flying out at Bourn Airfield.'

'So no interest in the opposite sex, then?'

'Not as far as I know, though that's not too unusual for Cambridge, or any university for that matter. I doubt there were many young females studying engineering that he could mix with, which is something my wife feels very strongly about, as I know to my cost. Perhaps there was an attractive aviatrix out at Bourn Flying Club who took Alan's fancy and he was impressing her by looping-the-loop at every given opportunity. Would you mind if I went out there and poked around?'

Mawson shrugged his shoulders. 'Suit yourself. I can't spare you any transport.'

'Please don't worry about that. Turning up in a blue-and-white Morris Minor might cramp my style. Besides, I've been offered a lift and a guided tour of the facilities by a fellow fly-boy, Luther Romo.'

'The Yank air-force officer?'

'Technically I think he's a sergeant, but he's definitely in the service, and a consultant to the Goshawk Project. You know him?'

'Our paths have crossed.' The inspector was uncommitted. 'He always shows up whenever any of the personnel from the base gets into trouble in town.'

'Does that happen often?'

'Rarely. They have their own cinema out there, along with bigger cars, cheaper cigarettes, and beer which they don't spit out for being warm. The only reason most of them drift into Cambridge is to take pictures of the old buildings on their expensive German cameras. Seen enough?'

'I suppose a quick peek in the rooms of Cuthbert Snow and Ted Toomey whilst we're here would be out of the question? I suspect the keys are on that bunch you borrowed from the landlord, aren't they?'

Mawson looked down at the keys in his hand as if seeing them for the first time, and he weighed them as if making a difficult decision.

'No, I don't think so, Mr Campion, not unless you can give me a damn good reason involving an immediate threat to life or you have a legal warrant in your pocket. I only do so many favours for friends of Scotland Yard.'

'Fair enough, Inspector. That's quite right and proper. Shall I lead the way so you can see me off the premises?'

Campion started down the stairs while Mawson locked up behind him; he had the door to the cupboard under the stairs open and the light switched on before the policeman reached him.

'What now?' said Mawson irritably.

'It fell open as I brushed past,' said Campion. 'It wasn't locked and I couldn't resist a peek. I've always been fascinated by what people hide under the stairs, haven't you?'

'Can't say I have, unless somebody tells me they've hidden a body there.'

Mr Campion feigned regret. 'Nothing so dramatic, Inspector, merely confirmation of our theory that poor Alan was planning to build his own bicycle.'

The policeman raised himself on his toes to peer over Campion's shoulder into the cupboard, which would have been big enough to fit a standing man had it not been crammed to bursting point with household accoutrements including a Hoover (clearly little used judging by the amount of dust on it rather than in it), a mop and bucket, two threadbare sweeping brushes, several lengths of clothesline and an ancient wicker basket of clothes pegs, as well as several metal parallelogram shapes made of tubular steel and a pair of large, rubber-tyred wheels.

'Those look like bits of a bicycle frame,' Mawson said into Campion's left ear, 'but those aren't pushbike wheels, they look as if they've come off a motorbike.'

'You are quite right, Inspector. Makes one wonder just what sort of a bicycle Alan was building.'

Campion walked back to Barton Road via the Market Square, where he treated himself to a large pork pie and a mug of tea in lieu of a missed breakfast, then he made the rounds of the stalls, purchasing fruit, lettuce, tomatoes and spring onions. At a butcher's he bought a selection of cold meats and liver sausage, and then added a loaf of bread and a bottle of Chablis to his shopping bag.

He had the front door to Professor Branscombe's house open and one foot in the hallway when he heard voices coming from the kitchen. He closed the door quietly and covered the distance to the kitchen in four quick, long strides.

'Oh, hello! I hope I'm not disturbing anything,' he announced as he entered, hefting his bag on to the kitchen table.

He was not really surprised to find Astra the housekeeper there, leaning back against the refrigerator, and only mildly surprised to see the boyish face and curly hair of Teddy Toomey, though he was slightly taken aback by how closely the young man's body was pressed up against her, his hands down by his side as though they had just been slapped there.

'Everything now is clean!' Astra squeaked – a line Campion imagined straight from a *Carry On* film – 'and I was just about to leave.'

Campion said nothing but raised an eyebrow in Teddy's direction.

'So was I,' said young Toomey, blushing. 'Only called by to deliver a package from Cuthbert,' he indicated a cardboard shoebox balanced precariously on the draining board, 'and when I cut across the fields, I saw Astra out in the garden and thought I'd say hello.'

'Very civil of you,' said Campion, suppressing a smile. 'Please do not let me detain you.'

He began to unpack his bag as Toomey, receiving no encouragement whatsoever from Astra to delay his departure, nodded and shuffled off towards the back door.

'You have bought food?' she asked as she pulled on a leather jacket. 'I could have cooked for you.'

'Did you not get my note? I will not be requiring supper tonight. I have made my own arrangements, and anyway, I simply cannot continue to eat the professor out of house and home.'

'Then I see you tomorrow?'

'Perhaps. I'm afraid my movements are a little unpredictable.'

Campion continued to put away his purchases, listening carefully for the sound of the front door closing, which was rapidly followed by the throaty roar of an engine. He made it to the front-room window in time to see a motorbike, complete with black-clad rider with Astra's arms around his waist, pulling away into the Barton Road traffic.

He returned to the kitchen and unpacked his groceries, making sure the Chablis had a secure place in the fridge. Then he familiarized himself with the contents of the cupboards until he found the professor's stock of glasses. He selected two wine glasses, which he washed thoroughly and left to dry.

Upstairs, in his bedroom, he collected his binoculars and did what seemed to be a perfunctory check of the suitcase and kitbag he had stored in the wardrobe and the few belongings scattered around the room, then he scampered downstairs and out into back garden.

By the stream at the bottom boundary, he trained the binoculars on the distant Goshawk hangar and the rough ground leading to it until he picked out the back of the trudging figure of Teddy Toomey, his reluctant delivery boy. Although perhaps not too reluctant, as he had clearly had an ulterior motive. Campion suspected he had volunteered to relieve Cuthbert of the task purely on the off chance that Astra would be in the house.

Convinced that he was not overlooked from any angle, Campion turned his attention to the summer house and used the spray can of WD-40 which Gary Cupples had given him on both the key and the lock. Satisfied that the key now turned easily, he opened the door and slotted it into place on the inside.

Without a second thought for the lovelorn messenger who

had brought it, he returned to the kitchen and the parcel from Cuthbert. On closer examination, it was not a shoebox but a box which had once contained spark plugs. Now it contained dust and dirt and smelled strongly of oil and grease.

Spreading a sheet of newspaper on the kitchen table, Mr Campion carefully emptied the box and, taking a fork from the cutlery drawer, began to comb through the inch-deep tilth he had created.

It took him only a minute of gentle tilling to find two items of interest among the muck, dead insects and cigarette butts: a twist of black insulating tape and a shiny ball-bearing about half an inch in diameter, which he held up between finger and thumb.

'Good old Lugg,' he said to no one but himself.

EIGHT
Magic Carpet

A casual passer-by, an innocent bystander or an evening dog-walker on Barton Road at about ten p.m. (fortunately there were none) could have witnessed a piece of pantomime which, even in Cambridge, might have tweaked their curiosity and possibly been reported to the police.

A small delivery van bearing the name and livery of Joshua Taylor & Co. Ltd, the respected department store on the corner of Market Street and Sidney Street, was parked outside number 112 with its lights off and its rear doors open. A large, shadowy figure with the proportions of a mountain gorilla, dressed in brown overalls and flat cap, was heaving what could only be a roll of carpet from the interior of the van to the tipping point where it could be flopped over his right shoulder.

It was not so much the fact that Joshua Taylor were not known for home deliveries at that time of the evening which was suspicious in itself, but the grunts and squeals which came from the figure as he staggered with the shouldered carpet to the front door were distinctly odd, and far too high-pitched for a healthy male gorilla.

The door of number 112 opened as if by magic, and the bulky figure with the upside-down U-shaped load squeezed into an unlit hallway, the door closing as soon as he was over the threshold.

In the living room, lit by a single table lamp and the curtains firmly drawn against (non-existent) passers-by, the large man carefully lowered his burden to the floor, where a convenient space had been made by withdrawing all the furniture to the edges of the room. Bent double and wheezing loudly, whilst muttering that he was not as young as he used to be, he flipped the roll of carpet gently so that it began to unravel. The contents of the carpet completed the manoeuvre with an exasperated squeal, a flapping of hands and a flurry of red hair.

'I spy *a bold coquette!*' said Mr Campion.

'What did I tell you to do, Lugg?' said Lady Amanda, who managed to dominate the room despite her supine position.

'Hit 'im on the nose with a rolled-up newspaper if he quoted Shakespeare on Cleopatra,' recited the fat man.

'I was quoting Plutarch, not Shakespeare,' said Campion, taking his wife's hands in his and helping her to her feet. 'He was describing Cleo being smuggled into Caesar's presence in a bed-roll by her Nubian slave. You and a roll of Axminster were the best I could come up with at short notice. And now you'd better return the carpet to soft furnishings before they realize it's gone. Tell them I'm sorry for the bother, but that pattern clashes horribly with the wallpaper and simply won't do.'

Lugg averted his eyes to the ceiling as Mr and Mrs Campion kissed passionately and allowed them a generous three seconds before coughing loudly.

'Don't the workers get the offer of a cuppa tea or p'rhaps something stronger for their trouble, then?'

''Fraid not, old chum. If anyone did see you arrive and thought it odd that a carpet be delivered at this time of night, then it might salve their curiosity if they see that carpet being removed a few minutes later, the delivery driver clearly having had a severe dressing-down for turning up at such an inconvenient time. So off you go, pick up thy bed and walk. Or rather stomp off and slam the van doors as if you're really miffed.'

'Reckon I could pull that off,' growled Lugg, 'though there's nobody about. I drove down the street twice to make sure. 'Ope it wasn't too bouncy in the back, Lady A.'

'I have made more demure entrances,' said Amanda, brushing dust from her clothing with the palms of her hands, 'and I could certainly do with a bath and a change of clothes.'

She was wearing the plain black Nina Ricci suit and high heels she had worn for her honorary degree ceremony underneath the official robes and bonnet. The suit, a favourite of hers, was badly in need of a stiff brush, and the skirt and her sheer black nylons were spotted with flecks of dark red wool acquired from the carpet.

'I'm sure that can be arranged,' said Campion, 'and I have your suitcase upstairs. I have also provided you with a bolt-hole in which to hide during the hours of daylight.'

'She's not turning vampire, is she?' asked Lugg with a music hall double-take.

'Don't be an oaf! For the purposes of our current subterfuge, Amanda has to stay out of sight during the day. Now pick up that carpet, sling it over your shoulder and sling your hook back to Bottle Street; and stay near the phone.'

Lugg tugged at the peak of his cap and attempted, but failed, to look humble. 'Yes, sir; certainly, sir. Three bags full, sir, even though it'll be well past last orders after I've returned the van and picked up the Jensen. Don't suppose I could break a few speed limits, could I?'

'Certainly not! Now off with you, you carpetbagger! But carry with you my thanks for all your help.'

Lugg held up a giant paw in dismissal. 'Don't mention it. Always a pleasure to help Lady A in one of her dramatic escapes.'

'I didn't mean *that*,' said Campion, 'or not just that, but your advice on the crane's control panel: you were right, it was a ball-bearing holding the On button down.'

'Glad to be of use,' said Lugg. 'Cheque in the post, is it?'

'Fat chance. Now wilt thou not be gone? And that *was* Shakespeare, or almost, and take your flying carpet with you.'

Muttering under his breath about the unfairness of life, Lugg dropped to his knees and rolled up the Axminster which, without its human passenger, he picked up, slung over his shoulder with ease and headed for the front door.

'I'll be leaving you now,' he said, his voice muffled by the carpet, half of which hung down his chest like an elephant's trunk.

Even for Lugg, it was an unusual exit.

'So how was your dramatic escape from our security services?' Campion asked as he escorted Amanda upstairs to the bedroom.

'Remarkably easy,' said Amanda. 'Went exactly to plan and, apart from the last bit in the back of a furniture van, was remarkably comfortable.'

'They treated you well? Gave you the third degree?'

'A bit like a glass doll; even got me last month's *Vogue* so I could read about Jean Shrimpton,' said Amanda, kicking off her shoes. 'I'm not sure if that was a hint of some sort, or whether it was part of their interrogation technique. On the whole, it was remarkably painless, until Lugg turned up, that is.'

'Yes, he is something of an escapee from the Natural History Museum, but he has his uses.'

'I take it my arrest caught the general imagination and stirred things up?'

'I think it did, but not in a way you will like.'

'What do you mean, Albert? What's happened?'

Campion eased her towards the bed. 'You'd better sit down, my dear.'

Amanda had inherited the Fitton shock of fiery red hair, which, it was automatically assumed by most if not all, came accompanied by a blistering temper. In her twenty-five years of marriage to Albert Campion, he had never given her cause to ignite that temper, although she had recently reminded him that the pilot light had not gone out and he had better not forget an important pending wedding anniversary.

But now, as she sat on the edge of the bed, her hands clenching and unclenching, plucking at her nylon-covered knees, she was angry. Not with her husband, but at the news he gave her, outlining the death of Alan Wormold. She knew Albert would have spared her the really gruesome details, but that he would also know she was familiar with the potential dangers associated with the machinery in the workshop. She had often thought, though she had never shared the thought with him, that the design, construction and testing of an aeroplane was a far more precarious endeavour than actually flying in one.

'Was it an accident?' she asked, staring down at the carpet.

'The police toyed with the idea of suicide but seem to have settled for industrial accident.'

'I didn't ask what the police thought,' said Amanda, eyes still firmly downwards. 'I want to know what you think.'

She noted the long pause before Campion answered and

knew that had anyone else asked that question, her husband would have removed his owlish classes and be vigorously polishing the lenses while he considered his response.

'Alf Bagley turned the power on, but the crane only started moving because the button on the control box had been pressed and held down.'

'So there must have been a third person in the workshop. You press the On button with your thumb and carry the box with you. If you take your thumb off the button, the crane stops.'

'You are correct, of course, but the button had been pressed and stayed pressed because someone had put a ball bearing into that depression and stuck it in place with black insulating tape. I took advice on the matter from Lugg, as I always like to consult the experts, and he said that's how he would have done it. The crane was technically already on, it just needed the electricity when the circuit was closed by poor Alf to set it in motion.'

'So it was murder; deliberate murder.'

'Well, it was a pretty elaborate method. It could have been designed to maim or at the very least terrify young Alan, but it was certainly premeditated, though not by Alf Bagley.'

'Of course not!' Amanda stamped a stockinged foot. 'I've known him for years, he's perfectly honest, completely loyal and wouldn't hurt a fly.'

'Somebody saw Alan Wormold as the fly in the ointment.'

'Not Alf, he's totally reliable.'

'Is that why you got him involved in your project?'

Amanda turned her heart-shaped face up to her husband to meet his concerned gaze. 'I know you never approved of the idea,' she said gently but firmly.

'I always thought it might prove a dangerous scheme,' said Campion softly, 'and Alf Bagley, with the best will in the world, is hardly equipped to cover your back.'

'And you, my dearest, always assumed that was your job,' she said, her eyes widening.

'Which of course it is, as I am your paladin, your sworn champion. I may not be as young as I was, nor as spry, and though I have the weak and feeble body of an old-age pensioner, I have the heart and stomach . . .'

Amanda reached out and took her husband's hand. 'Darling Albert, that's quite enough play-acting. I know you are only trying to soften the blow, but I need to think, and I need you to think as well.'

Campion squeezed his wife's hand and perched on the bed next to her. 'Very well, what little brain I have is yours, if you can locate it. Please, probe away.'

Amanda nodded her head silently, gathering her thoughts. 'I think the immediate problem is to discover whether Alan Wormold was killed because of something he knew or had discovered, or whether he was killed to implicate Alf, or at least distract him.'

'Or get him out of the way. Alf's on compassionate leave, thinking he was responsible.'

'Alf got on very well with Alan, with all Branscombe's students.'

'The rumour, though, is that you did not. A small matter of some missing tubing.'

'Oh, that! I gave him no more than a ticking off for not paying attention to stock control. Nugent Monck may have wanted to blow it up into something more serious, but Alan was no thief.'

'I think, technically, he was. In the house he shares with Ted Toomey and Crocodile Snow we found lengths of tubing. Perhaps Alan was going into business for himself.'

'I doubt that very much, but I would have believed you if you said he was building an aeroplane in the attic. He had an amateur pilot's licence, you know, but not a driving licence.'

'Yes, I was aware of that, which is why I intend to visit Bourn Airfield at some point.'

'Why?'

'As the Americans would say, I am covering all the bases. I've seen Wormold's workplace, I've seen his digs. The only other place he seems to have frequented is his flying club. I am of course working on the assumption that Alan's death was connected to your particular leakage problems at Alandel and now Goshawk.'

Amanda frowned and titled her head to one side. 'I don't see how he could be. The leaks started at Alandel before the

Goshawk Project was launched and before John Branscombe and his students joined the team here in Cambridge. I told you, there were always only four possible suspects.' She paused, moistened her lips with the tip of her tongue and allowed herself a modest smile. 'Actually five – if you include me.'

When Amanda had first raised the matter of a leak of Alandel's highly sensitive work to the company's board and certain officials of the security service, she had declared that she had narrowed down the suspects to the engineers with both access and understanding of the ongoing research. That meant, she put it boldly, 'There are four of them – and me' and did not attempt to downplay the importance of the leak.

Commercially sensitive information had been trickling out of Alandel for . . . well, nobody knew exactly, but as the firm attracted more and more government and military contracts, minor examples of industrial espionage had matured into espionage proper and a threat, if not directly to national security itself, then at least to the sleep patterns of the nation's allies. Those slumbers had been sorely disturbed over the past four years by a series of spy scandals which had resulted in red faces in Parliament and a massive boost in the sales of certain newspapers.

Having followed the string of exposés in the popular press, which were difficult to avoid, Amanda had more faith in the legion of fictional secret agents and spy-catchers which populated the shelves of every paperback bookshop, cinema screen and television drama these days, than in the actual security services. Thus, Amanda being Amanda, she decided to take matters into her own hands and the Goshawk Project was born.

Her plan, though she said it herself, was ingenious. Isolate the four senior engineers under suspicion from the ongoing research at Alandel and set them to work on a project of equal sensitivity and, importantly, one which would clearly be of interest to both a commercial competitor and an enemy state. And so the concept of the AAF-3, the Advanced Agile Fighter, became flesh, or rather lengths of angled metal twisted and tested to take unnatural levels of stress, each analysed by a thousand calculations done by hand, then triple-checked, and every nut, bolt and bearing scrupulously recorded on several hundred drawings and blueprints.

Not that the Goshawk, as the AAF-3 was code-named, was likely to get into front-line service or even be constructed in the near future. Such things took time, and the wheels of the Ministry of Defence were famous for grinding slow. And then there were the politicians who had shown, with the TSR-2, that they had no compunction about discarding years of research and a considerable investment of intellect and sterling if the mood took them.

But Amanda knew she would have no trouble in finding volunteers, even if they did not know they had been volunteered. The chance to work on something so revolutionary as a jet fighter with forward-swept wings, to make something aerodynamically stunning and be the first in the world to do so, was a temptation which could not be resisted by any aeronautical engineer worth his salt.

A chance meeting at the Institute of Electrical Engineering with John Branscombe provided Amanda with the location. Cambridge was safely distant from the Alandel headquarters and came with impeccable academic credentials. Even better, the university had a wartime aircraft workshop on its hands, and the professor was confident that Alandel could have the use of it if the university could claim joint credit on any successful outcome. It could even provide useful practical training for some of his brighter engineering students before they left the cocoon of college life and began to make their own way in the world.

It was not difficult to persuade her four key suspects to agree to be seconded to the Goshawk Project, thanks to her natural charm and the fact that she was respected as both engineer and employer. A fair amount of flattery and the oft-dropped hint that she was 'looking only for the best' undoubtedly helped.

Kevin Loder had, initially, been the only one to express hesitation, not on professional grounds but personal ones, pleading that he was reluctant to be relocated away from his wife, teenage daughter and recently bought seaside bungalow. Amanda's assurances that no weekend working would be required, the Goshawk Project could provide a rail warrant and that Cambridge wasn't really that far away, did the trick.

Nugent Monck – the 'squadron leader' – was instantly on board, having been told that he was the first of the senior engineers to be approached to join the Goshawk Project. It was a lie Amanda told with angelic innocence and absolutely no sense of guilt.

Melvyn Barnes had sucked on his pipe and rubbed his troublesome leg and agreed to join the team as (as he put it phlegmatically) somebody had to be there to take the squadron leader down a peg or two, and to help out as a translator, as no one in Cambridge would be able to follow Kevin Loder's Brummie accent. As he had left Amanda's office, she thought there may not have been an actual spring in his step, but his limp seemed less pronounced than when he had entered.

Gary Cupples, being American – and his short-sleeved shirts worn with a tie advertised his nationality as much as his passport – greeted the prospect with gleeful enthusiasm, almost as a child would receive a new toy. But then he was young and American, and Americans thrived on the prospect of something new over the horizon, although he too admitted that he would relish a continuation of his attempts 'to get a rise' out of Nugent Monck.

Once up and running, any advances made on the Goshawk Project which became known outside the secure circle Amanda had created should, in theory, lead back to the leak. Swept-forward wing technology was a research topic which many in aviation thought a luxury, if not downright esoteric, and one which had not been seriously pursued for fifteen years, when Soviet Russia had attempted to exploit Nazi Germany's experiments. Yet the fact that Alandel, Cambridge University and Amanda Fitton were putting their heads together and showing an interest in the subject would make sure that certain other parties sat up and took an interest too.

Mr Campion, a firm believer in the maxim that a trouble shared was two people worrying unnecessarily, had asked Amanda how and when she would know that 'certain other parties' had, so to speak, taken the bait. On this she had remained tight-lipped, offering no more than a taciturn assurance that she would know because she had her own, highly placed sources.

Her husband knew better than to take this as a slight. Amanda knew her business, its intricacies and its importance, Campion did not, yet he thought he had other skills and experience to offer.

When she had divulged her plan, or at least some of it, over dinner one evening, Campion had tried to make light of his concern.

'It sounds as if you are looking for a spy,' he had said casually, 'so why not set a spy to catch a spy, and if your trap is being set in Cambridge, surely a Cambridge man could help. I admit that, as an alumnus of St Ignatius, I may not have a convincing curriculum vitae. As we used to say, if you want a decent spy, you should pop across the road to Trinity.'

That at least had provoked a smile.

'And who was the wise man,' Campion pressed his case, 'who said that the ideal spy was the man with the best intellect but the outward appearance of a fool?'

'On those criteria,' Amanda had replied, 'you would certainly qualify, my darling fool, but you could not pass for anyone with a basic grasp of aeronautical engineering, or even a passing interest in the subject. You may bluff your way through a cocktail party, but the technical detail would be beyond you. You would have no idea what was worth stealing, let alone if it had been stolen.'

'But I simply do not like the idea of you getting involved in industrial espionage without someone to help you,' Campion had pleaded, and then quickly, for the sake of domestic harmony, qualified: 'Not that you are incapable of taking care of yourself.'

To his relief, Amanda had taken a moment to reflect and then allowed her husband a small victory.

'Actually, there is something you can do to help. At some point I think I will need what the professionals call a "safe house", and I think I have already picked one out. John Branscombe's house on Barton Road is ideally placed and I happen to know, because he has confided in me, that the professor is heading for an acrimonious divorce. I am sure he could be persuaded to stay in his rooms at Magdalene, which would leave the house free to be used by a wayward traveller for a few days.'

'You, my darling,' Campion had said, 'are frighteningly well-informed.'

'I really must have a bath and get changed,' said Amanda, pushing herself to her feet. 'Where's my case?'

'In the wardrobe.' Campion took a small key from his jacket pocket. 'It's locked, which is just as well, as if anyone had opened it I would have been hard-pressed to explain its extremely feminine contents.'

'I'm sure you would have come up with something amusing, perhaps something salacious, but I'm glad your blushes have been spared.'

'So am I, considering someone has searched this room.'

'Are you sure?'

'My few paltry belongings are in that old kitbag and my washbag is in the bathroom. Both have been gone through, though nothing taken.'

'The housekeeper?' Amanda spoke lightly, concentrating on removing her suit jacket and hanging it in the wardrobe.

'Almost certainly,' said Campion, 'and probably out of simple nosiness, though there was somebody else in the house today, one of Alan Wormold's friends, Ted Toomey.'

Amanda hefted her case on to the bed, unlocked the two brass catches, opened the lid and removed a make-up bag and began serious consideration of a change of outfit.

'Alan and Teddy were good chums,' she said, rejecting a salmon-pink blouse in favour of a dark blue sweater, 'always talking about bicycles. The only thing Alan could talk about other than flying. With Teddy it was girls and bicycles, though I'm sure he had far more experience on two wheels than he had success with anything on two legs.'

'They were building a bicycle in their digs, I'm sure of it,' said Campion trying not to be distracted as his wife rummaged through a profusion of lacy underwear.

'Well, that explains the missing tubing,' said Amanda, selecting and inspecting a pair of black ski pants which

Campion knew looked far more attractive when inhabited than when displayed empty.

'I thought so too, but it's hardly a reason to eliminate him.'

Amanda paused, elbow deep in the contents of her suitcase, and looked squarely at her husband.

'What do you mean by "eliminate"?'

'I'm not terribly sure, it's just a theory that is bubbling away at the back of my brain.'

Amanda remained silent, but her unblinking gaze into Campion's eyes was as good as a prompter's cue from off-stage.

'Your rather dramatic honorary degree ceremony was designed to shake things up, provoke a response, wasn't it? With the entire nation thinking you must be suspected of leaking your own secret research, the real source of the leak might be encouraged to give himself away, or at least make it easier to flush him out. That was basically the plan, correct?'

'Go on.'

'Well, what if it worked rather too well?'

'Explain yourself.'

'Wormold, as one of Branscombe's students, could not possibly have been involved in leaking secrets from Alandel prior to the Goshawk Project. But what if he had brought a fresh pair of eyes – innocent eyes – to the research being done here in Cambridge? What if he had seen something, or knew something, which would prove you were not the leak, *but someone else was*? And that someone knew he knew, and so thought it expedient to dispose of him.'

'Are you saying that I might be responsible for Alan's death?'

'Of course not.' Campion reached out and grabbed Amanda's arm. 'Whoever set that trap with the mobile crane was responsible. All you did was spook them into action, as the Americans would say. And now they're well and truly spooked, they will make mistakes.'

NINE

Bait

Mr Campion had long ago learned that when asked to pass an opinion on what his wife was wearing, it was best to assume a position of armed neutrality if either sudden deafness or being struck mute by divine intervention failed as a believable excuse. That night he was not asked for an opinion, but he was speechless all the same, for he had never realized what an attractive burglar his wife made.

Amanda had bathed and then joined her husband in a cold meal made from the provisions he had purchased. They made sure that one glass, one plate and one set of cutlery were washed and put away, leaving a third of the Chablis in the fridge to give the impression that Mr Campion had eased his loneliness with solitary drinking.

Then, just short of midnight, she disappeared upstairs and returned dressed head to dainty toe in black: a black sweater, black ski pants, black running pumps and a black knitted 'beanie' hat struggling to contain her hair. The last person he had seen wearing one of those had been Lugg and it had been pulled over his bald pate like an egg cosy.

Campion himself, wearing a chunky navy-blue sweater, brown corduroy 'gardening' trousers and a flat cap borrowed from Professor Branscombe's hallway hatstand to conceal his white hair, felt positively overdressed.

'Ready to go breaking and entering, darling?' Campion asked cheerfully.

'That would imply we are going to steal something,' said Amanda, holding up a long, unsealed brown envelope, 'whereas we are actual going to deliver something.'

'By breaking and entering your own research facility, although first we have to go on a commando night exercise across rough country. Wouldn't it have been easier to use the post?'

Amanda raised the hem of her sweater and slid the envelope down the front of her trousers until it was secured against her stomach. She pulled down her sweater and patted the imperceptible bulge just to make sure it was in place.

'We have torches?'

'One each,' said Campion, displaying them, 'both with fresh batteries.'

'Then with a bit of luck we won't twist an ankle or fall down a mineshaft. Shall we go for a romantic stroll in the moonlight?'

'Even dressed like this, and with the distinct possibility that we *will* trip and break our necks, it is always romantic when we take a stroll together.'

Campion led the way down the garden path, pausing at the summer house to illuminate it with his torch beam.

'I've oiled the lock and the key's on the inside so you can lock yourself in should you have to keep out of sight. It's pretty basic, but waterproof as far as I can judge.'

'It's not the Savoy, is it?' said Amanda.

'It's not even the Ritz, but hopefully, like the Ritz, you won't have to spend much time in there.'

Campion crossed over the brook at the bottom of the garden in one purposeful stride, his wife following with a delicate leap. Both had listened in vain for a tell-tale splash indicating that the other had got their feet wet.

From there on, there was enough moonlight to help them avoid the worst ankle traps of the rough ground, though both kept their torches on and pointed down at an angle on the look-out for likely obstacles such as those spotted by Mr Campion on his reconnaissance mission. By far the most daunting, and the most unavoidable, was the sunken firing range, but to circumvent it would involve having to negotiate a cat's cradle of random barbed wire and fence posts, an experience Campion did not want to put his wife through. With her safety in mind, he then suffered the indignity of stumbling down one slope of the range and having to have

Amanda help him scramble up the opposite slope on his knees, first by pushing from behind, then pulling from the front.

Campion cursed silently, admitted that he was getting too old for this sort of activity, and then immediately chided himself for complaining of that fact more and more often these days. It was not that he had, on principle, anything against the healthy exercise of a walk across uncultivated fields, but at a time of night surely beyond his bedtime? Perhaps he really was feeling his age, if not acting it.

As break-ins went, this one went like clockwork, the burglars having the distinct advantage of holding keys to both the heavy padlock which secured the main door to the Goshawk hangar, and to the office safe which held the Project's paperwork.

Campion closed the sliding door behind them as they entered and suggested they work by torchlight; he was unsure whether the hangar lights could be seen from outside, betraying their presence to a patrolling fox or a curious owl. In truth he had absolutely no idea whether the Goshawk hangar was light-proof or not and, even if light did spill out, at this time of night who was there to notice it – other than a passing fox or an inquisitive owl? The real reason he fought shy of illuminating the interior of the hangar was two-fold. He was unsure whether the lights worked from the central circuit box and was all too aware what had happened when Alf Bagley had innocently turned on the power and set the travelling crane in motion, and the fact that the Campions were at that moment standing directly under that crane concentrated his mind wonderfully. He was also intent on protecting Amanda, as much as he could, from visual triggers which might invoke a vision of what had happened to Alan Wormold, so if the scene of the crime – for he was sure it had been a crime – could be hidden in the shadows, then his wife might be spared a gruesome nightmare.

He let Amanda lead the way across the hangar floor to the office area, keeping close behind her and deliberately shining his torch to the right, away from the lathe which had devoured poor Wormold. Even so, some of the ghostly shapes thrown up as his torch beam flitted over the dormant machinery were worthy of a Hammer horror film.

The door to the office was not locked, and Amanda made directly for the floor safe, crouching down and inserting the key. By the light of Campion's torch she presented the perfect image of the romantic thief, the sort of cat burglar who stole diamond necklaces while the owner – almost certainly a beautiful heiress, probably titled – slept soundly in a four-poster bed nearby. But that would be in a villa overlooking the Riviera or Lake Como, not in a corrugated-iron construction on wasteland in Cambridge, and there would be no diamond necklace or anything else removed from the safe, rather something added.

Amanda riffled through the papers in the open safe and then pulled the brown envelope from her waistband.

'Exactly what sort of present are you leaving them?' Campion asked, his voice startlingly loud as it echoed round the hangar.

Amanda opened the envelope, pulled out two inches of a large, folded sheet and angled it under Campion's torch beam, which reflected a dark shiny surface with white lines which could have been a diagram, some examples of calculus, or even hieroglyphics as far as he could tell. 'It's an ammonia blueprint of my very own design, done in my own fair hand.'

'Gosh, blueprints really are blue; who knew? What is it a blueprint of? The Goshawk?'

'Hardly,' said Amanda patiently, 'just a few ideas about aerodynamic stability and airframe stiffness and suggestions for modelling.'

'You haven't had a "Eureka!" moment, have you? Have you solved all the Project's problems and this is in fact giving the team here their notice?'

'Far from it, but there are some rather advanced ideas in these plans which may nudge the research along.'

'Ideas which would mean absolutely nothing to a simpleton like me, but which will get the juices of your boffins flowing?'

'Don't put yourself down, darling, that's my job. You may not grasp the aerodynamics, but you're no simpleton. If someone dangled a tasty morsel like this under your nose, you'd be the first to smell a rat.'

'And your boffins won't?'

'I'm not presenting them with a gift-wrapped solution, but they will see some new lines which could advance the research. Even Nugent Monck should grasp that these blueprints represent a step forward, or perhaps half a step. They'll be so excited by the potential they won't question where the ideas came from.'

'Or the draughtsmanship?'

Amanda placed the envelope in the safe so that it would be all too obvious to the next person to look inside, hopefully an engineer and not a real, opportunist burglar.

'Like painters, we all have our little quirks, and some of the team are very familiar with my work, so Melvyn Barnes or Kevin Loder could probably spot it was my work. Young Gary, the American, hasn't been around long enough to pick up my signature and Nugent Monck would, automatically, assume they had been drawn by a man. There's not a problem with them knowing I drew the blueprints, and I do have rather a good reputation which will add to their value.'

'She said modestly.'

Amanda gave him scathing look which in the torchlight came across as quite alluring. 'Your job is to brief the professor,' she said, closing the safe door.

'I'm having lunch with him tomorrow in Magdalene,' said Campion, 'and I have one or two people to see in town, so you'll be on your own for much of the day I'm afraid.'

'I'll survive as long as you do some more food shopping. I don't mind living in a garret for my art, but I'm not going to starve in one.'

'It's not a garret, darling.' Campion placed the beam of his torch under his chin so that his grinning face lit up like a Halloween mask. 'It's an octagonal Victorian summer house.'

'It's a shed,' said his wife in a voice which brooked no argument.

Mr Campion had always disdained Lugg's use of the vulgar phrase 'caught with 'is trousers down' but he had to admit, the next morning at just shy of 8.30, that it would have been almost apposite. The earlier than expected arrival of Astra, whom he was beginning to think of as the overenthusiastic housekeeper, did not catch him trouser-less but still in his pyjamas.

He was at least awake and out of bed, and Amanda was not only awake but emerging from the bathroom dressed in her dark burglar ensemble of the previous night, when the revving of a motorbike engine outside the front of the house rattled the windowpanes and spurred the Campions into action better than any alarm clock.

'God, she's early! Action stations!'

'Does she have a key?' asked Amanda, hiding her make-up bag and suitcase in the wardrobe.

'Yes, but I slipped the bolt on, which should buy you enough time to scurry down the garden to your hidey-hole.'

'For goodness' sake, don't let her upstairs.'

'Don't worry, I'll make sure all your things are out of sight.'

Amanda was already heading for the stairs and she spoke over her shoulder. 'Think of an excuse to keep her downstairs. She's a woman, she'll sense my presence up here.'

Mr Campion saw no point in arguing such a female certainty and, in any case, Mrs Campion had already grabbed her handbag and was bolting downstairs two steps at a time.

At the window he twitched the curtain – something which happens in the best of residential streets – and peered out. There at the kerb was a motorbike, its engine idling, its black-helmeted, leather-clad rider talking to his passenger, who had just dismounted and was adjusting the strap of a large shoulder bag. Even looking down from his vantage point at her rear view, Campion could identify Astra's short but muscular frame.

He was on the landing when he heard the front door lock rattle as a key was tried and the roar of the motorbike pulling away. He waited until he heard the back door open and close, counted to five slowly to give Amanda a bit of a start, then started slowly downstairs as the doorbell began to chime rather aggressively.

'On my way! With you momentarily,' he shouted, not knowing whether his visitor could hear him.

A quick diversion to the kitchen window gave him the reas-suring sight of the summer-house door being pulled shut. Only then did he step lively into the hallway, offering loud apologies up to and including the moment he released the bolt at the top of the front door and pulled it open.

A pink-faced Astra Jarvela was revealed, holding a Yale key like a pistol pointed at Mr Campion's pyjama-jacketed heart.

'Why you lock me out?' she demanded.

'I did no such thing. I locked myself in – it's something we have to do in London to deter intruders.'

He followed her gaze, all the way down his striped pyjamas to his naked feet and curling toes, as he spoke.

'I forgot you were due – you're early, aren't you? – so forgive me for keeping you hanging around on the doorstep while I overslept. Now do come in and let me get dressed before I frighten any passing horses.'

The girl's reaction to that was itself horse-like as she snorted down a wrinkled nose and shook her head so violently that her long blonde, plaited ponytail ended up hanging over her left shoulder.

'There really was no need for you to call today,' said Campion, following her into the kitchen. 'I am perfectly capable of fending for myself.'

'I am not sure what "fending" means, but someone has to look after the cats.'

Mr Campion knew that any defence he might offer would be futile in the face of the inscrutable stares of Pratt and Whitney, who sat in the middle of the kitchen floor, accusing him with yellow-green eyes and drawn-in stomachs rumbling with hunger. To them, oversleeping by humans was no excuse in cat law, and the punishment was total disdain, the sentence to take effect immediately.

'I had not forgotten them,' said Mr Campion, squirming slightly, 'and fully intended to give them their breakfast, but I overslept.'

The accusatory mewling of the two cats as they circled Astra's legs, tails in the air, left Campion in no doubt that as witnesses for the prosecution they were successfully swaying the jury. Fortunately, their testimony was cut short by Astra's dexterity in opening a tin of cat food and dispensing it (in absolutely equal proportions) into two plastic bowls on the floor. The mewling ceased as the cats buried their heads, sank down on their haunches and let their tails go limp.

Only then did Campion feel confident to speak. 'Despite what Pratt and Whitney might tell you, Astra, I really am quite capable of looking after myself,' said Campion, realizing that still being in his pyjamas was not lending him the air of authority he had been aiming for, 'and there really is no reason why you should come here every day. In fact, I think you must be due a few days' holiday – with pay, of course – and I will square it with Professor Branscombe, with whom I am lunching today. Honestly, there's nothing for you to do whilst I'm here.'

The woman's blue eyes opened wide in disbelief.

'I am serious,' said Mr Campion. 'I can make my own bed, something in which I was trained mercilessly at boarding school, always brush my teeth morning and night, and I never spill red wine on white carpets; that is always someone else. In short, I am perfectly house-trained. There is absolutely no need for any hoovering, chimney sweeping, window cleaning or laundry to be done today.'

'What about breakfast?'

'My dear woman, I am as capable of burning toast as the next man.'

Astra pointed an accusing finger at her shoulder bag which she had deposited on the table. 'But I brought supplies: eggs, bacon, mushrooms and blood sausage.'

'How kind, and that does sound tempting,' said Campion, risking a swift glance out of the window into the garden. 'But I really shouldn't put you to the trouble.'

'No trouble,' said Astra, shrugging off her leather jacket and draping it over the back of a kitchen chair. 'I will cook, but you must put trousers on.'

Campion, grateful that his wife was out of earshot, agreed with alacrity. The combination of fried eggs and black pudding, preferably sandwiched between two slices of white bread, was, as Lugg often enthused, 'the proper ambrosia', but if it was a food of the gods, it was not one worshipped in any kitchen where Amanda ruled.

Upstairs he dressed quickly and tidied the bedroom, making sure any remaining detritus was definitely male, made the bed and even opened the window to expel any trace of Amanda's perfume. Then he hurried back to the kitchen, drawn by the scent of frying bacon, already rehearsing the excuses he would need to placate Amanda when she was released from solitary confinement in the summer house.

'I am quite serious, you know,' he told Astra as he ate at the kitchen table. 'I can manage perfectly well on my own, and I think you should take a few days off, starting today – once you've done the washing up, that is.' He treated the girl to his broadest smile, though it did not seem to reassure her. 'I'm joking. You should only do that if your conscience troubles you; otherwise take some time off and enjoy yourself. I will get Professor Branscombe to ring you when he wants normal service resumed.'

Astra remained unconvinced and turned silently to the sink, where she began to clean a frying pan under the running tap with short, efficient movements of her muscular arms. Campion could see, as she wore a short-sleeve top, just how muscular they were.

'I will finish the housework, then go,' she said when the pan was cleaned to her satisfaction.

'But there's absolutely nothing for you to do. I really am quite well house-trained and hardly ever here, and I promise I will keep the cats regularly fed and watered until your return. Go now, while the day is young! In fact, I will have to insist upon it as I am expecting visitors later this morning.'

'I could cook a lunch for them,' said Astra hopefully.

'No, no,' said Campion quickly, 'I'm having lunch with Professor Branscombe, and anyway, my visitors are here for a meeting not a free lunch. They're all policemen, you see, and if you give policemen food and drink, they never leave.'

'Then I will not get in your way.'

When Mr Campion knocked on the door of the summer house and told his wife the coast was clear, Amanda's opening gambit was: 'Did you get rid of her?'

'Very easily; once I discovered her weak spot.'

'You bribed her?'

'No, I did not have to.'

'You didn't try and seduce her?'

'Certainly not; I preyed on one of her basic fears.'

'So you did try and seduce her.'

'Don't be ridiculous – you know you are my only heart's desire. With Astra, all I had to do was suggest that a flock of policemen was about to descend on the house and that did the trick.'

'How odd,' said Amanda as they walked towards the house. 'You're not, are you? Expecting policemen, that is?'

'No, not at all, it was something I just made up on the spot. Now let's get you inside where I can cook you some breakfast. There's bacon and eggs but I'm afraid all the black pudding has gone.'

'That's a relief,' said Amanda, eyeing him suspiciously.

Once in the kitchen, Amanda settled for a slice of toast, not trusting her husband's skill with a frying pan, and a pot of tea, whilst writing out a list of provisions for which Mr Campion was to be responsible.

'If I have to spend any length of time out there in the Château d'If without even the company of a count from Monte Cristo, then I insist you hide an industrial-size tin of broken biscuits in there.'

'Hopefully, it won't be necessary for you to hide again, at least not from Astra,' said Campion. 'I've given her the week off.'

'So you expect me to do the housework?'

'How can I when you are not here but being held in custody by Her Majesty's security services? In any case, neither of us makes that much mess as a rule, and as long as the cats are kept under control, we should not knock too much off the rateable value.'

'Does John know you've furloughed his housekeeper?'

'He will. I told you I'm having lunch with him at Magdalene today.'

Amanda pursed her lips and put a forefinger to her chin. 'Mmmm,' she said dreamily, 'they keep a good High Table there. I'm sure they will do you proud. I, of course, will make do on whatever scraps you've left me.'

'But darling, I know you hate black pudding, so I took it

upon myself to remove it from your sight. What are you doing?'

Amanda was scribbling furiously, attacking the shopping list with her pencil.

'I'm crossing out sausages and adding lobsters.'

Mr Campion was shown into the Pepys Library at Magdalene to wait whilst Professor Branscombe concluded an internal college meeting. There were, he decided, few more pleasant waiting rooms on Earth; perhaps only in Florence – in rooms with a view of the Ponte Vecchio – might there be a contender.

In comparison, the lunch served in the professor's rooms was positively spartan, a portion of tinned salmon in a nest of damp, tired lettuce leaves, garnished with half a tomato and served accompanied by a bottle of Heinz salad cream. To drink there was a jug of the finest vintage the city's water pipes could supply.

'Going through a patch of austerity,' said Branscombe, coughing to cover his embarrassment, 'pending divorce proceedings, don't you know? Got to watch the pennies at the moment. Tuck in.'

Campion wondered whether the professor's economy drive was due to looming legal fees or a desire to make sure there were no assets for the future ex-Mrs Branscombe to appropriate.

'Anything wrong?' asked Branscombe, catching Campion picking at his lunch whilst gazing wistfully out of the mullioned window at the river Cam as it shimmered by.

'I'm sorry,' said Campion, 'but I could have sworn I just saw Cuthbert Snow sliding past the window, either walking on water, which would be a good trick, or gracefully propelling a punt.'

'That wouldn't surprise me; he earns a bit of pocket money taking tourists on punt trips. I'm told his running commentary on the history of the colleges along the Backs is highly entertaining, mostly inspired by *1066 And All That* apparently.'

'I've always found that a reliable text, but surely Cuthbert should be at work, shouldn't he?'

'He'll be on one of his days off. All the students we employed as workshop technicians are part-timers. The Goshawk budget wouldn't allow for more, but they seem happy with three or four days' work a week. It's the experience they're after, and it will look good on their CVs to be able to say they worked for Lady Amanda and Alandel.'

'Assuming Amanda isn't hanged for high treason.'

'Don't be ridiculous, Albert. How goes your hunt for the real spy?'

'Slowly but steadily. The picture is rather blurred by what happened to Alan Wormold.'

'Poor Alan. You think he was in on the leakage of information?'

'Well, there's the rub. The leaks started back at Alandel while Wormold was one of your students here, so at best he could only have been involved after Goshawk set up shop here.'

'You mean he was recruited by somebody?'

'It's possible. Are there any political skeletons in his cupboard that you are aware of?'

'Politics? None at all. The chap was an engineer and therefore a conservative by nature. I doubt he ever thought seriously about politics, which would also make him a conservative, come to think of it.'

'Do you know anything about his family circumstances?'

'You mean financially?' The professor paused between forks-full of lettuce until Campion nodded. 'His parents are a decent couple, shopkeepers from Leicestershire, I seem to recall, and Alan was a scholarship boy on a grant from his local authority. I don't think the family was particularly well off. Why do you ask?'

'His hobby. Flying is an expensive activity. I just wondered where the money came from. Do let me know if there is anything I can do regarding the funeral. I know Amanda would want to help.'

'That's kind of you, I will have to talk to his parents on that grim matter, I suppose, though they are still in shock as far as I can gather.'

'Understandably, it was a terrible business, and I cannot help thinking it is connected to our little . . . scheme.'

'So you are investigating Alan's death; actively, I mean?'

'Shall we say I am keeping a watching brief on that, but on our wider stratagem, I need your assistance, or at least your silent acquiescence.'

'Well, I've gone along with the Goshawk Project so far. What now?'

'We don't wish to get you too closely enmeshed in things, John; your role was always meant to be on the periphery – for the good of your reputation, and that of the university, of course. However, there is a little white lie I would like you to tell, if asked, and if you are not asked, perhaps you could drop it into the general conversation.'

'Sounds a little like perjury. Should I ask one of the law dons in for an opinion? We've got some top legal minds here at Magdalene.'

'Absolutely not necessary, John. In my experience one should only involve lawyers when all light has faded and all hope gone. All I want you to do, should anyone ask, is vouch for a set of blueprints which have magically – please do not ask how – appeared in the safe over at Goshawk. I would encourage you to be as vague as possible. If anyone asks how they got there, simply say that they came from Alandel, though you haven't had a chance to examine them yourself.'

'And these are blueprints of what exactly?'

Campion put down the cutlery he was toying with and held up his hands in surrender. 'Do not ask me, John, for I would have a better chance of understanding them if they were done in Chinese calligraphy. All I know is that they propose some new lines of approach on the design of forward-swept wings. Beyond that I can add nothing remotely sensible, you'll just have to trust me.'

Branscombe stared at his guest for a full minute, as if weighing up this mild-mannered, owlish elderly gentleman for an untenured teaching post or perhaps an applicant for a vacancy as a church warden. 'You're baiting a trap, aren't you?' he said at last.

'But my dear professor,' said Campion, 'the whole Goshawk Project is a trap.'

TEN

Almost a Gondoliere

As he sauntered over Magdalene Bridge and into town, Mr Campion was mentally listing the running order of the 'errands', as he liked to call them, which he had to run that afternoon when, out of the corner of his eye, he saw a familiar figure passing below. Cuthbert Snow was propelling a punt with as much ease and grace as a beefy six-foot-plus figure manipulating a long wooden pole could, whilst bending to go under the arch of the bridge, thus thrusting out his rear end (should that be undercarriage? Campion thought) and keeping his balance by using his bare feet as talons to cling to the stern platform sometimes known as the till.

As the bow of the punt emerged on Campion's side of the bridge, he saw that Cuthbert was carrying two passengers – a middle-aged couple who were holding tightly on to each other, but whether in affection or for safety it was difficult to say. The male passenger, who wore a green trilby with a red feather cockade in the band, was the first to notice Campion leaning over the parapet before Cuthbert, now with his back to the bridge, could respond to Campion's low whistle.

'*Herr Kapitän . . .*' said the green trilby, releasing his grip on the side of the craft in order to point over Cuthbert's shoulder.

'Please don't let me interrupt anything, Captain Snow,' Campion shouted as the punt drifted majestically over towards the old Quayside, where several dozen others lay at rest. 'But I would like a word at some point.'

Cuthbert twisted around and looked up to follow the voice, an action which in less experienced punt-pole-holding hands might have led to disaster.

'Oh hello, Mr C,' he said cheerfully, 'I'm just about to dock and put these two lovely people back on to dry land.'

'*Ja, ja. Bitte ja*,' said green trilby, and his female companion nodded enthusiastically, perhaps too enthusiastically.

'Then I'll meet you round on the quay,' said Campion, estimating how slowly he would have to walk in order not to arrive as Cuthbert was negotiating his fee, and possible tip, which might be generous given the obvious relief with which his passengers were disembarking.

'Nice couple, for Germans,' said Cuthbert, pocketing some silver coins and two green notes. 'Not sure they agreed with my version of Reformation history though.'

'They can be sticklers for accuracy,' said Campion sympathetically, 'and, after all, you didn't claim to be a historian, did you?'

'Well, not as such. Anyway, what can I do for you, Mr C?'

'Having seen your prowess with the punt pole, I really must hire you for a trip to Grantchester. Sunday, perhaps?'

Cuthbert, who had been securing the punt, straightened up to his full height and, holding the pole upright in his right hand, looked for all the world as if he was posing for a silhouette of an ancient Greek hoplite with his spear.

'Sundays I usually work down by Laundress Green, near The Anchor, which is good for Grantchester and avoids the amateurs messing about on the Backs. Will you be bringing a picnic?'

'I doubt it, I wasn't planning a romantic tryst.'

'Not to worry, it was just a thought. You see, I've made this collapsible cage thing which takes a bottle of champagne and you trail it in the water to keep it cool. I'm thinking of patenting it.'

'Sounds like it could be a money-spinner,' said Campion. Then with mock severity: 'Was it made on Goshawk time from Goshawk materials?'

Cuthbert looked surprised, but far from guilty. 'Only odd bits rescued from the scrap pile. The design was all my own and it's quite aerodynamic in its own way, though I was going for the rustic look rather than thinking about slipstreams.'

'You Magdalene men all seem to have a little sideline on the go.'

'I don't know what you mean, sir.'

Campion noted the 'sir' and marked it down as a sure sign of a guilty conscience, although he was sure that Cuthbert was such a decent chap that his conscience could be tricked into guilt with ease. An intelligent young woman would have great fun teasing Cuthbert in the future.

'Never forget, young Cuthbert, that I knew your grandfather. He always had an eye for a nifty business deal. I seem to remember him coming up with some scheme to export a consignment of gin to America, describing it as a vital medical antiseptic. That was in the dark days of Prohibition, of course. Not that I'm suggesting your patented wine cooler is on the same scale as your granddaddy's ambitions to be a bootlegger, but those digs you shared with Alan Wormold and Ted Toomey could be mistaken for a bicycle factory. Are you going into mass production?'

'Oh, you mean the Decameron,' said Cuthbert genially, shifting from one foot to the other, shifting the punt pole to the 'present arms' position.

'I do?' Campion attempted outrage but managed only surprised bemusement.

'That's what they call the bike they were building; it's a sort of extended tandem idea for multiple riders. Terribly impractical and commercially would be a disaster, but it will be a hoot during Rag Week. They were doing it for a good cause, but now Alan's gone, I suppose Teddy will be in charge. I'm not involved.' He patted his stomach with the flat of his hand. 'Too much bulk. I would upset the weight/balance ratio and probably affect the drag quotient.'

'I understood some of those words and am delighted that the problem is being tackled scientifically, though I would have thought a muscular specimen like you would have been a great asset on a giant tandem.'

'Apparently not.' A shadow of disappointment flitted across Cuthbert's face, but did not linger. 'Teddy thought the idea of a big, beefy rugger player would put off some of the girls from Girton and Lucy Cavendish he wanted as riders, but that's Teddy for you, always thinking about girls.'

Campion saw his opening. 'Ah yes, Teddy. He is quite struck on one particular young lady, isn't he?'

'You mean Astra? Yes, he's mad on her, though I don't think she's quite so keen on him.'

'Bad luck for Teddy, but a useful life lesson in the long run. What does he do on his days off?'

Cuthbert shrugged his impressive shoulders with such force that Campion imagined the tremors producing ripples on the Cam, causing the tethered punts to bob at their moorings.

'Goes off to study Russian, which is to say he moons around his teacher's house on Hills Road hoping to see Astra. That's not as desperate as it sounds. Astra's brother Jari is Teddy's Russian tutor and they live in the same house. I think that's how he first met her and he's been lovestruck ever since.'

'How does he pay for it?' asked Campion, who was unprepared for Cuthbert's shocked reaction.

'Steady on, Mr Campion! I don't think Astra's that sort of girl, and even if she was, Teddy would run a mile rather than—'

'No, no, you big ape, I meant the Russian lessons. Learning Russian is extra-curricular I presume, so he's paying for private tuition, unless Astra's brother is doing it out of the kindness of his heart.'

'I don't know where he gets the money for his lessons,' said Cuthbert, relieved that they were now no longer questioning Astra's honour. 'I guess he has an allowance, but I don't think his family is rich.' He snorted a derisory laugh. 'Mind you, my people *are* rich, but very little trickles down my way. Instead you find me performing for tips from bemused German tourists who were convinced I was going to sink the punt.'

'Perhaps they had heard of your grandfather,' said Campion with a twinkle behind the big round lenses of his glasses. 'So Teddy doesn't have a job on the side? Some little enterprise? Repairing bicycles, for instance?'

'No, I told you, all he thinks about is Astra. If *she* told him to go out and get a job, he'd be off pea-picking or bricklaying like a shot. He's a good engineer and he will get a good career out of it after his PhD, but that doesn't impress a girl right now, this minute. He's so impatient to make love to her I fear for his sanity sometimes.'

'Why is that?'

'I'm not sure I should tell you, it's personal and rather awkward.'

'My dear chap, you must think of me as a kindly uncle; an uncle whom you see rarely and who has neither power nor authority over any aspect of your life. It is therefore perfectly safe to tell him anything.'

'With due respect, I'm not too sure I believe that . . .' said Cuthbert.

Clever lad, thought Campion.

'But here goes. When he realized he was madly in love with Astra, he plucked up all his courage and went and bought a packet of you-know-whats.'

'I'm sorry, but why should I know what a "what" is?'

'From the chemist's,' spluttered Cuthbert. 'A pack of condoms. It nearly killed him to go in and ask for them.'

'Poor boy. Clearly he didn't have a regular barber who could offer him a little "something for the weekend, sir". You look confused at the reference, Cuthbert. Perhaps it's a generational thing. I am, after all, very old, but pray go on.'

'Well, having screwed his courage to the sticking-place – whatever that means – and bought the damn things, Teddy has an attack of the heebie-jeebies about even having them in his room, so he asked me to look after them. It's not even like we were still in rooms in college.'

'Oh my, the curse of Magdalene,' said Campion.

'You know the legend?'

'Oh, it's not a legend. It was after my time here, but I heard about it. A very bright student, who went on to become one of our leading literary critics, was sent down and banished from the city after a college servant found a packet of you-know-whats in his room. I heard that the college authorities referred to them as "engines of love". Do I take it that Astra never encouraged Teddy to start his engine?'

'I think that's a fair assumption – not that one likes to pry.'

'And one shouldn't, but I wasn't really asking about Teddy's sex life, or lack of one. I was prying into his financial situation, a far more acceptable form of snooping.'

'As I said, he isn't well off, but he isn't skint. He always has his share of the rent, but then he's often absent when it's his round in the pub. I just don't know, Mr Campion. My parents always said it was uncouth to talk about money.'

'People with money usually say that, but never mind. One other thing, though. Would you happen to know if Alan Wormold kept anything out at Bourn Flying Club?'

Cuthbert's brow furrowed at this new line of questioning. 'I'm not sure. Teddy might know, though wait a minute . . . He did have some sort of locker there, he must have. He had this wonderful brown leather flying jacket which I really coveted but he wouldn't leave it in the house in case anyone borrowed it – quite innocently, of course, always meaning to return it.'

'Of course.'

'It had a map of the Pacific printed on the lining in case the pilot got shot down. Of course, the scale was a bit of a problem. I mean, it's OK knowing that Java is to the south and you should head in that direction, but it could be a thousand miles and that's a long way to swim or paddle a life raft. Still, it was a cracking jacket, and Alan was very proud of it. He would have left it somewhere secure.'

'I'm going out to Bourn tomorrow, I'll ask around,' said Campion, 'and let you know on Sunday when you glide me along the river. You don't charge double for Sundays, do you?'

'Only to German tourists who don't appreciate my interpretation of Cambridge history.' Cuthbert grinned.

'Yes, well, I think we can dispense with that, though if you want to increase your tips, why not invest in a straw boater and a striped jumper and learn a few verses of 'O Sole Mio'. I think you'd make a first-rate *gondoliere*.'

Mr Campion marched into town on a south-easterly line, passing what were sometimes known as the 'lesser' colleges of Sidney Sussex, Christ's and Emmanuel. It was both misleading and cruel to describe them as 'lesser' for the simple misfortune that they did not have lawns and 'backs' leading on to the River Cam, and consequently could not offer photogenic vistas to the milling tourists, and particularly the adventurous who had hired themselves a punt and a Cuthbert.

In both academic standing and capacity of wine cellar, the colleges which straddled the spine of Cambridge, as formed by Sidney Street through to Regent Street, were the equal of any of those instantly recognizable from a hundred picture postcards or the covers of tourist board guides. Use of the pejorative term 'lesser' to describe them indicated only jealousy or snobbery or a complete lack of intelligence, for surely no college could be lesser than his own St Ignatius.

At the University Arms hotel, which guarded one corner of the twenty-five acres of common ground known as Parker's Piece, Campion set off across the east–west diagonal pathway until he reached the middle, then switched to the north–south diagonal, merging on to Park Side. It was a gloriously pleasant Cambridge afternoon and, for the duration of his stroll, Mr Campion had nothing more dangerous to worry about than avoiding stumbling over a family picnic laid out on the grass, or being mown down by a bicycle, its rider's black gown flapping like a bat's wings in the slipstream.

He announced himself to the duty sergeant at the Park Side police station and explained that Detective Inspector Mawson had arranged to meet him. The expression of the sergeant was that DI Mawson was welcome to his visitor, and the visitor was more than welcome to DI Mawson. Mr Campion surmised that the sergeant was one of the 'old sweats' of Cambridge City Police, who resented the recent transposition into the Mid-Anglia Constabulary.

Once Mawson and his visitor were ensconced in a windowless interview room and Campion, from bitter experience, had politely refused the offer of a police station brew of tea, the policeman came straight to the point. 'So what have you got for me, Campion?'

'Funnily enough, that's exactly what I was going to ask you, Inspector.'

Mawson leaned back in his chair and looked suitably affronted. 'I was not aware that I had any obligation to provide you with anything, Mr Campion, but you have a civic duty to help the police with their enquiries into a very serious matter.'

'So you are treating Alan Wormold's death as murder?'

'We have to keep an open mind, as I am sure the coroner

will. There is no doubt that it was Alf Bagley who set in motion the mechanics of Wormold's death; he admits that openly, claiming it was a tragic accident, and unless someone can show me how such an accident could have been engineered, I am tempted to go along with that.'

Campion nodded his head quietly, as if digesting the policeman's analysis. 'You have the means, but what about a motive? If it wasn't an accident, that is.'

'I was hoping that's where you would weigh in, Campion, as you have, I take it, been spending your time in Cambridge wisely.'

Campion smiled. 'I have never been accused of doing that, Inspector, but from what I have gleaned so far, no one had a bad word to say about Alan Wormold.'

'Except Nugent Monck.' Mawson said it as if laying down a winning hand of cards.

'From what I can gather, Mr Monck has few good words to say about anyone. Does his animosity revolve around missing stocks of steel tubing by any chance?'

'He may have mentioned such, but no more than four times an hour.'

'That one I think I can help with. You remember the bits of bicycle we found at Wormold's house? I said he was building a bicycle and I was right. Teddy Toomey was in on it as well; it's some sort of joke tandem for Rag Week, so all in a good cause. I don't think Alandel would begrudge the students a few offcuts of metal. In one respect it's a harmless crime.'

'Wormold was cutting tubing when that block and tackle knocked him into his lathe. I wouldn't call that harmless.'

'No, that was awful but surely coincidental, although the fact that he was doing it at that precise moment might not have been.'

'What do you mean by that?'

'Alan was known to come into work early so he could . . . shall we say, pursue his hobby. If anyone wanted to arrange an accident, that would be a good time and the method would throw suspicion on Alf Bagley.'

'That's all a bit elaborate and far-fetched, isn't it? Engineering an accident involving a travelling crane, a dangling block and tackle and a spinning lathe sounds like something out of a 1930s' detective novel.'

'It does rather,' conceded Campion. 'Somebody once said that a murderer who relied on such a convoluted method of disposing of his victim really ought to find a new line of work.'

'But you are convinced it was murder?'

'I would be if I could discover *why* Wormold needed to be murdered, and as yet I have not, though that reminds me to ask if his bank statements turned up anything interesting.'

'I cannot share any detailed information, but as far as I and his bank manager can see, it was regularly humdrum. No unexpected withdrawals, just the usual expenses, the main one being rent and small amounts of cash for groceries and maybe a pint down the pub.'

'Thank you, you've just reminded me of something else,' said Campion airily. 'I have to do some grocery shopping this afternoon myself. Was there anything on the deposit side of Wormold's balance sheet?'

'Nothing unexpected. There was a bursary from the college and some scholarship money from his local authority at the start of the academic year, but apart from that, just the few quid he's earned recently on the Goshawk Project. I doubt if he earns enough to pay tax on that, lucky blighter.'

'Not so lucky as it turned out,' chided Campion. 'Were there any cheques made out to Bourn Flying Club?'

'Only one, months ago, for his club membership, which his bank manager said was an annual thing. Are you sniffing something dodgy here, Campion?'

'Possibly, possibly not. I'm going out there tomorrow for a flying lesson, so I'll make some enquiries.' Campion caught the look of alarm on Mawson's face. 'Discreetly of course, assuming I'm not airsick or hanging from a tree by a parachute.'

'Dangerous business, flying,' said the inspector with total conviction.

'I will be in the hands of a very professional instructor,' said Mr Campion, secretly crossing his fingers.

'Somebody from the club?'

'No, well yes, I think he's a member, but more importantly

he's a jet pilot in the American air force, a senior master sergeant, no less. A very amiable chap with an awesomely vulgar automobile, called Luther Romo.'

'Romo?' The inspector sat up straight. 'We've had our eye on him for some time and not just because of that battleship of a car he drives.'

'It is rather difficult to miss,' Campion conceded, 'but I suspect police interest in Sergeant Romo is not limited to the Traffic Division.'

Mawson's body tensed and his eyes contained flint. 'That's where you're right and also wrong. Every time Mr Romo has come to our attention, interest in him has been rapidly limited – by higher authority.'

'I see, or I think I do. How exactly has Sergeant Romo come to your attention?'

'If he's a sergeant, then I'm the commissioner of the Met,' Mawson spoke almost with a snarl. 'We started getting complaints from the moment he arrived at Alconbury.'

'I thought the American base policed itself.'

'It does; whatever goes on out there stays out there, thank heavens. The complaints we got about Romo came from Cambridge, from the university. He comes across as all hail-fellow-well-met and does lots of what he calls *public relations* . . .' Mawson's lip curled in distaste at the words, '. . . inviting people out to look round the base in the name of Anglo-American relations. Then he checks up on all the university types who go there, asking all sorts of ridiculous questions about political allegiances. Not just the Labour party, but Marxists, Communists, Trotskyists and anarchists of various hues. Said it was all in the cause of base security, but he ruffled quite a few feathers among the dons. He was not exactly subtle, but then Americans never are, are they? Even had the cheek to request police files on some students.'

'Did you supply them?'

'Of course not! And when I reported Romo's snooping up my chain of command, the word came down that as he had no official standing, I was not required to assist him, but equally, I was told not to hinder him. You know what that means.'

'That he has important friends in high places?'

'Exactly.'

'I think you could be right, Inspector,' said Campion coyly.

Conscious that Amanda's shopping list was burning a hole in the inside pocket of his jacket, Mr Campion felt confident that the groceries, or 'iron rations' as his wife described them, could wait while he ran one more errand, especially as he was in the vicinity.

It was only a minute's walk around the top corner of Parker's Piece to the shiny new Parkside swimming pool, and into Mill Road looking for an address provided by Professor Branscombe. It was not a part of Cambridge he was especially familiar with, though he did remember the Playhouse, grandly styled a 'cinema theatre' in his undergraduate days but now proudly proclaiming itself to be a Fine Fare supermarket and, further along, a rough-and-ready pub called The Locomotive which, oddly, seemed to attract sailors rather than railway workers. He was unsurprised, and rather pleased, to see that multiple bicycle shops were still at the heart of the local economy.

What did surprise him was that the address he was searching for turned out to be a flat above an RAF recruitment office, the entrance being via a door to the side of a large window decorated with a huge RAF roundel obscuring any view of the interior.

There was a doorbell, which Campion pressed and then waited, listening to the muffled thud of descending footsteps, until a lock clicked and the door was opened by a gaunt and unshaven Alf Bagley, who stood blinking in the afternoon light as if just awakened from a deep sleep, which might well have been the case given that he was dressed in striped flannel pyjamas and fake fur slippers. The pyjamas had been laundered and starched to within an inch of their natural life and the left slipper had a ragged hole through which a big toe had been allowed to escape.

'Hello, Alf. I hope I'm not disturbing anything. Remember me?'

'Course I do, Mr Campion. Your good lady wife showed

you round the Alandel works two or three times before we
'ad this present nastiness.'

'I'm still no wiser as to what you chaps were up to back
then, so I'm mystified by this Goshawk Project. Sounds a bit
unnatural to the layman, you know, putting the wings on an
aeroplane backwards.'

'It's not quite like that, Mr Campion, but I don't think you're
here to talk about aeronautical engineering.'

'Well, no,' said Campion, 'at least not on the doorstep. May
I come in?'

'Lord bless me for a fool! What must you think? Please
come up.'

'Have I caught you at a bad time?' Campion asked, following
the pyjama'd legs and slippered feet as they swished up a
wooden staircase.

'No times a good time, these days.' Bagley's voice, over
his shoulder, sounded tired and slightly desperate. 'Can't sleep
at night without seeing Alan Wormold being chewed up by
that lathe, that's why I have to kip during the day. The dreams
don't seem to come so much during the day.'

The flat was sparsely furnished with mismatched modern
pieces, a Formica-topped table and a gas cooker with enough
chips in its white enamel to suggest that a frustrated previous
owner had attempted to kill it with a shotgun. From the one
main room, with its long, uncurtained rectangular window
looking out over Mill Road (and allowing passengers on the
upper decks of buses to look in), one door led to a bathroom
and another, open one, showed a darkened bedroom with an
unmade bed, a shell-burst of crumpled clothing on the floor
and several empty beer bottles.

'Take a seat if you can find one,' said Bagley, waving vaguely
in the direction of a small sofa strategically placed in front of
a large television set standing on four thin metal legs, which
ended in bright orange plastic tops the size of pong-pong balls
to save wear and tear on the carpet.

'I know it's a dump,' said his host, running fingers through
his thinning hair, 'but it's only temporary for the duration of
Goshawk, and it was cheap. The landlords were happy not to
have to let to students as they get enough peace protests and

anti-nuclear types banging on the window downstairs without having beatniks as lodgers upstairs.'

'I always saw you as the country cottage type, Alf, all gumboots and fly-fishing, or sitting on a deckchair in your rose garden.'

Campion realized with a jolt that he was already thinking of Alf Bagley as a retired pensioner, although he knew him to be nearly ten years younger than himself. He studied the frail, almost spectral figure before him and wondered how many years had been added, or possibly subtracted, by witnessing the fate of Alan Wormold.

'Tell you straight, Mr Campion, I'd like nothing better than to get back up to Norfolk, where I do have a cottage and a few roses, and my old job back at Alandel,' said Bagley, sinking into a chair. 'I only came here to follow Lady Amanda; I've always tried to look out for her. It's terrible what happened to her. I don't know how they dare; all she's done for this country.'

'Don't worry about Amanda, I'm sure she's in control of her situation. If anything, she's worrying about you.'

'You've seen her?'

'I have heard from her,' Campion said carefully. 'She's very worried about the senior staff and how they're taking it.'

'I couldn't really say,' sighed Alf, his head drooping, his gaze fixed on his slippers, prompting Campion to remind himself that he was the older man in the room. 'Professor Branscombe sent me home and told me not to think about work until' – he drew in a deep, quivering breath – 'the situation is *clarified*. Well, is it, Mr Campion?'

'I fear not. Have you been here alone since the accident?'

'The police have been round several times and I've had visitors checking up on me to make sure I hadn't put my head in the oven.' He caught the frown crossing Campion's face. 'Oh, don't worry, I'm not the sort to do anything like that. Mind you, Nugent Monck would be the first to move in if I did vacate these premises.'

'Just be sure it's only these premises you might be vacating, Alf. But why would Mr Monck move in?'

'Because of the RAF recruitment office downstairs. The

squadron leader was livid when he found out this flat was for rent and I beat him to it; thought it should be his by right. Tell the truth, I only took the place to get up his nose, but he was civil enough when he called round, even brought me a bunch of grapes like I was an invalid.'

'Has anyone else visited?'

'The professor came, of course, and then Melvyn Barnes clumped his way up the stairs. Mind you, he's old-school Alandel and knows how to behave. Kevin stopped by for a chat this very lunchtime on his way to the station.'

'Kevin Loder? He hasn't got digs in Cambridge. Has he?'

'No, he goes home to his wife and kids near Ely at the weekend, comes back Monday mornings on the milk train. Stays in a bed-and-breakfast four nights a week. He's a family man and he misses his family.'

'I'm sure he does,' said Campion. 'It must have been difficult for you all to up sticks and move here to Cambridge.'

'The work's the thing,' said Alf, but with all the enthusiasm of a depressed bloodhound. 'When there's a chance of working on a breakthrough in aeronautical engineering, you take it, especially if you're a brash young high-flyer.'

'I'm guessing you mean our American friend, Gary Cupples.'

'Oh, I don't mean anything by it; we were all his age once.'

'Some of us earlier than others.' Now it was Campion's turn to sigh. 'I take it young Gary didn't mind the move to Cambridge?'

'Jumped at it, he did. Good thing to put on his *résumé*, as he calls it, but then he also had an ulterior motive.'

'Did he really?'

'Got him closer to Alconbury and the American base.'

Campion peered over the top of his spectacles. 'I didn't have him down as a fly-boy or a plane-spotter, other than out of purely professional interest.'

'He's not, as far as I know. His interests are far more down to earth and involve the teenage daughter of one of the senior officers out there. Might even be a general – they have funny ideas about ranks in their air force.'

'So I've heard,' said Campion. 'Did Cupples come and visit you?'

'Aye, he did, last night, but he didn't stay long, he was off to some dance out at the base and was, as they say, hot to trot.'

'Did any of the chaps from Goshawk discuss work whilst they were here?'

Bagley shook his head slowly. 'No, I think the professor warned them off, not wanting to bother me.'

'Well, I certainly don't want to add to your burdens, but there is one thing I have to ask you, though it will be painful.'

'Will it help Lady Amanda?'

'Almost certainly.'

For the first time since he had entered the flat, Campion saw hope – indeed, life – in Alf's eyes.

'Then ask away.'

'Tell me, in as much detail as you can, about the other morning. Not the horror of Alan Wormold's death, but what happened immediately afterwards. In other words, not when you switched *on* the electricity but in the ten minutes or so immediately following you turning it *off.*'

ELEVEN
All That Glisters

Mr Campion walked briskly along the diagonal pathway across Parker's Piece to get back into the main shopping area of the town, the fresh air clearing his head of depressing thoughts about when, if ever, Alf Bagley would bounce back to his old self.

In St Andrew's Street he allowed himself a diversion into a newsagent's to buy an evening paper and a large box of Black Magic chocolates. The chocolates did not feature on Amanda's list of vital supplies, but he thought she would appreciate them as a reward for a day spent in solitary confinement and might make a suitable accompaniment to an evening watching television behind drawn curtains at Barton Road. He had already resigned himself to taking responsibility for the coffee creams for the sake of domestic harmony.

With a considerable effort of will, he followed Amanda's instructions and avoided the temptations of the second-hand bookshops in Petty Cury, once a medieval maze of inns and bakeries, which had been noted by Samuel Pepys – a Magdalene man of course – in his diaries.

It was another Magdalene man, however, a real live twentieth-century one, who crossed Mr Campion's path as he turned into Market Street. Halfway down the street, young Edward Toomey was showing a casual disregard for the traffic moving bumper-to-bumper and with little intention of slowing down, as he crossed the road.

The young man had clearly not seen Campion, who had automatically raised a hand in greeting; indeed, it was almost as if he did not see the cars threatening to run him over, so determined was he to get to his destination. For a moment, civic concern consumed Mr Campion, as surely Market Street was unsuited to this volume of traffic and crying out for pedestrianization, but it was only for a moment. What seized his imagination was Teddy's destination, a branch of a commercial high street jeweller's, which he entered with alacrity after a furtive glance over both shoulders to make sure he was not being observed.

With some trepidation Campion also crossed the busy road, feeling ridiculously proud that he attracted only one admonishing toot from a car horn and two shrill jangles from bicycle bells, along with muttered curses from their riders who passed so close they brushed the tail of his jacket.

Through the main window of the jeweller's, peering over and between the felt padded display boards of rings and sparkling bracelets, he could see Toomey standing before a display case, its wares being explained by a pretty blonde girl, her hair piled in a massive beehive, who was bent over the case offering her customer, through a straining white blouse, the prospect of other things which might be on offer. Young Teddy, though, seemed to have eyes only for the legitimate merchandise, making excited jabbing motions with a pointed finger into the glass case.

Clearly a decision was made or a deal struck, when Teddy reached for his wallet and the blonde removed something from the case and stomped on unfeasibly high heels over to the cash desk. Toomey concentrated on the contents of his wallet, totally ignoring the retreating, very rhythmic sway of the assistant's chassis and the shortness of the skirt which encased it rather snugly.

Unwilling to be seen lurking suspiciously outside a window well stocked with sparkling gems and expensive watches, something he had often cautioned Lugg against, Campion moved along the pavement and ducked into the entrance to Freeman Hardy Willis, pressing his face to the window glass, as if totally fascinated by the latest designs in both formal and casual men's shoes.

He angled himself so that out of one corner of one eye he could see the jeweller's, but when Toomey emerged and turned down the street in his direction, he turned his face back to the serious business of weighing the merits of smart brown brogues against some loud, tri-coloured pigskin Oxfords. Although the pigskin loafers did look comfortable, Campion admitted he had probably never been young enough to pull off such a garish piece of fashion, though consideration of them had served their purpose as Ted Toomey walked by within eighteen inches but oblivious to him, concentrating instead on the small brightly coloured paper bag he clutched in both hands.

Campion counted slowly to thirty under his breath then strode back to the jeweller's, entering with a suitably dramatic flourish to the loud ringing of the sprung bell on the doorjamb and making a beeline for the teenage blonde assistant.

'Can I be of assistance, sir?' asked the startled girl, her right hand drifting towards the alarm button almost certainly positioned under her counter.

'I do hope so,' said Campion from behind his most disarming smile, removing his hat as he approached her, 'though it is rather a delicate matter.'

The girl relaxed almost instantly. He was, after all, a well-dressed elderly gentleman with good manners, and when such white-haired gentlemen asked for assistance with delicate matters, it usually meant the selection of a gift for a female, invariably a much younger one. That in turn meant her opinion would be valued and, confident of her natural charm, that could lead to a sale worthy of commission. The gentleman's 'delicate matter' though, was far from straightforward.

'It concerns the young man you served so efficiently a mere minute ago,' Campion said gently, adopting the voice of a country vicar at a christening. 'He is my nephew and also my ward.'

Campion had added 'ward' to his subterfuge as he thought it might appeal to the girl's romantic instincts.

'Was there something wrong with his purchase?' she asked nervously.

'No, not at all, at least not as far as I know,' Campion reassured her. 'I am merely concerned with, as it were, your side of the transaction.'

He turned his head to make sure there were no eavesdroppers among his fellow customers and, having assured himself that there were no other customers at all, for the shop was empty apart from two other assistants attending to their displays, he leaned in over the counter and lowered his voice to emphasize the delicacy of his problem.

'You see, we in the family are rather worried about young Edward's finances. He doesn't have a good head for his finances and is rather impetuous at times. You know the boy I'm talking about? I missed him by a whisker, the one who just left.'

'The young chap who bought the eternity ring? He was ever so shy.'

'It's a family failing,' said Campion confidentially, 'and it affects poor Edward terribly. You see, he makes purchases without thinking of the consequences and then is too shy to admit the error of his ways.'

'He seemed perfectly happy with his purchase,' said the assistant, planting her fists on her hips as if defying the old man to prove otherwise.

'I'm sure he did, but that's not the point. It is not a question of the aesthetics of the brooch . . .'

'It was a ring.'

'Of course, you said it was an engagement ring.'

'An *eternity* ring,' she corrected. 'A girl has a right to something bigger and brighter if she's getting engaged.'

'Absolutely, my dear. Bigger, brighter and more expensive, I would think, which brings me to my point. You see, young Edward has no real concept of money. I'm not so much interested in what he bought, but how he paid for it.'

The girl's false eyelashes – was she really doubling up and wearing two pairs? – fluttered dangerously. 'Perhaps I ought to call my manageress, Mrs McCoy . . .'

'No need to trouble the lady,' said Campion, pulling out his wallet. 'I'm sure you can help me, and young Edward, out of our predicament. All I would ask is that you hand back Edward's cheque and allow me to cover the cost in hard cash. Edward should never have been allowed to wield a chequebook in anger, and it is my task and duty to forestall any embarrassments in financial areas where Edward is very much a stranger in a strange land.'

The girl's hand once more floated around the underside of her counter. She may no longer fear the old man as a robber, but it was clear to her that he was slightly mad.

'He paid cash,' she said, as though explaining the concept to a younger sister. 'Eighteen pounds, twelve shillings and sixpence.'

'How efficient and how clever of Edward. And you are sure that was the value of the ring he bought?'

'I made a note of it for my sales commission,' she said primly.

'Of course you did. Well then, I have been worrying without due cause.' Campion looked down at the display of rings under the glass-topped counter, as if noticing them for the first time. 'Was it one of these?'

The assistant pointed at a particular tray with a long, blood-red fingernail. 'One of those: a gold heart in a twist. It's one of our most popular lines.'

'I'm sure it is. Look, you've been terribly helpful to a silly old man, but I have one more favour to ask.' Campion opened his wallet as he spoke and realized he had the girl's full attention. 'Should Edward ever come in here again, I would appreciate it if you did not mention that his meddling old uncle was checking up on him – no pun intended.' Campion took a pound note from his wallet and slid it across the glass counter, and the girl speared it with a fingernail.

'Please,' said Campion, 'take that for your trouble and buy yourself one of those pop music long-playing records.'

The girl looked up at him through fluttering veils of eyelashes. 'LPs cost more than that.'

Campion added another pound note, closed his wallet and put on his hat.

It was only when he was outside on Market Street that he muttered something under his breath about the younger generation, which may have been condemnation but was lightly tinged with admiration.

Mr Campion completed his shopping list with impressive speed, thoroughly enjoying his exchanges with an amiable butcher over the merits of sirloin over rump steak and his triumph over a surly market-stall holder in an argument over the ripeness of his tomatoes. Other items were purchased in haste and without diversion, even in the wine merchant's, where he instantly chose a non-vintage Burgundy despite the disappointed vintner's offer of a tasting of superior alternatives, as the fact that Amanda had been left alone for the bulk of the day was weighing on his mind.

Barton Road was busy with traffic heading out of the city at the end of the working day, and though Campion, sauntering along with his shopping bags, took careful note of every vehicle he saw, none struck him as remotely suspicious.

After one final glance up and down the road, he turned his key into the lock of number 112 and staggered in with his purchases, to be greeted by the unnatural silence of an empty house which you know is not empty and then a ghostly low whistle coming from the kitchen.

'Kettle's on. I'm absolutely gagging for a cuppa.'

Campion relaxed at the sound of his wife's voice, though who else could have been in the house? What had he expected? A hairnet-and-curlers harridan hefting a rolling pin or, even worse, a belligerent Lugg who has found the last of the milk stout but lost the bottle-opener?

'How was solitary confinement, dear?'

'Solitary and very boring. I realize I am not cut out to be a peeping Tom or a nosey neighbour.'

'Well, that's good to hear,' said Mr Campion, placing his bags on the kitchen table where Amanda had placed two cups and saucers so that they flanked his binoculars standing on end. 'How about birdwatching?'

'No, I shan't be taking that up either.' Amanda leaned in to peck her husband on the cheek then turned back to the stove to transfer boiling water from kettle to teapot, 'but I got a good view of the Goshawk hangar from the back bedroom window.'

'Anything of intertest happen?'

'Not a thing. John Branscombe was not in today as he had college duties and, of course, he was busy lunching you quite lavishly, wasn't he?'

'I wouldn't go that far.'

'And then everyone seemed to knock off early, probably because there was nobody taking charge.'

'Didn't Nugent Monck assume command?'

Amanda raised one perfect, but quizzical, eyebrow. 'I rest my case. He was probably the reason people couldn't wait to get away.'

'I don't suppose you notice who left first?'

'Kevin Loder. He has special dispensation as he goes home for the weekend. He cycles to the station and catches a train to Ely where his wife meets him.'

Mr Campion began to unpack his shopping, presenting the bottle of Burgundy with the pride of a French sommelier. 'That fits. He called in to see Alf Bagley on his way there.'

Amanda poured tea. 'How is poor Alf?'

'Depressed and still in shock, with reason of course. The psychiatrists would have a name for it, but at least most of the Goshawk staff have made the effort to visit him.'

'And so must I, just as soon as . . .'

'He would appreciate that; he was worried about you. Kevin Loder was his most recent visitor, not long before me as it happens.'

'Is that significant?' Amanda unwrapped the paper around the two sirloin steaks Campion had bought, nodded approval and found a plate for them.

'Probably not, but there's something I must do before we eat. I thought baked potatoes, steak and a tomato and onion salad if that meets with your approval.'

'It certainly does, though I insist on doing the cooking. It's not that I don't trust your culinary skills, Albert my love, but this isn't our kitchen and I want to leave it pristine. Think of it as not leaving any fingerprints for John Branscombe or his housekeeper to find.'

'I doubt the professor would notice if we tested spaghetti by throwing it at the walls, and the lovely Astra . . .'

'Lovely?'

'I have very good reason to think Teddy Toomey thinks she is, but anyway, she won't be coming round here until after the weekend.'

'So what's the pre-dinner task we have to perform?'

'Do you have Kevin Loder's home telephone number?'

'Yes, it's in my diary, which is in my handbag upstairs. Why?'

'I just want to check what time he got home today.'

'I can't very well ring him; I'm supposed to be under arrest.'

'Don't worry, I will, on some spurious excuse. Then we can eat and drink and spend the evening snuggled in front of the television with a box of chocolates.'

With a final flourish Mr Campion produced a slightly battered box of Black Magic.

'We'll have them for dessert,' said Amanda, 'and there'll be no lounging round watching the goggle-box tonight. We're going out for a top-secret assignation.'

'We are?'

While Amanda busied herself in the kitchen, Campion settled himself at the small table in one corner of the front room which served as an altar for the house telephone squatting on an elaborately crocheted cloth, perhaps a reminder of the absent Mrs Branscombe. Next to the phone was a small leather message pad, on which was scribbled in pencil a single line of handwriting: *E at Pant A 9.*

Consulting the pocket diary Amanda had retrieved from her handbag – a place where no sane husband would ever usually venture – Campion dialled the home number for Kevin Loder and heard it ring six times before a male voice – sounding harassed and with a distinct Midlands drone – answered by repeating the exchange and number.

'Mr Loder? This is Albert Campion ringing from the Goshawk Project in Cambridge.'

'Campion? Bugger! What's happened now?'

'Nothing terribly untoward; in fact, something really quite trivial and completely unworthy of bothering you at home, but I missed you at the Project. I hope I'm not disturbing anything important.'

'I've hardly had time to take off my coat, as a matter of fact. My train broke down just outside Ely and we ended up an hour late. The wife tells me my dinner's ruined.'

'I'm so sorry about that, and do not let me delay you or Mrs Loder any further. I only wanted to ask if you'd picked up my lighter by mistake.'

'Your what?'

'My cigarette lighter. I don't smoke any more, but I notice all you boffins seem to be pipe men and I think I left it in the hangar the other day. You didn't pick it up by mistake, did you? It's got sentimental value, you see.'

'Not guilty, Mr C, I'm a Swan Vesta man. Don't hold with modern mechanical contraptions.'

'Spoken like a true engineer!' Campion laughed. 'Look, Kevin, I'm so sorry to have bothered you. I'm sure it'll turn up. I'll see you back on the front line next week. You take care now.'

'As we all should after what happened this week,' said Loder in a low voice, presumably because Mrs Loder was within earshot.

'Amen to that,' said Campion, who added a polite 'Good evening' and then replaced the receiver to find Mrs Campion within earshot.

'I gave you that lighter,' said Amanda. 'I had it engraved *To A From A*.'

Campion reached into his jacket pocket and held up a silver Ibelo Monopol.

'You mean this lighter? It was the first excuse I could think of for ringing him.'

'Was he at home?'

'I would say so. He said his train was delayed at Ely and his wife is giving him grief that his dinner will now be ruined. That sounds like an honest married man to me.'

'We could easily check whether the trains were delayed at Ely today.'

'Darling, you do have a suspicious mind at times.'

'And you, my dearest man, are too trusting. You'd make a terrible spy. Let's eat.'

Campion glanced down at the scribbled words on the telephone notepad and then at the handwriting in Amanda's diary which lay open at the pages reserved for names and addresses.

And so would you, my darling.

Amanda prepared their meal with the speed and economy of movement which had always impressed her husband, whose sole responsibility was to open the wine, and they ate at the kitchen table.

'Shall I go first?' asked Mr Campion between forkfuls.

'We don't usually talk business over dinner,' Amanda chided him gently.

'Then shall I start with gossip rather than business?'

'That sounds much more acceptable.' Amanda pointed her fork. 'You have the floor.'

Campion began by regaling her with the details of his spartan lunch in Magdalene with Professor Branscombe, and Amanda expressed surprise at the frugality of the hospitality on offer, adding that – although out of character for a Cambridge college – it hardly qualified as gossip. Neither did she regard the news that Cuthbert Snow moonlighted as a punting tour guide as particularly 'juicy'. It was not unusual for postgraduate students to take odd jobs to help cover the expense of six years of living in ivory towers, nor was it hold-the-front-page news that students from wealthy families were often the least well-off. In any case, Cuthbert was a great hunk of a lad who had brawn and energy to spare, and he needed to work it off somehow.

Amanda listened carefully to his report of his meeting with Detective Inspector Mawson and Campion thought he saw an eyebrow flick upwards when he précised the policeman's assessment – or should that be suspicions? – of the American air force's 'public relations' man Luther Romo. But to all intents and purposes, for Amanda, this still did not qualify as good gossip.

She was, naturally, totally attentive when Campion's agenda reached his visit to Alf Bagley and asked many questions about her loyal employee's physical and mental health, some of which Campion chose not to answer. It was only when Campion's narrative moved on to his description of Edward Toomey's entry into the jewellery market that Amanda accepted that, at last, here was something worthy of the description of gossip.

'An eternity ring, not an engagement ring? You're sure?'

'That's what the charming young shop assistant called it: a small heart shape with a thin gold band. One of their most popular lines.'

'But no diamonds?'

'I doubt it at that price, but even eighteen pounds is a fair amount, in cash, for an impoverished student.'

'The lovestruck little puppy might have been saving up all the Christmas postal orders he got from his granny for the last five years. Give him the benefit of the romantic doubt.'

'He hasn't known her for five years,' said Mr Campion. 'I suspect it has been less than six months, round about the time Astra Jarvela started working here as Branscombe's house-keeper and, coincidentally, roughly the time the Goshawk Project started up.'

Amanda frowned. 'Are you sure you're not adding two and two and making four-squared or even four-cubed?'

'Please do not try and baffle me with mathematics; you would win far too easily.'

Amanda reached across the table and gently stroked Campion's cheek with the back of her hand. 'I am not arguing with you, darling, I just hope you are not getting distracted. Like Teddy buying that ring, all that glisters is not necessarily gold.'

'The assistant assured me it was, and she had others on display. It certainly looked like gold, though I admit I didn't pick one up and try bending it between my teeth the way pirates or grizzled old prospectors in Westerns test gold coins.'

'I wasn't talking metallurgy, I just meant that you might be making too much of a naïve young man's infatuations, however amusing, or tragic, we may find them. Teddy's love life can surely have nothing to do with my central problem. The leakage of research information from Alandel started before we established the Goshawk Project, and before any of the Cambridge students were involved.'

'So why was one of them murdered?'

'You are absolutely convinced of that?'

'Yes, I am.' Campion took his wife's hand from his cheek, turned it gently and placed a supplicant's kiss on the palm. 'I know how it was done and I have a pretty good idea who did it, I just don't know why.'

'Oh dear,' said Amanda, 'I had hoped to keep you out of all this – well, out of most of it – but now I suppose there

will be no stopping you. I knew you wouldn't be happy with
the roles of messenger boy and look-out.'

Campion smiled. 'Those are both honourable tasks which
I am happy to undertake on your behalf. You know full well
that I am totally at your beck and call in all matters, darling,
but in the current circumstances, perhaps a slight promotion
through the ranks is in order?'

'By which you mean I should put you in the full picture,'
Amanda concurred gently.

'There are certain aspects of this whole affair,' Campion
began equally gently, 'on which I am far from clear.'

Amanda regained possession of her hand, extended a forefinger and pressed it to her husband's lips. 'I have been very
secretive, I know, but tonight, all will be revealed.' She stood
up from the table, her chair scraping across the kitchen floor
behind her. 'Once you've made the coffee and I've got
changed.'

'So we really are going out?'

'We certainly are, so be a dear and do the washing up, then
you can open that box of chocolates and do the honourable
thing.'

'Which is?'

'To eat the coffee cream, of course.'

Mr Campion followed his orders dutifully, unconcerned about
what surprises Amanda had in store for him that evening and
rather reflecting that whenever his wife had surprised him in
the past, it had proved a pleasant and rewarding experience.
He had long ago in their marriage realized that the greatest
surprise Amanda could spring on him would be the day she
stopped springing surprises.

That she was prepared to leave her self-imposed confinement had been the first surprise, that she promised to reveal
her overall plan, to which he had so far been privy to only a
part, without any pressure or coercion on his part, was the
second.

The third and most jaw-dropping of all was when Amanda
appeared at the kitchen door just as Campion was drying the
last of the cutlery.

She wore a man's pinstripe double-breasted suit, brown Oxford brogues, and her hair was encased in a black homburg. As she stepped into the kitchen, she opened the suit jacket wide and did a coquettish swivel of the hips to reveal a white shirt, a set of maroon braces and a salmon-pink and cucumber striped tie.

'When did you become a member of the Garrick Club, darling?' Campion asked once he had regained the power of speech.

'Oh, I'm not,' said Amanda, fluffing the tie to give it a life of its own. 'I'm not allowed to be a member. It's borrowed, as is the suit and the shoes. The hat is John Branscombe's. I found it in the cupboard under the stairs where he keeps his golf clubs and umbrellas, but he won't miss it for one night. What do you think?'

'I'm not sure how to answer that.'

'Do you think anyone will recognize me in this ensemble?'

'My dear, I had to look twice – and I like to look at you as often as possible.'

'But as it's after dark and if I keep the hat on, I could pass for a man, don't you think?'

'Well, this is Cambridge,' said Campion slowly, 'and if we stay out of any direct light which would reflect your beautiful eyes, then we might just get away with it. Where are we going? Not a dinner dance, I hope?'

'No dancing and, anyway, you've had dinner. We're going to meet an old friend of yours for a drink.'

'Is he expecting you in to appear in such . . . masculine fashion?'

'He's pretty unshockable,' said Amanda cheerfully, 'but before we get to him, we've got to go a-burglar-ing again, so grab a torch and let's nip over to the Goshawk hangar to see if the bait's been taken.'

Campion flipped a hand in a mock salute. 'As you command, Quentin.'

'Quentin?'

'Well, I can't call you Amanda dressed like that, can I?'

TWELVE
The Adorable Professor

The second officially sanctioned burglary of the Goshawk Project was carried out smoothly and with disconcerting ease.

With the help of a weak early moon and their torches, the Campions picked their way over the Bin Brook and the rough pasture towards the dark shadow of the Goshawk hangar, even managing to negotiate the sunken rifle range with the practised ease of a pair of well-dressed mountain goats. Soon they were crunching across the car parking area, now deserted except for the Project's Land Rover, and standing before the large sliding door of the dark hangar.

Amanda worked her deft magic with the padlock, Campion slid the door aside and they padded across the floor of the hangar, as if wary of disturbing a lurking ghost. In the office, the impressive-looking safe yielded easily to another key, causing Campion to wonder just how many keys there were to this establishment. Given the sensitivity of the work being carried out, the lack of security measures ought surely to be a worry to the Alandel shareholders, and then he remembered that he was one himself.

'The bait's been taken,' said Amanda, kneeling in front of the safe and shining her torch into the interior which, to her husband's eyes, contained the same disordered pile of papers and drawings which he had seen the night before.

'Are you sure?'

'Positive,' said Amanda, closing the safe and locking it.

'Not worried about leaving fingerprints, darling?' Campion asked, smiling in the dark.

His torch beam caught Amanda's pout perfectly.

'Why should I? It's my safe.'

'I suppose it is. You'll have to forgive me – my breaking-and-entering days are long behind me.'

'Don't let that old reprobate Lugg hear you say that. He'll think that all those years of personal tutoring and mentoring have gone to waste. Did you retain nothing from all your years learning at the master's knee?'

'The only thing learned at Lugg's knee these days is either sciatica or lumbago,' scoffed Campion. 'Are we done here? I thought you were taking me out on the town tonight.'

Amanda consulted the luminous dial of her watch. 'I think I should have said we are going *into* town tonight, not *on* the town. We need to be discreet as, after all, I am technically being held by our wonderful security services, but you're right, we should make a move. And should you be tempted to hold hands or put an arm around me, please remember how I am dressed. We do not want to draw attention to ourselves.'

Campion feigned surprise. 'But my dear, this is supposed to be the Swinging Sixties and we are in Cambridge. How could we possibly attract unwanted attention?'

Once outside, Amanda took the lead and walked the length of the hangar until they reached the access road which joined with the Madingley Road. When they were opposite the site of the concrete and glass structures of Churchill College, Amanda pointed out that full college status for the newest academic constituency of the institution that was Cambridge University was expected the following year and, though it was laudable that Churchill would concentrate on science and technology, it was such a shame that it did not admit women.

Mr Campion agreed wholeheartedly and, having allowed his wife to make two very good points, he decided it was the moment to pounce.

'Why are we taking this roundabout route, darling? We should have gone back across the fields to Barton Road. Surely that's the quickest way to get to The Panton Arms by nine o'clock . . .'

There was a momentary hesitation in Amanda's gait; not a stumble or a misstep, but a definite pause, then she picked up the pace again, if anything lengthening her stride.

'How did you find out?' she asked, her eyes, under the brim of the homburg, fixed straight ahead, pointedly not looking at her husband.

'There was a notepad by John Branscombe's telephone. You scribbled a little *aide-mémoire* saying *E at Pant A 9* which I deduced – something we great detectives do given the slightest encouragement – that you, or we, were due to meet someone called 'E' at The Panton Arms at nine p.m.'

'That was a guess.'

'Yes, but a good one, as most of the deductions done by the great fictional detectives tend to be. It's a well-known Cambridge watering hole, somewhat off the beaten track and therefore not plagued by tourists, and just the sort of place a wife should take her husband out for a drink, even if she is dressed as a man, although I repeat, we are going the long way round.'

'I needed to stretch my legs,' said Amanda, lengthening her stride to illustrate her point. 'You haven't been cooped up in that house all day. Anyway, I wanted to walk through the town out of devilment, just to see if anyone recognized me.'

'You had better hope they do not,' said Mr Campion. 'It's all very well strolling along with your hands in pockets or twanging your braces, but should a polite young lady hail you, you would surely, as a gentleman, have to remove your hat in greeting and that, my dear, would be your undoing. Those fiery locks of yours, which I have always thought one of your most attractive features, would be a dead giveaway.'

Fortunately, the situation did not arise, and the Campions remained unmolested as they crossed Magdalene Bridge and strolled into town, their only excitement being the need to swerve to avoid a speeding unlit bicycle and having to negotiate a group of young students, already unstable from an early evening intake of beer, who were blocking the pavement attempting to untangle two bicycles chained to a lamppost. Or perhaps they were trying to secure rather than free them, Mr Campion was not sure, but cheerfully wished them luck, adding that in 'his day' undergraduates were only allowed to ride penny-farthings, an observation which left them slightly bemused but, this being Cambridge, where eccentricity tended to be the norm rather than the uncommon, not at all surprised.

They followed the route of Amanda's congregational procession as far as Senate House, with Campion tipping his fedora as they passed the gates of St Ignatius, although Professor Branscombe's homburg remained firmly fixed on Amanda's head, a helmet to protect and hide her tell-tale red hair. There were no trumpets or church bells to accompany their gentle progress, only the distant tinkling of bicycle bells from darkened streets and alleys and, occasionally, a spectral chord or two from a college chapel organ.

They had negotiated the length of King's Parade, the frontage of Kings as impressive at night as on a bright summer's day when it posed for photographs, and had almost reached the formidable entrance to Addenbrooke's hospital on Trumpington Street before Amanda raised the subject of the question her husband had not asked.

'So you *deduced* that we were going to The Panton Arms, and you *deduced* it was to meet someone at nine p.m., but you didn't even hazard a guess at who we will be meeting.'

'Ah, the mysterious "E". Well, I naturally suspected that he must be one of your many admirers, perhaps an old boyfriend or even a current rival for your affections. As the very thought of that is so abhorrent, I immediately thrust it from my mind, so I have no idea who "E" might be. Let he – or she – be yet another of this evening's surprises.'

With the advantage of his height and the fact that his wife was looking straight ahead under the brim of her borrowed homburg, Mr Campion was secretly delighted that Amanda could not see his smile, nor, behind his round glasses, the twinkle in his eyes.

The Panton Arms, halfway down an ill-lit street, boasted a disused brewery yard which, once furnished with a few extremely rustic wooden tables and even more rustic wooden benches flanking them, was known proudly as 'the garden', despite the fact not a single green shoot striving for sunlight ever managed to force its way through the cobbles.

The 'garden' was lit by a single outside light which guarded the three doors into the pub, each leading to a different bar, doors which were clearly labelled Public, Saloon and 4-Ale, the latter not actually being a bar, but a small shop-like enclosure which sold bottles and jugs of beer, crisps and chocolate bars, for consumption off the premises. Light also spilled from the uncurtained windows of the two bars which were bars, so that it was possible to make out the silhouette, at one of the tables, of the single customer nursing a small glass, who preferred the dark solitude of the 'garden' to the companionship on offer in the bright interior, which throbbed with the hum of jovial voices.

Breaking away from Campion's side, Amanda strode across the cobbled yard towards the solitary drinker, who remained seated, his face contorted in confusion as he gradually realized that the smartly dressed gentleman was the normally very feminine female he had been expecting. As recognition dawned across his face, so too did it on Mr Campion's.

'E for Elsie, that is a surprise,' said Campion, allowing Amanda a small triumph. 'I suppose I should have guessed.'

'But he didn't,' Amanda told the man, whose quiet contemplation of a small brown ale they had interrupted. 'I was very strict about security.'

The man seated across the table from her seemed at a loss for words, transfixed as he was by the figure of indeterminate sex. An unlit pipe held between loosely clenched teeth began to wobble slightly, and only when he removed it did he recover the power of speech.

'Amanda! Good God, what do you look like? Was this your idea, Campion?'

'Not at all, Elsie,' said Campion, stretching a long leg over the chair next to Amanda's. 'It was my wife's desire to pass unnoticed and unrecognized through the town this evening, though I suppose I should have advised her to remove her lipstick.'

'Damn,' said Amanda to herself.

'Fortunately, we were not molested in the course of our perambulations, which were really quite thirst-making. Can I get anyone a drink? I take it we want to stay outside as it's a fine evening. Unless, darling, you'd like to test your disguise in the public bar and challenge the regulars to a game of darts.

Good manners would dictate that you might have to remove your hat, though.'

'We'll stay out here,' said the man known as Elsie. 'I can't stay too long as I have to get back to London and there's a car waiting round the corner. I'll take a drop of Scotch this time, Albert.'

'Of course you will; you've had a bit of a shock. You two stay here and try not to look like two East Germans plotting to jump over the Berlin Wall. Pretend you are two philosophy dons debating the morality of income tax; that should keep you engaged and make sure no one disturbs you.'

Mr Campion was one of a select few who could use the name 'Elsie' with impunity in the presence of its owner. It was a lazy nickname based on the initials 'L.C.' and although he had, at one point in his career, held the military rank of brigadier, he was officially – and there was rarely anything unofficial about him – known as Mr L. C. Corkran.

No accurate, detailed description of Mr Corkran's career had ever been made public, nor was likely to be. Only those brave enough to refer to him as Elsie knew that his working life had been to serve king, queen and country in a variety of roles within the often labyrinthine establishment loosely termed the security service. Campion had served under him for a time during the war, and had appreciated his advice – and sometimes his protection – in the years since. He knew and respected Mr Corkran and was somewhat relieved to discover that he was involved, hopefully as a guardian angel to Amanda, in this current Goshawk business, despite the fact that he must now be well beyond retirement age.

He chose the saloon bar door and, although not full to bursting, there were sufficient customers – exclusively male – in there to have produced a haze of smoke and the hum of a dozen indistinct conversations. Campion found a place at the bar with ease and ordered a large whisky for Elsie and a pint of bitter for himself then, out of devilment, a second pint for Amanda, also requesting a tray for the portage of the drinks 'to the garden'.

A blue-rinsed middle-aged barmaid in a black dress decorated with a large white bow tie served him with a smile. It was no concern of hers if customers wished to sit outside, and at least this bespectacled gent looked the type who just might bring the empty glasses back to the bar, unlike some of the university toffs who expected servants to be following in their wake to clean up after them. She actually warmed to this quietly spoken customer when he told her 'and one for yourself' and didn't think twice about the way he suddenly started, turned his body into the bar and pulled down the brim of his fedora after scanning the room and seeing something, or someone, he recognized in the large mirror hanging above the fireplace. That was none of her business, and the customer had taken his tray and was out of the door before she had poured herself her port and lemon.

The two figures at the table had almost merged into one dark shape as Campion approached with his gently rattling tray. Amanda and Mr Corkran had leaned into each other as though in close and confidential discussion, Amanda's head, and hat, turned to the right to make it impossible to see her face. For Campion's benefit, she lowered her voice and declaimed, 'And ninthly . . .'

'Very convincing,' said Campion, placing the tray on the table. 'Two middle-aged dons engaged in a civilized debate on which no passing stranger in their right mind would want to eavesdrop.'

'Steady on with the term "middle-aged", Campion,' Corkran huffed as he accepted the offered tumbler of whisky. 'For one of us it is inaccurate and ungallant, for me it is anachronistic.'

'As it is for me, Elsie, as I am also now officially of pensionable age and I know you have the edge on me in calendar years, so does that mean Her Majesty's government is reluctant to put you out to pasture? Or perhaps they dare not, you knowing which cupboards hold the skeletons they have hidden.'

'You've locked a few things in cupboards in your time yourself, Albert.' Corkran raised his glass in a toast. 'Not that they didn't need putting away, but any official standing I once had is now behind me. I am no more than a private citizen working in the private sector.'

'Really? A private sector for former spymasters? What's it called, Marks and Spies or Karl Marx and Spencer?'

'I suppose we're in the right city for undergraduate humour, if not the right mood,' scolded Corkran gently. 'Actually, I am a consultant with Omega Oils and my brief includes recommending measures to counter industrial espionage.'

'Which is why,' said Amanda, 'I turned to Elsie for guidance rather than seek it closer to home . . .'

'A wise decision,' said Campion, taking one of the pint pots of ale from the tray and sliding it gently in front of Amanda.

'What's this?' she asked, glancing up.

'To complete your disguise, my dear. Dressed as you are, I had you down as a beer man, as a Babycham with a cherry on a stick might have drawn attention, especially as a member of your staff is not very far away – in the saloon bar, as a matter of fact.'

'Who?'

'That nice young chap Gary Cupples.'

'The Yank?' said Corkran and Amanda nodded.

'Don't worry,' said Campion, 'he didn't see me. I can be quite invisible when buying a round in a pub, so Lugg tells me.'

'Was he with anyone else from the Project?'

'A couple of John Branscombe's students I think, but I'm not sure. I didn't get a good look at them, but they were not ones I instantly recognized.'

'Could he have been recruiting?' Amanda asked Corkran, after taking a suspicious sip from her glass, but before he could answer, Campion intervened. 'I think he was just enjoying a drink with some engineering friends. When I met him he mentioned he came here, and that's not a surprise – it is a very popular pub. Now can we concentrate on why I am here? I thought it was to learn something to my advantage, as the phrase goes.'

'We thought you might have questions about this little operation of ours,' said Corkran, his face illuminated as he struck a match and applied it to his pipe.

'I had,' said Campion, waving away a small cloud of pungent pipe smoke, 'but your very presence has answered most of them, so it's no use laying down a smokescreen.'

'Explain your thinking,' said Amanda.

'Spoken like a real Cambridge don.' Campion laughed. 'Very well, Professor Quentin, I will.'

'Who's Quentin?' asked Corkran.

'I couldn't call her Amanda dressed like that, could I? So I decided on Quentin. Elsie, meet Quentin, and pray that no one is recording this conversation; not that my reputation in these particular groves of academe could sink much lower.'

Campion drank deeply from his glass and, satisfied that he had their attention, continued. 'You call it "this little operation of ours", Elsie, but I suspect it was very much Quentin – sorry, Amanda's – brainchild. Aeroplanes are, after all, her passion, and if she suspects her research work is being stolen for commercial or military reasons, then she will go on the offensive. She has done that by building an elaborate trap, the Goshawk Project, but I always had the niggle at the back of my mind: *how did she know Alandel secrets were being stolen and presumably sold to competitors or foreign powers?* Is there some sort of industrial espionage stock exchange with a tickertape news service, which offers best prices for secrets on the market? I think not; therefore, Quentin here must have had someone advising him. A kindly uncle with an elaborate network of contacts, recently retired from the spying game perhaps, or should that be an aunty?'

'Cut the fooling, Albert. Yes, it was I who tipped off Amanda that Alandel designs and research were appearing on the black market, as we might call it. I may no longer hold an official position in the service, but I do remain in close contact with many colleagues and I hear things. Funnily enough, the first tip-off we got was from the Americans, when one of their aerospace companies was approached. For once, they did the decent thing and turned down the offer. A few months later, one of our chaps in Moscow reported that some Russian engineers had made interesting advances in work on a certain jet engine.'

'Advances similar to those made at Alandel?'

'Exactly.' Corkran removed his pipe and pointed the stem at Amanda. 'Given the specific nature of the information which had been stolen, your good lady was able to trace its theft backwards. That's something our American friends call "walking back the cat", though goodness knows why. It became clear that only the senior engineers at Alandel had access to the information in the right time frame.'

'One of them being Gary Cupples, who is sitting in a saloon bar not a million miles away from here.'

'Ah, yes, the Yank.' Mr Corkran's face hardened. 'He seemed remarkably keen on the move to Cambridge. First one to volunteer for Goshawk, wasn't he, Amanda?'

'He was enthusiastic at the prospect of a new challenge,' said Amanda, 'but then he's young and not as set in his ways as the others.'

'Perhaps it was Cambridge rather than Goshawk which attracted him,' said Mr Campion, raising his glass to his lips and observing Corkran over the rim.

'What do you mean by that?' growled the old spy-catcher.

'I understand Mr Cupples may have a romantic interest in the daughter of a senior officer out at Alconbury.'

'The American base? How did you come up with that one?'

'By listening to workplace gossip, of course. You really should try it, though I'm surprised your opposite numbers in American intelligence didn't let you in on that little secret.'

Mr Corkran replaced his pipe with his glass and drained the whisky from it. 'The Americans are not keen on sharing intelligence these days. They think we're a leaky ship; too many spy scandals in the papers in recent years.'

'One can hardly blame them,' said Campion, 'and moving sensitive research to Cambridge of all places cannot have inspired them with much confidence.'

'But it suited our purposes very nicely.'

'When you say "our purposes", you're not referring to Omega Oils, are you?'

L.C. Corkran had the good grace to look slightly embarrassed. 'Well, no. Omega is now officially my employer, but I am advising Amanda on an authorized basis.'

'Sort of unofficially official, or officially unofficial?'

Mr Corkran gave Campion a full minute of his trademark 'headmaster's stare' which had terrified subordinates for over two decades. 'I may be employed in the private sector now, but I have some expertise which may still be put to use for the public good. Much of the work at Alandel is of a military nature and therefore a matter of national security, going above and beyond what one might call normal industrial espionage. I was seen as a useful link, a liaison officer if you like, between Amanda's Goshawk initiative and our assets at Oakley.'

Mr Campion pursed his lips and nodded his head slowly, impressed at Corkran's disclosure that GCHQ Oakley in Cheltenham, the government's monitoring and code-breaking centre, were involved. He sipped his beer, waiting patiently for Elsie to elaborate, and he did not have to wait long.

'Almost immediately after the announcement that Alandel's Goshawk Project was moving to Cambridge, Oakley started to pick up some high-speed radio traffic in a fairly basic code, clearly aimed towards Moscow.'

'KGB?'

'No, the GRU, Russian military intelligence, and the code was recognized as one used by the GRU directorate which deals with science and technology. The transmissions Oakley has managed to decrypt so far show more than a passing interest in Goshawk.'

'So what are you telling us, Elsie? That there is an agent, or a cell, here in Cambridge to gather intelligence on Goshawk and pass it on eastwards?'

'It would appear so,' said Corkran, inspecting the bowl of his pipe for signs of life.

'Then I think it imperative that Amanda is removed from the equation immediately. We are not dealing with industrial espionage and competition between commercial companies here; this is a big boys' game.'

Campion had spoken calmly and with genuine concern, but he knew the reaction his words would provoke from his wife.

'Albert! I am perfectly capable of looking after myself, thank you very much.'

'Of course you are, darling, but allow me to be protective. It is, after all, my prime function in life where you are concerned, a responsibility which I accepted with gratitude from the day we first met.'

Amanda took her husband's face in both hands and brought

it close to hers. Mr Campion found himself, once again, entranced by that heart-shaped face and those moist honey-brown eyes, even if that countenance was bizarrely framed between a collar and tie and the brim of a homburg.

'But you are here,' she said softly, 'and just by being here you are protecting me and supporting me.'

Mr L.C. Corkran coughed diplomatically. 'If you two kiss,' he said gruffly, 'people will talk.'

'Let them talk!' scoffed Campion. 'As Quentin here is my wife, I am well within my rights.'

At which point Amanda collapsed into giggles and the homburg and the fedora retreated to a respectable distance.

'You need not worry about Amanda,' said Mr Corkran, happy that the dark evening was hiding the fact that he was blushing even if no one else was. 'We keep in touch by telephone and I think that house on Barton Road was a stroke of genius as a hideout.'

'The fact that my wife has to hide at all is far from comforting, especially as we do not know from whom she is hiding.'

'The whole point, darling,' said Amanda, 'was that with me so publicly out of the way and John Branscombe suddenly finding a lot of college work to keep him occupied, then without the supervision of the cats, the mice would play and hopefully give themselves away.'

'Some of your mice may be rats, darling, and react violently to being coaxed into a trap.'

'You're thinking of this Wormold chap?' Mr Corkran tapped the stem of his pipe against his teeth; a sign, Campion knew, that the old boy was also uncomfortable with any theory of a bizarre industrial accident.

'I think you are too, Elsie.'

'But I've told you,' Amanda said forcefully, risking a finger-nail by jabbing the tabletop for emphasis, 'the leaks started before the Goshawk Project and Alan joined the team.'

'And yet Wormold is killed, but why? Did he stumble on the leaker by accident, or was he somehow involved?'

'How could he be? He was one of John's students, not a senior engineer with access to all our research work.'

Campion peered over the tops of his glasses. 'We both know that the security precautions to protect your research leave a lot to be desired.'

'He could have been a postman,' said Mr Corkran.

'A what?' exploded Amanda.

'A postman, a messenger boy, a conduit,' Corkran replied.

'A sort of human dead letter box,' said Campion. 'Someone who passed the information on to Russian agents here in Cambridge.' He noted Amanda's scowl. 'It's just a theory.'

'Well, that's Elsie's side of things,' said Amanda firmly. 'My only interest is plugging the leak from Goshawk.'

'Strictly speaking,' interjected Mr Corkran, 'it's not my side of things, officially anyway. It would be MI5 or Special Branch and if there is any trouble' – he caught Campion's eye – 'or even a hint of a threat, then get in touch with Detective Inspector Mawson. I'll make sure he's briefed and he will have a hotline which he can use to call in the cavalry if they're needed. I hope that puts your mind at ease, Albert.'

'It does, thank you.' Campion placed an arm around his wife and squeezed gently. 'Though hopefully my wife will stick to her plan and stay out of sight.'

L.C. Corkran used his empty glass like a gavel and rapped on the table. 'Action stations! Look out, strangers about.'

Campion withdrew his arm as if it had touched an electric fence and followed Corkran's gaze towards the open door of the pub from which both light and customers materialized.

'Damn!' said Campion under his breath. 'It's Cupples. Why couldn't he stay in there until closing time like any other carefree bachelor?'

He stood, unhooking his long legs from the wooden bench and picked up the tray he had brought from the bar, loading it with empty glasses as if en route for a refill.

'You two, hunker down,' he hissed. 'You are engaged in a serious academic debate on something-or-other. Keep your faces turned that way.'

Then he himself turned towards the pub doors and strode across the cobbles to meet the existing customers, making sure that his body obscured their view of the two figures hunched over the table.

'Hi there, Al!' exclaimed Cupples, recognizing Campion as his eyes adjusted to the dark.

Mr Campion suppressed a shudder at the too-familiar greeting and hoped that Amanda would not give the game away by shouting in annoyance or, worse, shrieking with laughter.

'Mr Cupples,' he said, trying but failing to recognize the two young men, clearly students, with the American. 'I hope I'm not driving you out of your local.'

'Not at all, we're just about to change watering holes. These guys are taking me on a pub crawl.'

'Well, good for them.' Campion beamed. 'All you rebellious colonials should be reminded of what you gave up when you decided on independence.'

'That's what we've been telling him, sir,' said one of the undergraduates, gently urging Cupples on with a push in the small of his back. 'Come on, Gary, it's your round next.'

'Then let me not detain you one instant.'

Campion wafted the tray he was carrying in the vague direction of the gate leading to Panton Street. Behind him he could hear L.C. Corkran's low rumbling voice maintaining a diatribe against whatever hypothesis his more restrained drinking partner had proposed, and Campion caught the phrases 'You're just not thinking empirically, old chap' and 'It fails all the tests of Hobbesian logic . . .'

Cupples had also picked up on this one-sided debate and, even as he was ushered towards his next hostelry, he strained his neck to look over Campion's shoulder to try and catch a glimpse of the two philosophers hunched in the shadows.

Campion sidestepped to block his sight line. 'You carry on with your evening's revelries and leave me to my far less enjoyable duties.' He jerked his head backwards to the two figures in full hugger-mugger mode. 'I have to chaperone these two visitors as a favour to my old college.'

'Are they dons?' Cupples whispered through beery fumes.

'Professors Gallagher and Shean,' Campion whispered back, hoping that young Gary was not a student of the American vaudeville circuit of forty years ago.

Apparently he was not. 'Are they philosophers?' he asked, even as his friends began to tug at his arms.

'Worse than that,' Campion confided, 'they're from Oxford.'

'They look like OK guys to me,' said the American as he was frog-marched away.

'Oh, they're adorable,' said Mr Campion. And then, when Cupples and his fellow drinkers were safely out of earshot, he added, 'Well, one of them is.'

THIRTEEN
Tiger Moth to a Flame

M r Campion could tell, across an ominously silent Saturday morning breakfast table, that his wife was unhappy at the prospect of another day of confinement whilst he, no doubt, would be out enjoying himself. Sensibly he refrained from reminding her that this was her plan all along; she was to dramatically disappear from the scene, leaving the secret workings of the Goshawk Project to be riffled through, removed, and disseminated to parties as yet unknown. Campion's role was to act as Amanda's eyes and ears in the world beyond 112 Barton Road, trawling for scraps of information as to who might be servicing those unknown parties and to report back to her.

He had the sneaking suspicion that his regular reports had fallen short of Amanda's expectations, and she had openly expressed her irritation that her 'leg man' seemed to be more interested in Branscombe's postgraduate students, who were surely peripheral to the investigation; a result, perhaps, of Campion yearning for his own youthful days in Cambridge?

And now he was gallivanting off into the countryside with Luther Romo on what would certainly be another wild-goose chase. What had possessed him to agree to that and what would it achieve?

Campion had declared that he found Luther Romo, albeit on the strength of only one encounter, to be an interesting chap – for an American – with a wonderfully ostentatious car in which he had offered Campion a lift to Bourn Airfield. A visit there might shed some light on the activities of the late Alan Wormold, and the prospect of riding there in such style was something Campion found difficult to resist.

'You do know he's a spy, don't you?' Amanda had said just as Mr Campion was about to crack the skull of a boiled egg.

'I would have expected nothing less of a man who drives around Cambridge in a bright red sedan too wide for half the streets in the city. He is the perfect spy, hiding in plain sight, but he is on our side, isn't he?'

'Supposedly,' Amanda had said sulkily. 'He's the Project's liaison officer with the American air force, but his idea of cooperation is very one-sided. We don't trust America not to steal our research and the Americans don't trust us to keep secrets. Be careful what you say to him.'

Mr Campion had gently pointed out that he was the very last person likely to give away, even accidentally, any of the technical mysteries of the Goshawk Project, for the simple reason that he did not know any, and even if he did he would not understand them.

'And as you well know, my darling,' he had said to lighten the mood, 'I never sermonize on topics of which I am bliss-fully ignorant, unless I am addressing politicians or answering impertinent questions from the Inland Revenue.'

Amanda's 'fierce face', as their son Rupert had called it when he had misbehaved as a child, had melted into a wistful smile at the thought, but she still resented the prospect of another day alone in that house.

'Just make sure you don't have too much fun,' she had told her husband as she refilled his teacup, 'because after doing the washing up, I'll be spending the day staring at the wallpaper.'

'Come, come, I'm sure John Branscombe has some terribly dull engineering magazines somewhere, and anyway, *Grandstand* is on the telly this afternoon.'

Amanda had paused and pretended to consider the prospect seriously, but then decided: 'But at least that means there's wrestling on the other side, though it won't be the same watching it without Lugg's running commentary.'

'It will be quieter,' Campion had observed.

They were both upstairs in the front bedroom when Mr Campion's chauffeur for the day arrived. Campion was sitting on the bed tying his shoelaces. Amanda had been sorting through her clothing, debating with herself whether to risk using the departed Mrs Branscombe's relatively new twin-tub washing machine as a way of passing the time. Being nearest to the window looking out on to Barton Road, she noticed the car pulling up to the kerb before stepping back into the room so she would not be seen.

'There is a very large, very ugly, very red automobile outside the front door. It's the sort of car you would expect the Beach Boys to drive.'

Campion stood up and pulled on a lightweight linen jacket as the doorbell sounded downstairs.

'Well, he's punctual, I'll say that for him, so I'll be off.' He blew a kiss across the room. 'I think you think I have absolutely no idea who the Beach Boys are.'

'Do you?' Amanda asked, one eyebrow raised.

'Not a clue,' said Mr Campion. 'Cheerio.'

It was quite a car, and Mr Campion said so; rather like being driven whilst still sitting in a favourite armchair, although no floating fireside wingchair could have produced so many looks of curiosity mixed with reluctant admiration from the pedestrians it passed, not to mention glares of hostility from the many cyclists it narrowly avoided. Contrary to his fears that Sergeant Romo's Chevrolet Bel Air was a potential traffic hazard or a rather sluggish mobile traffic jam, Campion was amazed at how effortlessly the car seemed to negotiate the streets of a Cambridge bustling with Saturday morning shoppers, and the usual density of cyclists, streaming like a tireless army of ants on manoeuvres.

Perhaps it was because the car was left-hand drive that Romo could judge so accurately the proximity of cyclists and avoid accidents, though he could easily have reached out through his open window and provoked unexpected dismountings with the prod of a finger, or simply by shouting 'Boo!' into a cyclist's right ear.

Lounging on the edge of the front bench seat, his legs unbent and stretching before him, Mr Campion relaxed and eyed his chauffeur from what seemed a great distance.

'This really is a most comfortable ride,' he said, genuinely impressed with the way Luther Romo navigated the Chevrolet through the busy streets. And then he decided that 'navigate' was not the right word as that suggested sailing, and whilst the mental image of a sleek yacht under full sail might be a useful one to have in reserve for the open road, in the city the car moved more like a river barge, slowly pushing – as if by osmosis – all other traffic out of the way. 'I take it you didn't buy it here.'

'Nope, had it shipped over from the States,' said Luther Romo. 'Uncle Sam likes to provide all the comforts of home to his boys overseas.'

'I'm jealous. All our boys get is the chance of a record request on *Two-Way Family Favourites* – as long as it's not some raucous jazz tune, of course.'

When they reached the Madingley Road and were approaching the access road leading to the Goshawk hangar, Romo, with one hand on the steering wheel and the other reaching for the pack of cigarettes in his jacket pocket, asked what the 'mood music' at the project was.

'I take it you mean morale,' said Campion, waving away the offered Lucky Strike, 'on which score I must say it seems to be holding up well, despite the accident.'

'You're sure it was an accident?' Romo asked from behind teeth delicately clamped around a cigarette whilst lighting it with a battered, gunmetal Zippo.

'The police are not convinced otherwise.'

'You're not the kind of guy who swallows everything the cops say, though, are you?'

Mr Campion observed his young driver for a good half-minute but decided to speak only when Luther Romo returned his stare rather than watching the road ahead, as he did not share the American's faith that the car could steer itself unaided. 'Whatever makes you think that?'

'Security is part of my job description and I've done some checking up on you. You're an interesting kinda guy. You did some impressive work in Washington during World War Two – real down-and-dirty fighting, so I hear.'

'It was hardly front-line combat,' said Campion, his nose wrinkling as the car interior filled with the acrid tang of 'toasted' American tobacco. 'You cannot equate the cocktail lounges of Washington with Iwo Jima or Omaha Beach.'

'Hey, don't do yourself down, fella.' Campion was sure

Romo had put the mental brakes on, saying 'fella' rather than
'grandpa'. 'From what I hear you were a stand-up guy to have
at your side in a tight spot.'

'And where did you hear this, may I ask?'

'You certainly may, you being the polite English gentleman
that you are.' Romo grinned. 'More than one old veteran from
the OSS days said you were the politest man they had ever
met, as well as being brave and smart.'

'More than one, eh?' Campion said drily. 'I must have made
an impression all that time ago. Tell me, Senior Master
Sergeant, the OSS, as it was in the war – that is now the CIA,
is it not?'

'So rumour has it.' Romo's grin broadened and then he
disconcerted Campion completely by fumbling a pair of wire-
framed aviator sunglasses from the breast pocket of his shirt
and clipping them over his ears, having taken both hands off
the steering wheel.

'And does the CIA brief air-force sergeants as a matter of
course?'

'It does when they're responsible for the security of an
American base in the front line of a Cold War which might
just heat up at any moment.'

'And I was worthy of a security vetting? I suppose I should
be flattered.'

'Not so much you,' said Romo, looking at his passenger
through sinister mirrored lenses in which Campion saw himself
reflected as diminished and almost cowering in his seat.
'Mostly your wife.'

Stately as a galleon, the Chevrolet followed the main road
towards Bedford, passing Madingley Hall, which had been
King Edward VII's personal hall of residence when he was a
student at Trinity. Campion also noted, with fond memories,
signposts pointing off the road to villages and hamlets such
as Hardwick, Little Eversden and Toft, which he always
thought of as 'Cromwell Country', for whilst the Lord Protector
himself may not have lived here, good Puritan stock from
those villages were willing recruits to his armies. His fresh-
faced, crew-cut chauffeur, however, was hardly likely to be in

the mood for a history lesson, and anyway they had come upon the sign to Bourn and the Chevrolet had turned off and into a lane just wide enough for it and possibly a thin pedestrian.

There was no formal gateway leading into Bourn Airfield, and no barrier with sentries demanding that all passes had to be shown as there might once have been. The Chevrolet had suddenly turned through a gap in the roadside hedge and was bouncing slowly over a tarmac surface pitted with clumps of grass and cut with holes, as if the engineers who had laid it had used a slice of Emmental as template.

Campion counted three large domed metal buildings, which he presumed were aircraft hangars, though on a much smaller scale than the one the Goshawk Project had inherited; several low-lying concrete bunkers which might have been air-raid shelters when the situation demanded, and a single, two-storeyed building built in functionally bleak RAF style with a flagpole from which dangled a limp windsock.

There was a dark blue Standard Ensign saloon, almost certainly an ex-RAF staff car, parked outside the main building – clubhouse? Campion wondered – but no other sign of life, until a man wearing a dark blue pullover with shoulder and elbow patches and sporting a moustache big enough to act as a personal snowplough for his face, rounded the corner wielding a clipboard like a machete.

'Sergeant Romo!'

'Jimmy, my man! Looking good.'

Mr Campion doubted that any serving RAF officer had ever been thus greeted at Bourn, but Jimmy Norris, as Romo introduced him, although certainly ex-air force, did not seem to mind.

'Got your message, Sergeant. She's all fuelled up.'

Sergeant, twice in ten seconds. Must have been a flight lieutenant at least, thought Campion.

'This is Albert Campion,' said Romo, 'the guy I told you about.'

'Ah yes,' said Norris, shaking hands, 'you're all cleared.'

'To look in Alan Wormold's locker . . .' prompted Campion.

'Of course. Terrible thing to happen to the lad, please follow me, though I don't think there's anything significant left in there. All his personal knick-knacks were collected yesterday.'

'Really? By the police?'

'No, by the chap who always gave him a lift here.' Norris allowed himself a polite chuckle. 'Alan could fly but he couldn't drive. We didn't mind; everybody in the club agreed that he'd got his priorities right. Originally he used to cycle out here, but then his uncle started to drive him here whenever he wanted to go up.'

'His uncle?'

'Well, I assumed he was. Perhaps he was one of Alan's tutors. Older chap – could have been his father for all I know. I never really talked to him because he wasn't particularly interested in the club. He'd drop Alan off, then go for a drive or to a pub somewhere and come back an hour or so later and wait for Alan to land. He didn't come in the clubhouse – sorry, control tower' – Norris grinned sheepishly – 'just sat in his Land Rover and waited. I only really saw him close enough to exchange a few words and pass on my sympathies, and that was yesterday afternoon.'

'Who told you about Alan's accident?'

'The police did, the day it happened. They had some questions about him, mostly routine: how often he came here, how long he'd been coming, how he paid for his lessons.' Another snigger. 'Not that Alan needed lessons. He'd got his licence; he just wanted to get as many hours in on the Moth as he could.'

'The Moth is the club's Tiger Moth,' offered Luther Romo.

'I guessed that,' said Campion, 'but those moths don't snack on insects, they run on fuel, and I suspect they use almost as much as that car of yours. Who paid for his flying time?'

'He did, of course,' said Norris. 'Always in cash and always up front before he climbed into the cockpit, regular as clockwork. I wish all our members were such prompt payers.'

'And this "uncle" of his you say came yesterday. What did he ask you?'

'Just if he could check Alan's locker to see if there were any personal items that Alan's parents might like to have.'

'Were there?'

'I don't know, I left him to it. He had a key – Alan's key,

I assumed. He said he'd leave it in the locker when he'd finished, which he did. He must have got what he needed and went. He seemed a decent enough bloke, obviously cut up about what had happened to Alan, so I didn't press him.'

'You didn't ask his name?'

'It didn't occur to me,' said Norris lightly. 'I mean, it was clearly the man who used to drive him here in the same Land Rover. He arrived when our last flight of the day was coming in, so we were watching that landing. The chap looked harmless and pretty sad, for obvious reasons. He walked with a limp and I suppose I felt a bit sorry for the old boy, so I just let him get on with it.'

The flying club's six lockers were standard, full-length, ex-government stock opened by a small key in a lock which kept the door closed and the contents only minimally secure. Campion was certain he could have picked the locks with a hairpin, and absolutely sure that Lugg could have removed the entire door with one sweep of a paw.

The second locker along had the key in the lock. Norris confirmed that it had been the one allocated to Alan Wormold, and Campion opened it carefully, as if expecting treasure to spill out. Nothing fell out and Campion stared in at the contents.

The bulkiest item by far, hanging from a simple screw hook, was a leather flying jacket, which on brief inspection was lined with a map of the South Pacific printed on the silk. Apart from that, the locker held only a school exercise book with the words 'A. Wormold Flight Log' handwritten in blue ink, and some loose coins: three halfpennies, two pennies and a three-penny bit.

'Standard procedure,' said Romo, observing Campion's puzzled expression. 'You leave all your pocket change on the ground when you go looping the loop.'

'I see,' said Campion and, after a cursory glance, handed the exercise book to Romo. 'You'd better have this, it will no doubt make more sense to you, but it might be useful to know where Wormold liked to fly.'

'And you ought to take the flying jacket. It can get kinda breezy where we're going.'

'We?' asked Mr Campion.

'I didn't come out here just to be your chauffeur, so I booked a session on the club's Tiger Moth. I like to keep my hand in, as you Brits say, and if you want to know where Alan flew, I can show you for real. I went up with him once.'

'Checking him out, were you?'

'Not at first, didn't know who he was. It was just two guys sharing flight time. It was only later I found out he worked on the Goshawk – and he found out what I did.'

'And when he did there were no more jollies into the wide blue yonder together?'

'But I kept an eye on the air miles he clocked up – the club keeps a record – and Alan never strayed too far.'

'No secret night flights to Moscow, then?'

'Not in a Tiger Moth, but you might be interested to see the ground he covered from the air.'

As they turned the corner of the main building, Mr Campion said, 'Now that's what I call a proper aeroplane.'

Across the closely cropped grass outside one of the corrugated metal half-pipe hangars was a bright yellow biplane with the registration G-ANFI stencilled on its fuselage. From that distance, he was almost convinced that Luther Romo's Chevrolet was longer than the aeroplane; it almost certainly had a higher top speed, yet he was not being flippant. For Mr Campion, who had been born before the Wright Brothers had taken to the air, this was the image of an aeroplane which had first imprinted itself on a youthful brain. Compared to the highly polished metal tubes which could carry a man, and an atomic bomb, at supersonic speeds, the very sort of aircraft his wife designed and helped build, this flimsy bundle of struts and flaps seemed little more than a boy's toy. Perhaps it really had been built from a kit with the aid of a very large tube of glue, he mused, and for some reason the thought cheered him, or at least made him forget his age. And if he was being honest, if not modest, he did cut rather a dashing figure in Alan Wormold's leather flying jacket, and was secure in the knowledge that if they were forced to land in the South Pacific, he had a map.

'It's got the correct number of wings,' said Mr Campion as they neared the parked aircraft, 'in the right place, facing the right way!'

'You're not a fan of the Goshawk then?'

'No matter how many times Amanda has tried to explain it, no doubt breaking numerous clauses of the Official Secrets Act in the process, it remains a mystery. This old dog is beyond learning new tricks and the Tiger is definitely my vintage.'

'You've flown in one before?'

'Once, before the war and before you were born, but only as a passenger. I sit in the front and you are the back-seat driver. Correct?'

'You got it,' said Romo, 'and if you've flown in a Tiger before, you'll know to take your false teeth out.' Campion smiled to indicate that such advice was superfluous. 'They're also as noisy as hell and it can sound as if you're strapped to a tractor, so you'll find a helmet with headphones for the intercom on your seat. There are goggles too, which should fit over your glasses, though that could be uncomfortable. You might want to take them off.'

'Then I'd be as blind as a bat and miss the wonderful view. Come on, let us up, up and away.'

As Campion clambered up and into the front open cockpit, he remembered, from that first flight in a Tiger Moth, the angry shout of his then pilot to keep his 'bloody feet off the bloody rudder pedals!' There had been no intercom or radio in those days, and instructions and information from the pilot in the second cockpit had come via shouts or thumps on the back of the passenger's head. It had been drilled into Campion that, as he was a joy rider rather than a pilot in training, he should touch none of the controls – especially those bloody pedals – and ignore the mysterious black dials on the dashboard. His pilot had said yes, in films, pilots always tap them with a bloody knuckle in the hope that they might suddenly produce more bloody fuel or even altitude, but it doesn't do any bloody good at all, except his instructor had not been polite enough to say 'bloody'.

The memory came back to him as Campion struggled to fit his long length into the cramped cockpit, twisting his legs around the joystick to avoid touching those bloody pedals. The leather flying helmet felt uncomfortably tight but, to his relief, the goggles fitted over his glasses, countering the blast of the slipstream from the spinning propellor, and the headphones and intercom system worked well, despite the powerful roar of the engine only a few inches in front of his knees.

In his ear he heard Romo talking to the control tower as the aeroplane began to bounce gently as it taxied over the grass parallel to the concrete runway.

'Bourn Radio, this is Tiger Moth Golf Alpha November Foxtrot India, two POB, one hour local, now departing zero-one-niner left.'

Whatever reply Bourn Radio made was indistinct as the engine noise increased dramatically and Campion was momentarily disorientated as Romo swung the Tiger left and right in order to give him a clear view ahead around the bulk of the forward fuselage and the back of Campion's head. Once on the runway proper, the aircraft surged forward, shaking and vibrating so much that Campion automatically hunched down behind the Perspex windscreen which offered only minimal protection from the elements.

'Tail up.'

Campion realized that Romo was talking to him and that the Tiger's fuselage was now level rather than angled down at the tail. And then the shaking stopped and the ground fell away, the engine noise seemed to drop a tone and another sound harmonized with it – the thrumming sound caused by the taut bracing wires between the wings. Mr Campion did not need the white needles on the black dials on the dashboard in front of him to know they were airborne and climbing slowly.

Leaning into the small windscreen for any shelter on offer from the slipstream, and grateful for the flying jacket which he wore over his totally inappropriate linen jacket, Campion turned his head and tried to make sense of the patchwork of fields and trees expanding below. There was a long straight road, with Matchbox-sized vehicles on it, which Campion thought might be pointing north, though in truth he had no idea in which direction they were flying, and frankly did not care as he was finding the whole experience rather exhilarating.

To say that Romo's voice in his helmet's earpieces brought him down to earth was literally ridiculous, but it did remind him of his half-promise to Amanda not to have too much fun whilst she was entombed back at Barton Road.

'What was that?'

'I said do you want to grab the joystick in front of you and take her for a spin?'

'Goodness me, no. I'll leave it to you professionals. The last thing the flying club needs is an untalented amateur playing the fool at this height. How high are we, anyway?'

'Fifteen hundred feet.'

'That's a long way to fall and I think you forgot to pack the parachutes.'

Campion flinched as Romo's laughter came as a braying assault on his eardrums. 'No room for parachutes. I thought you said you'd flown in a Tiger before.'

'I did, though that was before they invented parachutes, and for navigation we relied on a sundial or a sextant.'

'The good old days, eh? What did they call it? Flying by the seat of your pants?'

'Or by the seat of the instructor's pants.'

That had certainly been Mr Campion's original experience when, thirty years before, he had been tempted to take that flying lesson, or rather had been pushed into taking one by a group of younger friends who had been enthusiastic followers of the Schneider Trophy circus and the National Air Races in America. His instructor, a war-damaged and foul-mouthed veteran of the Royal Flying Corps, with an impenetrable Somerset accent, had subjected Campion to an hour-long lecture, made somehow more sinister by his West Country intonation, on how the Tiger Moth's open cockpit and its Gipsy Major four-cylinder engine guaranteed a cold, windy and very noisy experience without any luxuries such as a heater, or brakes! He had then gone on to list the dangers of flying a Tiger Moth, and the dangers of flying the particular Tiger Moth they were standing next to. By the end of the lecture, he had convinced Campion that the Tiger Moth could be 'a right bloody handful' which, in the wrong hands (his, obviously), would lapse into a fatal stall or a spin and that the aircraft he was about to climb into had been cursed by gods who had never intended men to fly, by which time Campion was promising himself never to fly in anything small enough and light enough to be pushed out of a hangar by a single middle-aged man. Since then he had certainly kept to his resolve not to be a passenger on any aeroplane which did not provide a steward serving cocktails, nor to ask his wife for any gruesome details of the flights she took as part of her work as a matter of course, although she was often keen to share her more hair-raising experiences of the jet age.

'So where d'you want to go, Al? The world's our oyster, or at least for about an hour's flying time at eighty knots, that's about ninety miles in English. We can roam the skies or go crop dusting, it's up to you as long as we don't go south into the airspace of RAF Bassingbourn, they get kinda touchy.'

'You said you knew where Alan Wormold liked to fly,' prompted Campion.

'Sure did. He always took the same flight path when he had the Tiger, at least to begin with. It's not that far from the airfield.'

'So can we circle round and do that?'

'Sure we can; just hang on to your stomach as we bank and turn, if you're sure.'

'I'm sure. And my stomach is secure.'

'Well, if you say so, though I could never figure what you Limeys see in eyeballing a place of public execution.'

FOURTEEN
Gibbet

The Tiger Moth performed a long, slow turn and, as the wings dipped, Mr Campion felt sure that there must be a law of gravity which said he really ought to have fallen out of his seat by now. Having defied gravity, however, he relaxed and began to enjoy the view as the plane descended to around five hundred feet above the green and brown quilt that was the Cambridgeshire countryside. He got his bearings when the airfield at Bourn came into view, and was reassured to see that Luther Romo's red Chevrolet was parked where they had left it, though he admitted to himself that any opportunist thief hoping to steal a mode of transport from an airfield might have been less conspicuous if he had driven off with a Tiger Moth rather than the Chevrolet.

A narrow road appeared below them, running north and east (Campion had finally got his bearings), and it was a road so suspiciously straight that it had to be Roman rather than Anglo-Saxon. Up ahead, a mere half-minute's flying time away, it was crossed by the main road to Bedford.

'That is Ermine Street down there,' he said into his intercom microphone, 'a famous Roman road.'

'And up ahead, at the crossroads, there's the gallows,' came the crackled reply.

'Technically, it's a gibbet,' said Campion. 'I know it well.'

The gibbet at the Caxton crossroads had been known to travellers for more than two hundred years, according to local legend, though Mr Campion doubted it had been a continuous tourist attraction, especially since the public's taste for displaying the corpses of executed miscreants had waned some-what. There were references to a place of execution at those ancient crossroads from 1745, but the original fatal mechanism was long gone and in fact the gibbet which now acted as a

gruesome road sign was not much older than Mr Campion
himself, almost certainly erected by the enterprising landlord
of the nearby Gibbet Inn around the turn of the century.

Campion had visited that austere and rather gloomy hostelry
in his undergraduate days. In those days, the university strictly
prohibited the ownership of cars by students, although the
more enterprising ones had vehicles secretly garaged in nearby
Cherry Hinton, and the idea of a jaunt out into the countryside
to a well-known gruesome landmark and its associated public
house which was – supposedly – haunted was difficult to resist.

The expedition had disappointed, as most spur-of-the-
moment student japes did. The gibbet itself, if spotted at
twilight or through an early morning mist, was probably spooky
enough for most passing trade, but the Gibbet Inn, as it was
then called, provided no ghosts, only the opportunity for
juvenile humour. It seemed a good idea to test whether Paine's
beers, from Paine's brewery in St Neots, were really painful
– if consumed in copious quantities. Similarly, much childish
amusement was derived from the large metallic sign on the
inn's frontage advertising 'Thorley's Cake' when it was discovered that it referred not to the provision of a sweetmeat, but
to a brand of cattle and pig feed which might appeal to the
agricultural community.

'Can we get lower?' Campion asked his pilot.

'I'll bring her round for another pass,' Romo replied, 'and
drop to two hundred and fifty feet. Any lower and the club
will get complaints from the pub down there.'

Campion thought there was little chance of that as he could
see the pub's car park was empty, suggesting that any passing
trade, even on a fine Saturday afternoon, had kept on passing by.
The Caxton Gibbet Inn, as it now was, operated under the
disadvantage of not having a village around it from which to
draw customers. It stood alone, bleak and grey near the crossroads, with only the ghoulish lure of a gibbet, and a replica
one at that, to attract business. Unless, of course, the pub still
did a healthy trade in Thorley's cattle cake.

Romo guided the plane in a wide, gentle turn which did
not upset Mr Campion's stomach in the slightest. He was
actually beginning to enjoy himself, admiring the countryside

below and having become used to – or possibly immune to – the loud chattering of the engine and the icy slipstream which had numbed his cheeks and fingers. As they lined up for a second, lower pass over the inn and the gibbet, Romo's voice crackled again in his ear.

'So what's the difference?'

'Between what?'

'Between a gallows and a gibbet,' Romo said, as if it was the most natural enquiry in the world.

'A gallows simply does the job and hangs you,' said Campion, 'but a gibbet is where you get hanged and perhaps other unpleasant things are done to you and then you are left to dangle as an example to the general populace until the crows and nature finish off your mortal remains.'

'Cool,' said Romo.

'I hardly think so.'

'Wormold thought so. When I went up with him, he was very interested in what was going on around that gibbet, and – according to his log – he always flew this way when he went up alone.'

'That's interesting,' Campion strained his neck for a better view as the Tiger Moth's shimmering shadow crossed over the gibbet below, 'though there's not much to see.'

'Except the guy who was messing around down there.'

Mr Campion had a sudden, irrational desire to stand up, turn around and confront Romo face-to-face, but he wisely stayed in his seat.

'There's nobody down there. I didn't see anyone.'

'I didn't mean *now*, you goof-ball,' drawled Romo, 'but back when I went up with Alan that first time. He spotted a guy by that gibbet thing who looked like he was trying to dig it up. Alan got quite excited about it.'

'What did you do?'

'Do? We carried on flying. What should we have done? Circled round and machine-gunned him? He wasn't King Kong and that may be one of your monuments down there, but it ain't the Empire State Building.'

'Did you see who it was?'

'No, sir, the guy was purely bad-mannered and didn't look

up as we went over, though we were probably too high anyway. I'm pretty sure Alan recognized his vehicle, though.'

'Really?'

'Yeah, it was a Land Rover, like the one they have at Goshawk.'

'Can we go round again?' asked Mr Campion.

There was a loud noise in Campion's ear, which at first he thought must be a malfunction of the intercom system but then realized was a long, low sigh.

'Jeez! If you'd only wanted to come this far, we should have taken my car; we'd have burned less fuel.'

'I seriously doubt that,' Campion replied, 'but I'm more than happy to split the petrol bill for this little jaunt.'

'OK then, I'm just the cab driver. You'll be asking me to land there next.'

'Is that possible?' Campion snapped his head to the side and peered out and down, trying to survey the land around the gibbet, but the Tiger Moth had flown beyond it and Romo was already negotiating another majestically slow 180-degree turn.

'Actually, it is possible . . . kinda.'

'Are you sure? You don't sound terribly sure. Good grief, you're not thinking of landing on the road, are you?'

'That'd scare the local hayseeds for sure,' laughed Romo, 'but it'd probably get me a ticket for a moving traffic violation. Might be best to stay off the highway and use the landing strip.'

'You mean back at Bourn?'

'No, the strip near the gibbet, on the other side of that Roman road you're so proud of. It was designated a Relief Landing Ground by the RAF during the war, in case of emergencies. It's grass and maybe a bit rocky, but at least it hasn't been ploughed up. Didn't you see it as we passed?'

'No,' said Campion. 'I make a point of never telling a taxi driver the best route to follow. It's only good manners.'

'I'll take her down then. It might be bumpy but it's sort of legal – well, it would be if we had an emergency.'

'If anyone complains later, we'll say I developed a sudden and dramatic fear of flying and went into an absolute blue funk. You had to put down immediately and slap me until I came to my senses.'

'And I was happy to oblige,' said Romo rather disconcertingly.

The biplane made a broad sweep north of the crossroads and then, with the engine throttled back to an indignant grumble, began its descent towards the pub, the gibbet and a landing strip, which had probably not been used in anger for twenty years. At least Campion could see it now, or thought he could: a long rectangle to the east of Ermine Street where the grass was shorter and darker than whatever was growing to each side of the strip. Fancifully, Campion imagined the local tenant farmer grumpily mowing that long stretch of lawn when he would much rather be trundling a harrow over it and seeding it with something more profitable.

There were no farmers working the nearby fields – or 'local hayseeds' as Romo would have called them – to witness the Tiger Moth's frequent circling of the Caxton Gibbet and ponder that here was a peculiar moth seemingly attracted to a grisly flame. Nor did any outraged customers come rushing out of the Caxton Gibbet Inn as the plane swept over its roof, so low that Campion was sure he could hear the tiles rattle, and its shadow flitted across Ermine Street.

'Here we go,' instructed his pilot, and the ground came up to meet them. 'Keep an eye out for fences and telephone wires.'

'Right-ho,' said Mr Campion, his eyes firmly closed as the Tiger Moth's undercarriage connected with East Anglian pasture with a teeth-jarring thump.

The plane shook, rocked and shuddered, and at one point seemed in danger of tipping over and burying its snout – and Mr Campion – in the grass screaming underneath its wheels. From the grunts and blasphemies in his headphones, Campion could only guess that Romo, behind him, was fighting the controls to keep the aircraft straight as it bounced and skidded for what seemed an unfeasible amount of time. Suddenly their headlong progress came to a halt, the engine at idle and the propellor turning lazily, until Luther Romo switched off the magneto and it floated to a complete stop.

Campion felt a strong hand on his shoulder, as though someone was shaking him awake.

'*Terra firma*,' said Luther Romo. 'Let's walk on it.'

Mr Campion left his flying helmet and goggles on his cockpit seat and was delighted to be able to stretch his long legs, leading the way as they strode over the grass strip, back towards the road and the dark wooden silhouette of the gibbet, a giant upside-down letter 'L', standing on a small mound, which close up looked far less intimidating than it did from a distance.

'So what are we looking for?' asked Romo, patting the worn timber with one hand whilst lighting a cigarette with the other. 'If we had a length of rope, we could make a noose and pose for a picture.'

'We have neither rope nor camera,' said Campion, 'and I have no idea what we're looking for. You brought me here.'

'Hey – I just flew the plane.'

'But you said Alan Wormold spotted something here.'

'He certainly did when I flew with him, and his flight logs show he always buzzed this place every time he went up.'

'That first time, you said there was a man, a man who didn't look up.'

Romo laughed, exhaling a cloud of smoke. 'Well, you know what they say: never go on vacation to a country where they look up in wonder when an aircraft goes over.' He caught Campion's deadpan expression. 'Guess that's not helpful, eh?'

'That wasn't exactly the point I was making, but never mind,' said Campion. 'Wormold saw someone here doing something – but what?'

'Could have been a tourist.'

'I don't think so, because I think – I'm sure – that Alan knew who it was.'

'The Land Rover?'

'Exactly, the same Land Rover that gave him a regular lift to the Bourn Airfield and which turned up there yesterday.'

Romo drew on his cigarette and leaned casually against the gibbet. 'You've thought this through,' he said.

'That's what I do.' Campion grinned. 'I have no useful skills of any kind.'

Mr Campion looked around him. He looked across fields, he looked up and down the roads both ancient and modern, he looked across at the gloomy pub, he even examined closely the gibbet itself from the grassy mound in which it was embedded, up its dark, gnarled length to the sinister span which topped it, and he slowly shook his head.

'No flashes of inspiration?'

'Not a spark. There's nothing here.'

Romo patted the upright of the gibbet with the flat of his hand. 'I suppose they put these things at crossroads so they could display the victims to passing travellers as a warning to keep their noses clean.'

'*Pour encourager les autres*,' said Campion.

'If you say so,' Romo said with a shrug, his eyes masked by his reflective sunglasses. 'Crossroads are surely crazy places. We have a story about a black guitar player who sold his soul to the devil at a crossroads at midnight, so he could become the best blues player in the world, and then ain't it vampires you're supposed to bury at a crossroad? Or is that werewolves?'

'That's it!' Campion exclaimed, not only surprising Romo, but himself, or rather the two images of him reflected in the gleaming lenses of the aviator glasses. 'The chap you and Wormold saw could have been burying something.'

'He didn't have a pick or a shovel or anything.'

'There's no sign he was burying a vampire or a werewolf, so it could be something fairly small. Maybe he was leaving a message for someone.'

'Like a dead letter box? You know that expression?'

'I'm afraid I do,' said Campion, bending over and peering at the ground around the base of the gibbet. 'Let's look for it, it's got to be easy to get at. Anyone hanging around here for too long would look suspicious.'

Romo barked out a laugh as he tugged up the creases of his trousers and sank to his knees. 'Hanging around . . . That's very good. Is that what you Limeys call "gallows humour"?'

'Yes, it is,' said Campion, now also on his knees and wafting the palms of both hands over the clumps of grass on the gibbet mound. 'Though we spell humour properly.'

Romo grunted a mild expletive, which Campion thought at first was a reaction to his comment, then he realized that the American was sucking the heel of his right hand. As he brought it away from his mouth, Campion could see an inch-long scratch glistening red.

'I think I've found what you're looking for,' said Romo, 'and there's two of them.'

After some scrabbling and at least one broken fingernail each, they extracted two steel tubes, each about a foot long and an inch and a half in diameter, with one end having been hammered flat and folded into crude points, the other, circular end being plugged with what was clearly a piece of wax candle, complete with a white, unburned stub of wick.

'Why don't you look surprised?' asked Luther Romo, shaking loose dirt from one of the tubes. 'Come to think of it, you never look surprised.'

'I went to an English public school,' said Campion, examining the other tube, 'and am therefore well practised in curbing my enthusiasm.'

'But you've seen these things before.'

'Yes, I have. They are pieces of Reynolds steel tubing, which is used at the Goshawk Project for modelling airframes as well as other things. Nugent Monck reported that supplies of it were being pilfered and I think he was right. I saw some of it stashed at Alan Wormold's digs.'

'And somebody made tent pegs out of it?'

'They look like that so the pointed end can be pushed into the ground easily. The other end is sealed with a candle to keep whatever's in there waterproof.'

'So what do we do? Open one up, see what's inside?'

'A quick peek,' Campion was firm, 'then we put them back exactly how we found them and we tell the police.'

Luther Romo, still on his knees, pulled down his sunglasses and looked at Campion over the mirrored lenses. 'You already know what's in these tubes, don't you?'

'I have a pretty good idea.'

Romo eased out an inch-long stub of candle by its wick as gently as a sommelier opening the most expensive wine on his list, and with one finger scooped out a twirl of a tightly rolled document coloured blue.

'As I thought,' said Campion.

'And when were you going to share your thought?' countered the American, tapping the paper down into the tube and twisting back the candle-wax stopper.

'Whenever you decided to tell me what your real interest in the Goshawk Project is.'

'We've still got some flying time due to us,' said Romo as he helped Campion back into the front cockpit of the Tiger Moth and strapped him in. 'It might look suspicious if we get back to base too soon.'

'Good point,' admitted Campion, pulling on his leather helmet. 'My wife thinks I'm out on a jolly this afternoon, so let's have a bit of a jolly. Will there be any problem taking off?'

'Well, unless you want to harvest some wheat or whatever it is growing in that next field, I'll turn us around so we can take off into the wind, such as it is. There should be enough room for us to miss the gibbet and hopefully clear the pub.'

'Your choice of words such as *should* and *hopefully* inspire me with confidence,' said Campion drily. 'Do you want me to get out?'

'No, stay where you are. I can handle it.'

Campion did as he was told, and once again pondered the folly of two grown men trusting their weight, and lives, to a machine flimsy enough, as Luther Romo was demonstrating, to be turned completely around by one man putting his shoulder to the tail end of the fuselage. He promised himself that his next trip into the wide blue yonder would be in nothing smaller than a Boeing 707, but thought it diplomatic not to share this thought with his pilot who, satisfied that the Tiger Moth was pointed in the right direction, was leaning into the rear cockpit fiddling with controls, but not climbing aboard.

Romo jumped down off the plane and jogged to the front, where he set the position of the propellor after a couple of turns, then nipped back to his cockpit again to turn on the magnetos. This ritual, for Mr Campion, was the most unnerving part of the drama involved in getting airborne, for he knew what came next. Romo once more returned to the propellor, flipping a casual salute towards Campion before placing his right hand midway along one blade and applying all the force of his shoulder into a mighty heave with a rolling motion, which took him out of reach as the engine caught and the blades began to rotate.

The engine noise settled into a steady idle, with a distinctive crackling sound coming from the exhaust stubs, and the aircraft began to vibrate. Mr Campion took a deep breath and reassured himself that, through the sheer force of his will, the Tiger Moth would not take off under its own steam whilst he was alone in the cockpit and the professional pilot was still on the ground.

He was startled out of his reverie by Romo's voice over the intercom. 'OK, here we go. Cross your fingers and say a prayer.'

That settled it, thought Campion – his next flight would be first class on Pan-Am.

The engine roared and the Tiger Moth rumbled then surged forward, the wings rocking violently. To Campion, it felt like a ride on a broken rollercoaster, and the end of the landing strip, flagged by the ominous outline of the Caxton Gibbet and the roof of the Caxton Gibbet Inn, seemed to be approaching far too quickly.

Then Romo worked his magic with throttle, joystick, and the help of whichever gods pilots pray to, and the Tiger Moth left soil and grass behind and ascended into its natural element, clearing both gibbet and its namesake hostelry with ease.

'I thought we might fly up to Godmanchester before turning back, just to see the sights and use up the fuel you're paying for.'

'Sounds good to me,' said Campion into the intercom, now oddly more relaxed that they had left the ground. 'There's a wonderful medieval bridge there over the river into Huntingdon.'

'I somehow figured you'd know that. Medieval bridges seem far more your thing than swept-forward wing jet fighters.'

'Do I detect an invitation to talk shop, as we innocent English might say?'

'If you mean getting down to business, then yeah, and you ain't goin' anywhere, are you?'

'Apart from back to earth in one piece, I hope. Are you suggesting, as you quaintly put it, that we share information?'

'Got a better idea for some in-flight conversation?'

'Lots, actually, but you're the one controlling this machine and therefore, as you Americans would say, you are the one calling the shots. Why don't you go first? Let the interrogation begin.'

'It's kinda difficult asking questions to the back of a guy's head. How will I know if you're giving me straight answers?'

'My dear chap, this was your idea. Why not just assume that everything I say is obfuscation at best, at worst a down-right lie?'

'Because I don't think you are a very good liar.'

'I shall take that as a compliment. Ooh look, there's the Godmanchester bridge, built in the fourteenth century, if memory serves.'

'I'll take your word on that.' Romo's tone was impossible to gauge over the crackling intercom. 'Now tell me something I don't know but might be interested in.'

'If I can.'

'Why is Lady Amanda persevering with the Goshawk design?'

'It's her job, her vocation, her passion. It is what she does, why should she not?'

'Because it won't work. Modern jets have wings swept *back* at an angle of thirty degrees, swept-forward wings are just a theoretical concept. Alandel doesn't have the computing tech-nology to make the thing fly – nobody does.'

Campion said nothing and the Tiger Moth performed a long and lazy right turn, leaving Godmanchester and its stone bridge behind and picking up the line of Ermine Street again.

It was Luther Romo who broke the silence. 'That's the point, isn't it?'

'I don't know what you mean,' said Mr Campion.

'The whole Goshawk Project is a goldarned set-up, or my name's Chuck Yeager, and what was in those metal tubes at the gibbet? That was bait, wasn't it?'

'That could be one interpretation.'

'Don't give me that! You know what a dead letter box is, you said so. That gibbet is a dead letter box, and whilst you might be interested in the postman who delivers there, I'm more interested in the guy picking up the mail.'

The aircraft was approaching the Caxton crossroads and, although higher than they had been on previous passes, Campion could clearly see the gibbet below. 'I think that might be him, down there, right now.'

'What?'

'By the gibbet.' Campion put his arm over the side of the cockpit and pointed downwards. 'A man on a motorbike has come to collect his post.'

From that height and distance, it was impossible to distinguish any detail other than that it was quite definitely a human figure, a black ant, moving in an upright human way from the gibbet mound back to the road to mount a shiny black motorcycle.

Romo played with the controls and the right wings of the Tiger Moth dipped slightly to give him a better view. 'Shall we buzz him? It would scare the hell out of him.'

'And probably me too,' replied Campion, concentrating on the bike rider, who he realized was dressed in black leathers and helmet. 'He hasn't noticed us, so let's keep it that way, just see where he's going.'

'We can't follow him. That bike can outrun us on the straight and flat, and all the roads round here are straight and flat.'

'Can we sort of circle innocently again and keep an eye on him, see which way he goes?'

'Wilco.'

Below them the motorbike pulled away from the gibbet mound, heading for the crossroads with the main A428 road. A left turn would be towards St Neots and Bedford, right would be back into Cambridge. The bike turned right and accelerated away.

'How far are we from Bourn?' Campion asked into the intercom.

'About five minutes to touch down.'

'Good, I need to use a telephone.'

'We have a radio, you know,' said Romo. 'We could ask Bourn to call the cops for you, save some time.'

'No, thank you,' Campion replied. 'Let's keep this to ourselves, shall we?'

There was an unexpected silence in Campion's headset, then Luther Romo surprised him and made him grin broadly. 'I like the way you think, Mr C. I'm figuring it's going to be fun working with you.'

FIFTEEN
Lady in Waiting

Amanda had been determined to be bored and had no interest whatsoever in an afternoon of televised sport. After feeding the two cats, who had promptly disappeared having urgent business elsewhere, she had drifted around the Barton Road house, idly wondering how John Branscombe's wife would have filled her Saturdays if the outside world had been denied her. And then she had gently bitten her lip and blushed – if it was possible to blush when no one was there to witness it – as she remembered that Mrs Branscombe had indeed had a hobby which had occupied her spare time, and he was an astrophysicist.

The positioning of the house meant that there were no easily available neighbours to distract her or – to put it more bluntly – to spy on, even though she had Mr Campion's small but powerful binoculars and lots of lace curtains to hide behind. There was, however, one neighbour she could observe from the back garden without being herself spied upon, and that was the Goshawk hangar across the rough open ground beyond the Bin Brook.

It was nothing more than an idle whim on her part when she took the binoculars, strode across the little stream, and brought the Goshawk building into focus. Being a Saturday and a day of employee rest, Amanda expected little more than the reassurance that the building was still there and intact.

Instead, she saw more people than she could count or recognize milling around the open main doors. Indeed, there seemed to be quite a party going on over there, and for a moment considered ringing John Branscombe at Magdalene to ask if he had authorized a disconcertingly large amount of overtime. There again, she was bored and had nothing better to do that morning, and so decided to investigate herself.

She had, of course, every right to go round there and demand to know what was going on, but that would have been an overly dramatic – and not easily explained – reappearance on site of the technical director of the Goshawk Project, who was supposedly detained at Her Majesty's pleasure with a rumoured charge of treason pending. On balance, a more subtle approach was required, along with clothing more suitable to a rough shoot or a spot of deer stalking rather than the role of the bored housewife.

Back in the house she exchanged her skirt for a pair of black ski-pants and liberated a dark green pullover from her husband's luggage to cover her floral-patterned blouse. As camouflage, it would have to do, but what really needed hiding was her hair, and for that she used the tartan headscarf she always carried in case of sudden thunderstorms. It was less than ideal, but it did contain most of her pinned-up red mane and was infinitely less ridiculous than resorting to John Branscombe's homburg again. Their absentee landlord, however, could provide the requisite footwear needed.

Amanda had, whilst idly touring the house, done the only natural thing in such circumstances, and opened every unlocked door and cupboard in order to orientate herself. A large cupboard under the stairs seemed to double as a wardrobe as well as storage space for Branscombe's golf clubs. She had already borrowed the homburg from there, and now she helped herself to the smallest pair of Wellingtons which, with the application of two pairs of socks, fitted her dainty feet.

Thus prepared, with the binoculars hanging around her neck, Amanda strode into the garden again, this time splashing into the Bin Brook and began to follow its course in what she estimated would take her in a right-hand flanking movement at least as far as the disused rifle range (or sunken tennis court as she imagined it), which should give her a clear view of the open door of the Goshawk hangar. By keeping low and sticking to the stream, which hardly covered her ankles, she was sure she could not be seen from the Goshawk building, even if anyone was looking in her direction, and she began to feel, with a frisson of excitement, that she was a Red Indian scout creeping up on a camp of unsuspecting pioneer settlers in a bad 'B' Western.

These particular extras from *Wagon Train* certainly did not appear to suspect that they were about to be attacked, or even casually observed, for as she got nearer, Amanda could distinctly hear music floating across the open ground. It was not loud enough to annoy any of the residents of Barton Road and the closer she got, the tinnier the sound became, betraying the fact that it came from a transistor radio. As a senior executive of the Goshawk Project, she was irritated that some of her staff were making unofficial use of supposedly sensitive and secure premises. As a wife, she was secretly delighted that she recognized the song being broadcast – 'Bring It on Home to Me' by a pop group called The Animals – where her husband would certainly not.

Standing upright, her feet still in the brook and her eyes glued to the binoculars, she could make out at least three female figures milling around the entrance to the hangar, which was rather disconcerting, not to say hurtful, as Amanda had on numerous occasions taken Professor Branscombe to task for not having any female postgraduate students.

Then she spotted two males she thought she recognized and one she definitely did: Ted Toomey, who seemed to be marshalling the troops – or was it a workforce? She had to get closer to be sure.

Here the Bin Brook cut into and across the shallow end of the rifle range. This would be where raw recruits had lain prone and shot across the little stream, aiming at the target butts way down to her left in the deeper cut of the trench. Stepping out of the stream, the length of the trench stretched before her, a long sunken rectangle, which she agreed with Albert was like being in an empty swimming pool. It was featureless apart from a rusting oil drum lying on its side at her end. As she walked by it, just to make sure it was empty, she kicked it and heard a reassuring chime like that of a dinner gong, then she cursed as she had to forcibly remove her Wellington-booted foot from the hole it had made in the lid of the drum, now paper-thin with rust.

As she reached the far end, she dug footholes with her heels in the side wall to make herself a 'firing step' (just as they had in trenches on the Somme) and, with the aid of a tussock of grass, hauled herself up until her head was, as Albert would have said, above the parapet.

She recalled her husband's description of feeling as if he was 'going over the top' as he climbed out of the sunken feature, and she could not help but think of old newsreels of trenches in World War One, the image reinforced by the fact that the ground ahead contained a random spread of broken posts bedecked with limp strands of barbed wire.

With the binoculars she had an excellent view of the hangar doors, now wide open, and a glimpse of the shadowy interior, although Ted Toomey and his student friends seemed to have retreated inside. Somebody had turned off the radio, but muffled sounds floated across the rough ground; sounds of machinery and the clanking of metal, along with sharp but indistinct commands being shouted, interspersed with bursts of high-pitched, almost certainly female, laughter.

Then there was movement as something slowly began to emerge from the hangar.

With all her experience of aeronautical engineering and a natural instinct to tinker with, and hopefully improve, anything mechanical, Amanda had seen nothing like it.

First came the front wheel and handlebars of a bicycle, except it wasn't a bicycle's front wheel – it looked more like a transplant from a motorbike, but the frame was that of a bicycle and it had a chain and pedals and a seat, from which dangled a pair of shapely bare legs which started in very short white shorts and ended in bright white tennis shoes.

Yet it was not those legs – the flesh so pale against the stark gunmetal frame as they pumped the pedals – which hypnotized Amanda, but rather that they were followed by a second pair. Where a normal bicycle's back wheel should have been, the frame had been extended to take another set of handlebars, another pair of pedals, and another female rider, this one wearing what looked like cricket flannels rolled up to the knee and black ballet shoes.

Neither girl appeared to have been press-ganged into providing the motive power for this tandem; indeed, they were smiling and laughing, their hair flying over their faces. But then, it wasn't a tandem.

A third co-joined rider appeared, and then a fourth, both females, as the frame of the machine went on and on. By the time Amanda recognized the fifth rider as Ted Toomey, the engineer part of her brain had worked out that she was watching the birth of a mechanical Frankenstein's creature, bicycle frames made from Reynolds steel tubing, she noted wryly, welded together to make a single unwieldy, highly impractical and probably illegal vehicle.

Finally, the back wheel, another motorbike cast-off, and the last rider, pedalling furiously, emerged from the hangar and Amanda did a quick recount. There were, amazingly, ten riders between the two wheels, which explained why they were not regular bicycle wheels, but wider, stronger ones from a motor-bike, because of the strains and stresses of the lengthy frame, something she could only think of as its fuselage. Despite the squeals of laughter from its riders – or should that be 'crew'? – the majority of whom were female, this behemoth of a machine remained shakily upright as it snaked out of the hangar and turned slowly on to the car parking area.

The mechanical part of Amanda's brain whirred into action as she worked out how the students had performed this feat of engineering, by manufacturing ten small basic frames from the Reynolds tubing, then slotting or soldering them together and adding the required number of seats, one set of handlebars over the front wheel forks for steering and controlling the brakes, if there were indeed any brakes, and then nine decora-tive ones, useful for the riders to hang on to. It had taken quite some imagination – not to mention skill – to organize its manufacture, and a good deal of nerve to volunteer as a rider. It would require a good deal of blind faith in the 'driver' on the front set of handlebars and, she suspected, the final position had the responsibility of shouting at the riders, rather like a cox in the Boat Race, to make sure they remained upright and did not unbalance the whole structure.

She was proved right when the contraption (would it be a *decadem*?), after travelling a good thirty or forty yards, was brought to a sudden stop with a cry of 'Brake!' and a yell of

'Left!' from the cox. With perfect coordination, all the riders took their left feet from the pedals and placed them on the ground, and the machine came to a quivering but at least upright halt. A small cheer went up from the ten riders, and Ted Toomey dismounted nimbly in order to address his fellow cyclists – or was that to take their applause, as several were clapping enthusiastically.

Amanda could not make out the exact words, but Teddy was clearly indicating that his cycling display team needed to practise their skills along the length of the car park and then back again. Then he remounted seat number five, the mid-point of this most bizarre velocipede, one foot poised on a pedal until, at a shout from the rear-gunner position, all ten riders pressed down with one foot whilst lifting the other off the ground and the metal monstrosity snaked off down the length of the hangar and then performed a painfully slow and wobbly right turn, with several of the riders sticking out their right arms in accordance with the rules of the Cycling Proficiency Test, others clinging to their handlebars for dear life.

Having turned back on itself, the machine picked up speed for the return journey, with commendable efficiency if not grace, directed by shouted orders from the 'pilot' at the front and the 'cox' at the rear. Amanda was impressed by the fact that these two key positions were occupied by females and did a quick headcount, noting that seven of the riders were female and only three were male, almost the reverse of the sex ratio among Cambridge students. It made her wonder how Ted Toomey had managed to recruit so many girls. Perhaps he was what Lugg would call 'a bit of a dark horse'.

After two more runs the length of the car-parking area without serious incident, although there were a couple of severe tremors in the stability of the machine, resulting in excited shrieks of surprise rather than injury, the machine turned, rather sedately, back towards the hangar doors and disappeared inside, like a snake sliding into its nesting hole or the burrow of some potential prey.

Standing on her makeshift firing step, Amanda dug her elbows into the earth on the top lip of the sunken range and brought her binoculars to bear again on the open door of the hangar. After a few minutes, a pair of girls emerged wheeling bicycles – regular ones, suitable for only one rider at a time, with carrying baskets on the front. They waved over their shoulders to those still in the hangar, mounted and pedalled off towards the access lane and the Madingley Road. Another pair of girls wearing scarves with twin red and white stripes, which identified them as students of Girton College, emerged arm-in-arm and followed the same route on foot, then three more girls and two boys appeared as a group, all pushing bicycles and chatting animatedly amongst themselves.

Amanda had no thought of being spotted, as only the top of her head was visible at ground level, and the tartan headscarf she had thrown on had colours dark enough to be almost perfect camouflage for the terrain, but none of the students – and more college scarves proved they were students – so much as glanced in her direction across the wasteland. Why would they?

Then the last of them, Ted Toomey, was sliding the hangar's door closed and locking it before not only looking in Amanda's direction, but striding purposefully towards her.

Instinctively she ducked her head and jumped down on to the floor of the rifle range, certain – well, almost certain, that he could not have seen her. She scuttled back towards the other end, pausing after ten yards to claw her way up the side again, her boots scrabbling for a brief foothold, so that she could peep over the edge. By pure luck, the top of her head emerged level with a thick clump of dock leaves which, she reasoned, not only provided something to hide behind but might come in useful to ease the nettle stings she was acquiring on her hands and wrists.

Confident that Ted Toomey had not spotted her yet, she was disconcerted to see that he was heading for the very place she had just abandoned. To avoid the barbed-wire entanglements and wire fences on the open ground, he would almost certainly cut across the rifle range as she and Albert had on their excursions from Barton Road. No sooner had she thought this through, the realization struck her that Toomey must be making for Barton Road himself, and almost certainly number 112

– where else? – and if he dropped down into the trench, he could not possibly fail to see her.

In the sunken shooting range, she was as exposed as a spider in an empty shoebox without a lid; there was nowhere she could scuttle to, no place to hide. Except one place, behind the one thing which might conceal her.

Not helped by the borrowed Wellingtons, she ran back to the far end of the range almost to the point where she had entered it, to where the rusting oil drum lay on its side. She flung herself down behind it, adopting a foetal position and checking that her boots were not sticking out beyond the end. She reached above her head with both hands and her fingertips grasped the top rim, hugging the drum close to her body and keeping her lips tightly together to avoid tasting the tiny flakes of rust which floated from it.

She was convinced that Toomey, if he had dropped into and crossed the range, could not see her but, there again, she could not see him; he had, she thought, been downright unhelpful by not coughing loudly, or whistling a catchy tune to reveal his progress. She counted silently to one hundred then risked raising her head to peep over the curve of the oil drum to discover if the coast, or at least the rest of the range, was clear. Which was just as well, for as she moved, so did the drum. It rolled only a few inches, a half-turn at most, but it did so with the audible clinking sound of something rolling around inside it. That turn of the cylinder also revealed that a series of neat holes, all in an area which could be covered by a playing card, had been punched in the side of the drum.

Amanda made a mental note but dealt with her primary concern of where Toomey was, which involved launching herself across the trench and establishing a foothold in the side which enabled her to, once more, put her head above the parapet.

The inelegance of her position, clinging to the side wall like a starfish on a rock, coupled with the fact that her clothes were now stained with dirt, crushed vegetation and brown patches of rust, was alleviated by the sight of the back of Ted Toomey as he continued towards the back garden of 112 Barton Road.

She decided that the best route was to trace her watery steps back through the Bin Brook, which would bring her, hopefully, to a position where she could see what was going on without herself being seen. She could not, however, resist returning to the oil drum which had sheltered her.

She raised the drum until it stood on one end, the wafer-thin rusted end which she had punctured with a casual kick, and examined the neat holes in the side; then she grasped it firmly with both hands and shook it, listened carefully to the metallic rattle coming from within it then laid it back down on its side. The end of the drum, which she had already punctured, gave way completely to three rapid kicks and she was able to get a good view of the dank interior.

Very gently, to avoid cuts and scrapes from jagged edges, she ran her fingers through the dust and fine particles of rust which she had shaken free and located three small nodules of solid, rust-free metal.

She might not have the experience of her husband in such matters, but she knew spent bullets when she saw them.

She returned to the Bin Brook, and by wading in midstream and crouching, she was confident she could not be seen. When she risked standing up straight she could see no sign of Ted Toomey; her obvious conclusion was that he had entered Branscombe's house via the garden and back door.

The only reason she could think of for his action was that he was hoping to find Mr Campion at home and waiting for *Grandstand* to come on the telly. Either that or, knowing that Campion was out, he was starting a new career as a burglar. Amanda had to find out, which meant getting nearer and possibly confronting Toomey, even if it meant having to explain why she was no longer in custody, though given the filth which had accumulated on her hands and clothes, and probably on her face, there was a good chance she could pass for an escaped convict and scare him away without having to admit anything.

The realization that one of her boots was letting in water did not deter her from pressing on down the brook until she reached the gap in the hedge at the bottom of Branscombe's garden. From there she had a clear view up the garden path, past the octagonal summer house and water butt to the back door, which was ominously wide open. Taking a deep breath, she stepped out of the brook and, bent almost double like a pantomime witch, scurried up the path trying to ignore the sloshing sound coming from her right foot.

She was at the door and, technically, her head was inside the house before she heard voices coming from the kitchen, one of them certainly female, and her stomach churned at the realization that she could easily have been seen through the kitchen window as she approached.

The male voice she recognized as Toomey's; he was not so much talking to the female as pleading with her.

'Please . . . please take it. I have done what you asked, now do this for me . . .'

But the only responses he received were in the negative.

'No! I cannot accept, it is impossible. You should not be here . . . we should not be here.'

'It's safe. I told you, he's out for the day, gone flying with that American officer.'

'Even so, this is not the time or the place for the making of love. Now you must go and so must I before I am seen.'

'Please—'

'Enough! Go and take this with you. Give it to some English girl.'

If Ted Toomey was not quick enough to take a hint, Amanda certainly was and, preferring concealment to confrontation, she turned away and scurried for her emergency refuge, the summer house, thankful for Albert's precaution of ensuring it could only be locked from the inside.

Secured in the semi-darkness, she kicked off the Wellingtons and peeled off the socks trusting her stockinged feet – one of them very damp – to reduce the chance of a creaking floorboard giving away her presence. There were enough cracks and knotholes in the structure to give her a view, albeit limited, of the path up to the back door, and she pressed her face to one at the most convenient height even if, in doing so, she felt dust and cobwebs settle on her nose and in her hair.

Through her adopted spyhole, she saw Ted Toomey emerge from the back door. She realized she had not bolted for cover a moment too soon and was relieved that she had not sought to confront him, despite having every right to do so. She had, after all, every right to be in the house; he had not.

And apart from the fact that she must look as if she had been dragged through a hedge backwards, it was never a good idea, unless one was blessed with supreme amounts of patience and charity, to engage with a young man who had clearly had his amorous advances rebuffed. Toomey made a sorry sight as he slouched by the summer house clutching a small box, the sort which might contain a ring from a high street jeweller's.

Amanda was so intent on tracking the heartbroken swain's progress, diving from one octagonal panel to the next, that she almost missed the fact that the object of Teddy's desire was closing the back door.

She was young and blonde, quite petite but solid in frame – would 'muscular' be too unkind? – with her hair tied back in a long ponytail. She was wearing black motorbike leathers, which did nothing to soften the chunkiness of her figure.

So that was Astra, who was not supposed to come to the house this weekend. If her motives were innocent, and as a lovers' tryst it had seemed innocent enough, then she would do what any good housekeeper would, knowing that the occupant of the house was out for the day, and lock the back door. If she did, it would mean Amanda was locked out until Mr Campion returned from his jolly day in the countryside, which made Mrs Campion grind her teeth for forgetting to bring any keys with her.

But if she did not lock the door, she would be leaving it as she had found it and thereby not betraying the fact that she had been in the house at all. Which would confirm Amanda's suspicion that Astra knew full well she *shouldn't* have been in the house.

Amanda held her wristwatch up almost to her nose in the gloom of the summer house, and patiently waited while the second hand revolved twice before opening the summer house door an inch in order to get a better view of the kitchen window. When she could see no movement behind the transparent half-curtain, she risked putting her head around the door and checking the garden path, to be rewarded with the sight of Ted Toomey's back as he trudged with slumped shoulders across the wasteland, the very embodiment of spurned love.

Emboldened, Amanda tiptoed daintily in her stockinged feet up to the back door, where she knelt down and pressed her left ear to the keyhole. Teddy might have left the premises, but she had no way of knowing if Astra had.

Delicately she tried the handle and exhaled with relief to find that the door had not been locked, though that did not answer the question of whether Astra was in the house or not.

Amanda pushed the door open wide enough for her to put one foot and her upper body inside, pulled off her headscarf and listened. She could see no sign of life, but she could hear a voice. As she concentrated, she realized it was a voice speaking on the telephone in the front room, just around the corner from the kitchen and the small cloakroom in which she cowered.

From the tone of the female voice, which surely must be Astra's, the telephone conversation was getting heated, at least at this end of the line, but Amanda could not follow the argument.

Her Russian simply wasn't good enough.

When she heard the ominous click of a telephone receiver being replaced, Amanda decided on discretion being the better part of valour. She closed the door quietly and scurried back to the summer house to think.

She had no intention of confronting Astra, even though right was on her side, at least not in her present bedraggled state. The feet of her stockings were not only laddered but shredded into flapping ribbons, and her leaking Wellingtons did not appeal as a fashionable solution to her lost dignity.

She could, she reasoned, remain in hiding until she heard a motorbike out on Barton Road. Astra had been wearing biking leathers, after all, and Albert had mentioned that was how she arrived to work. She was confident she would hear a bike's engine from this side of the house, but to be sure she held the door open.

The first sound she heard, however, was that of the back door opening, and then the clump of boots as a black, leather-clad Astra stomped down the garden path directly towards her.

For the next few minutes, Amanda forgot to breathe, or blink, or move a muscle apart from pulling the summer-house door closed as slowly and softly as possible, then stepping over to the knothole she had used before. This gave her a limited but clear view of the younger woman, her face rigid with concentration as she approached, seemingly on a collision course.

Yet Astra's eyes were not on the summer house but fixed off at an angle, and the only thing Amanda imagined she could be looking at was the large water butt which stood independent of the summer house but only a foot or so away.

Amanda switched her position to find a better spyhole, this time a vertical crack between two upright boards, which allowed her to see most of the water butt. By now Astra was standing next to it. Although she was not much taller than the butt, she gave Amanda the impression that she could wrap her arms around the bulbous wooden cask and, with those powerful shoulders, pick it up and throw it, just as a burly Highlander in a kilt would toss a caber.

Astra did extend her arms around the barrel, but only at the rim. With minimum effort she lifted the wooden top free, along with the connecting pipe which supplied the rainwater from the guttering of the summer house, revealing a dark surface of liquid.

In her role as voyeur, Amanda watched Astra look to her right and then left to make sure the coast was clear, then dip her fingers into the water and flutter them around the edge of the butt until they located a length of wet string. She pulled gently at first, then with increased effort the string emerged, tied to a thicker length of what could have been a washing line. Whatever curious fish Astra had caught, it now took both hands and a heave to land it.

But Astra was not fishing.

What the water butt gave up was a lengthy parcel of tightly wrapped plastic which, even with water dripping from it and her limited field of vision, Amanda could see contained the all-too-solid outline of a rifle.

This time Amanda definitely heard the sound of a motorbike engine, but she still waited a full five minutes, huddled in the gloom of the summer house, which she was convinced had been occupied by a family – hopefully not a colony – of rodents at some point, before venturing out and into the house.

There was no sign – no proof – that Astra and Ted Toomey had been in the house. Had it all been a dream? No, she knew what she had seen and Albert would believe her version of events, if only because, in his time, he had believed far more ridiculous scenarios without any empirical evidence.

But first things first: she needed a wash and a change of clothes.

Carrying the borrowed Wellingtons back to the understairs cupboard, she glanced at the telephone in the hallway and wondered if Albert knew a way of discovering who Astra had been talking to, and in Russian. She was sure it was Russian . . . why wouldn't it be?

It made as much sense as anything she had experienced in the last two hours. An unofficial (and unpaid) workforce occupying a sensitive, if not quite top secret, research facility, seemingly manufacturing a never-ending bicycle; a young couple trysting in a private house that neither had the right to be in, treating it as casually as a high street Wimpy Bar whilst the person who did have a right (sort of) to be there cowered in a musty shed in the garden; not to mention a rifle emerging like Excalibur from a water butt and the small slugs of deformed lead which she had rescued from the oil drum.

Her brain whirred, trying to process it all. Her hands were scratched, her nails chipped, her stockings were torn, her feet had picked up splinters from the summer house, her face and hair felt dirty . . . she must look a mess. What other confusion could befall her?

She opened the hallway cupboard, prepared to fling Branscombe's Wellingtons inside, and screamed as a forest of golf clubs cascaded on to her toes.

SIXTEEN
Thieves and Spies

'She must have stolen John's golf bag to carry the rifle in,' said Amanda, as if it was the most unusual thing that had happened to her that day.

'But of course, my dear,' said Mr Campion soothingly. 'She couldn't ride a motorbike through the groves of academe with a rifle slung around her neck. The good burghers of Cambridge might notice and suspect the revolution had finally arrived. A bag of golf clubs? On a Saturday? No one would bat an eyelid, unless she started to tee-off on the greensward on King's Parade, and even then they'd only ask if she'd seen the *Keep Off the Grass* signs. The golf bag could have been a neat piece of improvisation.'

'You sound as if you admire her.'

'I'm merely trying to put myself in her shoes, darling. You say she was on the phone before she retrieved the rifle?'

'Yes, and she was talking Russian.'

'That could have been her brother. I understand he gives Russian lessons on the side and Ted Toomey is one of his pupils. That was how he met Astra, and I have a feeling they used this house as a romantic rendezvous, though in this case the young swain's advances appear to have been rebuffed.'

'It certainly sounded that way, but I couldn't catch all of what they said. I was too busy skulking in the undergrowth.'

'I'm sure you skulked beautifully, my dear, but let me be sure about the sequence of things. Teddy saw Astra, plighted his troth or whatever . . .'

'He said something about doing what she'd asked.'

'Which presumably wasn't buying her a ring.'

'No, I think that was an unpleasant surprise.'

'But not nasty enough to make her run and retrieve the rifle she had hidden in the water butt?'

'Oh no, Teddy went quietly, without being threatened with a firearm, unlike some of the men I've met in the past.'

'A long time in the past, I hope,' said Mr Campion, peering over the top of his spectacles. 'So can we assume therefore that Astra collected the rifle *after* the phone call?'

'You mean she was given instructions?'

'Possibly. She certainly knew where it was hidden, had almost certainly hidden it there herself.'

'And probably,' said Amanda, pointing to the spent bullets she had placed on the kitchen table where they were drinking coffee fortified with Professor Branscombe's whisky, 'it was her using the old rifle range for target practice. I saw the grouping of the shots she put into that oil drum. She's a pretty good shot.'

Mr Campion appeared to study the bent pieces of lead on the table, even poking one with an inquisitive forefinger, then he looked at his wife over the tops of his spectacles.

'Wouldn't the neighbours have heard?' he said airily, then answered his own question. 'No, a clever girl like her would make sure they didn't.'

Mr Campion had returned from his aerial excursion over the wilds of Cambridgeshire to find his wife sitting on the edge of the bed in their appropriated bedroom, wearing a silk dressing gown and dabbing at damp hair with a towel, a trail of crumpled dirty clothing leading to the bathroom.

He had much to report but he knew instantly from the unwavering glint in her eyes that Amanda had also had quite a day, and so he tactfully gave way and listened attentively while she recounted her adventures as she dressed and occasionally cursed the departed Mrs Branscombe for taking her portable hairdryer with her – though which woman going off to live with her lover would not?

Campion refrained from any comment on the Branscombes' domestic situation (which included a diversion on why there were so few mirrors in the house), allowing his wife to tell her story without interruption as they moved downstairs into the kitchen, where he put the kettle on and reached for the Scotch.

He recounted his own day's activities, admitting that they were far less dramatic than Amanda's, and asked her to clarify several points of timing.

'Astra was wearing motorbike leather gear, right? From my vantage point, soaring like an eagle as I was above Caxton Gibbet, I saw a motorcyclist go to exactly the spot where those tubes were buried and remove them. But if your estimate of the time is right, *she* could not have got out to the gibbet, so my guess is the biker I saw was the someone she telephoned. It's just a theory, of course, and I can't prove anything until we know how the whole chain works.'

'The tubes you found . . . they definitely contained Goshawk material?'

'The very blueprints you planted in the safe during our reverse-burglary.'

'That was careless,' Amanda observed. 'The fact that they were missing would be noticed at some point.'

'Careless, or perhaps the thief simply didn't care about covering his tracks any more.'

'Still, no harm done there,' said Amanda, cheerfully toasting her husband with her coffee cup.

'Because your blueprints were fundamentally unsound.'

'But good enough to fool most people.'

'They would certainly fool me,' said Campion, 'though that would not be a challenge. I had trouble with Rupert's Meccano set. I'm not sure they were good enough to fool all the people all the time.'

'What do you mean by that?'

'I've spent the day with Luther Romo . . .'

'Oh, *him*. I told you he was a spook.'

'Indeed he is, but hopefully on our side. He had some very interesting things to say about forward-swept wing fighter planes, some of which I almost understood, as well as a lot of other very useful background information.'

'Did he now? Do tell. I'm dying to hear what a master sergeant in the American air force has to say about advanced aeronautical engineering research.'

'I don't think Mr Romo is a sergeant in anything, at least not any more. I suspect he's quite a high-ranking officer in the CIA, but he does know his aeroplanes and he doesn't think your Goshawk design is viable, or at least not until we have computers good enough to help fly them.'

Amanda remained silent, but Mr Campion noticed that one of her eyebrows had risen slowly.

'Romo thinks the whole Goshawk Project was a ruse, right from the start, designed – by a very clever person of course – to distract from the Alandel work on high-bypass jet engines. At least I think that's what he called them. As you know, I am easily confused by technicalities.'

'And why would that very clever person' – theatrically she flicked an imaginary lock of hair from her eyes – 'create such an elaborate diversion?'

'To bait a trap and catch a mole, of course,' said Mr Campion, 'which seems to have worked.'

'It has?'

'Let me use the telephone and we'll find out.'

In fact, Mr Campion made several phone calls, and when he returned to the kitchen, he found Amanda applying her make-up with the aid of the small, circular mirror from her powder compact.

'You've been while. I hope one of those calls was a reservation for dinner.'

'It was,' said her husband, 'for the University Arms, and I will ring for a taxi when madam is ready.'

'Madam is not quite presentable yet, but she is hungry. Any other news?'

'Yes, but first let me show you the spoils of my escapade this afternoon.'

He carefully placed the black bundle he was holding under one arm on the kitchen table and waited patiently for Amanda to be reassured that her lipstick was perfectly applied.

'A leather jacket? You're not think of taking up motorcycling at your age, are you?' she asked, snapping her compact closed, as if that put an end to such thoughts.

'It's a flying jacket,' said Campion, 'and a very warm one too. It belonged to Alan Wormold, but look inside.'

Amanda pulled the sleeves, and the jacket unfolded to reveal two pointed metal tubes resting, as it happened, on a silk map of the South Pacific.

'So that's where my Reynolds steel tubing has been going.'

'I suspect quite a bit went into that bicycle you saw this afternoon. Cuthbert Snow told me they were cooking up something called the Decameron, but I never put two and two together to make ten.'

'Decameron?' Amanda said vaguely, concentrating on one of the tubes.

'Ten stories, seven told by women, three by men. The name chose itself. Pull the candle in the end out and win a prize.'

Amanda used her fingernails to grasp the wick and gently removed the candle stub, then knocked the upturned tube on the table. Like a cigar out of its cylinder, a tube of brown ten-pound notes slid out. They had been rolled tightly lengthwise and secured with a rubber band.

'You're a winner!' gushed Campion. 'You picked the right tube and won a prize! Roll up, roll up! The other one is empty, by the way. Probably just a spare, or maybe one was the inbox and the other the outbox.'

Amanda eased the rubber band from the notes and began to uncurl them in front of her.

'There's a lot of pictures of the Queen here.'

'A total of £250 in new notes,' said Campion. 'I counted them on the way back. After we landed back at Bourn, Luther Romo drove me out to Caxton Gibbet and we retrieved them.'

'A tidy sum.'

'Especially if it's delivered regularly on demand.'

'But you didn't see who delivered this windfall?'

'I would think of it more as a pay packet rather than a windfall, and I could not identify who left it, but the real question is: who was supposed to pick it up?'

'And have you narrowed it down?'

'Almost. Now I'll phone for a taxi whilst you put your glad rags on and I climb into a clean shirt and tie. We must make an effort for the University Arms.'

'You mean I can't dress as your adorable professor from Oxford again?' asked Amanda with a fake pout.

'No. Happily I think we are way past that by now.'

Amanda finished her make-up regime and changed into the black dress she had worn for her honorary degree ceremony, which she had fortunately remembered to brush and hang in the wardrobe that morning. The black stockings she had worn were still slightly damp from a quick rinse through in John Branscombe's bathtub, but as they were the only intact pair she had, she struggled into them.

She was easing her way into her shoes when Mr Campion called up the stairs, 'Your chariot awaits!' and was only mildly surprised to find that the chariot he had summoned was not one of the contentious 'minicabs' which had got London's black cab drivers so hot under the collar, but a police car complete with a uniformed police driver.

'Courtesy of Inspector Mawson,' said Campion, opening the rear door of the saloon for her, 'on condition that we don't use the bells and we make our own way back, and that we run an errand en route.'

'What sort of errand?'

'Oh, just a small piece of housekeeping and I didn't think you'd mind. Actually, your presence could be invaluable – if you don't scare the poor chap to death.'

'Lady Amanda! My God, what have they done to you?'

Amanda was taken aback. Hadn't she made an effort, after all the physical exertions of the last few days of hiding, being rolled in a carpet, and doing the equivalent of an army assault course? And then she realized that Alf Bagley was probably referring to her legal condition.

'If you mean the police' – Amanda took a sidestep to allow Alf a clear view of the police car purring softly on Mill Road – 'they have merely offered my husband and me a lift to the University Arms, but we thought we'd pop by to see how you were coping.'

She felt she would have been justified in turning Bagley's question back on him and asking what 'they' had done to him, except that she knew what he had gone through. Even so, this was not the fiercely loyal, always cheerful Alf she had known for many years, the Alf who was younger than her husband but now looked ten years older, with his grey stubble, uncombed hair and sunken, red-rimmed eyes, wearing pyjamas that were desperately in need of a laundry, or possibly a rag-and-bone man.

'Are you being looked after?' Amanda asked as she followed him up the stairs to his flat above the RAF recruitment office, though she had already decided that he clearly was not.

'Seein' you has cheered me up no end. Can I offer you anything? I wasn't expecting visitors, but I could brew a pot of tea . . .'

'Please, don't trouble yourself, we are merely passing by,' said Campion, slipping his arm around Amanda's waist as he joined them. 'You were, very graciously, concerned about Amanda's recent altercation with the powers that be, and so I thought I would bring her to show you that she was safe, well and at liberty.'

'That's kind of you,' said Bagley with a sigh. 'Puts my mind at ease knowing they didn't get away with a trumped-up charge like that. It was just shocking the way they treated you.'

'It was all a silly misunderstanding,' Amanda told him, 'and what I went through cannot be compared to how you must have suffered.'

From Bagley's hangdog expression, he clearly agreed, but Amanda's words provided little solace.

'We have no wish to revive unpleasant memories, Alf,' Campion intervened, 'but there are several matters concerning the Goshawk Project we need to clear up. Call them house-keeping issues, and we think you can help us.'

'If I can . . .' Bagley spread his arms, palms outward.

'The Project's Land Rover,' said Campion. 'Who drove it?'

Bagley glanced at Amanda, seeking permission to answer, and only did so when Amanda nodded. 'We all did, Mr Campion. All of us were insured for it, all the Alandel people that is, and Professor Branscombe, though not any of his students.'

'Was there any rota as to who used it?'

'No, we were free and easy about it, but there's a little red notebook in the office and drivers write down the mileage they've done, then put money in the petty cash for the petrol. We worked it out as five bob a gallon and that she did twenty miles to the gallon. That book was like an honesty box – none of us cheated.'

'I'm sure no one did, but did anyone run up more miles than anyone else?'

Alf shrugged his shoulders. 'I suppose that would be Melvyn, all those times he ran Alan out to the airfield at Bourn. He always paid up his petrol money, though.'

'I don't suppose you would know if anyone took out the Land Rover yesterday – say, late afternoon?'

Alf waved his arms to indicate the confinement of his flat. 'I was stuck here, so how would I know? But I can tell you for nothing that if Melvyn Barnes was driving it, he would have logged the mileage. Dead honest is Melvyn,' he said, turning to Amanda. 'Been with Alandel almost as long as I have.'

'Somebody hasn't been totally honest with Alandel property, though, have they?'

The polite sympathy she had shown for Alf on arrival had disappeared as Amanda exerted her managerial authority. To Mr Campion, poor Alf visibly deflated into the posture of a peasant still loyal to a liege lord (in this case, lady) having to explain a shortfall in the harvest, his only defence being embarrassed silence.

'Nugent Monck was convinced someone was stealing from our stock of Reynolds tubing,' Amanda continued in the manner of a prosecuting counsel, 'but because it was Nugent and we all knew he was a bit of a worry-pants, I did not take him seriously. Until this morning, when I saw that quite a bit of it had ended up between two wheels.'

'Ah,' said Bagley, with the pained expression which usually came with trapped wind, 'you've seen the cycling contraption the young 'uns were making. I never thought it would work.'

'I assure you it does.'

'How many was it for in the end?'

'If you mean riders, there were ten of them and seven were girls. I suppose they were there to ease the weight ratio.'

Bagley shook his head. 'The original design was for seven riders, all girls, because they came up with the idea.'

'They did?'

'Yes, they're all students from Girton or Newnham, and they wanted to do a charity stunt. One of them designed the thing, said she always wanted to be an engineer but neither her parents nor her college would give the idea house room.'

'I suppose they needed the boys to get the tubing,' said Mr Campion.

'I didn't think there was much harm in it,' said Bagley with a faint whine. 'Most of it was offcuts going for scrap anyway, and to be honest I never thought the thing would fly. If they've got it going, then they'll be doing a trial run round the town tomorrow with the collecting tins out, catch people when they're coming out of church and before the pubs get going. All I did was turn a blind eye to it. Suppose I was wrong – it was theft, after all.'

'Let's worry about that later,' said Amanda. 'Do you happen to know the name of the girl who designed the bike?'

'I don't, Lady A, but Cuthbert Snow does. I think he's a bit sweet on her. Is she going to get into trouble over this?'

'Actually, I was thinking of offering her a job.'

The Campions dismissed their police driver, choosing to walk across Parker's Piece to the University Arms. At a safe distance along Mill Road, Amanda spat out a curse with such venom that Mr Campion – so shocked by the action itself – was unable to judge whether such an accusation about Alf Bagley's parentage might be founded on fact.

'Sorry about that,' Amanda said immediately, once she had composed herself. 'I just can't get over the fact that dear old Alf – trusted, loyal Alf – knew about the tubing being stolen all along. When Nugent Monck kept banging on about it, Alf assured me it was nonsense. But he knew about the theft all along and I am not sure I can forget that.'

Mr Campion put a comforting arm around her shoulders.

'I think poor Alf will have trouble forgetting too,' he said as they walked. 'When Alan Wormold died so horribly, he was in the process of cutting lengths of tubing, but what you must remember is that this is not just about thievery. Those tubes were used for more than making bicycles.'

He touched her cheek lightly with his fingertips, turning her face towards his.

'Remember what the Italians say: *Chi non beve in compagnia o è un ladro o è una spia* – he who drinks alone is either a thief or a spy.'

'What on earth does that mean?'

'It means that we are neither thieves nor spies, we are together, not alone, and I am sure we are both dying for a drink.'

'For once, my darling, you are talking complete sense.'

They enjoyed their drinks and dinner at the University Arms without anyone seeming to recognize Amanda, despite her being, at least to those who sat and pontificated around many a high table in Cambridge, still something of a *cause célèbre*, if not a traitor to the realm or – as some dons insisted – a traitoress.

'I suppose I can come out of hiding now,' Amanda announced over dessert.

'You mean escape from custody?'

'How about we say I was let off with a warning? Or what's that verdict in Scotland? Not proven. I like that.'

'My dear, this is Cambridge. People will assume you are upholding an ancient Cambridge tradition going back to Christopher Marlowe, and you actually are a spy, or they will think it was all a publicity stunt. In either case, most are too well-mannered to even broach the subject in polite company, so I think it's safe for you to re-enter society. Did you have any plans? Lunch with the vice chancellor, perhaps?'

After checking that no one was observing them, Amanda put her tongue out at her husband before answering him.

'I was thinking of wandering into town tomorrow to cheer on the Decameron and, if it stays upright, I might try and have a word with the girl who designed it. Call it talent spotting if you like, but I've seen it and it is a ridiculously impressive machine.'

'Keep an eye out for young Mr Toomey – discreetly, of course. I think I may need to have a word with him.'

'He can only be on the periphery of things. I've always known that the leaks must originate with the Alandel team.'

'Which is why I will be spending tomorrow having a nice long chat with our prime suspect.'

'You're sure?'

'As sure as I can be. It wasn't a difficult choice. I automatically discounted you, my darling . . .'

Amanda made a fanning motion with one hand and said in a stage *Gone with the Wind* accent: 'Why, thank you, kind sir.'

'And you would never have let me consider Alf, the faithful retainer. The tubes Luther Romo and I found out at Caxton Gibbet dead letter box were certainly made at the Goshawk Project. Nugent Monck suspected something and tried to tell you.'

'Which rules him out?'

'I would say so. And whoever it was that took the Goshawk Land Rover out to Bourn yesterday, it wasn't Kevin Loder, as he was on his way home on a train.'

'Do we know where Gary Cupples was yesterday?'

'That doesn't matter . . . well, not in this instance.'

'Why not? The Americans have a terrible track record when it comes to pinching our ideas.'

'Be that as it may, but Mr Cupples has been vouched for by Luther Romo.'

Amanda sat back in her chair, indignant. 'And you trust him? If anyone's a spy, he is.'

'He certainly is,' said Mr Campion, 'and so is Gary Cupples; he is also CIA and was put into Alandel because our trans-Atlantic cousins initially suspected you!'

To Mr Campion's surprise, and relief, Amanda responded to this revelation with a wry smile, then she rearranged the cutlery on her empty plate and looked her husband in the eye. 'Which leaves Melvyn Barnes.'

'Who has agreed to join me tomorrow for a leisurely punting

expedition along the Cam, powered by Cuthbert Snow, another young man who may have something to tell us.'

'Somebody else on the periphery of things.'

'I agree entirely, but so was Alan Wormold, and look what happened to him.'

SEVENTEEN

Can You Punt a Little Faster?

Whether it was called the Cam or the Granta, depending on which side of the Silver Street bridge it was being observed from, Mr Campion had always been convinced that the waterway which ran through Cambridge perfectly fitted the definition of *Rivers: for the messing about on*. The ideal craft for doing so, of course, being a punt, propelled in gentle stateliness by a muscular young man in flannels and white shirt, preferably wearing a straw boater.

It was the perfect morning for such a scenario, the sun shining, the river placid, church bells ringing and ice-cream vans staking out the most profitable territories, even though the tourist season had not fully tightened its grip on the city. Along the length of King's Parade, students wearing black gowns happily celebrated the end of term by posing for photographs in front of college buildings for complete strangers; others in more casual attire dispensed printed flyers advertising accompanied river trips by punt at 'mostly competitive' rates. Mr Campion noted, with grudging admiration, that several had gone to the trouble of quoting their prices in US dollars, French francs and Deutsche Marks, though at exchange rates which were far from competitive.

Campion had no need to hail a passing punt or take a flyer from a strolling hawker, for Cuthbert Snow had been ready and waiting near Laundress Green, his bare feet firmly planted on the till, that flat counter of dark wood in the stern of a punt, holding a sixteen-foot pole in his right hand in the Greek warrior stance he clearly thought his most photogenic pose. He had had no doubt that Cuthbert would be there as arranged, and was already thinking of him not so much as a watery chauffeur but as a propulsion unit. That sounded far more suitable for an engineering student, and he certainly looked impressive enough in white flannels tied at the waist with a rope belt and the sleeves of his open-necked white shirt rolled up above the elbows. Pity about the lack of a straw boater, though. Perhaps Campion should have specified one.

He felt he too was dressed appropriately, in cornflower blue cotton trousers and a lightweight linen jacket, complete with powder blue pocket square, his favourite fedora having to act, hopefully, as a stand-in Panama to keep the sun at bay. Only Melvyn Barnes, approaching with limping gait from The Anchor, let the sartorial side down, dressed as he was more for gardening than a leisurely float along the river.

Melvyn's army-surplus brown leather jerkin over a green shirt and khaki trousers might have given the initial impression that he was going into combat with a particularly vicious rose bush, but with his pipe clenched between his teeth and his uncombed hair, he could, thought Campion, be mistaken for an eccentric don, at least from the riverbank.

'Melvyn, so glad you could make it. We may not be wearing straw boaters and we do not have a dog, but we are three men in a boat. You know Cuthbert Snow, of course.'

Barnes returned the greeting with nods to both. 'When you phoned last night, you said we needed to talk – privately,' he said, his eyes flicking towards Cuthbert, who was busy plumping, or rather punching, the punt's bench-seat cushions into place.

'What better place for a private chinwag, out there on the river where we can only be overheard by the swans, or duck-lings, or the odd Canadian goose? And don't mind Cuthbert, he's here as our driver, or our captain, navigator and chief stoker all rolled into one. I couldn't resist employing him as I remember his grandfather, positively a legend in and on the Cam, though I think this bit of the river is known as the Granta. I always found that confusing. Permission to come aboard, Cap'n?'

Cuthbert manoeuvred the twenty-four-foot-long punt parallel to the bank, to allow his passengers to step aboard, keeping it steady by balancing the pressures and stresses between the soles of his feet and the pole he had pushed into the muddy bottom of the river.

'We'll take the Oxford end,' said Campion, stepping into the well of the shallow craft, which remained rock steady.

He indicated the furthest of the two cushioned seats which faced each other in the centre of the punt.

'So the Oxford end is the front? The blunt end?' Melvyn asked.

'I think both ends are pretty blunt, but in Cambridge the punter stands on that platform, which is called a till, as Cuthbert is demonstrating, to wield his pole. The awkward squad at Oxford, however, prefer to do their punting from the other end, turning the till into the bow, but then that's Oxford for you. We called it "the other place" in my day.'

Campion sat on the right side of the bench seat and stretched out his long legs, his feet tangling with the short wooden oar that came with every punt, should some emergency paddling be required. He waved Barnes to sit next to him, which was just about possible, though their shoulders brushed, thanks to Campion's thinness.

Campion had a sudden vision of Lugg occupying the same seat. There would be no room whatsoever for a second person and, perched there in glorious solitude, Lugg's Buddha-like proportions would have strained the thwarts of the punt; although in fairness a much more rugged Viking longship might also have had problems keeping on an even keel with a Lugg on board.

'This way,' said Campion, 'we get a ringside view of our pilot, entrusting him to take us smoothly and safely to our destination, without the need to see where we are going.'

'And where are we going?' Barnes tamped his pipe with his thumb and produced a box of matches, shaking them until they rattled to reassure himself. 'Or should I ask where *this* is going?'

Campion did not answer immediately. Rather he seemed to be admiring the smooth hand-over-hand efficiency with which Cuthbert was using the sixteen-foot pole of polished spruce to propel them out into the middle of the river. He allowed his left arm to flop over the edge of the punt and his fingers tickled the surface of the water only a few inches below.

'Nautically, we are going upstream towards Grantchester, where we will turn around and come back again. For the duration of our little trip, though, I would like to think that we are in international waters, beyond the three-mile limit as it were, even though we are less than three yards from dry land. If you are agreeable, that is.'

'And what's that supposed to mean?' Melvyn asked between smoke signals from his pipe.

'Well, it means I can't arrest you,' Campion said, leaning in so that Cuthbert on the till could not hear. 'Not that I have that power on dry land, but I know several gentlemen who do and they are relatively adjacent.'

A punt carrying two giggling students and two unimpressed girls passed them heading back towards The Anchor, without giving them a sideways glance.

Barnes struck a match, lit his pipe, replaced the spent match in the box and puffed in silence for half a minute before stretching out a hand to massage his left leg just above the knee.

Campion broke the silence, saying, 'Did you ever tell me how you got that limp?'

'Don't think you ever asked.'

'It wasn't a war wound?'

'No, it was an accident, a car accident, before then. During the war I was in a reserved occupation at Bristol Aero. Lady Amanda knows that; everybody knows that, even you.'

'I wasn't referring to the Second World War,' said Mr Campion.

For a moment, the dominant sound to be heard in the punt was the clack of Melvyn's pipe stem as it rattled against his teeth, louder it seemed than the rhythmic slap of Cuthbert's pole entering and leaving the water.

'What do you think you know?' Barnes spoke softly and calmly.

'I know what our American cousins think they know.'

'Pah! Them?'

Barnes gave a snort of derision which made his pipe jerk

up and down, issuing a small puff of acrid smoke which made Campion recoil.

'You may not think much of them, Melvyn, but they have certainly taken an interest in you. In fact, they have taken a great interest in everybody at Alandel in the past few years, my wife included. Not in the Goshawk Project *per se*, but in your research on high-bypass jet engines.'

'Aye, they would, the thievin' buggers. It's common knowledge they're working on them.'

'Then we should not be surprised if less friendly nations – to the east, shall we say – are interested in them as well. I do not pretend to understand the intricacies of such things, but I realize they are sensitive and that our American friends take them very seriously. Thus, they have been very thorough in researching – they call it checking out – all the people involved in the research.'

Campion glanced to the stern to see that Cuthbert had inched his way forward on the till and was leaning towards them, his ears pricked up.

'Eyes on the road, Cuthbert,' said Campion. 'We don't want any collisions or sinkings.'

Cuthbert grinned sheepishly, slid his feet back six inches and straightened up.

'No chance of that, Mr C. I think we have the river to ourselves today.'

Campion turned to look at the river ahead, conscious of Barnes's eyes boring into him. They had passed the university swimming club and were very much out of the city and in the countryside, the quiet river entering a series of lazy turns, its banks lined with reeds and dangling willow branches. Cuthbert was right – there was no other river traffic ahead. Apart from whatever wildlife lurked on the riverbank, they were alone and unobserved.

'Slow ahead, Mr Snow, we're in no hurry.'

'Aye, aye, Cap'n.' Cuthbert grinned, using his pole as a rudder rather than an engine.

Campion turned back to face Barnes. 'Of course, that's not strictly true. I may not be in a hurry, but you are running out of time.'

Barnes removed his pipe and pointed the stem at Campion. It was not a threatening gesture, rather one of a schoolmaster picking up a reluctant pupil on a point of Latin grammar, and Campion found that somehow more insulting.

'Go on then, spit it out.' Barnes's tone was composed, his demeanour unruffled.

'As I said, the Americans have looked into you, far more deeply than our own much-maligned security services. They tell me that your limp is indeed the result of a war wound, received during the Spanish Civil War where you fought with the International Brigade. At the time you were a member of the Communist Party and, whilst your active participation may have fluctuated over the years, at heart you remained dedicated. You must have gone through numerous crises of belief over the years – the Nazi–Soviet Pact, Hungary, the Berlin Wall – but you stayed loyal.'

Barnes's face remained emotionless. 'Americans could see reds under beds in a convent,' he said. 'So I was a firebrand young socialist, so what? I was twenty-two when I went to Spain. First – and last – time I've been abroad. I never fired a shot in anger, but that didn't stop me getting shot. Went with an ideal, came back with a gammy leg two weeks later. Hardly something to be proud of, so I never talked about it.'

He held Campion's gaze.

A cool customer, thought Campion. He is saying: *Prove it.*

'Let's leave your motivation for a moment and concentrate on what you did rather than why.'

Barnes gave a slight shrug, as if he could not care less.

'You started selling details of Alandel research on the open market,' said Campion, 'although black market might be a better description. Then, for some reason, you opted to sell into only one market, the Russian one. It must have been very convenient to find that your ideological comrades were also good cash payers.'

'Generous enough to support my lavish lifestyle, you reckon?' Barnes reversed the stem of his pipe so it pointed at his chest. 'Look at me, Mr Campion. I'm a working-class lad from the Black Country who found a trade and stuck to it. Can you see me in Savile Row suits? Do I drive a flash car?

Go on fancy holidays? You won't find any wine, women or songs in my life, no matter how much checking up your Yankee friends do.'

'Or you could simply be clever enough not to give yourself away like that.'

'And you could be bluffing, just touting for a scapegoat to get your wife off the hook.'

'Oh, my wife is off the hook already. She was never really on a hook at all, and in fact it was she who baited a hook by planting those blueprints in the office safe for you to steal.'

'What blueprints?' Barnes said without flinching.

'The ones you took out to Caxton Gibbet, where you planted them like saplings which would grow into money trees. And don't bother trying to reclaim them; I have, so to speak, collected your mail for you, and your latest stipend is safe in my wallet.'

Barnes's expression did not so much as flicker, and Campion, who was physically close enough to him to detect the slightest tremor, had, reluctantly, to admire the man's nerve.

'Did you actually see me do any of that?'

'I did not, but there is a witness who will put you at Bourn Airfield on Friday afternoon.'

'So what? I often went there.'

'Yes, you did, with Alan Wormold.'

Even as he said the name, Campion noticed that Cuthbert had tensed his upper body and leaned forward. He was a large, muscular young man and his looming posture was sufficiently disconcerting to produce the faintest bead of sweat on Melvyn Barnes's upper lip, which persuaded Campion to press home his advantage.

'What were you hoping to find when you raided Alan's locker out at Bourn?'

When Branes said nothing, Campion continued. 'Let me guess, it was a couple of those tubes for your dead letter box. Well, I can tell you those blueprints were collected and your postman left your payment. I saw that with my own eyes. Though I wouldn't be at all surprised if your paymasters demanded their money back.'

'I've no idea what you are talking about,' said Barnes,

making a half-hearted attempt to pat his pockets, looking for his matches.

'I think you have, and because I do not think you are stupid, I think you have known for some time.'

'Known what?' said Cuthbert suddenly, leaning menacingly forward in his stance.

Campion turned on him sharply, raising the palm of a hand. 'Cuthbert! You promised to behave.'

Cuthbert nodded acquiescence and retreated into an upright posture, plunging his pole into the water with far more force than was necessary. Campion returned, expressionless, to face Barnes.

'The Goshawk as a forward-swept wing fighter is not going to work, is it?'

'I didn't know you were the aero-engineer of the family,' Barnes's mouth twitched into a smirk, 'but if you want my honest opinion, the answer would be no, at least not yet. We need new metals to take the stresses in the airframe and we need a computer to help a pilot control the aircraft. We don't have those things, but we will, in time.'

'But not in your time,' Campion said coldly.

'So you say, Mr Campion, so you say.'

'I am confident of it. Just when did you realize you were selling duff information to your Soviet customers?'

'I'm not saying anything. You'll not get me to incriminate myself. If you have a shred of proof, you would have used it by now, otherwise you're just fishing.'

'Well, we are in the perfect vehicle for a bit of fishing, are we not? And you could say that the bait we dangled had been swallowed.'

'And this is you reeling in your catch, is it? Can't say I'm impressed.'

Campion sighed, shook his head slightly, and then looked up at Cuthbert Snow, towering like a Colossus on the till of the punt, the pole sliding through his hands in smooth, regular movements.

'Cuthbert, listen to me,' said Campion, as though addressing a child on a school sports day, 'you must promise me you will do your very best to behave yourself.'

Cuthbert stared at Campion in confusion. 'Yes . . . sure . . . whatever you say.'

'You promise?'

'Of course.'

'Good lad.'

Melvyn Barnes followed this exchange closely, at first puzzled, then wary. The mask is ready to crack, thought Campion. He knows what's coming.

'I am not trying to impress you, Melvyn, I am trying to understand you. Industrial espionage, whether for some extra cash on the side or motivated by political ideology, is one thing. Cold-blooded murder is quite another, and the one you committed was particularly cold-blooded.'

'I have no idea what you're talking about,' said Barnes, but there was a catch in his voice.

'Yes, you do, because you very cleverly arranged the death of Alan Wormold, a truly horrific death, and you were quite happy for Alf Bagley to be scarred for life by it. It was supposed to look like an accident, wasn't it?'

Barnes was silent but Campion could hear Cuthbert's loud and irregular breathing.

'But it couldn't have worked if Alf hadn't been there to flick the circuit breaker. You knew that, and thus you have two lives on your conscience.'

'This is ridiculous. How dare you suggest—'

Campion held up a hand in the universal 'Halt!' gesture, but it was aimed at Cuthbert, not Barnes.

'I didn't want Cuthbert to have to relive the death of his friend, and I am relying on his sense of self-control not to rip your head off, but I dare suggest it because Cuthbert found the proof for me. Proof that would, in happier days, have seen you hanged – and that is not something I have ever wished on anyone, though for the sheer *engineering* of your crime, I will make an exception.'

Barnes remained silent, his eyes locked on Campion's, but there was a noticeable movement in his throat as he swallowed nervously.

'You carefully made sure you were not present when Alan had his accident, though it was anything but an accident, yet you were very quickly on the scene. It was you who went straight to the control box. It looked as if you were trying to switch the crane off, trying to help. In fact, you were removing the ball-bearing you had taped to the ON button before anyone could see it. In the horror of the scene, nobody would notice you dropping a bearing and the strip of tape on to the dirty workshop floor. Nobody did, but I got Cuthbert here to sweep up that day and bring me the detritus from the floor. Do you know how long fingerprints stay on black insulating tape?'

Campion hoped he did not, as he himself had no idea.

Now the first twitch of fear cracked Barnes's stony expression and he glanced anxiously towards Cuthbert, whose feet had not moved, but whose upper body seemed to be looming closer.

'It wasn't supposed to kill him,' said Barnes, 'just frighten him off. A nasty industrial accident. They happen all the time.'

'But they're not usually so well planned, are they? What I can't work out is *why* you needed to frighten him.'

Once again Barnes's eyes flicked towards Cuthbert. He was right to be worried, thought Campion, as Cuthbert's knuckles had whitened as he gripped the punt pole.

'He was getting greedy,' said Barnes, his voice a whisper but simply not quiet enough.

'You utter pig!' snarled Cuthbert, who pulled the pole out of the water and held it like a long-staff.

'Cuthbert! Keep your station,' snapped Campion. 'Please control yourself.'

With a growl the young man returned to propelling the punt, breathing rapidly and loudly through his nose, his chest heaving. When Campion judged Cuthbert had regained control of himself, he rounded on Barnes.

'So Wormold was your contact here in Cambridge?'

'Messenger boy, not contact, and yes, he was one. Toomey was the other.'

'What? That's piffle!'

Cuthbert spat the word, his whole body shaking, and as it did, the punt began to rock.

Melvyn Barnes, to Campion's surprise, did not recoil at the outburst, did not even flinch, but his eyes narrowed and there was, yes, there definitely was, a hint of a smile at the corners of his mouth. Barnes was beginning to take some sort of masochistic pleasure in his situation.

'They didn't cut you in on the deal, did they?' he taunted Cuthbert. 'They couldn't trust an oaf like you to keep his mouth shut.'

'Ignore him, Cuthbert,' ordered Campion. 'He's just lashing out. Rats, when trapped, do that. And you really are a rat, Melvyn, burrowing your way into Alandel, and who-knows-where before that? Was the motive money, or the valiant nature of the working-class struggle?'

Barnes looked at his inquisitor with disdain. 'What would you know about either?'

'Of the former, I believe that having some, honestly earned, is far preferable to having none, or it being dishonestly acquired at the expense of someone else. As to the latter, by birth and breeding I am no socialist, but when I see injustice in society, I would hope I would recognize and challenge it. You are not denying that your motives were mercenary, are you? Remember, I have your latest stipend in my possession.'

Barnes examined the bowl of his pipe, apparently surprised to find it had gone out. The man was simply too calm, thought Campion. It was unlikely that he was planning anything violent – the odds would be two-to-one and the wrestling ring was basically a long wide plank of wood floating down the middle of the river. Admittedly, the river wasn't very deep and certainly not fast flowing, but it was wet, and plunging overboard didn't seem a sensible escape route. That left two explanations: Barnes did not believe he would suffer for his crimes, which was ridiculous as the man was not stupid, or he simply did not care any more. The latter could make him more compliant, or more dangerous.

'It wasn't about the money, not at first,' he said, tucking his pipe away into a jerkin pocket and using his free hand to massage his leg once more. 'I was an idealist once, before the war, that's why I went to Spain. During the war with Hitler, it was a fight for survival. That was all that mattered, but afterwards I saw how the Americans had become the Fancy Dans, the show ponies of capitalism, and how they bullied and stole what they couldn't buy. I saw how they took our research, on aircraft, rockets, jet engines and nuclear power, treating us like the Red Indians they took the land from.'

'Yet you sold Alandel secrets on the open market and Americans were among your buyers.'

'Never anything essential, and sometimes things which were useless or downright wrong, but they were stupid and they paid top dollar for any old rubbish rather than risk the Russians getting it.'

'Your comrades,' said Campion.

'At one time I thought they were, now I'm not too sure. I was going to find out in my retirement.'

'I somehow don't think you'll be collecting a pension.'

'I have made my own arrangements on that score,' said Barnes, making a noise somewhere between a hiccup and a laugh. 'My plan was to retire at fifty-five. My wife died a few years back and I reckon I could have put up a good case for saying it was time for a new start abroad, in sunnier climes.'

'Back to Spain?'

'God, no!' Barnes rubbed his leg harder. 'Too many bad memories.'

'But you said you hadn't been out of the country since then.'

'Haven't, but I've done a lot of reading up on Cuba and that sounds like the place for me. Dollars and pounds sterling go a long way there, though I don't suppose getting a passport will be easy now, will it?'

'I suspect not,' said Campion.

He glanced up at Cuthbert to see how he was taking Melvyn's *ad hoc* confession, if indeed it was a confession. The student gave him a look which suggested confusion and frustration, but the rhythmic movement of his arms and shoulders never faltered.

The punt, still midstream, was turning slowly into one of the many sharp bends in this section of the river and, between Cuthbert's right thigh and the angle of the punt pole, Campion saw another punt floating on the same track, though still some distance behind them.

What caught Campion's eye was the fact that this punt did not have a muscular young man standing in the stern providing propulsion. In fact, at first glance it seemed to be an empty vessel, then Campion realized that there was an occupant and he (or she) was using the wooden paddle supplied with one hand whilst lying prone in the punt, only the top of a head showing above the square bow at the Oxford end.

'Cuthbert,' said Mr Campion, 'could you punt a little faster? I think we're being followed.'

Before Cuthbert could fully turn to look behind him, the first bullet smacked into the stern of the punt, gouging out a six-inch splinter of wood which went spinning away across the water.

EIGHTEEN
On a Bicycle Made for Ten

D inner at the University Arms may have been Amanda's first exposure to public scrutiny since her spectacular fall from grace at her congregation at Senate House, but it, and the walk back to Barton Street in the dark, had hardly been a true test of her notoriety. This morning's excursion into the centre of Cambridge – where she would mingle openly in broad daylight with students, dons and the church-going populace – would provide a better assessment of how she was regarded by both gown and town.

There was, of course, the possibility that she would pass completely unnoticed, but to counter that, she decided to look her best, or as good as the limited wardrobe at her disposal would allow. Her biggest act of defiance – though she was not quite sure who she was defying – would be to comb her hair out, allowing the Fitton family colours to fly freely and uncovered, truly a red rag to any bull daring to challenge her right to roam innocent and free.

She deliberately did not leave the house until an hour after Campion had, as she had no wish to confront Melvyn Barnes and, knowing her husband's plan to go upstream towards Grantchester, she chose to walk down Queen's Road and on to the footpaths over the Backs, crossing the river by King's College Bridge and through the college itself, until she reached King's Parade. She was almost disappointed that no one challenged her. Not a single pointed finger or shout of 'Traitor!' marked her passing, though she was certainly buoyed by the admiring glances and, in one case, a low, barely audible wolf-whistle, from two different groups of male students as they left the chapel, their Sunday morning duty done.

She put that down to the numerical imbalance between male and female students in the university rather than her natural

sex appeal or fashion sense. Certainly, compared to the examples of red velvet minidresses she spotted on King's Parade,
she was the acme of propriety in the flowery summer frock
and lightweight jacket she had salvaged from her meagre
travelling wardrobe.

Automatically she turned her head as she walked by Senate
House, in case it had not forgiven her for disrupting the congregation ceremony or, more importantly for many of the dons
who had been present, the reception. She could well imagine
that in some eyes, her being arrested for espionage was a lesser
crime than interrupting the flow of champagne and cucumber
sandwiches and, having enjoyed the freedom of walking
openly in public for the first time in several days, and even
secretly relishing the admiring glances she had received, she
suddenly decided that here was a location where she did not
want to be recognized. With fingers crossed and head down,
she quickened her pace as she turned into Trinity Street and
ran headfirst into the one don who recognized her instantly.

'Good God, Amanda! Have they . . .?'

Amanda was delighted to find that Professor Branscombe
was more surprised to see her than she was him, and he
clutched the brown paper parcel he was carrying tightly to his
chest, as if he was frightened she might be intent on robbing
him.

'Sent me to the Tower via Traitor's Gate? No, I am a free
woman taking the air on this fine Sunday without a care in
the world, or so I would like to think.'

'You're not waiting for anything, are you?'

'Do I look as if I'm loitering?'

'No, not all, I just thought you might be waiting for Albert.
I rang the house about twenty minutes ago but there was no
answer, so I thought I'd look in at St Ignatius, see if he was
there.'

'He's on the river, punting with Cuthbert Snow,' said
Amanda, deciding not to mention Melvyn Barnes.

'Is he now? Well, it's a nice day for it.'

'Did you need to see him?'

'I wanted to speak to him . . . about something.' Branscombe
was flustered, there was no doubt about that, but standing on

the pavement being bustled by what seemed to be an increasing number of pedestrians was hardly the place for a heart-to-heart. 'Can we step into St Ignatius for a minute? It's reasonably adjacent.'

Amanda leaned to her right, peering around Branscombe and his parcel, until she could see the far from imposing frontage of her husband's alma mater.

'I'm told Saint Ig's doesn't exactly welcome women across its threshold, but as it is such a nice day, we can at least sit on the threshold, if it is permitted.'

Branscombe followed her gaze to the three worn steps leading to the studded oak door of the college, which most visitors to Cambridge pass without noticing and which most Cambridge dons pretend does not exist unless pressed.

Amanda settled herself on the cold stone and pulled the hem of her dress down over her knees as Branscombe sat down gingerly beside her, still clutching the brown paper parcel to his chest.

'The thing you wanted to talk to Albert about,' Amanda began, as if the pair of them had just taken their seats at the opera, 'would it have anything to do with bicycles?'

The professor squirmed slightly, something which Amanda did not ascribe to the effect of hard cold stone on his nether regions.

'You've heard about the Decameron then?'

'I have actually seen it! Quite a remarkable machine, but I am puzzled as to why I had not heard of it, as it seems to have been made out of steel tubing paid for by my company.'

Branscombe squirmed again, this time with embarrassment. 'They said they would only use offcuts and that it was in a good cause. It's to raise money for charity and it will appear regularly at Rag Weeks. Today is a trial run, but there will be plenty of students on the streets with collecting tins, so I hope you are carrying lots of spare change.'

He risked a look at Amanda but found her expression as cool and unmoving as the stone step under him. 'It was all the idea of some female from Girton,' he said, as if that explained, and excused, everything.

'She sounds a bright girl.'

'Yes, she is. Very sound ideas on design and construction, and understood stress levels without any instruction from me. She's a born engineer and I don't know why she's wasting her time with medieval erotic poetry or whatever it is she's studying. I didn't think you – of all people – would mind giving a girl like that a chance.'

Amanda had the distinct feeling that Branscombe was playing a mental chess game and had just advanced to check if not mate.

'Put like that, I would probably have offered her a job. I still might. What's her name?'

'Marigold? Petunia? Rose? I'm not sure, but it was something floral. One of my students will know.'

'I'll be sure to ask them,' said Amanda, resisting the urge to bite her tongue, 'and if she impresses me as much as she did you, then I might not report your students for theft of materials. I'm intrigued as to how they did it, though. Nugent Monck spotted that tubing was going missing and surely he would have noticed someone welding together a bicycle made for ten in the corner of the workshop.'

'I gave them permission to store the finished frames at Magdalene. We have a lock-up workshop just up the road near the old Norman castle. The plan was for them to each carry their own segment round to the Goshawk Project to put it together for a test flight, so to speak.'

'Which I witnessed yesterday.'

'Really?'

'Quite by accident. The good news is it worked; the less good news is that I recognized what it was made from.' Amanda had deliberately lightened her voice to signal that she had accepted the situation, but Branscombe seemed far from comforted and clutched his parcel even tighter.

'It wasn't the only thing they made there,' he said solemnly, 'which is why I wanted to talk to Albert.'

'Tell me, John, and I'll tell him.'

'I think it might be inappropriate . . .'

'Don't talk rot, John, spit it out. It's to do with whatever you've got wrapped up like a pound of wet fish in that parcel, isn't it?'

The professor's chin dropped and his arms relaxed, so that the parcel slid slowly on to his lap. It was not tied or secured in any way and a flap of brown paper fell open, inviting inquisitive fingers to reveal its contents. It was Amanda who did the unwrapping, whilst Branscombe remained sullenly immobile, rather like a sulking Buddha. Amanda's furious curiosity – why couldn't the man just show her? – was tempered by the thought that many a student of St Ignatius's hallowed hall must have sat on these steps over the years, regretting an examination failed, a thesis torn apart in a tutorial, a love rejected, or even their decision to apply there in the first place.

'I know what those are,' she said, as two lengths of familiar steel tubing, each at least a foot long, were revealed.

'You do?' Branscombe came to life suddenly. 'I'm astonished. I thought Albert might, with his history, but you . . .?'

'They are bits of *my* Reynolds steel tubing and I saw a pair exactly like them yesterday. Albert found them on his travels. They're pointed at one end like tent pegs so they can be pushed into the ground and . . . wait a minute . . .'

She picked up one of the tubes and weighed it in her hand.

'This one isn't pointed and it's not hollow – there's something inside it.'

She held the tube up to her eye like a telescope, pointing it across the street to the frontage of Trinity college. John Branscombe wriggled uncomfortably and looked around frantically to see if they were being observed by the passers-by.

'There's something stuck in there,' said Amanda, oblivious as to whether she was offering a free spectacle to pedestrians. 'They look like washers, or small sprockets from a gearing mechanism.'

'Baffles,' said Branscombe gloomily.

'Yes, I am baffled as to why . . .'

'No, baffles. They're called baffles, you know, as in to baffle a sound in an exhaust pipe. I would not have noticed them, but Ogden did.'

'Ogden?'

'Our head porter at Magdalene – good chap, very keen. After the students finished working on the Decameron, he popped around to the workshop first thing this morning to make sure they had left it in a fit state, and heaven help them if they hadn't.'

'First thing on a Sunday morning? That is keen. Go before Mass, did he?'

'Mr Ogden is a bit of a stickler and thinks my students take advantage of me, and anyway, he goes to early morning service. For once, though, I am grateful for his devotion to duty and his years of active service in the Royal Marine Commandos, because he spotted what they were immediately.'

'Do I get three guesses?' Amanda pointed the tube at the professor's chest. 'Or are you going to tell me?'

'Well, these two are probably prototypes which had been abandoned. Ogden found them in a pile of waste ready for collection by the scrap-metal dealer. It was clear to him that someone had been experimenting in how to make a suppressor.'

Amanda dropped the tube back into Branscombe's parcel as if it had just ignited.

'In the movies they're called silencers, though that's not strictly accurate,' he added, although the look of horror on Amanda's face should have told him further explanation was superfluous. 'They're for guns.'

Amanda composed herself instantly with the skill of an experienced actress, so that her expression was ready for its close-up, should Professor Branscombe examine it to detect whether she was lying – which she proceeded, convincingly, to do.

She did not consider it lying, merely the withholding of certain facts, at least until she had a chance to consult her husband. With almost childlike innocence, she asked Branscombe if the tubes could be explained away as an experiment by his students into the dispersion of gasses or pressures involved in the firing of a bullet. The professor had shaken his head, muttered something about ballistics and then asked, in an angry whisper, where would his engineering students have got hold of guns and bullets?

Amanda, naturally, had no idea, despite her recent discoveries in and around the professor's own house in Barton Road. Without much conviction, she suggested that the tubes might have been part, then aborted, of the design of the Decameron's construction, but Branscombe only shook his head.

'Well, somebody on that freakish machine must know,' she said to break the sullen silence, 'so we should ask them. Where's the best place to observe their maiden flight?'

'King's Parade will get them their biggest crowd,' Branscombe said, distracted.

'Then let us go and mingle with the crowds,' said Amanda, getting to her feet and brushing off the back of her skirt.

The professor folded up his parcel and, hugging it close to his chest, he followed Amanda as she retraced her steps round to King's Parade, where the crowds had indeed congregated and space on the pavements was at a premium.

Being a Sunday there were few motorized vehicles on the streets, but the Sabbath clearly put no restrictions on bicycles, as conventional ones – ridden by students and academics with gowns flowing and panniers solid with books – streamed in both directions, almost as a curtain-raiser to the main show.

And the star attraction, that most unconventional bicycle, sounded its approach by a rolling murmur which passed through the spectators, and applause which, though sporadic, was definitely getting louder.

Jostled by parents struggling to lift complaining children into higher viewing positions, and a scrum of bearded young men whose clothes gave off a distinctly herbal scent, Amanda and Branscombe were soon parted, but by repeating a polite 'Excuse me' like a mantra, and with the judicious use of her elbows, Amanda forced her way to the kerb.

The bicycle made for ten sailed majestically into King's Parade, prompting some of the older generation of onlookers to break into an erratic rendition of 'Bicycle Made for Two', asking 'Daisy' to give them their answer do. Amanda could not resist smiling at the thought that the female who had designed the Decameron might be called Daisy. It would be just too twee, and had not Branscombe said her name was 'something floral'?

Whatever her name, Amanda was convinced that the attract-ive, freckle-faced girl in the driving seat, as it were, was not only the pilot but also the brains behind the Decameron. The fact that she was blessed with a fine, curly mane of hair the colour of bright copper did not affect her judgement.

As the machine went by Amanda, along with most of the onlookers, counted the riders. There at number five was Ted Toomey, grinning like a loon, and when the tenth rider, the girl acting as the coxswain – and it was easy to think of the machine as a boat as all the riders were dressed in light blue rowing shirts – had passed, applause rang out and tins and buckets began to be rattled noisily.

Amanda looked around for the professor, though failed to locate him in the crowd, but as she was on tiptoe and looking around, she became aware of the sound of an engine which cut through the general hubbub.

The motorbike came out of Trinity Street in the middle of the road in the wake of the Decameron. It was not speeding, but clearly was intent on overtaking its pedal-powered cousin. The rider, head down over the handlebars, was encased in black leather riding gear, helmet and goggles with a black scarf covering the lower half of the face, ensuring complete anonymity.

At first, Amanda thought it might be a police outrider, there for reasons of road safety or traffic control, but it soon became clear it was not a police bike. As far as she was aware, the maiden voyage of the Decameron had been a spontaneous event which had not been advertised; knowing students, it was unlikely that official permission had ever been sought.

She stepped off the pavement and into the road to get a better view as the motorbike approached the rear of the Decameron. The girl acting as coxswain stuck out an arm to wave the bike on, indicating that it was safe to overtake. The bike rider took up the invitation and pulled out until the machines were in parallel as they passed the frontage of King's, where many a spectator had chosen to ignore the *Keep Off the Grass* signs.

Observing from the rear, Amanda saw the motorbike's brake light flicker as it slowed halfway along the length of the Decameron, which was still being applauded by spectators, then with a growl it speeded up and rapidly disappeared. Amanda stepped back on to the pavement and joined the throng, having now also lost sight of the Decameron.

She had taken no more than five or six paces when the screaming started.

If she had been instructed as child never to run into a burning building, approach a firework which had not gone off or stroke a cat to whom she had not been formally introduced, these and many other cautionary guidelines were thrown to the wind as she began to run down the road. Her view of whatever lay ahead was already obscured as pedestrians spilled off the pavements, some wishing to get a better view, some hurrying confused children away.

The Decameron had progressed into Trumpington Street and had come to halt, with a crowd gathering around it, by the stone façade of Pembroke College. The machine was being held upright by four of its riders and, as she ran, Amanda did a headcount, locating three others, all girls, standing in a semicircle, their hands held to their mouths.

The eighth rider, one of the boys, and the ninth, the flame-haired captain of the crew, were on their knees in the road, the girl clearly in charge as they leaned over a figure lying there. Despite the snapped instructions of the girl to pull himself together, the boy was whimpering, or perhaps praying, whilst the red-head used a bunched-up university scarf to try and staunch the flow of blood which was already trickling in a thin stream into the gutter.

A breathless Amanda had no doubt that it was life blood, and that it was draining out of the tenth rider, Ted Toomey.

'Oh my good God.'

Amanda felt the words hot on the back of her neck, just as she felt a hand clasp her shoulder.

'What's happened?'

'There's been an accident, John,' she said, turning to see a flushed Professor Branscombe behind her. 'It's Toomey. Do you know any of the others?'

'Not the girls, of course' – Amanda noted the qualification – 'but that big cissy down there is one of my undergrads.'

'Perhaps he doesn't have much experience of dead bodies,' said Amanda coldly.

'Oh dear, yes . . . er . . . Hey! Jiggins! What happened here?'

Jiggins, the weeping student, looked up and picked out Branscombe in the crowd of onlookers, but replied only with a chest-heaving sob. The red-headed girl answered for him.

'He slumped over the handlebars about two hundred yards back and then fell off as we got here. No one noticed the blood at first.' The girl spoke in a voice which did not expect to be contradicted or interrupted. 'The Pembroke porters have already called for an ambulance.'

Amanda leaned back into Branscombe's chest and spoke out of the side of her mouth.

'Get to the porters, John. Tell them to ring for the police as well. Teddy's been shot.'

Branscombe pushed his way to the gates of the college whilst Amanda squeezed her way nearer to the casualty, easing aside fretting mothers whispering that they thought 'that contraption' was a deathtrap as soon as they saw it, and grumpy men muttering that there were far too many bicycles in the town and something like this was bound to happen sooner or later.

Unlike the crowd of onlookers, and even the two young people attempting first aid, it occurred to Amanda that she was perhaps the only one in the vicinity who had actually seen a bullet wound before. To avoid panic, it was not information she was willing to share, and in particular she had no wish to frighten the red-headed girl who was remaining remarkably calm under such pressure.

'Help is on the way,' she reassured her, when she was close enough to be heard above the general gabble and the hooting of car horns questioning why the thoroughfare was blocked with bystanders.

The girl looked up and nodded a silent 'Thank you', without releasing her grip on the scarf she was pressing into Toomey's chest, holding it with hands that were bloodstained up to the wrists.

'Can you tell me what happened?' Amanda asked quietly.

'I don't know. Everything was going well. We didn't crash into anything and nothing crashed into us, but suddenly Teddy's feet slipped off his pedals and he just toppled off. I braked as soon as I felt his weight shift. I don't know how all this blood happened and I don't know how to stop it.'

'You're doing exactly the right thing. Stay calm, stay brave. An ambulance will be here any moment.'

'Amanda!'

She looked up to see Professor Branscombe coming through the crowd, dragging by the arm a woman whose coat was flapping open to reveal a nurse's uniform.

'This is Nurse Johnson,' said Branscombe, pushing the woman forward. 'She was on her way to work at Addenbrooke's and I sort of hijacked her.'

'Well done.'

As the nurse sank to her knees beside the inert Toomey, the red-haired girl stared up at Amanda in surprise. 'You're Amanda Campion?'

Amanda leaned over the girl, carefully avoiding looking at the bloody corpse she was tending, and said quietly, 'We will talk later.' Then she took Branscombe by the arm and pulled him aside.

'John, listen. When the police turn up, I'm likely to be more of a distraction than a help. I don't want them to waste time on me. Toomey is the one they should concentrate on and make sure that Inspector Mawson is informed of events.'

'What did you see, Amanda?'

'It's more what I *thought* I saw, and perhaps it was nothing at all, just a subliminal suggestion, probably entirely fanciful.' She paused as if the thought had just sprung into her head. 'Your housekeeper, au pair girl, Astra . . .'

'What about her?'

'Albert says she rides a motorbike.'

'I know her brother sometimes gives her a lift to Barton Road on the back of his, but why . . .? Do you know Astra?'

'No, I've never met her, but I need to ask her a question. Where does she live?'

The professor could not quite understand why the question was important, but because it was being asked by Amanda, it had to be answered.

'It's called The Halfhouse on Hills Road, way down Hills

Road, almost to where they're going to relocate the hospital. If you have to see her, I'll go and get my car.'

'No, you stay here.' There was no doubt Amanda was in charge and she caught a glimpse of the red-headed student watching her. 'Teddy was your student; you'll be needed here. I'll take a taxi if you can tell me where I can find one.'

'By the station, I suppose.'

'I know where that is,' said Amanda, holding out a hand. 'Lend me five pounds and take care of the students. They've been through something horrible, but they don't quite realize it yet.'

Then, to the girl, kneeling dirty and bloodied in the gutter by Ted Toomey, she said 'Good luck' and began to run again.

Amanda, breath rasping in her throat and Branscombe's five-pound note crumpled in her fist, found a taxi on the station rank. To her great relief, it had a driver who knew where The Halfhouse was.

'Funny noime that, don't get many o'them. Zounds like a pub it do!'

Amanda nodded enthusiastically, attempting to indicate urgency rather than a willingness to engage in conversation and compete with the local accent, rare though it was becoming these days.

Hills Road was blissfully deserted, and the taxi sped down the long avenue of large houses masked by trees and flower beds. Just as Amanda felt sure they would shoot off the end and find themselves out of the city and in a country field, the driver pulled in to the kerb by a wooden sign declaring 'The Halfhouse' in gothic lettering.

The reason for the name was instantly clear. A large Victorian villa had been divided, not exactly in two, but near enough to show this was a house divided and not a purpose-built semi-detached. The right half had retained its sash windows and faded paintwork, whilst the left had been modernized in the worst possible taste, a brick garage tacked on the side. The garage door was open and Amanda could see a motorbike resting on its stand.

Of the two front doors before her, Amanda chose the left

and pressed the bellpush. The door opened almost immediately.

The fact that Astra Jarvela was wearing black motorbiking leathers was hardly a revelation, as Amanda had only ever seen the girl dressed that way. The pistol she held levelled at Amanda's midriff, however, did provide something of a surprise.

'The Lady Campion,' said Astra. 'Please come in. Indeed, I insist on it.'

NINETEEN
Duck Shoot

Cuthbert Snow had never been shot at before, and the realization that his baptism of fire was in progress did not immediately interfere with the steady plunging and pulling of the punt pole under his muscular guidance. At Campion's warning, he had turned to see the punt on the last bend in the river, a seemingly harmless empty punt drifting in their wake. It was only when he registered the chunk of wooden till fly off from between his feet and splash into the water that he realized something was seriously wrong, despite the eerie silence being broken only by birdsong and the lapping of the river.

'Cuthbert! Head for the bank. Quickly!'

From his position, Mr Campion had a far better view of the danger and, unlike Cuthbert, had some experience of finding himself in the firing line. It still took several seconds for his brain to register that the punt pursuing them had stopped dead in the water, that the now prone figure had abandoned the wooden oar used for one-handed propulsion and was instead pointing the long metal barrel of a rifle in their direction. It was the ancient technique of wildfowling with a punt gun as used by duck hunters on the Fens since the days of the flint-lock. The hunter would approach his swimming prey silently, with little or no profile, then fire birdshot at water level, usually claiming several victims with one shot. This hunter, though, was not using birdshot and his prey were not ducks.

There was a thud, and a splinter of wood landed on Campion's outstretched legs. At first he could not see where they had been hit, until a spurt of water from beneath the till appeared at his feet, suggesting they had been holed below the waterline.

'Quick as you can, Cuthbert.' Campion turned in his seat, pushing Melvyn Barnes's head down as he did to get his bearings.

There was another left bend in the river ahead and, on the Trumpington side, the bank was shrouded in a curtain of willows weeping into the water. It did not look a promising place to land, but it might be a place to hide.

Campion judged that they would have a few seconds' grace where they would be out of sight of their now stationary pursuer as they rounded the bend. 'Swing us into those trees, Cuthbert. Full speed.'

'What's happening?' squealed Barnes.

'We're being shot at, you fool!' Campion snapped, grabbing the punt's wooden oar and twisting his body until he was on his knees facing front and able to paddle.

'I don't hear gunshots.'

'Because he's using a silencer!'

As if to illustrate Campion's point, a spout of river water erupted a yard ahead of them.

'And he's adjusting his sights to compensate. Get us into those trees.'

With a last frantic push from Cuthbert, the punt entered the hanging curtain of willow branches and Campion had just enough time before the curtain closed to see their hunter was kneeling up in the bow of his punt, paddling in pursuit with deep and determined strokes.

'What now, Mr C?' Cuthbert crouched on the till, holding the punt pole like an unwieldy lance. 'Jump ashore and run for it?'

'No,' said Campion firmly. 'Once we rise up he gets a clear shot, and my running days are behind me. If we stay here, he'll have to come closer.'

'And we want that?'

'Yes, you do.'

'I do?' Cuthbert was incredulous.

'Because it's time for the crocodile,' said Campion. 'You with me?'

Cuthbert nodded enthusiastically and began to take off his trousers.

His grandfather, the original Crocodile Snow, would have been proud, Campion was to say later.

Cuthbert, down to his underpants, slipped carefully over the side of the punt, the water shallow enough to allow him to touch the muddy bottom and steady the punt with his hands. Campion used the oar to row as far as he could without breaking the cover of their willow shelter. Motioning Barnes to stay down and keep still, Campion stood upright and, using the oar, parted the curtain of leaves.

The pursuing punt was closing on their willow hide, the hunter paddling with deep strokes to build momentum, and then allowing his craft to drift towards the bank, exchanging his wooden oar for his rifle, which Campion could now see was a short carbine elongated by the addition of a thick tube at the muzzle. The gunman was no longer bothering to lie prone for his duck shoot. There seemed little need for stealth – the ducks knew he was there.

When Campion saw the hunter performing the unmistake-able action of working the bolt action of his rifle to push another round into the chamber, he nodded to Cuthbert, who was standing up to his neck in the river, his fingers hooked over the side of the punt.

'Twenty-five yards,' he said. 'Can you do that?'

Cuthbert nodded, took a deep breath, and disappeared under the surface leaving barely a ripple.

'Stay down,' Campion ordered Melvyn Barnes, though his instructions were superfluous. Barnes had lain down in the well of the punt and pulled the cushions from the rear seat over his head.

Holding the oar, Campion strode to the stern, not really worried if he stepped on Melvyn, and knelt down on the till. Cuthbert had left the punt pole sticking upright in the riverbed mud, the upper half of it now surrounded by the willow's foliage. Campion put down the oar and grabbed the pole with both hands, turning it and shaking it in its muddy socket. The result was a rustling and flurry of leaves, followed by a disturb-ance and a shredding of some of the leaves as a bullet whipped through them, inches above his head. This time, he was convinced he heard the 'phutt' of a silenced weapon, a sound far too close for comfort.

He pushed against the pole and as the punt inched forward,

took up the oar and began to row; with three deep, strong strokes, the bow of the punt thrust through the trailing branches and back into the river proper.

Campion, crouched on the till, willed himself to be as small a target as possible as he left the cover of the willow tree. He also said a silent prayer that he had given Cuthbert enough time to do his crocodile party piece; if not he would be only a few watery yards from the hunter taking aim.

He could not have timed it better if they had rehearsed it, for as Campion emerged from the foliage, his kneeling body hunched over and anticipating the impact of another shot, he did indeed see – and much closer than he had feared – the hunter's punt, the hunter, and his rifle, with that inelegant, bulging extension to its barrel.

Yet he was not afraid, because the Crocodile was doing what crocodiles do best and the hunter's punt was not flat on the water but tipped at an angle of about sixty degrees to the surface. The hunter was no longer on board but falling head-first into the river.

'Oh, well done, Cuthbert! Crocodiling of the first order!'

Cuthbert, his wet hair and several fronds of green vegetation plastered to his head, grinned inanely and released his grip on the sides of the enemy punt, so that it slapped down flat in the water. Campion could not tell whether he was standing on the riverbed or effortlessly treading water whilst getting his breath back, but Cuthbert had the presence of mind to look around him and shout a warning.

'Where is he?'

Campion, acutely aware that their hunter may be down but not out, dug his oar in the water until the two punts were nudging each other.

'There!'

Cuthbert 'Crocodile' Snow did not have a monopoly on swimming underwater, and their assailant had surfaced, spluttering, and was now striking out for the opposite riverbank where a gentle, muddy slope led to a water meadow. The river was not wide, and the Grantchester bank was within easy reach of even the weakest swimmer. Campion realized that if he found firm footing, their assailant could be quickly out of the river and across the fields and standing at the bar of The Red

Lion, a public house not unused to serving drenched and dripping customers who had been baptized in the Cam.

'We've got to nab him before he gets away. Can you give us a push?'

Cuthbert nodded enthusiastically and grabbed the stern of Campion's punt, his legs kicking behind him as a human outboard motor. With Campion paddling, they covered the distance as if jet-propelled, and came level with the swimmer just as he was finding his feet on the muddy bank.

The shallow draught of the punt allowed it to slide alongside the shipwrecked assassin, who barely seemed to register its presence as he waded through knee-deep mud and water.

Campion rose to his feet on the till and swung the wooden oar in what the cricketing manuals would have called a front-foot pull shot.

The flat blade of the paddle connected with the back of the hunter's head with a satisfying thump and he went face down into the mud.

'As I'm not dressed for swimming,' Campion said, looking down at Cuthbert, 'and you are already very wet, could you be an angel and pull him out? I really don't want him to drown before I've had a chance to berate him for his damned unsporting behaviour.'

With a look which reminded Campion of Oliver Hardy at his exasperated best, Cuthbert pushed Campion's punt into the shore then splashed his way over to the inert figure, grabbing two handfuls of shirt and dragging it up on to the bank, where he flipped it from prone to supine and noticed the muddy brown bubbles emerging from the nose.

'He's still breathing.' Cuthbert sounded almost disappointed.

'Well, one can't have everything,' said Campion, brandishing the short wooden oar like a club. 'Now would you mind rescuing his punt before it drifts off into the sunset whilst I go through his pockets.'

'Now who's not being sporting?'

'Oh, come on! You tried to drown him and I tried to bash his brains out. A bit of petty larceny is hardly worth mentioning.'

Campion knelt by the waterlogged figure, brushing a strand

of weed from the face and then prising his fingers into the wet pockets of the man's trousers.

'Nothing here except some keys,' he said over his shoulder. 'Anything in his punt, Cuthbert?'

Chest-deep in the river, having claimed salvage on the vessel, Cuthbert shouted his reply.

'A leather jacket, a crash helmet, a few spent cartridge cases and – would you believe it – a bag of golf clubs. I mean a bag for golf clubs; there aren't any actual clubs in it.'

'The bag belongs to Professor Branscombe and he'll be delighted to have it back. I take it that our friend's rifle is at the bottom of the river?'

'You don't want me to dive for it, do you?'

'No, let the police drag the river. You come ashore and help me secure our prisoner of war.'

Campion became aware that Melvyn Barnes had risen from the bowels of the punt and was stepping cautiously across the muddy bank, peering over Campion's shoulder.

'Why was that chap trying to kill you?' he asked.

'Oh, I don't think he was trying to shoot *me*,' said Mr Campion.

'Who is he?'

'Don't you know?'

'I've never seen him before in my life.'

'Neither have I . . . Well, I may have, but we've never been properly introduced.'

Cuthbert splashed and scrambled up the sloping bank until the punt he was dragging was grounded, then he sat down on the grass and exhaled loudly, his forearms around his knees which, down to his feet, were brown with mud.

'Is there anything in the punts we could use to tie up our prisoner?' Campion asked him, but when Cuthbert shook his head wearily, he turned on Barnes. 'In that case, I'll be needing your belt and your shoelaces, Melvyn.'

'Why?'

'To secure our would-be sniper until we get back to civilization and, as an added bonus, to prevent you doing a bunk.' Campion stood and confronted Barnes with an outstretched hand. 'Come on, belt and laces – and that's an instruction you'd better start getting used to. Cuthbert, put your trousers on before you frighten the horses, or the charge list against us might get even longer.'

Barnes dropped to one knee and began to untie his shoelaces. As he did so he studied the face of the unconscious gunman. 'I honestly do not know who that is, Campion,' he said, 'or why he would try to kill you.'

'I told you,' said Campion, 'it wasn't me he was after. I'm pretty sure it was you.'

Cuthbert, pulling up his trousers over damp legs, hopped towards them and peered down at the figure lying on the grass. 'Why was Astra's brother trying to shoot Melvyn?' he asked innocently.

Barnes stared at the student. They made an incongruous sight: Cuthbert tucking his shirt into his trousers as he dressed, Barnes pulling the belt free from the loops on the waist of his trousers as though preparing to strip.

'Who's Astra?' said Barnes.

'Professor Branscombe's housekeeper,' Campion answered, 'and her brother . . .'

'Jari,' supplied Cuthbert, 'Jari Jarvela.'

Campion nodded to acknowledge the information. 'Her brother Jari, who is, I believe, a tutor in the Russian language, among other things. I'm amazed you didn't recognize him, Melvyn, as he's been your paymaster since you came to Cambridge.'

Jari Jarvela announced his return to consciousness with a long, low moan, but by then he was bound at the ankles, with his wrists tied behind his back, and lying in the bottom of Campion's punt. Melvyn Barnes had not helped in the process, but had stood to one side, holding the front of his trousers in a bunch at his waist.

When Cuthbert had paddled Jarvela's punt back across the river to retrieve their punt pole from their hideaway in the willow tree, it had left Campion and Barnes alone on the Grantchester bank in an uneasy silence. Campion did not think Barnes would turn violent, nor would he be stupid enough to try and run away now that he was handicapped in the trouser and footwear departments, as well as by his limping leg.

On Cuthbert's return, he presented Campion with three brass cartridge cases, which Campion pocketed, then they combined to pull Jarvela's punt out of the river. They transferred the golf bag, jacket and crash helmet to their craft, then clambered on board, being careful – but not too careful – to avoid stepping on Jarvela. Naturally, Cuthbert resumed his duties on the till as their propulsion unit for the journey downstream back to Cambridge, although as the city boundary ran down the river here, technically they may never have left it.

They had travelled perhaps half a mile, hugging the western bank when the afternoon silence, sprinkled only by birdsong until then, was punctured by five loud blasts on a car horn.

'Left-hand down a bit, Cuthbert,' said Campion with a grin, 'and pull in here. That's the sound of the cavalry arriving.'

'The cavalry?'

'Well, the Americans. Late to the fray as usual, but very welcome nonetheless.'

Campion's meaning, if not his humour, became clear when the punt nudged into the bank as rising out of the grass to greet them was the figure of Luther Romo. He wore a Brooks Brothers' seersucker suit, white shirt and tie (almost certainly a clip-on, thought Campion), his reflective aviator sunglasses masking most of his face.

'Are y'all having fun down there in your little boat?' he called out.

'We certainly are,' Campion replied, 'but you've missed all the good bits. It's been jolly exciting. What are you doing in the middle of this wetland wilderness?'

'Hardly a wilderness. I'm standing on a public footpath, not wallowing around in the mud like you guys. If you've finished splish-splashing, would you like a lift? My car's just here.'

Campion exchanged grins with Cuthbert as Romo strode down the bank towards them. 'Only an American would go for a trip on a river in a Chevrolet.'

'I was following him,' said Romo, pointing a finger at the trussed Jarvela in the punt.

'You were? That was very astute of you.'

'Dumb luck, really. After our talks yesterday, I thought I'd keep an eye on *him*' – the finger moved until it was aimed at Melvyn Barnes – 'and I spotted that he had a tail, so I tracked the tracker at a safe distance. He's resourceful, I'll give him that, and a quick thinker. You guys piling into that punt threw him for a couple of seconds. How was he gonna follow you on his bike?'

'He was on his motorbike? That explains the leather trousers and jacket,' said Campion. 'Not the usual fashion choice for an afternoon on the river. Where did he get the punt?'

'I told you, he was cool. Once he saw the direction you were taking, he took the Grantchester Road and I followed at a distance.'

'Quite a distance, for that car of yours not to be noticed.'

'Hey, don't tell grandma how to suck eggs. I know how to run a tail. Our biker friend spotted a couple of lovebirds canoodling in the long grass with a picnic. They were far too interested in each other to notice their punt being stolen by chummy there. You guys had just sailed right by them.'

'It would have been extremely rude to point and stare,' said Campion. 'Do you think they are still *in situ*?'

'Guess so. They were heavily into their picnicking, if you know what I mean. I found our guy's bike where he'd left it and moved it behind some bushes, then I followed the path and caught the final reel of you chaps playing at submarine warfare. I was too far away to help, but you seemed to have things under control.'

'It didn't seem like it at the time.'

'Nah, you were fine. That was a neat trick, hiding in that tree and launching young Cuthbert as a human torpedo to sink the enemy warship. Where did he learn to do that?'

'It's a family trait,' said Campion to save Cuthbert's blushes. 'His grandfather perfected the technique. I just knew it would come in useful one day.'

Jari Jarvela was beginning to come round and squirmed like a landed pike as Cuthbert and Luther Romo carried him by the head and feet up to the footpath and then to the Chevrolet parked at the side of Grantchester Road. Campion followed, supervising Melvyn Barnes, who was more concerned with holding his trousers up than in objecting or resisting.

That the Chevrolet was hardly the ideal vehicle for transporting prisoners did not bother Romo, who pushed Jarvela and Barnes unceremoniously into the back seat. Then he turned to Cuthbert.

'As for you, big feller, you can scootch up front with me and Albert, or you could ride this guy's motorbike back into town, if you can find the keys on him.'

'I have them,' said Campion, noting the huge grin on Cuthbert's face which indicated that he had chosen the motorcycle. 'Run back to the punts and grab his jacket and helmet, see if they fit. We can abandon our craft here and report its location later, but I feel guilty about the one Jari stole from the young lovers.'

'Leave that too,' said Romo. 'They've probably not even noticed it's missing. They had other things on their mind.'

'Very well. I suggest we rendezvous at Magdalene. John Branscombe deserves to know what's been going on and it is Cuthbert's college. He, and it, deserve a Triumph – in the Roman sense, that is, not just the motorbike.'

Luther Romo leaned into the Chevrolet and opened the glove compartment. 'That was your famous British humour, I guess, but just in case our back-seat passengers don't get the joke, you may need this.'

He handed Campion an automatic pistol with the prancing horse trademark of Colt embossed on the butt.

Campion did his best to look disappointed. 'Oh dear, are my jokes really that bad?'

TWENTY
The Gun She Came in With

For a few uneasy seconds Amanda misread the situation, and then the real danger she was in began to dawn on her.

'Astra, I have come about your brother,' she said in a rush. 'You must get away from him and come with me.'

The shorter, younger blonde woman looked up into the face of her hot and flustered visitor, her own a blank, emotionless canvas.

'My brother is not here,' she said in a dull monotone.

'But his motorbike is outside . . .'

'That is my motorbike. Jari has his own.'

Amanda would never tell anyone, not even her husband, how she gasped for breath and felt ice form in her stomach at that precise moment, not when Astra had opened the door and recognized her, nor when she had registered the fact that Astra was holding a gun – an ugly black automatic with a bulbous addition to the barrel made of all-too-familiar tubing – but when the girl calmly confirmed that she too owned a motorbike.

She would never admit to that sudden feeling of dread, for she was furious with herself for not noticing immediately that Astra was wearing black leather from neck to ankle. The realization that there were two motorbikes and, what is more, two guns in the equation, and her own folly in presenting herself, alone and unarmed, into the camp of the enemy struck her like a thunderbolt.

'It was you, wasn't it, who shot Teddy Toomey on King's Parade?'

'I saw you with Professor Branscombe,' said Astra calmly, 'so perhaps you saw me.'

It was an admission of sorts, but a long way from a confession, and Amanda had the gruesome thought that if she had confessed, then her chances of leaving the house alive would have been nil. But why was she deluding herself? Her chances were nil anyway.

'You knew who I was?'

'I was well briefed and have observed you several times at the Goshawk facility.'

'From Barton Road, of course, which is where I saw you yesterday.' There was a flicker of something – interest perhaps, certainly not concern – in the younger woman's eyes. 'But that was not the gun you collected from the house, though perhaps the silencer was.'

'You saw me?'

'I did, and I have been briefed on you also.'

'Yet you came here alone.'

'I may have misjudged the situation,' said Amanda quietly.

'I would say you most certainly have. Now put your hands on your head, kneel down and face the wall.'

Mr Campion had always held to the belief that the porter's lodge of a well-run Cambridge college – St Ignatius, on various grounds, being exempt – was something akin to a cross between the safety-deposit vault of a city bank and the private chapel of a powerful Renaissance family in an Italian cathedral. Things could be deposited there and only withdrawn after strenuous identity checks and no one, but no one, was allowed to misbehave in there without incurring the wrath of the incumbent priest, the head porter.

It was therefore fortunate that Professor Branscombe was on hand to smooth the feathers of Magdalene's own Praetorian Guard when their lodge was invaded and it was demanded that it act as a temporary prison for two inmates, one dripping wet and bound at the wrists and ankles, and an older man who could have passed for a visiting academic, despite the fact that his trousers were in imminent danger of falling down. The porters' blood pressure was raised further by a request to unlock the gates to the Fellows' Garden in order that a motor-bike be parked there, and the fact that these demands were being made by a loud *American* and a thin, bespectacled gentleman who spoke politely and precisely, but had the disadvantage of being recognized as a St Ignatius man.

John Branscombe's presence went a long way to restoring order and, after nodding a greeting, rather quizzically, to both Romo and a grinning Cuthbert, who arrived with a deep-throated engine roar, he grabbed Campion by the arm and pulled him to one side.

'That's Jari Jarvela. He's the Finn who teaches Russian.'

'Or the Russian who happens to speak Finnish,' said Campion.

'Has he said anything?'

'Almost nothing, in either language, just a few choice swear words. He's keeping his mouth shut and working out his options. I would do the same in his position, given that we are unlikely to subject him to the torture I might have expected in Moscow if our positions were reversed. Nobody except the *Daily Express* wants yet another spy scandal, so he would do well to keep quiet and hope for a trial *in camera* followed by a quiet exchange in Berlin for one of our chaps. I'm afraid it will be Melvyn Barnes who the police will be arresting for murder. Jarvela might have had a good go, but he hasn't actually killed anyone.'

'Then his sister might have,' said the professor grimly, 'and your wife's gone after her.'

'You thought I was Jari,' said Astra Jarvela.

Amanda's mouth had gone dry and she had to lick her lips before answering.

'On King's Parade, on the motorbike? Yes, I did.'

'But you do not know us.'

'I told you, I saw you in John Branscombe's house.'

'Impossible.' Astra said the word as if it ended an argument.

'I saw you with Teddy in the kitchen and I know he offered you a ring, as well as other things. I think Teddy also told you that Melvyn Barnes had taken the Land Rover out to Bourn, which was easy for him to discover as Melvyn always logged his mileage. That was the regular signal for your brother to go out and check his dead letter box, which was probably what you told him when you were talking on the telephone. And then he asked you to retrieve the rifle for him from the water butt in the garden. How am I doing? Still impossible?'

'You know nothing.'

Internally, Amanda screamed in frustration. There seemed to be no shaking the girl, who, frighteningly, seemed to know exactly what she was doing. She had made Amanda drop to her knees in the narrow hallway of the house and had then taken up a position behind her, carefully staying out of range, not that – from a kneeling position with her hands on her head – Amanda posed much of a threat.

The only weapon available to Amanda was speech; keeping the girl talking might just distract her from pulling a trigger.

'You tried out that rifle with a silencer in the old rifle range, didn't you? That was so convenient – you just couldn't resist taking pot-shots at that old oil drum. We found the bullets, you know, inside the drum.' Being made to face the wall meant it was impossible for Amanda to tell if her revelations were having any effect. 'I'm sure you were careful to collect your cartridge cases, what the Americans call their "brass", but you forgot about the bullets. The shooting was good grouping, though, very accurate.'

Behind her, Amanda could hear Astrid stepping from foot to foot as she patrolled the hallway. It was the lithe movement of a tigress, hardly the sound of someone shaking in their boots.

'You know so little I almost pity you.'

'Really? I think I know a lot. I know you took John Branscombe's golf bag to hide the rifle. Why did your brother want it?'

'Unfinished business,' said Astra, her voice cold and emotionless.

'You didn't need it to kill Teddy,' Amanda hoped she did not sound as frightened as she felt, 'and he was in love with you, wasn't he? That was brutal – and to do it using a silencer which he made for you! That wasn't just brutal, that was evil.'

'He was young and stupid and, also, he was unfinished business.'

Once again there was no inflection, no emotion in Astra's almost robotic response. It was, Amanda thought, like talking to the wall, which was exactly what she was doing.

'The police, I take it, are aware of things,' Campion said to Branscombe, after the professor had outlined the incidents on King's Parade.

'They were on the spot fairly quickly, taking statements; they probably still are, there were a lot of witnesses.'

'But it seems only Amanda suspected Astra?'

They were talking in whispers, away from the lodge, where the porters were struggling to remain polite and professional as their sanctum was invaded.

'I think she thought it must be the brother and she felt the need to warn Astra. Clearly it could not have been Jari if he was out on the river with you chaps.'

'We weren't exactly having a picnic. He was shooting at us with a silenced rifle which Astra kept hidden at your house.'

'Good God! In my house? That's devilish cheeky.' Then, as an afterthought, he added: 'Why was he trying to shoot you?'

Mr Campion pushed his spectacles higher up the bridge of his nose with a forefinger.

'Why does everyone assume he was trying to kill *me*? It was Melvyn Barnes he was after.'

'But why?'

'I think he was tying up loose ends, and in a sense Melvyn brought it on himself when *he* started to tie off a loose end by killing Alan Wormold.'

'And what about Teddy? Was he just another loose end?'

'I'm afraid he probably was. Listen, John, don't say anything in front of Cuthbert just yet. He's pumped up and excited after his exertions on the river – where he was magnificent, by the way. But finding out he's just lost another housemate would be a cruel way of bringing him down to earth.'

'I agree,' said Branscombe, 'but what about Amanda. Is she in danger?'

'It is very likely,' said Campion, 'that she has walked unsuspecting into the lioness's den. She saw Astra collect a rifle, presumably for her brother, and she knew Jari rode a motorbike. But Jari had the rifle and his bike when he followed Melvyn Barnes to our punt trip. Amanda did not realize that there were two weapons and two motorbikes.'

'And I gave her their address; even the loan of the taxi fare . . .'

'Did you tell the police at the scene that?'

The professor's face fell. 'No, they only asked me if I had seen Teddy come off that damn stupid bicycle, which I hadn't, but because he was a Magdalene man, they would want a statement later. We must telephone them.'

Mr Campion took off his glasses and began to polish the lenses with his handkerchief.

'Of course we must, but there's someone else I need to ring first.'

This was not going to plan, thought Amanda, but then it had never been much of a plan to begin with. What was it that they said about policemen, that they walk unarmed into danger to protect the innocent? What had possessed her to think she could fill their boots?

It wasn't as if she had a Plan B, other than the one which always uncoiled in the final scenes of films and television melodramas, where the fiendish villain (or villainess) has the hero (or heroine) trapped, but then embarks on a monologue revealing his or her plans for world domination for so long that the police/army/cavalry have plenty of time to arrive in the nick of.

There seemed little chance of Plan B having any traction, as Astra Jarvela was not forthcoming in the monologue department and preferred to speak only in short, sharp commands. She might be tight-lipped, but rather that than trigger-happy, and even as she thought this, Amanda had another, almost optimistic realization. Astra was clearly not given to panic or she would have used that gun by now, so perhaps she did not see Amanda as a threat. What would it take to unsettle her and hopefully provoke her into a misstep?

How about if Amanda proved she was a threat? What if

Amanda gave the villainess's monologue instead of the
villainess? It could buy her some time – or an early bullet.

'You must have thought all your Christmases had come
at once,' she said, hoping that her voice sounded more
confident than she felt, 'if you people believe in Christmas,
that is.'

She received no answer and there was no bullet, which she
took to mean that Astra was willing to listen, if not speak.

'I mean when you found the Goshawk Project was coming
to Cambridge. You probably couldn't believe your luck. You
already had your sights on John Branscombe and his research
work, and your job at Barton Road gave you plenty of opportunity to go through any papers he casually left lying around
at home which, being an academic, he almost certainly did.
Just to make sure, there was Teddy Toomey, who fell into your
lap, perhaps literally, when he turned up here – this very house?
– for some extra-curricular Russian lessons with your brother
Jari. There was another route in to Branscombe's work, if he
could be manipulated, and from what I saw, that wasn't a
problem for you. It would not have taken you long to seduce
an innocent boy like Teddy.'

Ignoring the discomfort in her knees due to the hard floor-
boards of the hallway and the cramp in her tensed shoulder
blades, Amanda strained her ears for any reaction from her captor
standing behind her. She heard nothing to break the clammy
silence, except she thought she detected a sharp intake of breath,
but could not be sure that was when she mentioned Teddy or
brother Jari by name.

'I'm sure you were aware that someone in Alandel, my
company, was selling research information to whoever would
pay for it. And now he was here in Cambridge and working
at Goshawk, with access to all our designs and research into
materials and, what's more, he was willing to sell. Your masters
in Moscow – which is it, by the way, the KGB or the GRU?
– well, they must have been delighted. What I cannot understand is why Alan Wormold had to die.'

'We did not harm him.'

At last, a reaction, though it was hardly an emotional breakthrough. By turning her head ever so slightly, Amanda could

see, out of the corner of her eye, the bulbous barrel of the pistol held rock-solidly in Astra's unwavering hands.

'But he was harmed. In fact, he was murdered.'

'By that fool Barnes, that greedy, stupid fool.'

'But Teddy thought you were responsible and that's why he had to die.'

'Pah!' scoffed Astra, startling Amanda. 'You understand nothing. Teddy thought it was an accident. He was easily fooled.'

'In more ways than one,' said Amanda through gritted teeth, 'but if so, why kill him?'

'He was a loose end.'

'That's quite a brutal way of tying off loose ends.'

Amanda suddenly realized the implication of what she had just said.

'Does that mean I am a loose end as well?'

'That is for my brother to decide.'

Amanda risked turning her head until she could see Astra's dispassionate face. 'And where is Jari?'

For the first time the pistol quivered as the girl shrugged her shoulders. 'Taking care of unfinished business.'

'Melvyn Barnes,' said Amanda softly, 'on the river, with the rifle. Dear God, I sound like I'm playing *Cluedo*.' She registered the puzzled flicker in Astra's eyes. 'That was a poor joke in dubious taste.'

'English humour when distressed.'

'Something like that.'

Without knowing how or why, Amanda felt a surge of confidence, possibly even bravery, or perhaps simply stubborn defiance. She let her hands drop from where they had been clasped above her head and shuffled around on her knees until her body faced Astra's. The girl took a step back down the hallway to stay out of reach just in case a suicidal Amanda launched herself in a rugby tackle at her. The pistol, steady as ever, was aimed at the centre of Amanda's face.

'You're waiting for Jari to return, aren't you? He gives the orders, doesn't he, and you've got no orders to dispose of me, not yet anyway.'

And Jari, she hoped, a flare of panic going off inside her, did not have orders to dispose of Albert.

'When is he due back? Shouldn't he be home by now?'

Amanda realized that it was never wise to poke and prod a dangerous animal, but a mixture of frustration and anger spurred her on.

'You've both been out tying up your loose ends, as you call it, though most people would say you've been busy committing murder. What do you think is going to happen next? Are you planning on going back to cleaning house for John Branscombe tomorrow? I don't think so. Industrial espionage is one thing, cold-blooded murder in broad daylight is quite another, and that won't be forgotten or swept under the carpet. Your problem is whether Jari gets here before the police, or has he cut and run already, leaving you to take the rap, as our American friends would say? Of course, we haven't hanged a woman for several years in this country, and the death penalty is about to be abolished for good this year, although not, I believe, for espionage. What if your dear brother has thought it through and decided his best chance is to cut and run?'

'Shut your mouth!'

The gun shook in Astra's hand and Amanda felt a cold trickle of sweat run down the back of her neck.

Then the tension was broken by the shrill ringing of a telephone.

Before Amanda had fully realized that the sound was coming from what must be the front room of the house, she found herself being dragged there, arms flailing, still on her knees, by Astra, who had grabbed a fistful of her hair with one hand whilst pressing the pistol to her forehead with the other.

Squealing with discomfort and the humiliation of being led like a recalcitrant dog, Amanda was dragged into the room and pushed down face-first on to the carpet. Spluttering with inhaled dust, she tried to get her bearings. The room was sparsely furnished with just two mismatched armchairs and a small card table, on which sat the vibrating telephone demanding to be answered.

'Stay down,' said Astra, moving to the table, keeping her eyes and her gun pointed at her prisoner whilst reaching for the receiver.

'Hello?'

There was a pause after she answered the call. A long pause. So long that Amanda began to mentally count the seconds of silence.

She estimated that almost two full minutes had passed before Astra looked down at her and said, 'It's for you.'

TWENTY-ONE
Magdalene Bridge of Spies

'Oh, hello. Albert Campion here, may I speak with my wife?'

Mr Campion could not recall when he had ever allowed himself to make a private telephone call with such an attentive audience hanging on his every word. There were three college porters, all trying to retain their composure as their temple became ever more like a scene from a Marx Brothers' film, despite soothing noises praising their patience from Professor Branscombe. A still-damp Cuthbert put himself between Melvyn Barnes and the door to prevent any escape attempt, whilst Luther Romo hovered on the shoulder of a stonily silent Jari Jarvela, with one hand firmly jammed into a bulging jacket pocket, a pocket which Campion knew contained the small Colt automatic because he had, with commendable sleight-of-hand, returned it to its owner without anyone noticing.

'Albert, is this the most prudent course of action?'

'Probably not, John, but I must do this first, then we can call the police. May I have that number, please?'

Branscombe held out a pocket diary, opened at a page reserved for useful telephone numbers, and pointed to a Cambridge number in red ink.

'You sure you know what you're doing?' Luther Romo asked as Campion appropriated the porters' telephone and began to dial.

'In general, rarely,' said Mr Campion, 'but in this case I am sure I want to get my wife back in one piece.'

'So you're gonna negotiate?'

'Something like that.'

'Astra, Astra Jarvela,' Campion said into the silence which followed the answering. 'Hello.'

'I know it's you, Astra, and I know my wife is with you. I would like some assurance that she is in good health and not in any immediate danger. If that is the case – and for now I will take your silence that it is – then I have a proposition for you.

'Firstly, you should know that I have your brother here with me. He is unharmed and is not yet in the custody of the authorities. Happily, he failed in his mission to eliminate Melvyn Barnes, who *is* now in custody, a factor which signals the end of your interest in the Goshawk Project. But you knew that well enough. It's over, Astra, as is your time in Cambridge, and I would not be surprised if you had your bags packed and were ready to do a moonlight flit, as the lower criminal classes say.

'You could stay put, I suppose, but you would be pestered to an inordinate degree by the police and security services. You may wish to report back to your Moscow overlords, though whether they will be pleased to see you is a moot point, as the technical information you have been passing recently is, as I understand it, wildly optimistic about the prospects for swept-forward winged flight, not to say fundamentally unsound. But I suspect your brother knew that well enough when he saw the last lot of blueprints left out by Caxton Gibbet yesterday. The game is up, Astra.

'We have our traitor and we have your brother; we even have his motorbike. You have my wife, and before we go any further, I insist on talking to her.'

'Albert? It could only be you.'

'Of course it is, my darling. Now be very careful what you say, as I am assuming you are not exactly a free agent at the moment.'

'You could say that.'

'And I take it that our conversation is not exactly private.'

'Not comfortably so, no.'

Amanda had actually bitten back a squeal of pain as Astra had put the receiver down on the table, in order to grab a handful of red hair and pull Amanda, on her knees again, towards the telephone. Amanda had placed the receiver to her right ear as the girl pressed the muzzle of her weapon uncomfortably into her left.

'Then tell me you are unharmed,' said Mr Campion down the wire, 'but nothing else.'

'A bit battered and bruised,' said Amanda, 'but still breathing.'

'Excellent, now make those breaths deep ones, ask no questions and trust me. Put the girl back on and just go along with what happens thereafter.'

After *what*? Amanda wanted to scream, but submissively she offered the receiver back to Astra.

'I am honour bound,' said Campion into the telephone, 'to reciprocate the gesture by proving that I have your brother here and he is unharmed. If you wish it, you may speak to him, but I insist you talk in English. If I hear Russian or Finnish spoken, I will hang up immediately. Is that understood?'

'I understand. Let me speak to Jari.'

Campion held out the receiver and Luther Romo gently pushed Jarvela forward, keeping his body close to his own. When he was sure he could not be seen by the porters, he slipped the Colt from his pocket and jammed it into the Finn's side at kidney height.

Campion held the receiver just out of Jarvela's reach. 'English only,' he said, 'or there will be consequences.'

Jari nodded and took the instrument. 'Astra? Jari. Yes, I am fine. No, my business remains unfinished. Listen to what the man Campion says. I think he has a plan we can follow.'

However hard she strained her ears, Amanda could only hear one half of the conversation, and the fact that the pistol Astra was holding never wavered did not help her concentration.

That Albert was allowing her to speak to her brother meant he had some sort of private plan of action, as allowing a social telephone call between two conspiring murderers was surely not standard police procedure. If the police were running the operation, they would be outside The Halfhouse laying siege by now, but there had been no battering at the front door, not even the clump of a size twelve police boot on the driveway.

When Astra said into the receiver 'Did you finish your business?' Amanda struggled to read the expression on the girl's face as she got her answer. Could it be that Jari had failed to tie up his 'loose end' and that Albert had saved Melvyn Barnes and, if so, was that on the plus side of the equation? Jari might be a thief and possibly a blackmailer, given that he was certainly a spy, and theft and blackmail were a spy's favourite tools, but perhaps he was not a murderer. Did that leave Astra feeling exposed and thinking she had been left to carry the can, because she certainly was a killer. Amanda knew that, but did the police?

If possible, it made Astra, and Amanda's predicament, even more dangerous.

Albert's plan had better be a good one.

'We need somewhere to secure our prisoners, John,' said Mr Campion. 'Actually two places, where they can be kept under lock and key apart from each other.'

'You don't want them cooking up something between them?'

'Actually, I'm more worried they might kill each other, so find me two places with stout doors, hefty iron locks and no windows. A college this old ought to have a surfeit of them.'

'There's the wine cellar,' suggested the head porter, still silently fuming at the way his staff and headquarters were being treated.

'Come now, Mr Ogden, that's rather drastic,' said Branscombe quickly.

Mr Campion allowed himself a broad grin. 'I can think of a situation where locking someone – and I have in mind a specific reprobate acquaintance – in the wine cellars would be positively dangerous and severely undermine the college's financial security, but Melvyn there would probably behave himself as he knows the game is up.' Campion stopped grinning and stared at the downcast Barnes. 'Plus I doubt he would fancy being left alone with the Soviet agent whose career he has successfully ended.'

'We could stick the foreign gentleman in the cleaners' store cupboard, sir,' said Mr Ogden, recognizing Campion as the man who could get this mob out of his lodge, thereby restoring the natural order of things. 'There's a lock of sorts on it and I could have one of my men stand guard.'

'An excellent idea, Mr Ogden, and I am sure Cuthbert here will help with guard duty.'

'Just make sure the storeroom doesn't have the fixings for anything explosive,' interjected Romo. 'Cleaning materials can be pretty volatile.'

'Some of our more mischievous young gentlemen discovered that many years ago, sir, so we do take precautions,' Ogden told him with puffed-chest pride.

Branscombe and the porters led Barnes and Jarvela away, with Cuthbert, bouncing on the balls of his feet, keen to reinforce them, until he was asked by Campion to bring in the leather jacket and crash helmet worn by Jari Jarvela.

When he and Romo were left alone in the porters' lodge, the American stood four-square in front of Campion; a stance which suggested he was about to ask questions to which he expected answers.

'Did you have any authority to offer the deal you just did?'

'None at all,' said Campion.

'But you think she'll go for it? An exchange – her brother for your wife?'

'She has gone for it. She'll bring Amanda to the other side of Magdalene Bridge in about half an hour, so we must be ready.'

'A prisoner exchange across a bridge, like for spies?'

'I believe they are all the rage in Berlin.'

'But if you intend to exchange Jarvela for your wife, why have him locked in the cleaning cupboard?'

'Oh, I never intended to swap *him* for Amanda.' Campion smiled. 'I'm exchanging you.'

Astra Jarvela replaced the telephone receiver and waved her pistol to indicate that Amanda should stand up, which she did stiffly and with trepidation. What the girl said next made her sore knees tremble.

'I am taking you to your husband, so you must behave. If you do not, it will be bad for you.'

'Where is he?' she asked, still tasting the carpet dust she had inhaled.

'With Professor Branscombe at his college – we will meet on the bridge there. Now say you will give me no trouble.'

She waved the snout of her weapon like a wand for emphasis. Amanda was once more surprised at how ridiculous the pistol looked, with its bulbous home-made suppressor made from a bicycle part. She would have dismissed it as a boy's toy, had she not seen with her own eyes that it worked only too well.

'I promise to behave,' she said in a childlike manner, almost tempted to make the cross-my-heart gesture with a finger.

Satisfied with Amanda's answer, though not enough to lower the gun, Astra grunted 'Kitchen' and indicated they should move back into the hall.

The kitchen at the back of the house was as spartan as the front room had been. Every surface had been cleaned and there was not a pot, pan or plate in sight. Amanda also suspected that all the cupboards were bare, which meant only one thing: the Jarvelas were pulling out of their base and almost certainly Cambridge, but whether that was to her advantage or not she was not sure.

'Stand there and do not move,' said Astra, pointing to a blank piece of wall, and as Amanda complied she sank down on one knee, opened the small cupboard under the sink, reached in and pulled out a length of clothesline.

Keeping her eyes fixed on Amanda, she placed her gun – still within easy reach – on the draining board, and quickly fastened a crude slipknot in the rope, forming a noose at the end.

Arming herself again, she advanced on Amanda, casually flipped the lasso over her head and pushed the knot so that it was secure but not likely to choke.

'Are you intending to drag me through Cambridge like a dog on a lead?' Amanda said, tight-lipped.

'No,' said Astra without a shred of emotion, 'we are going for a ride.'

John Branscombe caught up with Campion and Romo in the Fellows' Garden, having made sure that Magdalene's most reluctant visitors were secure, if not comfortable.

'I say, Campion, when you were speaking to that horrid little woman, you didn't mention Toomey's death or that we have called in the police.'

'No, John, I didn't. I preferred to let her think I was unaware of Teddy's death, as she was hardly likely to bring Amanda here if she thought a platoon of coppers were waiting to arrest her. The brother played into my hands somewhat, which helped no end.'

'He did?'

'When he said his business remained unfinished. That was clearly their code for his failed assassination of Melvyn, so Astra knows we haven't got him for murder or manslaughter.'

'And that helps?'

'It makes it more likely she will do a trade. She must know we would not let a murderer go, but we might swap a mere spy.'

'And when is this exchange going to take place?'

'In about fifteen minutes,' said Campion, after a glance at his wristwatch.

'And the police are happy with this plan?'

'Oh, I shouldn't think so for a minute, but now might be a good time to ring them and ask them to pop along, discreetly of course.'

The professor struggled to find a reply, but Campion had already turned to address Romo.

'Now, Luther, for my peace of mind, would you take out that neat little Colt and remove the magazine, please? I'm relying on you to handle the situation without starting a gunfight with my wife in the middle.'

The American raised his eyebrows, shrugged and produced the Colt, slipping out the magazine in one swift movement, offering it to Campion.

'Now the round in the breech, please.'

Romo worked the slide on the pistol and caught the ejected bullet.

'Now put all the ammunition in one pocket and the Colt in the other and give me your jacket.'

'So you're sending me into battle unarmed,' said Romo. Then, noticing the shocked look on Branscombe's face: 'That's hardly cricket, is it, Prof?'

'None of this is cricket! It's insane.'

'Now keep calm, John,' said Campion. 'Luther here is young, fit and highly trained. I'm sure he can handle himself against a young girl half his size.'

'There's something I meant to tell you,' said Romo, handing over his jacket. 'I got a package from Langley this morning about the Jarvela siblings. Came with a picture of the two of them, taken at the 1960 Winter Olympics in Squaw Valley, California, at the biathlon event. The Finns took the silver medal, the Russians the bronze. Guess which team both the Jarvelas were pictured with?'

'Which?' said Branscombe.

'The question was rhetorical, John,' soothed Campion, 'and a skill on skis, even at Olympic standard, should not worry us.'

'I'm talking about the biathlon, Al,' said Romo. 'Used to be known as Military Patrol. It involved cross-country skiing *and shooting*, a tough sport and they both trained for it. Get what I'm saying?'

'You mean she might almost be as tough as her brother who, despite being armed with a rifle, was laid out and captured by the weak and feeble old-age pensioner you see before you?' Campion hoped the American could see the twinkle in his eyes.

Luther Romo flexed his biceps and gave a body-builder's grimace. 'I can take her,' he drawled.

If she had been frightened before, Amanda was truly terrified riding behind Astra on her motorbike and was to describe the experience as her 'Isadora Duncan moment'. It was not that she was scared of motorbikes as such, or even riding as a pillion passenger, though on the few occasions she had, it had been with an overwhelming feeling of powerlessness as she was not at the controls. Her journey through Cambridge that Sunday afternoon offered an extra layer of distress in that she was tethered to the driver.

She had hitched up her skirt and mounted the bike as instructed and, as also instructed, put her arms around Astra's waist. Her captor had then taken the end of the clothesline which still formed a noose around her neck, wrapped a loop of slack around her forearm and then used the remaining length to tie Amanda's wrists together. A casual observer would have seen a leather-clad, helmeted bike rider with an affectionate female passenger, her arms around the rider's waist, her face pressed into the back of his leather jacket. The observer might have thought that the female was poorly dressed to go motorbike riding and that, in all honesty, she was possibly a little too old for such a recreation, but then this was Cambridge and far stranger sights had graced its streets.

Amanda knew that she must be giving the impression of an adoring pillion rider. On the plus side, her position did provide some protection from the slipstream, and she kept her eyes and mouth shut tight, trying not to think what her hair looked like or what would happen to her if she came off the bike at speed without the benefit of any protective gear. Not that her coming off the bike was a possibility, unless Astra crashed the infernal thing, and any attempt to destabilize the bike would result, she had been warned, in Astra slamming her crash helmet backwards into Amanda's face.

The journey – she had no idea how long it took – passed in a nightmarish blur, and only when the bike finally slowed and then ground to halt did Amanda risk opening her eyes. She was conscious of the engine being turned off and Astra kicking down the stand before fumbling with the rope which bound her wrists. She was also aware when Astra slid off the bike and felt she really ought to make a move herself, only to find she could hardly move. She had not realized how cold she was; her legs felt as if they were encased in ice and it took a great effort of will to lift her feet from the bike's passenger foot pegs, noticing as she did that both her comfortable suede shoes were stained with engine oil.

Her stiff dismount was both clumsy and undignified, and she was begrudgingly grateful when Astra appeared to offer to help her, though her motive was to remove the 'dog lead' noose around her neck.

'Stand over there,' Astra said, her eyes dead, 'and do not move until I tell you.' She removed her helmet, balancing it on the bike's petrol tank, then unzipped her leather jacket and plunged her right hand inside, withdrawing it just enough to show Amanda the butt of the pistol.

Massaging her wrists where they had been tied, and sporadically trying to slap some warmth into her thighs, Amanda concentrated on the view in front of her.

She was on the eastern bank of the river, standing on what had been the quayside of the Anglo-Saxon settlement. Directly across the water she instantly recognized the outline of Magdalene College and, slightly to her left, the Great Bridge.

At the Magdalene end of the cast-iron bridge stood a figure in a black leather jacket and motorcycle helmet and goggles, holding the handlebars of a stationary motorbike. He was flanked by the unmistakeable John Branscombe and the gloriously familiar Albert Campion.

Mr Campion took hold of his trusty fedora and raised it high above his head.

'That's the signal,' said Astra. 'Walk, do not run.'

'Walk, don't run,' said Mr Campion, patting the leather-jacketed figure on the back to send him on his way, head down, pushing the motorbike alongside him.

Being late Sunday afternoon there was little traffic to or from the city centre, and the sight of a motorcyclist whose machine had perhaps run out of petrol was unlikely to raise any suspicion or even a second look.

Certainly the woman walking towards him in a slightly odd, bow-legged fashion, did not give him a second look, not even when they passed each other on the pavement less than a yard apart. The woman stayed close to the iron railings, the man kept to the kerb edge, the wheels of his silent machine in the gutter. His eyes, behind the goggles, were fixed on the pavement immediately in front of him; she only had eyes for the far end of the bridge.

Magdalene Bridge may be a Great Bridge, but it is not a long one. And what happened after the two figures passed each other happened very quickly.

The man wheeling the motorbike was within four yards of

Astra Jarvela when she realized something was wrong and the smile that had started to form on her lips disappeared in an instant as she reached for the zip of her jacket.

Reading the unmistakeable signs that he had been recognized – or, more correctly, *not* recognized – Luther Romo let go of the motorbike and lunged the last few steps towards her.

The machine falling on its side with a loud crash undoubtedly distracted the girl, and Romo moved with lightning speed, the heel of his hand descending in a perfect karate chop on the side of the girl's neck.

Astra Jarvela collapsed like a dropped sack of malt against her assailant.

On the other side of the bridge, Amanda fell far more enthusiastically into the outstretched arms of Mr Campion.

TWENTY-TWO
The Blind Cell

'So this 'ere Gos'awk of yours never could fly backwards?' asked Lugg as politely as anyone could who was not remotely interested in the answer.

'That was never really the intention,' Amanda answered with the patience of a kindly infants' schoolteacher, 'though in theory a jet fighter with swept-forward wings will be possible in the future, we just haven't got the right materials or technology yet.'

'So what you were doin', it was like something out of science-fiction?'

Lugg was still smarting from having been declared surplus to requirements in Cambridge and forced to sit by a telephone in London which did not ring until everything remotely interesting had happened and all that was required of him was to play the humble chauffeur and return Mr Campion's Jensen to him.

'Well, it was certainly fiction of a sort, designed to draw the people stealing our research out into the open.'

'So you 'ad Reds under yer bed up at Alandel, did yer? That's why you've been down Mayfair this morning, innit? You wasn't shopping, were you?'

Two days after returning home, the Campions had been summoned to Leconfield House at the Park Lane end of Curzon Street – the headquarters of MI5 and certainly not a department store – for a detailed debriefing. They had decided to stay at the Bottle Street flat and take in a show whilst in town and had asked Lugg to make sure it was presentable.

Lugg, offended that he had been excluded once again, was determined to extract every detail, preferably the embarrassing ones, by forcing the Campions into partaking of 'afternoon tea', an uncomfortable ceremony at the best of times, but a positively exhausting one when Lugg was in charge of the menu.

He had gone to considerable lengths, laying on a spread of neat salmon paste (triangular, white bread with the crusts cut off) and egg-and-cress (rectangular, white bread *avec* crust) sandwiches, a slab of ham-and-egg pie which resembled a section of railway sleeper, cream horns and a Battenberg cake. As a crowning glory he had also made, with his own fair hands, a blancmange using only a pint of milk and the contents of a packet mix. When Mr Campion had enquired as to its flavour, Lugg had scratched his bald pate and said simply, 'Pink.'

Producing a teapot big enough to have served in a NAAFI canteen – which indeed it had – Lugg had joined them at the feast table, poured strong brown tea into their cups, loosened his belt and sat back in his chair waiting to be entertained as he ate.

It was clear that Lugg was prepared to interrogate them just as thoroughly, if not more so, than the grey men at Leconfield House and, on one of his several trips to the flat's kitchen, the Campions had conspired together and agreed that they would not get any peace until they had satisfied the fat man's curiosity.

'It can't do any harm to tell him what went on in Cambridge,' Amanda had said. 'It's only Lugg, after all.'

'The chaps at MI5 this morning would argue against it until the futures of Melvyn Barnes and the Jarvelas have been decided,' Campion had advised.

'Frankly, I wasn't impressed by them. We did their job for them and all they could do was whine about why we had to involve an American.'

'I am very glad we did, my dear. I'm pretty sure – no, I'm certain – I could not have handled Astra as efficiently as Luther Romo did. Anyway, I agree, we must tell Lugg the basic facts or, heaven knows, he might cook dinner for us.'

'He's building up to some sarcastic put-down, I can tell,' Amanda had said, 'so let's get it over with.'

'The Goshawk, as such, was a fiction,' said Amanda, when Lugg had settled himself, Buddha-like, back in his chair, 'but it was a tempting one. It just might have been practical if we had made a breakthrough inventing new materials, and a computer better than any in existence now. The theory was good, the design perfect, though I say it myself. The only problem was it didn't fool enough people for long enough.'

'I thought your business was making aeroplanes that flew proper, not ones that didn't fly at all.'

Here it comes, thought Amanda, the smug look on Lugg's face was advance warning of a barbed comment in the forging.

'Did you copy it from an Airfix kit?'

'Don't be rude, old fruit,' said Campion, 'Amanda's keeping it simple for you, just like she had to for me. Don't get her started on high by-pass engines, because those were the real story and the Goshawk Project was to divert the attention of the spy inside Alandel. It was just too good an idea not to tempt them out into the open.'

'Such a good idea they gave her that honourable degree at Cambridge, even though it was all make-believe?'

'It was an honorary doctorate and well deserved, and provided a dramatic scene which got the ball rolling.'

'Rolling right over that young lad Wormold from what I hear.'

'Go carefully, old boy. Amanda is in no way responsible for anyone's death. Melvyn Barnes arranged that, perhaps with the intent of frightening Wormold, but it went too far. It was all planned, or rather *engineered*, before Amanda caused her little scene at the Senate House. In any case, he's admitted it.'

Lugg scrunched up his face, as if pondering the meaning of the universe. 'So he had the means and the h'opportunity, but what was his motive?'

'We think Alan Wormold was demanding money from Barnes,' said Amanda, taking over the narrative. 'More than was required for his flying lessons, and probably to keep Teddy Toomey happy as well.'

Lugg slurped tea, put down his cup and piled three more sandwiches on to the plate balanced on his knees before rubbing his hands together in glee.

'This sounds more like it! What was going on there? A bit of blackmail or more Reds under the bed?'

'Blackmail may be going too far, but certainly Toomey was getting money from Wormold, who was demanding more and more from Melvyn Barnes. The police have looked at the bank accounts and both Toomey and Barnes have unexplained cash deposits, in Melvyn's case quite substantial ones, going back quite a while.

'I think it started out as an ideological act as far as Barnes was concerned,' Mr Campion continued. 'He went to fight the fascists in the Spanish Civil War and he had dreams of retiring to that workers' paradise of Cuba. He was very open about that when we went punting.'

Lugg's face creaked into an expression of mock outrage. Here it comes, thought Amanda.

'Let me get this straight.' The fat man put his plate back down on his knee and clasped his hands over his chest, fingers intertwined like links of sausages in a butcher's window. 'You 'ad a Communist sympathizer who sold secrets to the Russians and had already knocked off one of them young students, and you took him sailing down the river? I thought there were supposed to be brains in Cambridge. All those clever people with their parchment scrolls and their caps and gowns tossing their top 'ats in the air when they get a prize for doing their homework . . .'

'I think that's Eton,' said Campion, 'not Cambridge, but your point, so subtly made, is well taken. It was perhaps a foolish move on my part, but I did have a guardian angel with me in the shape of a pet crocodile.'

'Just as well. Sounds like Lady A could have used one herself.'

Amanda braced herself. 'But I had one,' she said, 'a rather muscular young American air-force officer.'

Lugg snorted. ''Ad to rely on the Yanks, did yer? As usual.'

'Mostly for their rather elaborate motor cars – oh, and their flying skills,' said Campion. 'Our American angel was rather useful, I suppose, and he helped me understand how the blind cell worked.'

'What's one of them when it's at home?'

'The mechanism they used for stealing the Goshawk research material. It was quite clever really because – the way they worked it – Melvyn Barnes never actually saw the Soviet cell who were his customers. They had already planted Astra in Professor Branscombe's house and had recruited one of his students, Teddy, thanks to his Russian lessons and infatuation with Miss Jarvela. We are pretty sure he built silencers for the Jarvelas' guns, and may have come up with the idea of the metal tubes as a letter box. Taking Teddy's friend Wormold out to Bourn for flying lessons gave Melvyn a perfect excuse for disappearing from site every week so he could leave documents and pick up his paycheques. Teddy would tell Astra when Wormold had gone flying and her brother would zip out to Caxton Gibbet to collect the goods. Melvyn Barnes only had to deal with the students, which was hardly suspicious as he worked with them every day. He never had any dealings with the professional agents who were running him, and was genuinely bemused when Jari tried to shoot him. He didn't know Jari from Adam, that was the beauty of a blind cell.'

'If it was such a clever set-up, how come they started killing each other? Did they realize the game was up when they gave the missus her certificate at that posh Speech Day we went to?'

'It was a well-deserved honorary degree from an outstanding university,' said Campion firmly, 'which recognizes innovation and advances in . . .'

Amanda reached out and put a hand on her husband's knee. 'Don't,' she said, 'it's not worth it. The honorary doctorate was genuine, Maggers, so I am now Doctor Campion if I need to pull rank. That little stunt of having me arrested in public was meant to flush out the traitor in our midst, but the writing was already on the wall for our little nest of spies.'

'They rumbled your little charade, did they?'

'Yes, but not in the way you think,' said Amanda, determined to wipe the smugness from Lugg's face. 'I think Melvyn who, for all his faults, was a good aeronautical engineer, had realized that the plans for the Goshawk were never going to work and what he'd been passing over to the Russians were neither practical nor useful.'

'And not worth the dosh they'd already paid out to him.'

'Exactly, plus the fact that they might have been tempted to set up their own expensive research project.'

'Did they know they'd bought a pig in a poke?'

'I'm sure the Russian government has a whole ministry devoted to buying pigs in pokes,' said Campion. 'Goodness knows, our government does.'

'The point is,' continued Amanda, 'that Barnes knew it was only a matter of time before they realized he was selling them shoddy goods, and when Alan Wormold started demanding more money from him, probably at Toomey's insistence, he decided to give Alan a scare by staging an industrial accident. Sadly, he staged it too well and, once he started to panic, the Jarvelas decided to wind up the cell and cut their losses. Killing Teddy was eliminating the one person who could incriminate them. Trying to kill Melvyn Barnes was in revenge for supplying them with bad material.'

Lugg shook his massive head slowly and made a tut-tutting noise between pursed lips. 'There's just no honour among thieves or spies any more, is there?' He looked down at the plate balanced on his knee, was astonished to find it empty, and then patted his orb of a stomach. 'Just remembered, I got some tinned herrings in the kitchen. I'll dish them up once I find the can opener. Best we have them before the sweet stuff.'

Lugg heaved himself to his feet and glided into the kitchen, leaving the Campions facing each other over a table-top vaguely resembling a battlefield.

'At least we won't have to worry about reserving a table for a pre-theatre dinner,' said Mr Campion.

'We could always fill my handbag with sandwiches,' said Amanda. 'Still, it was nice of him to make the effort. I thought he'd be in more of a sulk and I was expecting more cheek from him.'

'Give him time.'

Even as Campion spoke, there came a loud metallic crash from the kitchen and the sound of a Lugg bellowing at full volume.

'Ow! Gordon Bennett! I've cut me fingers on this tin of herrings and there's blood everywhere! Is there a *doctorate* in the 'ouse?'

AUTHOR'S NOTE

I am greatly indebted to Antoni Deighton for fielding numerous questions about aircraft and jet engine design in a painfully simple way so that even I could understand the answers.

The idea of a jet aircraft with swept-forward wings is not fanciful. Apart from Luftwaffe experiments during World War Two and by Soviet Russia immediately afterwards, the Germans developed the Hansa HFB 320 business jet to compete with the American Lear Jet in 1964. The most well-known example of a warplane with swept-forward wings is probably the Grumman X-29, developed jointly by NASA and USAF, which flew at supersonic speed during tests in 1984, although only two were built. They are now on display in museums at Edwards Air Force Base in California and the Wright-Patterson Base near Dayton, Ohio.

I have no idea whether Margery Allingham was inspired by the life in aircraft design of Maxine 'Blossom' Miles (1901–84), when she decided the career path of Lady Amanda Fitton, but I have been.

In Cambridge in the 1960s there were, according to local witnesses, 'large and mysterious black sheds', visible from Barton Road across rough ground and university playing fields. I have situated the Goshawk Project there, but by 1974 the site had become home to the far more prestigious, and useful, Cavendish Laboratory. Although I have taken a few liberties, a rifle range on that ground existed from the 1890s. Now relocated outside of Cambridge near the village of Barton, it retains the name Barton Road Rifle Range. I am, as usual, indebted to Roger Johnson for his cartographic skills.

The student referred to in Chapter Ten, who was banished from Magdalene when 'engines of love' were found in his room in 1929, was the literary critic (Sir) William Empson.

Caxton Gibbet still exists but The Gibbet Inn, as it was

when Albert Campion was an undergraduate, does not. Land nearby was used during World War Two as an emergency landing strip for the RAF training base at Bourn and, during raids by the Luftwaffe, several Tiger Moths were shot down or destroyed on the ground. The renamed Caxton Gibbet Inn eventually became the Yim Wah House Chinese restaurant until destroyed by a fire in March 2009. The redeveloped site is now home to some well-known fast-food outlets.

GCHQ, the British government's signals monitoring and cyber-security centre, was based in Oakley in Cheltenham from 1951 until operations moved fully to the new 'doughnut' complex in nearby Benhall in 2012 and the Oakley site redeveloped for housing.